Praise for *New York Times* bestselling author Diana Palmer

"Palmer proves that love and passion can be found even in the most dangerous situations."
—*Publishers Weekly* on *Untamed*

"You just can't do better than a Diana Palmer story to make your heart lighter and smile brighter."
—*Fresh Fiction* on *Wyoming Rugged*

"Diana Palmer is a mesmerizing storyteller who captures the essence of what a romance should be."
—*Affaire de Coeur*

"The popular Palmer has penned another winning novel, a perfect blend of romance and suspense."
—*Booklist* on *Lawman*

"Diana Palmer's characters leap off the page. She captures their emotions and scars beautifully and makes them come alive for readers."
—*RT Book Reviews* on *Lawless*

Dear Reader,

I can't believe that it has been thirty years since my first Long, Tall Texans book, *Calhoun*, debuted! The series was suggested by my former editor Tara Gavin, who asked if I might like to set stories in a fictional town of my own design. Would I! And the rest is history.

As the years went by, I found more and more sexy ranchers and cowboys to add to the collection. My readers (especially Amy!) found time to gift me with a notebook listing every single one of them, wives and kids and connections to other families in my own Texas town of Jacobsville. Eventually the town got a little too big for me, so I added another smaller town called Comanche Wells and began to fill it up, too.

You can't imagine how much pleasure this series has given me. I continue to add to the population of Jacobs County, Texas, and I have no plans to stop. Ever.

I hope all of you enjoy reading the Long, Tall Texans as much as I enjoy writing them. Thank you all for your kindness and loyalty and friendship. I am your biggest fan!

Love,

Diana Palmer

NEW YORK TIMES BESTSELLING AUTHOR

DIANA PALMER

THE TEXAN WAY

4 Heartfelt Stories

Drew, Jobe, Tom and *Grant*
(previously published as *Paper Husband*)

HARLEQUIN SPECIAL RELEASE

HARLEQUIN® SPECIAL RELEASE

Recycling programs
for this product may
not exist in your area.

ISBN-13: 978-1-335-45439-3

The Texan Way

Copyright © 2022 by Harlequin Enterprises ULC.

Drew
First published in 1997. This edition published in 2022.
Copyright © 1997 by Diana Palmer

Jobe
First published in 1997. This edition published in 2022.
Copyright © 1997 by Diana Palmer

Tom
First published in 1997. This edition published in 2022.
Copyright © 1997 by Diana Palmer

Grant
First published as Paper Husband in 1996. This edition published
in 2022. Copyright © 1996 by Diana Palmer

For questions and comments about the quality of this book,
please contact us at CustomerService@Harlequin.com.

Harlequin Enterprises ULC
22 Adelaide St. West, 41st Floor
Toronto, Ontario M5H 4E3, Canada
www.Harlequin.com

Printed in U.S.A.

CONTENTS

A prolific author of more than one hundred books,
Diana Palmer got her start as a newspaper reporter.
A *New York Times* bestselling author and voted one of
the top ten romance writers in America, she has a gift
for telling the most sensual tales with charm and humor.
Diana lives with her family in Cornelia, Georgia. Visit her
website at dianapalmer.com.

Books by Diana Palmer

Long, Tall Texans

Fearless
Heartless
Dangerous
Merciless
Courageous
Protector
Invincible
Untamed
Defender
Undaunted

The Wyoming Men

Wyoming Tough
Wyoming Fierce
Wyoming Bold
Wyoming Strong
Wyoming Rugged
Wyoming Brave

Visit the Author Profile page
at Harlequin.com for more titles.

DREW

CHAPTER ONE

"How are you today?" Drew Morris asked his first patient of the day, smiling in his usual remote, but kind way. "Mr...." He glanced at the file, glanced at the patient, bit back a curse and smiled in a different way. "Excuse me just a minute, will you?"

Before the patient could say a word, Drew was out the door and marching down the hall to his receptionist's desk. He threw the file down in front of her with curt irritation.

"I said Bill Hayes, not William Haynie," he said shortly.

Kitty Carson grimaced, and the green eyes behind her large wire-rimmed lenses winced. "Sorry, Dr. Morris," she stammered, jumping up to thumb through the files until she found the right one and handed it to him. "If Mrs. Turner was here, I wouldn't get so rattled," she defended, mentioning the office nurse who was off sick today.

"Bad way to start off the day, Ms. Carson," he muttered and went straight back to his patient.

Kitty sat down, hard, letting out the breath she'd been holding. The former receptionist, Mrs. Alice Martin, had retired two weeks previously, and Kitty had been hired through a local professional agency in Jacobsville, Texas, to replace her. She hadn't met Drew Morris when she applied for the job, which was a good thing. If she'd met him first, she wouldn't be working here.

On the other hand, it was nice to be treated like a normal employee. She was asthmatic, and in at least one job, her well-meaning boss had been so wary of triggering an attack that he actually had another girl in the office ask her for pressing work. He was sweet, but her asthma wasn't brought on by emotional upheavals; it was triggered by pollens and dust and smoke. Probably since Dr. Morris did some pediatric work, he knew more about asthma than any routine employer. An increasing number of children seemed to have the chronic illness.

She pushed back a wisp of dark hair that had escaped the huge bun at her nape and stared blankly at the file he'd given her. She got up again to replace it, but by then the phone was ringing again—both lines.

It wasn't that she couldn't handle the pressure of a busy doctor's office, but she did wish he'd take a partner. He had no life at all. He worked from dawn until dusk daily through Saturday, and on Sunday he had an afternoon clinic for children. He did minor surgery through the week as well—tonsils and adenoids—and he was always willing to stand in for other doctors in the local hospital's emergency room on weekends. No wonder Mrs. Turner had come down with the flu, she mused. It was probably exhaustion. It didn't surprise her that Dr. Morris wasn't married, either. When would he have the time?

He'd been married, though. Everyone talked about

his eternal devotion to Eve, his wife of twelve years until her untimely death of cancer. No woman in Jacobsville ever set her cap at Drew because of the competition. His marriage had been one of those rare, blissful matches. It was said that Drew would much rather have his memory of it than any new relationship.

Not that Kitty was interested in him that way. She had her eyes on a local cowboy named Guy Fenton, who was something of a rounder but a nice man when he wasn't drinking. He'd broken a bone in his hand the day after Kitty started working for Drew. He'd known Kitty for years, but only then had he noticed that she'd grown up. He seemed to like her, too, because he teased and picked at her. He had a habit of stopping by the office at lunchtime to talk to her, and he'd just asked her to go to the movies with him on Saturday night. She was so flustered that she was all thumbs. Dr. Morris, she reflected, had no patience with the course of true love.

By lunchtime, she'd dealt, calmly and efficiently, with two emergencies that required Drew's presence at the local emergency room, and a waiting room full of angry, impatient people. Her soft voice and reassuring smile defused what could have been a mutiny. She was used to calming bad tempers. Her late father had been a retired colonel from the Green Berets, a veteran of Vietnam with a habit of running right over people. Kitty, an only child, had learned quickly how to get along with him. He was difficult, but he was like Drew Morris in one respect; he never overemphasized her asthma attacks. His very calmness helped avert many of them. But if they led her to the emergency room, he was always the soul of compassion.

Her mother was long dead, so there had been just the two of them, until six months ago. She still missed the old man terribly. The job she'd left to come here had held just too many memories of him. Her father had known Drew, but only socially, so there were no close associations with him in this office.

"Don't daydream on my time," a harsh voice called from the doorway.

She jumped, glancing toward Drew, whose dark eyes were filled with dislike. "I'm…on my lunch hour, Dr. Morris," she faltered.

"Then why the hell are you spending it staring into space? Go eat."

As she got up, she caught her sleeve on the knob of the middle desk drawer and was jerked back down onto the chair.

"Oh, for God's sake…!" Drew moved forward and caught her just as the swivel, rolling desk chair crashed to the floor. He stood her upright with an angry sigh and noticed at the same time that the buttons on her bulky gray cardigan were done up wrong.

"You are an albatross," he muttered as he undid buttons, to her shocked surprise, and efficiently did them up again, the right way. "There. I'm amazed that the agency would risk sending me a receptionist-stenographer who can't even button a sweater properly."

"I usually can," she said nervously. "It's just that Guy asked me out. I'm a little unsettled, that's all. I'm sorry."

His dark eyes cut into hers. They were alarming at

close range, big under a jutting brow. The pupils were black-rimmed. "Guy?" he asked curtly.

"Guy Fenton," she said with a demure smile.

His eyes narrowed. "Broken metacarpal, left hand," he recalled with a frown. "Works for the Ballenger brothers out at their feedlot. And drinks to excess on weekends," he added firmly.

"I know that. He won't drink when he's with me, though. We're just going to a movie," she said, and began to feel as if her father had come back.

His eyebrows lifted. "Don't you date much?"

She flushed. It was too much work to explain that she didn't, and why. Her father, God rest his soul, had terrified most of the shy young men she'd brought home. Eventually she stopped bringing them home. The thought flashed unwanted through her mind that her father would have made mincemeat of Guy Fenton. She wondered how he would have stood up to Dr. Morris, who was quite obviously the offspring of adders and scorpions.

The thought almost brought a laugh from her pretty mouth. She barely bit it back in time and transformed it into a cough.

"Watch yourself," Drew said. "Fenton's trouble, any way you look at it. His ex-girlfriend would eat you for breakfast."

"Ex-girlfriend?"

He glanced impatiently at his watch. "I have rounds to make. I don't have time… All right, his girlfriend dropped him because of the drinking, but she still feels that he's her personal property and she doesn't like him seeing other women."

"Oh."

"I'll be back at two," he said, shedding his white lab coat as he headed to his office. "How many more appointments do I have?" he asked without looking back.

She picked up her pad and followed him, almost running to keep up with his long-legged stride. She read them off. She managed to run right into him as he barreled back out into the hall, dignified in a gray vested suit and red striped tie. He made another impatient sound and ran a hand through his thick dark hair, making it just a bit unruly.

"Do you have to walk into me every time you come down the hall?" he muttered.

"Sorry. New glasses." She grinned gamely and pushed them back on her nose again.

He kept walking. "If I run a little late, make the usual excuses." He turned with the doorknob in his hand. "And try to keep the files straight, will you? I'm all for true love, but I have a practice to run."

He went out while she was still searching for a reply.

HE GOT INTO his new black Mercedes and slammed the door impatiently. The girl was going to have to go, that was all there was to it. She was a positive disaster when she wasn't trying to get involved with a man. Fenton's presence was going to make her into an accident waiting to happen.

He started the car and pulled out into traffic. Really, it was too bad that she had no one. She needed looking after. She was all thumbs when he spoke harshly to her, and she drank far too much coffee. She couldn't seem to button blouses or dresses or jackets with any degree of competency. Once she'd come to work wearing two different shades of ankle-high hose, looking like a refugee from two-tone body tanning.

A faint smile touched his firm mouth. All the same, the patients seemed to like her, especially children. She was good with asthmatics, too, possibly because she was one herself.

One day when his nurse had been out sick—funny just how often Mrs. Turner was sick lately, he mused—he'd come to get a small patient from the waiting room and found her sitting on Kitty's lap while she typed up forms. The child had a sprained wrist and had been wailing, accompanied by a grandmother who didn't seem to care much whether she was seen or not. Kitty cared all too much.

The memory touched him in a way he didn't like. His late wife, Eve, had been sensitive like that. She'd loved kids, too, but they'd lost the only one Eve had been able to conceive due to a miscarriage. Despite their lack of offspring, it had been an idyllic marriage. He missed Eve. He still spent holidays with his in-laws. It was like being near her. He didn't date and he didn't want involvement, despite the unending efforts of local people to set him up with eligible young women. His twelve years with Eve were precious enough to last him the rest of his life.

Kitty, with her foibles, wasn't enough to threaten his

peace of mind, but if she kept mixing up patients, she was going to endanger his practice.

On the other hand, if Fenton was really interested, she might be the making of him. A man in love was ready enough to give up bad habits. Everyone knew that Fenton drank to excess; no one knew why. Drew had tried to drag it out of him while he was putting the man's hand in a lightweight cast, but he couldn't make him talk. Fenton just ignored him.

The tall, gangly cowboy didn't seem as if he were Kitty's sort of man, really. He might like her, but he had a reputation and he dated a variety of women. Kitty was naive. She could get into real trouble there, if Fenton was just playing around. And he didn't seem the sort of man to worry overmuch about Kitty's asthma. Drew himself pretended that it didn't exist, but he kept a close eye on her just the same. He'd talked with her own doctor and discovered that in the past she'd had to be rushed to the emergency room with those attacks, especially during heavy pollen levels in spring.

The hospital loomed ahead in the gray misting September rain and he put Kitty and her problems right out of his mind.

GUY FENTON WAS TWENTY-NINE, dark-headed and gray-eyed with a lean physique and a wandering eye. He wasn't handsome, but Kitty found him very attractive. Actually she found his attention attractive. In her young life, attention had been a luxury. She was making up for lost time.

She'd bought new makeup and learned how to apply

it. She'd given up her high-necked blouses and started wearing things that were flimsier, looser. She wore her hair in a braid coiled around her head instead of in its former tight bun. And sure enough, Guy had noticed her and asked her out to this great movie.

The thing was, she was watching it, and he was leaning over the next row of seats talking to Millie Brady, a cute little redhead who worked in the local bank where Guy did business.

Kitty was feeling left out and miserable. She'd worn a pretty pink-and-gray-plaid skirt with a nicely fitting pink sweater, and her hair had been curled and intricately pinned up. She looked very nice indeed, glasses and all. But that didn't make up for the sort of personality that little Millie had in such abundance. Perhaps Millie hadn't been raised in a military environment where her life was filled with orders instead of affection.

Even now, Kitty found it difficult to interact with people. She had very few social skills. She'd had classes at business school in human relations, but that hardly made up for a lifetime of being loved and wanted. Even if the late Colonel Carson had been a well-respected military war hero, he'd been a dead bust as a loving parent. In his way, he'd been fond of his daughter, but he'd lived in the comfort of past glories, especially after his wife's death.

She sighed without knowing it. If she'd stayed home, she could be watching one of her favorite television programs, about a duo of detectives tracing down exciting phenomena. Instead she seemed to be double-dating with Millie.

She tapped Guy on the shoulder. "I'm going to get some popcorn," she said.

He didn't even look her way. "Sure, you go right ahead. Now, Millie, let me explain to you how that roping is done. It's sort of tricky…"

He was going on and on about how to sit a quarter horse while bulldogging a calf in the rodeo ring. Although Kitty liked him, she couldn't have cared less about horses and ranching. She was a city girl.

She went to the snack bar, paused, and suddenly turned and walked right out the front door. She only lived two blocks from the theater. It was a cloudless summer night and the air smelled nice.

Just as she made it to the corner, a carload of bored teenage boys pulled up to the curb, with the windows open, and began to make catcalls.

She tried ignoring them, but they only got louder, and the car began to follow her. She wasn't frightened, but she might yet have to go back to the theater. It would be the perfect end to a perfectly rotten date.

Furious at her predicament, she whirled and glared straight into the eyes of the boy in the passenger seat. "If you want trouble, you've come to the right place," she assured him. She dug into her pocket for a pencil and pad and walked right to the back of the car to write down the license plate number.

When they realized what she was about to do, they took off. One of the real advantages of living in a small town was the fact that most cars were instantly recognizable to the local police; and they knew where the owners lived. A license plate number would make the search even easier. But these guys weren't too keen to be located. They left rubber on the street getting away.

She stood staring after them with her eyebrows raised, the pencil still poised over the blank paper. "Well, well," she murmured to herself. She made a check on the paper. "That's one for my side."

She turned the corner and walked briskly to the alley that cut between one street and another. It took her right to her apartment house. She went inside and up to her small apartment, muttering furiously to herself all the way. Some great date, she thought furiously. Not only had her date ignored her, but she'd been catcalled on the street like a streetwalker.

"No wonder Amazons only used men for breeding stock," she told her door as she inserted the key in the lock.

She went into her lonely apartment, locked the door and unplugged the telephone. She had a small glass of milk and went to bed. It was barely nine-thirty, but she felt as if she'd worked hard all day.

Somewhere around eleven she heard knocking on her door, but she rolled over and pulled the pillow over her head. Guy Fenton could stand there until hell froze for all she cared.

THE NEXT MORNING she went to church, surprised to see Drew Morris there. He went to the same church, but he didn't often attend services, due to his erratic schedule. Several times she'd seen him check his beeper and leave right in the middle of the offering. A doctor couldn't be certain of any sort of normal social attendance, especially a family doctor who specialized in pediatrics. It must make his weekends nerve-racking, she thought.

After the service, he stopped her on the sidewalk, his face somber.

"What happened last night?" he asked abruptly.

Her eyebrows arched. "What?" she exclaimed, shocked.

"I saw you," he said impatiently. "You were walking—no, you were running—down an alley, alone, about nine-thirty last night. Where was Fenton?"

"Enjoying his date. Sadly it wasn't me."

"I beg your pardon?"

"He likes Millie," she explained. "She was sitting in front of us, and she's much more interesting to talk to than I am. She actually likes rodeo."

Her tone tugged a corner of his mouth up. "Imagine that!"

"I hate cattle," she said.

"Our economy locally would suffer if we didn't have so many of them," he said pointedly.

"Oh, I know that, but I thought we were going to see a movie," she muttered. "It was a fantasy movie," she recalled wistfully, "with a computer-created dragon that looked so real…" She flushed at the amusement in his eyes. "I like dragons," she said belligerently.

"I'm partial to them myself."

She shrugged. "I'll see it another time," she murmured. "It wasn't important."

He barely heard her. He was amazed to find himself outraged on her behalf. Kitty wasn't bad-looking at all. She had pretty legs and a neat little figure. She was intelligent and she had a fine sensitivity that was refreshing.

Millie, on the other hand, was a born flirt and something of a man-eater. She had a reputation locally for stealing men away from their girlfriends. She and Guy Fenton were a match made in heaven. Poor Kitty.

"I have to go," she said with a quiet smile.

She walked to the small used foreign car she drove, patting its white hood affectionately before she got in and started the engine. Dr. Morris was so nice, she thought, smiling as she watched him get into his Mercedes. He was a handsome man, too, and despite his impatience and sometimes unexpected bursts of temper, she liked him. If she wasn't careful, he could become very important to her, and that would never do. He lived with a beautiful ghost. No mortal woman could ever compete with his Eve.

She spent an uneventful day watching old movies on television and went to bed early. Guy Fenton didn't phone. She didn't really expect him to. She decided to write him off as a bad experience and get on with her life.

SHE LEARNED THE office routine slowly but surely as the summer ended and autumn began. As the weeks slipped away, her filing improved, too. So did her people skills. She got to know the patients who came in regularly, and as the holidays approached, she found herself on the receiving end of all sorts of delicious recipes for turkey and dressing and pies.

She noticed that Guy Fenton didn't come back to

have his cast off and mentioned it to Nurse Turner, to be told that he'd gone to the emergency room for the procedure. She supposed he'd been too embarrassed about their disastrous date to come to the office. It was history, anyway.

She accepted jars of preserves with enthusiasm. She didn't bother to put any of her own up, as she had nobody to cook for except herself. Thanksgiving and Christmas came and went and she spent them alone, having no close relatives to consider. Dr. Morris, as usual, went to his late wife's family for both occasions.

Winter turned slowly to spring and Kitty began to feel like part of the office furniture, in the nicest possible way. Dr. Morris had started calling her "Kitty Cat," to the amusement of some of his smaller patients who wanted to know if she could purr.

She marveled at the change in Dr. Morris's treatment of her. His gruff, abrupt manner at first had given way to a casual friendliness that stopped just short of affection. He was forever dressing her, though, unfastening buttons and doing them up the right way, righting hair bows, grimacing when she wore one dark blue sock with one dark green one because she couldn't see the difference between dark shades.

"I can't wake up on time," she muttered one day when he was rebuttoning her patterned blazer on a nippy day. "I'm always in a rush when I leave home."

"Go to bed earlier," he advised.

"How can I? The neighbors below me have one of those monster sound systems," she muttered. "They like to listen to it until the wee hours. My floor vibrates."

"Complain to the landlord," he persisted.

"The landlord lives in Kansas City," she said irritably. "He doesn't care what they do if they pay the rent on time."

He smiled wickedly as he finished the buttons and dropped his hands. "Buy a set of drums and practice constantly. Better yet, get bagpipes."

Her eyes brightened. "But I have a set," she said, laughing at his amazement. "They belonged to my father's cousin, and we inherited them when he died. I never learned to play them."

"No better time to practice."

She chuckled. She hadn't thought of her taciturn boss as a kindred spirit. "I'll get them out tonight and see if the moths have eaten them."

"Do you have Scottish ancestry?" he asked suddenly.

"Yes. Clan Stuart."

"My mother's forebears were Maxwells," he mused. "They came over just after the Revolutionary War."

"I don't know anything about mine," she replied. "Dad was too busy talking about wars to care much about ancient history. He was a retired colonel in the Green Berets. He served three tours of duty in Vietnam."

He searched her eyes quietly. "You poor kid."

She flushed. "Why do you say that?"

"Your mother died when you were in grammar school, didn't you say?"

She nodded.

"Just you and the colonel and the war," he pondered

aloud, dark eyes narrowing. "I'll bet he scared the hell out of any prospective dates."

"You don't know the half of it," she murmured, recalling some fraught encounters. "He tried to teach one of my dates a hand-to-hand combat move." She grimaced. "He accidentally threw him out the window instead. Fortunately it was open at the time and on the first floor. He actually left his car, he was in such a hurry to get away."

He tried to smother a laugh. "I get the idea."

"Dad loved me, in his way," she continued wistfully. "And I loved him. But I didn't like growing up like a soldier."

"Taught you everything he knew, I'll bet."

"Oh, I could win medals in target shooting and karate," she agreed. "But it would have been so much nicer if I could have learned to cook and sew. I liked those 'sissy' hobbies, even if he didn't. I had to sneak over to my girlfriend's house to knit, for God's sake!"

"But you miss him, don't you?"

"Oh, yes," she confessed. "Every day. But he was a horrible father."

"I'm not surprised." He checked his watch and grimaced. "I've got to get going. I'll be late for rounds, and there's a hospital board meeting tonight."

"You'll be medical chief of staff one day," she said proudly.

He chuckled. "Not if I start being late for meetings." He heard her sigh—actually heard it, with its accompanying wheeze.

His eyes narrowed thoughtfully. "Used your preventive medicine?"

She gaped at him. "What?"

"Your nedochromil sodium," he replied, and then added the brand name she was prescribed.

"Yes," she said shortly. "That and the albuterol as well. Religiously. I don't like ending up in the emergency room."

"See that you keep using them properly. You've got a wheeze."

"Cold nights and warm days for a week," she said.

He shrugged. "Yes. I've noticed the increase in my little asthmatics' visits." He picked up his jacket. "Is the medicine giving enough cover?"

His concern touched her, but she wasn't going to let him know. "Yes, sir."

"Good." He checked his watch, nodded and left her in the waiting room as he went out the back way to his car. She felt a warm glow at the personal conversation they'd had. Nothing in their relationship had been the least personal until now.

But when she realized what she was thinking, she clamped down hard on her wandering attention. She'd have to be crazy to let Dr. Morris get under her skin. Even crazier than she'd been to go out with Guy Fenton.

Dr. Morris was just being the ideal boss, concerned for his workers' welfare, she told herself. So she'd better concentrate on just doing her job and not trying to make intimate comments out of impersonal observations about her health. He was a doctor, after all. It was natural for him to be concerned with someone's health.

CHAPTER TWO

IN THE MONTHS since their disastrous date, Kitty had put Guy Fenton out of her mind. She knew that he and Millie had a brief fling together, of sorts, but it didn't seem to last long. And not because of any interference from Guy's ex-girlfriend. In fact, there were rumors that she was seeing someone else.

Kitty hadn't expected Guy to ever apologize for his behavior on their one and only date, but he did, when he came to have a routine physical for a new insurance policy, long after his cast had been removed—a procedure that she remembered he'd had done at the hospital rather than at Drew's office.

"Letting you leave the theater that night without even noticing was a low thing to do, and I'm sorry," he told her. "I love bulldogging. Millie was hanging on every word, and I'd been sweet on her for a long time. But that was no excuse for ignoring you until you left and went home alone at night. I'm really sorry—several months too late," he added with a sheepish grin. "To tell you the truth, I was too ashamed to call you afterward."

"No harm done," she'd told him.

"Lucky for me," he added vaguely. "Your, uh, boss had quite a lot to say about it."

She was shocked. "Dr. Morris?"

"The very same. He dragged me out of bed in the bunkhouse at the ranch the day you told him and read me the riot act for ten minutes in front of the whole crew." He quirked an eyebrow. "Wouldn't have taken it from anyone else, but he had a point. I should have checked to see where you were when you didn't come back with popcorn. Anything could have happened to you." He stuck his hands into his pockets and shrugged. "There's another reason I stayed away. I thought he might have designs on you." He noted Kitty's sudden color. "My mistake. I guess he only felt responsible for you since you work for him."

"Yes," she said, her head whirling, "I suppose so."

He glanced at her with amusement. "I don't suppose you'd like to try going out with me again? Even if I swore I wouldn't talk rodeo with anybody in a nearby seat?"

She smiled pleasantly. "No, thanks." She looked at the intercom and saw the light flashing. "You can go in now."

He hesitated, but then he gave her a rueful smile and walked on down the hall. They had too little in common to make many waves together, anyway.

Later she was curious enough to ask Dr. Morris about what he'd said to Guy.

He gave her one of his blandest looks. "You could have been assaulted, walking around town alone at night, even in Jacobsville. Somebody needed to put him straight."

"Shades of my dad," she murmured.

Something changed in his expression. He studied her far longer than he meant to before he shrugged and turned away. "Just the same, pick your dates more carefully in the future, would you? I've got better ways to amuse myself than play nursemaid."

"Such as?" she blurted.

He stared at her blankly.

"What better ways do you have to amuse yourself?" she persisted. "You work all day and then you help out in the emergency room if you don't have late hours, which you mostly do. On weekends, you cover for doctors who are going on vacation or spending time with their families. I doubt you've dined out, taken in a movie or gone bowling in the past five years."

He was clouding up again, like a thunderstorm waiting to crash down on her head. "My private life is no concern of yours," he said pointedly. "Just do your job."

She searched his hard face quietly, seeing deep lines there, and the beginnings of gray at his temples. He'd been a little overweight when she'd first come to work for him, but he'd lost the extra pounds and now he was streamlined; probably from all the work he did.

"There's a whole world out there that you can't even see," she said, thinking aloud. "Children playing baseball, old men talking about past glories on their bench in the grocery store, gardeners telling lies about their prize roses over the fences. You don't see any of that because you run past it." She saw him tense, but she didn't stop. "Dr. Morris, the only thing you're going to accomplish is to put yourself in the grave next to your wife."

"Stop it."

His voice cut like a lash. "I'm sorry," she replied. "Nobody else seems to care if you kill yourself. Being a workaholic is fine, for a while, but it catches up with you eventually. You should already know that you're a prime candidate for a heart attack. Or is that why you push yourself so hard?" she added softly. "Is life so unbearable without her that you're trying…"

"I said, stop it."

This time there was no mistaking the threat. Any minute now, she was going to be minus a good job.

She backed off mentally, holding up her hands in mock defense. "Okay, I quit," she said. "I'll be a model secretary-receptionist from now on, seen but not heard."

"Great idea, if you plan to keep working here," he said, putting what he felt into words. He didn't need to. The black fury in his eyes was threat enough. "If you want something to worry about, try having someone sort your hose so that you can wear two of the same shade!"

He indicated her feet. She looked down and grimaced. Peeking out from under her charcoal gray slacks were a pair of knee-high hose so obviously different that she flushed.

She looked up, tossing her head. "Done on purpose," she proclaimed triumphantly. "I'm setting a new fashion trend."

He made an odd sound. His eyes twinkled but he turned away before the grin inside him got loose.

"Get to work," he muttered.

"Yes, sir!"

She whirled and headed back to her office, so flushed that Nurse Turner stopped her and felt her forehead.

"I'm fine," she assured the middle-aged nurse. "I've just been rushing again."

She glanced back toward the doctor and said loudly, "You've got workaholitis. It's contagious!"

"There goes your Independence Day bonus," he called over his shoulder without breaking stride.

Nurse Turner made a face at him.

"I saw that," he called from his office without looking back.

"See?" she told Kitty. "You can't win."

"I already knew that."

Nurse Turner took her by the arm and pulled her into the receptionist's cubbyhole, closing the door carefully behind her.

"Don't mention his wife, ever," she cautioned gently. "He tends to brood around the time she died. It makes things worse for him."

"When did she die?"

"Six years ago tomorrow," the nurse said in a quiet tone. "The first year after it happened, he ran his car into a tree. Fortunately he was only mildly concussed. After that, Dr. Coltrain started keeping an eye on him. They're friends, you know. Dr. Louise Blakely went out with him a time or two, and people began to wonder if he wasn't getting over his wife, but then she married Dr. Coltrain. He's been a real hermit ever since she married."

"It's his life, I guess," Kitty replied. "But it's such a

shame. He's a good man. Surely his wife wouldn't want him to live alone forever?"

Nurse Turner shook her head. "She was a tender-hearted little thing. She'd never have wanted that. But he misses her something fierce. Always has. Pity they couldn't have a child."

"Yes, isn't it?" Kitty replied.

SHE DIDN'T SAY anything else to Drew, but it was obvious by the next day that she'd already said too much. The first thing he did when he came in that morning was to give her a black glare and read her the riot act about the condition of the waiting room.

"Those magazines are two years old," he said shortly. "Throw them all out and get subscriptions to new ones. Meanwhile, buy some at the drugstore."

"Yes, sir," she said, and resisted the urge to salute.

He sighed angrily. "And do something about that stupid rubber plant in the corner. It's dying."

"You'd die, too, if little boys dumped gummy worms and old soft drinks and used bubble gum on you," she murmured.

"Fertilize the thing and keep it watered or get rid of it," he muttered. "And your desk…"

"It looks better than yours," she snapped right back, losing her temper. "At least I don't save year-old sale papers from variety stores and parking tickets that I don't pay!"

He opened his mouth to speak, closed it again and marched off down the hall so loudly that Nurse Turner came out of the filing room and stared after him.

From that point on, the day deteriorated. Grown-up people who came in for minor complaints got lectures, children went away sulky, Nurse Turner finally hid in the bathroom and Kitty was thinking seriously of sitting under her desk until quitting time.

The telephone rang noisily and she answered it, painfully aware that Dr. Morris was standing nearby, visibly hoping for someone he could attack on the other end.

"It's Coltrain," came the deep voice over the line. "Are the closets full yet?" he added with faint amusement.

"Every one," Kitty said. "Not to mention the bathroom."

"Let me talk to him while there's still time."

She handed the receiver over smartly. Drew came to stand beside her, far too close, while he spoke tersely to Dr. Coltrain. One hand was in his pocket, moving his car keys and loose change around. His arm in its lab coat brushed against Kitty's with the movement, and she felt odd sensations all over her body. It disturbed her. She tried to move away, but there was nowhere to go. She was already wedged against the desk.

Drew asked Dr. Coltrain something and then listened. While he was listening, he happened to glance down at Kitty and his black eyes met her searching, uneasy green ones with an impact that stopped her breath. It felt a little like asthma, when the air got trapped in her lungs and she couldn't get it out again.

He didn't look away, and neither did she. The sudden tension in the office was almost tangible. She saw muscles move in his jaw as his teeth clenched. His eyes began to glitter faintly, and she became aware of him as she never had been before.

"What?" he murmured into the telephone, because he hadn't heard a word Coltrain was saying. He blinked and managed to look away from Kitty's eyes. Odd, how he felt, as if he'd stuck his fingers in an electric socket. It made him angry, that he should feel such things today of all days. "Yes, I'll meet you at the restaurant," he said. There was a pause and he glanced at Kitty as if he suddenly hated her. "No, I don't want to bring anyone," he said deliberately.

Kitty dropped her eyes and didn't move. He was still too close and she didn't trust her voice, either. She wanted to get up and run away.

"Yes, I'll do that," Drew finished. He hung up the telephone and abruptly bent, jerking Kitty's chin up so that he could search her eyes. "Have you been talking to Lou?"

Her breath fluttered in her throat. "Dr. Lou?" she faltered. "I…I haven't seen her since Christmas."

"I don't need the Coltrains to play Cupid for me, and I don't want you as a dinner date," he said flatly. His eyes ran over her angrily, noting the rise and fall of her firm breasts, the increase of her breath. She was aware of him, and he knew it, and hated it. "I don't want you, period. You're an employee. Nothing more. You make that clear to the Coltrains."

"I'll do that very thing," she said, losing her own temper. "And for your information, I am not interested in you in any respect at all. I don't date people who are married to ghosts!"

He glared at her even more as the sound of footsteps coming along the hall diverted him. He realized that he was holding Kitty's soft little chin in his long fingers and he dropped his hand abruptly before Nurse Turner came into Kitty's office.

"Doesn't anybody work around here?" he demanded when he saw his nurse standing behind him.

"It's lunchtime, Doctor," Nurse Turner stammered.

"Then why the hell don't you both go and eat something?" he demanded. He stormed off back to his own office, leaving Kitty and Nurse Turner and the last patient of the morning openmouthed.

IT DIDN'T GET any better after lunch. There were three small emergencies that held up office hours, so that it was after seven when they ushered the last patient back to Dr. Morris.

"Run for it," Nurse Turner advised, grabbing her sweater and purse. "When he comes out of there with no patients as buffers, you're going to need an asbestos shield."

"I can't," Kitty groaned, "I have to put everything away."

"I'll pray for you," Nurse Turner said sincerely, glanced down the hall from which an audible roar could be heard and shot out the front door.

The patient, middle-aged Mr. James, came rushing down the hall despite his painful arthritis, grasping a scribbled charge slip.

"Here," he said, thrusting it to Kitty with a quick glance over his shoulder, like a drowning man expecting an imminent shark attack. "I'm to stop smoking, lose thirty pounds and move the building five feet to the left," he added with grim amusement. "I'll send a check right along, and you can give me another appointment for my arthritis in three months on whichever day you think he might be in a *good* mood!" He turned and fled for his life. "On second thought, I'll phone you about that appointment!" he called as he left.

He went out the door just as Drew came into the hall, and it seemed to Kitty as if flames were following right behind him. He paused at her desk, his black eyes glittering at her as if all his problems were her fault.

There was only one thing to do. She stood up, sighed and held her hands high over her head as if she were an escaped prisoner trying to give up while there was still time.

He started to say something and suddenly burst out laughing. "My God, is it that bad?" he asked.

"Mrs. Turner left skid marks. She offered to pray for me," she informed him. "And I wouldn't bet good money that Mr. James will ever come back."

He let out a weary sigh and leaned against the door facing, checking his watch. "I'm late for dinner, to boot." He glanced at her almost sheepishly, for him. "Go home."

"Post haste," she promised, grabbing her jacket and purse. Her hands were all thumbs as she tried to mate buttons. She was out of breath, not only due to Drew's bad temper. It was hard to make her lungs work. The pollen count had been extremely high.

"Good God, Kitty, you're hopeless," he said impatiently. He took the purse from her nerveless fingers, put it down on the chair and pulled her close. He slowly fastened the buttons, his mouth just inches from her forehead. She could feel his warm breath there, his knuckles moving gently against her breasts, and her legs trembled under her.

Drew was feeling something equally powerful and trying with all his might to resist it. This was the day, the anniversary of his beloved Eve's death. He felt guilty that he was attracted to Kitty at all. It had made him irritable and impatient all day.

He looked down at her soft mouth and his hands stilled as he wondered how it would feel to kiss her. He hadn't kissed a woman, touched a woman, since his wife's lingering death. He was hungry and alone and miserable.

His fingers slid up to Kitty's face and cradled it, lifting it slowly. His eyes lingered on her lips while he fought his own need, and hers.

Inevitably he bent those few inches, drawn like a puppet on a string, and he heard her soft intake of breath as his mouth pushed very gently at her set lips. His fingers tightened to hold her there; unnecessarily, because she couldn't have drawn away to save her own life.

He made a rough sound and his mouth pushed down against hers with years of hunger behind it, grinding her lips under his. He moaned out loud, his arms dropping, enfolding her, lifting her to the length of his hard, fit body.

Somewhere in the back of her mind, Kitty knew that he was using her, that in spite of the fervor and heat of his passion, she was standing in for his late wife. But it didn't seem to matter. No one had ever kissed her with such anguished need, with such hunger. She gave in to him at once, swamped by his fervor and her own curiosity and need. She knew what it was to be alone. She understood his grief. He only wanted comfort, and she could give him that. She sighed and pressed into him, not counting the cost, not looking ahead even by a second. Her arms clenched at his back and she gave him what he wanted.

Time seemed to stop while they kissed like starving people, there, in the silence of the office with only the big grandfather clock in the waiting room to be heard above their own rough breathing. She felt Drew move, leaning back against the wall so that he could, more comfortably, take her weight. His hands slid up and down her back, smoothing her against him. He became aroused, and his groan was rough in the silence as he turned her quickly, so that she was against the wall and his full weight was pressed to her.

He felt her quiver with pleasure and he had to drag his mouth away from the nectar of hers. He looked into her eyes with blinding passion, racked with desire he hadn't felt in ages. He knew his body was trembling, but so was hers. He hesitated, trying to clear his mind just enough to allow for rational thought. He couldn't even focus. She tasted like the sweetest kind of honey under his mouth, generous with her kisses, her embraces. Generous, like his Eve…

Eve.

He jerked away from her, his eyes full of the shame

and guilt he felt. He didn't even have an excuse. He'd lost his head so completely that he could barely form words in his mind, much less voice them.

To his amazement, she reached up with a soft hand and stroked his cheek. Her eyes, far from being shamed or puzzled, were full of understanding.

"It's all right," she said softly, her voice breathless from the kiss. "I understand. You must miss her terribly, today of all days."

His heart caught in his throat. He couldn't speak.

She stepped against him, demurely this time, so that she didn't make things any worse, and slid her arms around him. It was an embrace of comfort and tenderness rather than impassioned need. Fascinated, he felt his own arms enclose her as he fought and controlled his desire.

He hadn't had comfort. Not like this. Eve's parents missed her, of course, but they weren't warm and loving people. They welcomed Drew like an old friend when he came, but not with this sort of uninhibited affection. He'd never had it before.

She nuzzled her cheek against his shoulder with a smile. "Are the Coltrains taking you out to eat?" she asked softly, trying to hide her outrageous reactions to him.

His hand idly smoothed over her hair in its neat bun. He allowed himself for just one minute to wonder how it looked hanging loose down her back. There was so much of it that it must reach her waist...

"Yes, they are," he replied deeply. He sighed, closing his eyes. He was in no hurry to move, none at all. In fact, his arms contracted gently.

She didn't move. She could see the big grandfather clock against the wall from her vantage point. They'd both have to leave soon. But just for a minute or so, this was very nice. She'd had no one to hold her when her father had died. She wished she'd known Drew then.

"Do you have any family?" he asked at her ear.

She shook her head. "I only had Dad."

His hand stilled and then moved again on her hair. "You had no one when he died."

"No." She remembered the loneliness of it very well. "You had her people, at least, didn't you?"

"They don't…touch," he said after a minute. "They're very reserved, all of them, even Eve's younger brother." He smiled ruefully. "I didn't realize how comforting it was, to be held…"

He stopped, as if he was giving away something he didn't want to admit.

"No one held me, when I lost Dad," she said, easing him past the bad moment. She sighed and closed her eyes. "Maybe they're right. Maybe everyone really does need a hug, now and again."

He murmured softly. His own eyes closed. He drank in the subtle smell of her body, a fragrance like gardenias. She always smelled nice, and she was a neat little thing, except for buttons that never seemed to be done up properly. He was sorry that he'd been so efficient earlier about buttoning those buttons, because he'd have liked to feel her breasts against him closer than this.

The route of his thoughts startled him. He mustn't

let this situation deteriorate. He couldn't afford to get involved with his receptionist.

He eased her away finally, breath by breath, and coaxed her eyes up to his.

She searched them, quiet and curious, like some contented cat. Her breath was still ragged.

He thought about the scent she was wearing and frowned. "Doesn't perfume bother you at all?" he asked suddenly.

"Perfume? Why, no, I don't... Well, I've never actually thought about it. Why?"

"You sound raspy." He left her and went back into his office. He returned a minute later with his stethoscope.

He plopped her down on the edge of her desk and slid his hand inside her blouse to listen to her chest.

Her sharp intake of breath was as loud as the sudden frantic beating of her heart. He smiled as he listened, flattered by her reaction. Then he scowled. He heard the rasp of her breath as she exhaled, along with the telltale wheezing.

"Take a deep breath. Hold it. Now breathe out, as hard as you can. Once more," he instructed.

He lifted his head and removed the stethoscope, scowling. "How long have you been wheezing like this?"

She was still getting her heart calmed down. "Just... just today."

"How long have you been wearing that perfume?"

"It's new," she faltered. "I bought it yesterday. This is the first time... You think it's the perfume?"

"Yes, I do. Don't wear it again. If you're not better

in the morning, I'll send you over to your allergist and let him listen to you. Meanwhile, drink more coffee. The caffeine will help."

"I know," she said gently, having learned long ago that it helped attacks.

"You've got my number if you get in trouble during the night?"

She was really touched now. "Yes, sir."

"Use it if you need me." He touched her cheek lightly, his earlier bad temper forgotten in his concern for her. "I have to go," he said then.

She managed a smile and stepped back. "So do I."

He picked up her purse and handed it to her, trying to dismiss the taste of her mouth that still clung to his lips. He liked the taste of her, the feel of her. He was worried about her. He needed a drink, he decided as he stared at her.

"I'll lock up," he said. "Go ahead."

She nodded. "Good night, Dr. Morris."

He caught her by the sleeve. "Drew."

She bit her lower lip. "I couldn't. It wouldn't be quite proper."

His annoyance made a frown between his dark eyes. "Was kissing me that way quite proper?" he taunted.

She searched his face. "Probably not, but I wouldn't feel right to work with you on a first-name basis." She lowered her eyes. "Sometimes people do things totally out of character," she added vaguely, "things that they regret the next day."

"Do you think I'll regret this?"

"Yes," she said honestly. Her eyes were clear and

very bright. "But you shouldn't. You've had a rough day
and the memories must be pretty terrible from time to
time. You acted like any other human being who was
hurting and needed someone to hold on to, just for a
little while. As you said, it was nice to be held and comforted. I enjoyed it, too, but you needn't worry that I'm
going to go all soppy and start getting ideas about my
place in your life."

He folded his arms across his chest and studied her
curiously. "You're blunt."

"I grew up with a soldier. He taught me never to tell
lies. Well, I wouldn't tell Nurse Turner that orange lip-
stick made her look like a dried-up lemon, but that's
not exactly lying," she amended.

He chuckled. "Neither would I. She has boxes of nee-
dles," he murmured with a conspiratorial smile.

She smiled back, and he thought that he'd never realized until now how much he enjoyed watching her
smile. They seemed to have reached a new level of
comfort with each other.

"I don't want wild sex or another wife," he replied
after a minute, with equal honesty, "but I have to admit,
being hugged could be habit-forming."

"You're sure about the wild sex part?" she asked
with wide eyes. "Because if you ever change your mind,
here I am."

"Have you ever had wild sex with a man?" he teased.

She shrugged. "I've never had sex, period, but I'm
long overdue for a feverish initiation. Just so you know,"
she added with a grin. "But give me plenty of warning,
because I just know I'll be a fanatic about prevention."

He burst out laughing, and she blushed.

"Get out of here and go home!" he roared, choking on mirth. "For God's sake, have you no shame? Propositioning your own boss!"

"If you don't want to be propositioned, don't make passes at me," she returned with mock hauteur and twinkling eyes. "Now, I'm going home."

"The Coltrains said I could bring you along."

She wanted to go with him, but she forced herself to shake her head nonchalantly. "Thanks all the same." She hesitated. "Thanks for…being concerned about me, too. I'll deep-six the perfume. And next time I'll be careful what I put on. Good night."

He wondered why she'd refused to go to dinner with him. But he smiled casually and opened the door for her, and then walked her to her car after he'd locked up. He stood there watching her drive away, aware that she was grinding gears like mad. He wondered if he was losing his mind. She was only his receptionist.

CHAPTER THREE

THE COLTRAINS NOTICED a difference in Drew, and it wasn't because he was grieving. He seemed oddly thoughtful, and when Jeb mentioned Kitty, his hand jumped, as if just the sound of her name startled him.

Jeb and Lou were much too cagey to come right out and ask questions. They kept the conversation on work right through the main course. But over dessert, they probed a little.

"How's your receptionist working out, now that you've had her around for almost a year?"

"She's doing fine," Drew said without looking up from his cheesecake. "At least, as long as she stays away from perfumes with a woodsy tone," he added thoughtfully, and described the asthma that had surfaced with the wearing of her new perfume.

"A lot of our patients don't connect perfume with asthma attacks or severe headaches," Lou mused, smiling. "It isn't something you consciously think about."

"She'll think about it now," he reflected.

"Do she and Nurse Turner get along well?" Lou probed.

He chuckled. "They conspire," he murmured. "To-night they drew straws to see who got to leave first.

Kitty lost the draw." He sighed and shook his head. "I'd been pure hell to get along with all day, but she didn't say a word."

"What did she do?" Jeb asked curiously.

"She put both her hands straight up over her head and I burst out laughing."

"She's a doll," Jeb chuckled. "I remember her as a little girl, trotting along behind her dad when they went to the store together. He had her marching like a proper soldier. I felt sorry for her. He was badly wounded in Vietnam, you know, and had to take a discharge that he didn't want. They offered him a job at the Pentagon, but he was too proud to take it. So he stayed here in town, reliving past glories and making his wife and daughter suffer for his losses."

"He didn't hurt her?" Drew asked before he took time to think what he was saying.

"Not at all," Jeb assured him. "He wasn't a cruel man, but he was domineering and demanding. Kitty never had boyfriends. Nobody got past the old man, even when she graduated from high school and started taking those business courses. He intimidated the young men."

"I'll bet he did," Drew mused, thinking privately that he'd have given the old buzzard a run for his money. He moved his cheesecake around on the plate. "She must have had at least one steady boyfriend," he said probingly.

"Nope," Jeb returned. "No chance of that. The old man went down with a stroke the year she enrolled in business college. She had to nurse him and work to supplement his government pension." He shook his head. "In between, she spent a lot of time in the emergency room with what she thought was coughing fits until they diagnosed her as asthmatic. It took a while to get her medicines set to contain them, too. It's better now, but she has fits when the grasses start blooming."

"I'll keep a close check on her," Drew promised.

"She could use one," Jeb replied grimly. "Kitty's had no fun at all. That's why I suggested that you might bring her along tonight," he added with a rueful grin. "I wasn't trying to matchmake. She works for you and I like her, that's all."

"I'm sorry," Drew said, and genuinely was, now. "If I'd realized that…"

"We know better than to try to pair you off with anyone," Lou affirmed, smiling. "Least of all, Kitty."

He frowned slightly. "Why do you say that?" he murmured curiously.

"Well, she's not your type, is she?" Lou asked, averting her eyes to the table. "She's unsophisticated and unworldly. She'd rather tend her garden than go to a cocktail party, and she doesn't have a clue how to dress properly."

He wondered for a minute if Lou was making digs at his receptionist, but he realized almost at once that she wasn't. She seemed to genuinely like Kitty.

"She'll never get a boyfriend, the way she looks," Lou continued sadly. "Drew, couldn't you do something, point her to the right sort of clothes, get her to a hairdresser? Guy Fenton is still interested in her, but she's just not the sort of girl a man wants to show off. You know what I mean?"

"You mean that she doesn't dress like a young and attractive woman looking for a soul mate," he translated.

"That's exactly what I mean."

"Why don't you take her in hand?" he asked Lou.

"How would I go about it, without making her look stupid?" she asked honestly. "She doesn't really know me."

"She only works for me," Drew replied.

"But she looks up to you. You know, sort of as a father figure." She looked down so that her eyes wouldn't reflect her delight at the way that remark made Drew tauten and look irritated.

"I'm not old enough to be her father," he said shortly.

Coltrain cleared his throat to choke back helpless laughter. "Lou didn't mean it that way. But she does look up to you. What would it hurt to help her change her image? Married receptionists never quit their jobs."

"She can do better than Guy Fenton," he said, remembering vividly how Fenton had already treated her. "As I recall, she dressed up for him, and he ditched her in the middle of a date."

"Her idea of dressing up is a new shirtwaist dress," Lou muttered. "And she never lets that hair down."

Drew tried not to think about all that hair. He had frequent longings to start tearing pins out of it, just to see how it looked when it was loose.

"She needs someone besides Guy Fenton," Jeb remarked coolly. "Guy keeps dark secrets, and he drinks too much. But there are plenty of eligible men in town. Matt Caldwell, for instance."

Matt was rugged and outlandish, but he was also single and well-to-do. Drew didn't like the idea of him. He didn't like the idea of any man, actually. And because he didn't, he agreed to Lou's proposal. He wasn't going to get involved with Kitty. Getting her involved with another man was the ideal way to protect himself.

"Jeb and I are on the orphanage committee here in town," Lou reminded him, "and we're hosting a Summer Charity Ball to raise money to build a new wing onto the orphanage. I'd like you to come. You could bring Kitty—and then I can introduce her to the eligible men."

Drew frowned.

"All you have to do is bring her, Drew," Lou persisted, "not propose to her. You can have her meet you there if you don't want to be seen with her."

"Oh, for God's sake, I don't mind asking her," he grumbled.

"Good," Lou replied, smiling at him. "And if you can get her refurbished in time, there's no telling what might happen."

"Matt likes her—" Jeb put his two cents worth in "—and they've got a lot in common."

"Was he afraid of her father?" Drew asked curiously.

"Not at all," Jeb mused, grinning so that his freckles stood out. "In fact, they came to blows over Operation Desert Storm—Matt's reserve unit was called up during it, you know. He laid the colonel out in the middle of the local McDonald's and poured a milkshake over him. I don't think the colonel ever got over it."

Drew chuckled. "What did Kitty say?"

"Nothing. She didn't dare. But you used to be able to just say the word 'milkshake' to her, and she'd collapse laughing."

Drew found the idea amusing. He'd have to try that one day. He toyed with his fork. "All right, I'll take her to the ball. When is it?"

She told him. "And it's formal. Very formal."

"I'll wear a dinner jacket," he said reluctantly. "I guess Kitty can come up with a dress."

"Help her find one," Lou suggested. "And you might point her toward the cosmetic counter and a hairstylist and contact lenses. She'd be pretty if she worked at it."

HE WAITED UNTIL she came to work the following Monday, and when Nurse Turner went out to lunch, he asked Kitty to come into his office.

She'd spent an uneasy weekend remembering what they'd done together and her lack of sleep was evident in the dark circles under her eyes. She noticed that he looked tired as well, but considering how hard he worked, she couldn't attribute it to anything other than his job. She didn't know that he'd spent his share of sleepless nights trying to decide how to put the experience out of his mind.

"Are you still sweet on Guy Fenton?" he asked bluntly.

She didn't ask why he was probing into her private life. She moved restlessly in the chair. "I used to like him. I still do. But I don't want to go out with him any-more."

"I don't blame you. How about Matt Caldwell, then?"

"Matt doesn't know me from a peanut," she informed him. "He and my father never got along at all."

"Neither do he and I from time to time, but he's coming to the Summer Charity Ball at the country club and I thought you might like to go with me," he added, not looking at her.

She looked at the wall and wondered if she was having delusions. Perhaps that glass of wine she'd consumed with her dinner Saturday night had had a delayed reaction...

"Could you repeat that?" she asked. "I think I may be in the midst of a drunken stupor."

"On what, coffee?" he asked, diverted.

"I had a glass of wine Saturday night," she volunteered.

His mouth curled up. "Did I drive you to drink?" he chided, and then felt guilty when she blushed. "Never mind. I asked you to go to the Summer Charity Ball with me. Lou's hosting it with Jeb, and they're inviting all the single men and women in town, including Matt and Guy." He glanced at his hands. "The Coltrains particularly wanted you to come."

Kitty studied his face uncertainly. He sounded as if he hated the idea of asking her at all, and she knew without being told that it was the Coltrains who'd put him up to this. Funny how disappointing that was, although she couldn't deny that she knew how he still felt about his late wife. She must have been temporarily out of her mind to think that he'd asked her for his own sake; or to allow herself to build one kiss into a future.

"I don't really think I want to…" she began politely.

He looked up, his dark eyes so intent that they stopped her protest before she could get it out of her mouth. "I want you to come," he said deliberately.

Of course he didn't. But her stubborn refusal irritated him. She was young and sweet and she had a lot to offer. Matt or Guy would be lucky to have such a woman find them attractive. She deserved a little happiness.

She misunderstood his determination, and she smiled warmly. "Really?" she asked breathlessly.

He turned away from that bright-eyed surprise. "Sure."

"Well, I guess I could."

"You'll need a dress," he continued, toying with a sheet of paper on the desk. "Something pretty and formal."

"I'll…I'll have to buy one," she faltered.

"And you could have your hair done."

She touched the bun defensively. "Cut it?"

"No!" He caught himself before he sounded even more of a fool. "I meant, you could have it put in one of those complicated styles. Cut it?" He looked absolutely shocked. "It would be a crime to cut hair like that." His eyes reluctantly slid over it, confined as usual in a huge bun behind her nape. "It must fall all the way to your waist when it's down."

She smiled self-consciously. "A little farther than that," she confided. "I don't ever wear it down anymore."

"Why?"

She shrugged. "My father said I looked like 'Alice in Wonderland.'"

"Bull," he muttered.

"Anyway, it gets in my way when I'm working."

"You could braid it," he suggested.

She laughed. "I can't do it myself."

He had to bite his tongue to keep from offering to help. For a long time now, he'd wondered how Kitty's hair would look when it was loosened. It was a lovely dark shade of brown. She had just a faintly olive complexion and those soft green eyes dominated her delicate oval face. Despite the glasses she insisted on wearing instead of contact lenses, she was very attractive. Her figure was as good as any he'd ever seen. If only she took advantage of her assets and didn't downplay them so drastically. On the other hand, that might be a good thing. He could see himself trying to diagnose and treat illnesses with Kitty running around the office looking like a nymph.

"Never mind," he murmured. "Do what you like with it. But get a pretty dress to wear."

"Which one of them are you planning to throw me at?" she asked.

He straightened. "I beg your pardon?"

"Who's being sacrificed for me, Guy or Matt?" she persisted. "I gather that you and the Coltrains are determined to save me from spinsterhood?"

His face grew stern. "I thought, as they do, that you deserved a little fun. We aren't throwing you at anyone. We only want to…improve you."

"I see."

"Like hell you see!" he burst out, irritated by his own thoughts as well as her resistance to having people remodel her for her own good. "You can't see anything! You dress like a bag lady, you screw your hair up into those god-awful buns, you walk around in a permanent daze and then you probably wonder why men never come on to you!"

She wasn't just shocked; she was downright hurt. She hadn't thought he had such a low opinion of her. Apparently nothing about her appealed to him at all. She wasn't sure if he was genuinely trying to help her find a man, or if he had plans to marry her off so that he could get her out of his office for good.

She lowered her eyes to the floor, hiding rage and shock. "I didn't realize I had so little to offer."

"It isn't that," he grumbled. "You have plenty to offer, that's why I hate to see you waste it! You're very attractive, but you could be a lot more appealing if you just worked at it. Your father isn't around to chase away prospective suitors anymore, Kitty. You don't have to downplay your looks. It's all right to dress up and make the most of your assets."

She sighed angrily. "Okay," she said tightly. "I'll just do that little thing."

Her eyes sparkled like emeralds in a pale face. He hated what he'd said to her, but if it woke her up to the possibilities, it was for the best.

"Get something dark green," he said out of the blue. "Tight in the waist and low-cut. It will do wonders for those eyes. They're incredible," he added softly. "Like living emeralds."

Her heart jumped. "I beg your pardon?"

He cleared his throat and glanced quickly at his watch. "I have a meeting with the hospital board of directors in thirty minutes," he said abruptly. "We're going to try to convince them to hire a full-time physician for the emergency room so that the rest of us can have a little peace after hours."

"Good luck," she said, and meant it, because she knew how hard the local doctors had to work to keep that emergency room going.

"We'll need it. Indigent care is killing the budget."

"A lot of people can't get insurance," she reminded him, glad to be off the subject of her own physical shortcomings. "And some people can't afford it."

He agreed. "It's a sad world in some ways, isn't it, Kitty?" he murmured. "Money shouldn't be the determining factor in a life or death situation. It isn't, here in Jacobsville, despite the budget. But hospitals can't operate on goodwill and hope."

"I know that." She shrugged. "I guess it's more complicated than it seems to a layperson."

He nodded. "It's complicated even to the professionals."

She moved toward her desk.

"What about the ball?" he asked curtly. "Are you going with me?"

She didn't look at him, but at her computer. "I'll go," she said, but without real enthusiasm. She knew, even if he wasn't admitting it, that he was only taking her so that she could be offered up to Guy and Matt. It hurt her as nothing had in recent years. That, too, was disturbing.

"Good," he said. He couldn't think of anything else to say, so he went back to get his jacket and soon afterward, he left the office.

KITTY WENT SHOPPING all by herself. Thinking that he'd made suggestions and shouldn't push his luck by offering to accompany her, Drew never said another word about the dress or the hairstyling.

She went all the way to Houston, in the end, to look for a dress, leaving very early on Saturday morning in her little car. The drive was nice, even though it was drizzling rain. Tree colors were so varied and pretty, hazes of green, hundreds of shades of it, in the trees that grew along streams and near houses in the distance. There were calves in the pastures, too, because it was that time of year as well. In summer, everything seemed to come alive on the earth. She thought about a young man's fancy turning to thoughts of love and laughed out loud. Drew was neither young nor interested in her, so she'd do well to ignore these strange feelings he engendered in her. Despite his collusion with the Coltrains, she had to remember that he wasn't interested in dolling her up for himself. He only wanted to sacrifice her to Guy or Matt.

Well, she thought, she might as well let him. If he thought she had potential, perhaps she did. All her life, she'd deferred to her father as far as the opposite sex was concerned. It hadn't ever occurred to her how alone her father was or how much he depended on her at home. Perhaps the thought of losing her was really terrifying to him and he had too much pride to admit it. That would explain his reluctance to let her get involved with men, or to think of marriage. He seemed very self-reliant and domineering, but underneath, he had many insecurities, all of which had grown much worse with the death of her mother.

She remembered her mother sometimes, marveling at the way the seemingly gentle and unassuming little woman had handled her father's moods and demands. Only someone close to them would have ever realized that Martha was her husband's strength, and when she died, he collapsed. From that day on, Kitty became his strength, and he depended on her more and more. Despite her frequent asthma attacks, he clung. When he had the stroke, the dependence became complete. Only then was his fear visible, because he no longer had the strength of will to conceal it. Kitty had learned to use her medicines conscientiously for her father's sake. It was crucial that she keep well to look after him. Even so, there were times when she had to depend on kind co-workers to get her to the emergency room. She didn't even tell her father about the attacks that precipitated more and more medicine changes. Finally a preventative added to her regular regimen made trips to the emergency room almost a thing of the past.

Kitty became the colonel's substitute mother for the last few pitiful years of his proud life. But at the end, he had enough consciousness to call her mother's name, once, achingly…

She blinked away sudden tears. Her parents had been married for thirty years when Kitty's mother, Martha, had died. Perhaps that was how Drew had been after his Eve died, lost and alone and afraid. But he hadn't even a daughter to console him. No wonder he was impatient and ill-tempered and overworked. His job had probably been all that stood between him and madness just after his wife's untimely death.

Houston loomed ahead, its familiar skyline bringing back the present. She couldn't live in the past, although Drew seemed determined to do just that. She had to look toward the future. Marriage had seemed like an impossible dream, but now it might be accessible. If she worked at her appearance and tried to be outgoing, the possibilities were unlimited. Her asthma was under tight control and she could look nice if she worked at it. Who knows, she might actually interest a man enough to turn his thoughts to marriage. It would be nice to have a home of her own, someone to share her spare time with, children.

She sighed. It was going to take a lot more than a new dress to inspire anyone to marry her. But they did say that fine feathers made fine birds. It was worth a try.

SHE LOOKED THROUGH several stores before she came across a dress very much like the one Drew had described—dark green taffeta with a low neckline and short, puffy pale green chiffon sleeves. It was ankle-length and when she tried it on, she was astonished at the change it made. The cut emphasized her firm breasts and narrow waist subtly, and there was a wispy chiffon scarf that matched the sleeves to go over her hair. It was like something out of the forties, a glimpse of bygone elegance that took her breath. She couldn't really afford it, but she bought it anyway, and white satin pumps and a white satin evening bag to go with it.

The hairdresser's was next, where she had her exquisite locks trimmed but not altered in length. The beautician enthused over the length and texture of her hair and talked her into a wavy style much seen on television and in movies. She was hesitant, but hours later when the curlers were removed, she was shocked at the face that looked back at her, surrounded by exquisite flowing waves. She went right to the optometrist and got herself fitted for contact lenses. They would be in long before the ball. She was going to make it a night to remember.

JUST FOR FUN, Monday morning she put on a lacy white dress that she'd bought during a trip to San Antonio with a cousin three years before. It was a Spanish style that suited her dark hair and olive skin, with lace and soft off-white embroidery around the flounced top and the long skirt.

She wore high heels and stockings with it, and wore her hair down for the first time ever. It was a dressy getup to go to work in, but she felt like a new woman. And after all, there was no time like the present to try out her new look on her boss.

She stood in front of her full-length mirror and marveled at what was reflected back. Even with her wire-framed glasses, she looked nice. She'd taken pains with her makeup and the new hairstyle made her feel very feminine.

As she gathered her purse and lacy shawl, she wondered what her boss was going to think of it.

She'd prepared herself for every sort of reaction, from mild surprise to indifference. What she got was a total surprise.

He was in his office when she arrived, engrossed in a patient's file. He hadn't shaved, an indication in itself that he'd been up either all night or since very early that morning without a chance to go home.

He didn't even look up at first. He heard her footsteps as she tapped on the door.

"Bring me a cup of coffee," he murmured. "Please," he added, still without looking up.

Vaguely disappointed that he hadn't taken time to even glance at her, Kitty went to the small kitchen and made a pot of coffee. She put a cup and saucer and napkin, a spoon and the sugar and cream holders on a tray and as an afterthought, added some almond cookies. He wouldn't eat breakfast, she knew that from Nurse Turner, but he was bound to feel a little hungry if he'd been up all night.

She edged in the door and put the tray on one of the retractable leaves of his oak desk.

"Thanks," he muttered, still absorbed in his file. Then he caught a glimpse of something long and flowing and looked up.

Kitty thought that, as long as she lived, she would never forget those few seconds.

He actually dropped the file. His black, shocked eyes

went from her crown down her body to the exquisite, endless small curls that plunged down her slender figure all the way past her waist.

"Good God," he breathed, and it sounded reverent.

His unblinking intensity made her self-conscious. "You mentioned getting it styled…" she faltered.

He got up from the desk, oblivious to the notes, and moved to stand just in front of her. Like a sleepwalker, like a man possessed, his hands gathered up her long, silky hair and tested its softness as he searched her eyes. His lips made a thin line in the fraught silence of the office, and the contraction of his fingers began to be a little painful.

His closeness was affecting her. Her heartbeat against the flounced bodice was now noticeable, and her lips had parted under the force of her breath.

His eyes fell to them and held there for an eternity as his hands tugged and he moved closer, all in the same breath, until his legs were touching hers.

"You smell like a hundred varieties of roses," he whispered, breathing in the perfume that clung to her. "I wonder…if you taste of them?"

Almost in a trance, he started to bend to her while the silence in the office intensified.

Then, as his lips hovered just above hers, so that she could almost taste them, the front door suddenly opened and closed. Nurse Turner had arrived.

Drew released her at once, and his eyes blazed. "Go home and put on something appropriate for an office," he snapped, unbearably outraged by her appearance and his unexpected reaction to it. "Right now, Miss Carson!"

The bite in his deep voice was painful. She couldn't understand the sudden rage, as if the sight of her offended him. Was she dressed like some sort of call girl?

"And do something about that damned mane of hair!" he added furiously.

She stared at him with wounded eyes. She'd felt so wonderful when she left her apartment, and now she felt dirty and naked. Without another word, she went out the door and past the stunned nurse.

"Well, look at you!" Nurse Turner exclaimed. "Kitty, you're gorgeous!"

"No, I'm not," Kitty said through building anger and tears, grabbing her shawl and purse. "I've got to go home and change my clothes and do something about my awful hair. I'll be back as soon as I can."

She went out the door, her first thought that she was going to grab the nearest pair of scissors and cut her hair to the skull!

CHAPTER FOUR

DREW COULD BARELY THINK. He'd been at the hospital until dawn with a small patient who was going to live despite the odds against him from a burst appendix and peritonitis. Now he'd been cruel to Kitty, whose only crime was to look like a ministering angel in white. The sight of her had hurt him, taunted him, reminded him all too blatantly of Eve in a similar dress the evening he'd asked her to marry him. Eve had blond hair, not brunette, but hers had been long and she'd worn it similarly to that beautiful curling mass that Kitty had entered his office displaying.

The thought occurred to him at once that Kitty would be on her way home now in tears, thanks to his unreasonable anger, and probably the first thing she'd do was look for scissors…

It horrified him beyond all rationality to imagine that Kitty would butcher her hair. He got up from his desk, barely able to reason from lack of sleep, and rushed out the door.

"I'll be back. An emergency," he murmured to Nurse Turner on his way out.

It was thankfully too early for patients. In fact, he was due at the hospital to make rounds, but this couldn't wait. He got into his Mercedes and burned rubber getting to Kitty's apartment house.

He walked right in behind a young woman with a key who'd just entered it.

"You can't…" she blurted.

"The hell I can't," he muttered, going up the steps in twos as he rushed to stop Kitty from what he knew she was going to do.

The pounding on the apartment door was loud and violent. Kitty glared at it from her bedroom, but if she didn't stop it, the other tenants were going to be furious. Some of them worked nights.

She went to the front door and looked through the keyhole, knowing before she did who was going to be standing there.

"Go away!" she raged.

"No. Open the door."

He looked as if he planned to spend the day on her doorstep. She thought for a minute and finally decided that it would be easier to lay a skillet across his thick skull if he were inside the apartment, so she opened the door.

He came in and closed the door, breathless from his rushed trip over here, and stared at her. She was wearing a bathrobe instead of the dress. She had a pair of scissors in her right hand, and apparently he'd been in the veritable nick of time. She was flushed. Her eyes were red from crying. Tracks of tears were visible on her cheeks. Even tangled, her hair was glorious.

He reached down and took the scissors out of her hand. "Not to get even with me," he said quietly. "Not even if I deserve it. It would be a crime to cut it, Kitty. It's beautiful."

She glared at him with trembling lips.

He tossed the scissors onto the table and pulled her into his arms with a heavy sigh, wrapping her up against him. Odd how familiar it felt, how comfortable…how exciting.

His face nuzzled that thick mane of hair and found its way under it, to her neck, to her soft throat. His mouth pressed there, gently at first and then hungrily. His arms contracted. He bent and lifted her in the instant that his mouth searched for and found hers.

He tasted of the endless cups of coffee he'd had at the hospital, and the bristles on his face were rough and vaguely abrasive, but Kitty didn't care. Her arms went around him and she held on for dear life.

"I love your hair," he breathed into her lips as he laid her down gently on her bed and eased down beside her. "I love the feel of it, the smell of it, the glorious length of it. You can't…cut it," he murmured roughly as he began to kiss her again.

His hands were in it, gripping, savoring, and then they were under the bathrobe, against her thin slip, then under it, touching and tracing, delicately probing until she arched up with a moan that he took into his hungry mouth…

A LONG TIME LATER, he managed to pull away, his eyes full of her flushed face with its swollen, red mouth and wide eyes.

The robe was gone and her gown was around her

hips. He looked down at the vivid mauve tips of her firm breasts and the faint marks his mouth had made on the rest of them. She hadn't protested anything he'd done to her. Her eyes were still on him as she lay there like a creamy sacrifice, watching him, searching his face like loving hands.

"I haven't had any sleep," he began gruffly.

"Is that an excuse?" she asked breathlessly.

"I don't need an excuse. If you ever come to work again dressed like you were this morning, women's liberation notwithstanding, I'll lay you down on the floor in my office!"

He was breathing heavily. Of course, so was she. Her arms were beside her head and she felt hot and trembly all over. She'd read in books that men touched women in the ways he'd touched her, but she hadn't understood what it felt like until now.

She moved experimentally. Her body still felt shocks of pleasure go through it with every movement. She shivered a little.

He watched her with indulgent amusement. He hadn't meant to let things go so far, but her shocked pleasure had made it impossible for him to stop. He enjoyed her fledgling responses to his lovemaking. He enjoyed all of her. It had been years since he'd indulged in anything remotely resembling this heavy petting. He found that his body still responded sharply to a woman's, and it pleased him that he wasn't completely dead from the neck down.

He traced her face with his fingers, lightly touching, teasing. He sighed and eased down, stretching, before he pulled her completely against him and held her there, her bare breasts against his hair-roughened chest. His shirt was on the floor somewhere, along with his belt and her robe. They were both disheveled as hell, and he didn't care.

His hand fumbled for the telephone. He lifted his head long enough to punch in numbers.

"Nurse Turner?" he murmured drowsily. "Call the hospital and tell them I'll be two hours late for rounds. I've got to have some sleep. They can reach me by my beeper. Yes. Thank you. She hasn't? Well, we'll start in two hours, I imagine she'll be back by then." He chuckled drowsily. "Oh, I think she'll get over it. I'm not easy to get along with when I haven't had any sleep. Yes, I will. Thanks."

He hung up and pulled a stunned, still drowsy Kitty closer. Seconds later, they were both asleep.

Used as he was to grabbing odd moments of sleep, Drew woke in a little over two hours, feeling an unfamiliar weight on his arm. He opened his eyes, turned over and stifled a gasp at what he saw.

Kitty was lying beside him, her firm, pretty breasts bare, her glorious hair making a veil over the upper half of her body. She looked like a painting he'd once seen of a fairy, almost glowing, beautiful, vibrantly alive.

His hand lifted involuntarily and he touched her breasts, tracing their firm contours, delighting in their instant response. Even asleep, her body recognized him and lifted toward his searching fingers.

He groaned deep in his throat and moved again, tracing Kitty's warm, soft flesh with his mouth.

She stirred then and moaned breathlessly, lifting again.

Something was touching her. She felt wanted, beautiful, wanton. She cradled the dark head to her breasts and moved sinuously, enjoying the unfamiliar warmth of Drew's hungry mouth against her bare flesh.

"God Almighty," he breathed roughly, leaning his forehead against her while he fought for control, "what am I doing?"

"Don't ask me," she whispered shakily, "I'm a novice myself." She laughed softly as she moved against the sheets. "But I wouldn't mind if you kept doing whatever it is."

He lifted his head with a heavy sigh and looked down at her. She met his eyes with curiosity and drowsy pleasure. She smiled. Unthinking, uncaring, he smiled back.

His lean hands cradled her face. He bent, kissing her tenderly. "I have to make rounds," he whispered.

"I have to go to work," she whispered back.

His body moved restlessly against hers. He ached all over with desire. He could have her. He knew it without a word passing between them. He was more than prepared, there would be no risk, none at all, of a child.

But what then? His mouth lifted from hers with reluctance. He searched her soft eyes for a long moment.

She could see him deliberating. Seconds later, she knew that he'd taken several mental steps away from her. Nothing else was going to happen. That iron control wasn't going to let him lose his head completely.

Her arms fell away from him and she lay there, just watching him, without speaking.

He rolled away from her and got up, shrugging into his shirt before he replaced his belt.

She watched him do these routine things with pleasure. She should have felt embarrassed, she supposed, but she didn't. It occurred to her in that moment that she was in love with him.

His eyes slid to where she still lay on the bed and she tried not to let the possessiveness she felt for him show.

"Get dressed," he said quietly. "We both have work to do."

She didn't look at him as she sat up and replaced her slip. She got out of bed, pushing her hair back over her shoulders.

He took her by the shoulders, smoothing his hands over the soft, warm skin. "I won't lie and say that I didn't enjoy it," he said quietly. "I did. But it's still too soon for me," he added.

She looked up into his eyes, searching them quietly. "Was it me?"

"It was you, not a ghost," he replied, understanding the question. "You're very attractive, and I think you already know what effect that hair has on me. You saw it in the office, when I lost my temper. I was so afraid that you'd cut it before I could get here." He laughed flatly. "I think I'd have cut my own throat. It's glorious hair."

She pushed it away from her face. "Why were you so angry?" she asked belatedly.

"The night I proposed to Eve, she had her hair in a similar fashion and she was wearing a white lacy Spanish dress," he explained. "I wasn't at all prepared for the way you were going to look in your new image."

"I see. I'm sorry," she said through her teeth.

"There's no need to apologize," he replied at once. "You look delightful, Kitty Cat," he teased softly. "Wear your hair like that anytime you please. I'll try to restrain my enthusiasm."

"Is that what it was?" she asked demurely.

He linked his hands behind her waist and pulled her close. "It was affection punctuated with the purest lust I've ever felt," he replied, looking at her possessively. "I want you. I mean it. I'm not thinking of any other woman, either, when I touch you."

"But it makes you feel guilty."

His shoulders rose and fell. "Yes, it does. I loved Eve. I've never been able to let go of her memory." He looked her straight in the eye. "I never will. I loved her too much. I can offer you some passionate kisses. I can sleep with you. God knows I want to. But that's all it would be," he added, trying to be honest with her. His hands contracted. "Sex wouldn't be enough."

Her eyes fell to his hair-roughened chest. She wanted to touch him there, caress him, but she didn't. He wanted her. But he still loved Eve. It was always going to be like that.

"We can be friends," he said. "Even intimate friends. I like you a hell of a lot. You're good company and you aren't afraid to speak your mind."

She looked up. "Friends."

"Lovers, if you like," he added bluntly.

She managed a soft laugh. "With everyone in town knowing?"

"I'm afraid so. Your face is a dead giveaway right now."

"I suppose it is." She moved away from him, reaching to the floor to pick up her robe and wrap it around her. She felt cold.

He went to her, and tilted her face up to his. "I can't love you," he said shortly. "I can't offer you marriage."

"I know that." She tied the robe. "And I can't accept anything less." She moved away from him. "I want a husband and children."

He drew a long, sad breath. "I'm sorry."

"You can't help it. If I'd had someone that wonderful in my past, maybe I could settle for memories, too. I don't blame you." She turned to look at him. "But I'm only twenty-four and I have my whole life still ahead of me. I don't have any memories to live on."

He stuck his hands into his pockets. "I guess not."

She took a deep breath and coughed, then grimaced. "The pollen count's terrible today," she murmured, searching in her purse for her inhaler. She kept them everywhere: one in the bedside table, one in her purse, one in the pocket of the jacket she wore on walks. It staved off attacks if she used it soon enough.

She did her spaced inhalations and then sat down, breathing better. "I walked to work this morning," she murmured.

"Stupid."

She shrugged. "It was beautiful outside, and I love flowers," she said with a nostalgic smile. "Life isn't fair, is it? I used to keep a garden when I lived with Dad. It was hard on my lungs when everything was blooming, but I wore a mask and hoed right on."

"At least you don't mind using your medicine. I have patients who never fill the prescription."

"The same ones you have to see in the emergency room at two in the morning," she ventured.

He smiled. "Exactly."

He picked up the watch he'd laid on her bedside table and grimaced as he looked at it, shaking his head. "I'm really late."

"So am I."

He buttoned his shirt and put the watch back on, reaching for his jacket. He pulled out his comb and stopped in her bathroom long enough to put his hair back in its pristine condition.

"You need a shave," she murmured when he came out.

"Tell me about it. I was planning to have one when you walked into the office looking like Venus rising."

"You said to get my hair fixed and buy new clothes," she said pointedly.

"To attract Guy Fenton and Matt Caldwell," he shot back, scowling. "Not me!"

She wrapped her arms around her breasts. "Sorry."

He ran a hand through his thick hair, mussing it again. He couldn't bear to look at her. It made him hungry.

"I'll see you at the office. I told Nurse Turner that you were probably upset and might be late getting back. She knew that I'd upset you." He sighed deeply. "I'm sorry," he added. His eyes went to the bed and then back to her. "But I don't regret one minute of this."

Her arms tightened around herself. "Men never do," she murmured.

He cocked an eyebrow. "Would you like to explain that?"

"Not really." She walked toward the door.

He caught her hand before she could open the door-knob and turned her to face him. "You're still going to the ball with me," he said firmly.

"Are you sure you want me to?"

He nodded.

"All right, then."

His dark eyes slid over her body in the bathrobe, down to her pretty feet and back up to her flushed, sad face. "It's hard for me to remember that I'm a doctor sometimes. You have lovely breasts."

She flushed.

"Embarrassed?" he asked softly, and moved even closer. "There's no need. I'm not going to tell a living soul what I know about your body. Ever," he added solemnly.

The flush got worse. She dropped her eyes to his chin. "I never did that before."

His chest rose and fell. He touched her long hair gently. "You're young enough to enjoy first times."

She met his eyes, worried. "You didn't enjoy it?" she blurted out.

His jaw tautened. His eyes glittered. "Hell, yes, I enjoyed it," he said through his teeth. "Did you think your innocence didn't show?"

"You…laughed."

"Yes." He bent, brushing his mouth gently over her eyes. "It was so sweet when you convulsed, and I heard you cry out because the pleasure was so overwhelming. Your first time…and it was with me."

"It wasn't…your first time," she whispered.

"My first time was very much like yours," he whispered, smiling as he recalled it. "With an older girl who was too afraid of getting pregnant to let me go all the way. But it was sweet, just the same."

"Were you ashamed, afterward?"

"A little," he confessed. "I was brought up to believe that certain things only happened between married people."

"So was I." She wouldn't look up.

He tilted her face up to his. "You have a beautiful, innocent body. I did nothing to threaten your chastity."

"I know that. But it was so intimate," she emphasized.

"Yes." He kissed her forehead gently, feeling things inside himself that he'd forgotten he could. "Intimate."

"I wouldn't, couldn't, let anyone else do that to me."

He put her away from him. "I'm going home to shave. You'd better have lunch and go to work. We're going to have a busy afternoon."

"I guess we are."

He started to open the door. His black eyes snared hers. She looked vulnerable, somehow. He didn't want to leave her like that.

"Don't beat your conscience to death, Kitty," he commanded.

"Won't you?" she asked bitterly.

He scowled. He didn't want to think about that. It probably would. He shrugged, smiled faintly in her direction and left.

KITTY WENT BACK to work, pretending that nothing more than Drew's outburst of temper had affected her. Nurse Turner, knowing no better, accepted the explanation. But she noticed that Kitty had her hair bundled up again and that she was wearing the old nondescript clothes she'd always worn to work. Drew might be sorry for what he'd said, but Kitty wasn't taking chances.

He came back from making rounds at the hospital, glanced at her with strangely wounded eyes and went back to wait for his first patient.

Kitty knew from his behavior that he was going to pretend it never happened. She went along. It would make things at the office more bearable if they could just be boss and receptionist. She tried. Only at night, when the memory made her twist and turn with painful longing did she give in to what she felt for Drew. And he wouldn't know, because she was adept at hiding her feelings.

SHE DRESSED FOR the grand charity ball feeling like a limp Cinderella in her green satin gown. She was sorry that she'd bought it, because when Drew saw it, the first thing that would occur to him was that he'd suggested the color. That couldn't be helped. She couldn't afford to buy another, not on her budget.

But it didn't really surprise her when he sent word

that he was called to the hospital for an emergency case and she'd have to meet him at the country club. She smiled to herself, knowing full well that any other doctor on staff would gladly have covered for him if he'd really wanted them to.

She drove herself to the ball, crushing her pretty taffeta dress in the small confines of the little white car. She got out, her glorious hair in a becoming tangle down her back, her evening purse gripped in her hand, and went inside.

The Coltrains were at the door to greet their guests, since they were the organizers.

"Don't tell me," Lou said when she greeted Kitty, "Drew's been called to the hospital."

"Fortunes of war," Kitty mused.

Jeb didn't say a word. He smiled and said the conventional things and watched Kitty go to the refreshment table alone.

Lou's hand clung to his unobtrusively. "He's fighting it."

"Damn it," he muttered, contracting his fingers around hers. "He could have gotten someone to cover for him at the hospital."

She moved closer to him, momentarily resting her blond head against his shoulder. "The road to true love is rocky."

He looked down at her, his blue eyes narrow and full of love as they searched her pretty face. He smiled. "But worth the climb," he murmured.

She smiled. He bent his head and kissed her softly.

"Cut it out," Matt Caldwell teased, grinning at them.

They both flushed a little, still feeling like newly-weds after more than a year and several months of marriage.

Matt had a hand in his pocket, and he looked devastating in an evening jacket, his black wavy hair neatly combed above a lean and dark face with dancing dark eyes. He was the most eligible bachelor left in Jacobsville, but no woman ever seemed to touch his heart. All the same, he never lacked for dates as a rule. But tonight he was alone.

"Where's Kitty?" he asked, tongue-in-cheek.

They both flushed even more. "Now, Matt," Lou began.

He held up a hand. "It's all right. I knew why I was being invited. I like Kitty. I didn't have anyone in mind to bring anyway. Where is she?"

"By the punch bowl," Jeb sighed. "She was supposed to come with Drew, but he had an emergency."

Matt was looking past them at Kitty. He scowled. He'd known her since high school, although she was four years behind him, but he'd never seen her look like that!

"Poor man," he mused. "His loss is my gain. See you."

He went straight to Kitty like a shot, barely acknowledging the people who spoke to him as he walked through the crowd. He stopped in front of Kitty, towering over her.

"Cinderella, I presume?" he mused, giving her a bow. "The prince is here."

She laughed. Her sad face was radiant as she went gratefully into his arms, feeling like the belle of the ball.

The number they were playing was an exquisite waltz, and it was one dance she did very well. So did Matt.

He whirled her around the floor with pure delight, noticing that the other dancers moved aside for them. He had eyes only for pretty Kitty, with her contacts in and her glorious hair flying as he whirled her to the rhythm. Despite the fact that his name had been loosely linked with that of widow Elysia Craig Nash, he seemed to find Kitty enchanting.

It was at that moment that Drew showed up, his emergency having been little more than a scratch that needed a single stitch. He greeted Jeb and Lou, but they were engrossed in conversation with Jane and Todd Burke, so he waved and went forward, hands in his pockets, to see what the crowd was watching.

The sight that met his eyes had a strange effect on him. There, in the middle of the floor, was his receptionist dancing with the richest, most eligible bachelor in Jacobsville. And judging from the look on her face as they danced, she was floating on a cloud.

CHAPTER FIVE

KITTY FELT LIKE a princess as she twirled gaily in Matt's arms to the rhythm of the waltz, her eyes half-closed, her face radiant and almost beautiful in the brilliant light from the chandeliers. She was breathless, oblivious, in those few moments. There was no past nor present, only now and the music and the brilliant color.

The waltz ended, though, and people applauded wildly. Matt hugged Kitty close and she returned his affectionate embrace, still exhilarated from the breathless joy of dancing for the first time in years.

"Oh, that was fun," she exclaimed at Matt's ear. "That was so much fun!"

He chuckled. "You're some dancer, Miss Carson," he mused, smiling down at her.

"So are you. You're wasted on business."

He shrugged. "Can't make much money dancing, but I do all right at buying and selling horses."

"All right" meant that his Caldwell Enterprises was listed in the Fortune 500 companies. His business empire was so diversified that even if one company failed, there were a hundred more successful ones to take up the slack. Matt was the original hometown boy made good, except for that one black incident in his past...

"Enjoying yourself, I see, Miss Carson," a cold voice murmured behind them.

Kitty turned, flushed and breathless, to meet the icy dark eyes of her boss.

"Indeed I am, Dr. Morris," Kitty said with a breathless laugh. Her green eyes flashed at him. "I haven't danced in years."

Drew's gaze had gone all over the green satin dress twice. He couldn't seem to drag his attention away from it. Matt lifted an eyebrow and quickly glanced past them.

"Excuse me, won't you?" he asked politely. "I have to talk to Justin Ballenger about some stock he and Calhoun are feeding out for me. Be right back, Kitty."

He winked at Kitty and nodded at Drew before he strode off toward the Ballenger brothers and their wives.

"If you came on my account, you needn't," Kitty told Drew, and without resentment; he couldn't help the way he felt about his late wife, after all. "I'm sure Matt wouldn't mind taking me home."

He looked really out of sorts, despite his striking appearance in evening clothes. His hands were in his pockets and his face was drawn and stiff with banked-down anger.

"Do you want to get something to drink at the refreshment table?" she asked when he didn't speak. She glanced around to see eyes watching them surreptitiously. "People are staring at us."

"They're staring at you, in that dress," he replied quietly. "You look devastating. I'm sure Matt's already told you so."

"No, not really. But at least he smiles at me."

His shoulder moved restlessly. "I don't feel like smiling. I don't want to be here."

Her heart plummeted. "I guess not. You've already put in a long day. Why don't you go home? You don't need to stay on my account, honest."

"I might as well," he said half under his breath, as Matt came back toward them. "I seem to be superfluous."

Matt joined them, catching Kitty's hand in his. "Glad you could make it, Drew. Did you bring anyone?"

Drew glanced at Kitty, who refused to meet his eyes. "No," he said flatly.

Matt laughed pleasantly. "I'm not surprised. You never do. It's good to see you mixing socially, just the same. A man can't live in the past." His smile was bitter. "I ought to know."

Kitty looked up and for an instant, the friendly, familiar Matt she knew was someone else, someone who'd known pain and sorrow.

He glanced down at her. "Let's dance. Unless you have anything else to say to Drew?" he added with a pleasant smile.

"No," she replied quietly. "No, I haven't. Did you take care of your emergency case?" she added.

"Yes," he said, "but it wouldn't hurt to check on him before I go home," he added, not revealing that his "emergency" was one stitch in a torn finger.

"Good night, then," Kitty said, trying not to look as miserable as she felt.

Drew watched her walk away with Matt Caldwell,

saw them holding hands. Guy Fenton was standing beside a pretty little brunette at the refreshment table. He greeted them and gave Kitty a soft, low whistle of appreciation. Drew cursed under his breath, turned and stalked out of the country club.

"Would you look at that," Lou Coltrain murmured to her husband. "I don't think I've ever seen Drew so disagreeable."

"Why did he bother to show up at all?" Jeb Coltrain asked curiously. "He didn't want to come. All he managed to do was to make Kitty feel even more miserable." He glanced at her solemn face, all the gaiety gone out of it with Drew's absence. "She put up a good front."

Lou shook her head. "Poor thing. I suppose she'll choke back tears for the rest of the… Well, would you look at that?"

She stopped dead as Drew suddenly turned around and marched right back into the hall.

Jeb grinned. "Miracles will never cease," he mused.

Kitty was staring into her punch with dead eyes, barely aware of the soft music playing while Matt and Guy talked about bloodlines beside her.

Before she realized what was happening, the punch glass was taken out of her hand and placed on the table, and Drew was leading her onto the dance floor.

He pulled her close, tucking her against him while a soft, seductive ballad sung by Julio Iglesias filled the room with exquisite sound.

Kitty's heart was racing wildly. Drew's hand contracted, his fingers locking with hers. His cheek moved against her temple, coaxing her to rest her head on his shoulder. His movements were deft, fluid, as he guided her around the room.

"You dance like a fairy," he murmured at her ear.

She shivered. The shock of having every single dream come true at once had reduced her to speechlessness. He came back. He came back!

His arm contracted, bringing her closer. Her softness went right to his head. He hadn't realized how possessive he felt about Kitty until he watched Matt hold her hand. He wanted to rip the man apart, an odd notion for a man who abhorred violence.

She smelled nice; her perfume was light and floral. She wasn't wheezing, either.

"You dance very nicely," she murmured, her eyes closed as she drifted between heaven and earth.

"I used to love it. I haven't danced for years, either." His fingers curled closer into hers. "You're going home with me. Even if I didn't bring you, you're mine for the evening. You aren't leaving the building with Matt Caldwell, and I don't give a damn if he does waltz like Yul Brynner."

Her heart jumped wildly. She moved her face into his warm throat and shivered again. He made a sound deep in his throat. He couldn't remember the last time he'd felt like this. It had to be several dates after his first one with Eve. He was a boy again, all aches and daydreams.

His lips brushed against her ear. "I was right," he whispered huskily. "The green suits you right down to your toes. Perfume not bothering your lungs?"

"Only…a little," she managed to say in a shaky tone. His nearness was making her hungry. "Actually some of the ladies are wearing musky perfumes and they're uncomfortable to breathe." Even as she spoke, she coughed spasmodically.

He stopped in the middle of the dance floor, without letting her go. "Where's your spacer?"

She opened her purse and fished for it. She used it quickly, grimacing when she noticed that it was almost empty.

"Don't you check the damned thing?" he muttered, because he'd heard the sound it made. "Dangerous, Kitty."

"I've got another at home, I think. I'll be okay."

"I've got my bag in the car. If worse comes to worst, I can give you epinephrine to break up an attack, or drive you to the emergency room. Stop being careless."

"I was excited about tonight," she murmured defensively.

He drew in a long breath. "So was I," he replied. "And the emergency was real," he added, "not an excuse to get out of bringing you. It was the Adams boy, the one with cystic fibrosis. He cut his finger. You know how his mother is."

"Yes, I do, poor thing," she agreed, smiling, because he hadn't wanted to stand her up.

He searched her eyes, reading their expression easily. "Did you think I wanted a way out? I didn't. I'd been looking forward to it, too."

"You were going to leave me here with Matt."

"At first," he agreed quietly.

"Why did you come back?"

His arm drew her right up against him. "When I figure it out, I'll tell you. Dance."

She did, ignoring her reservations and clinging like a limpet to his strength. They danced with no one else for the rest of the evening, and he drove behind her until they reached the parking lot of her apartment building. Even then, he got out and escorted her right to her door.

"Going to church in the morning?" he asked, in no hurry to leave.

"Thought I might," she replied.

"I'll pick you up at ten-thirty, if nothing comes up. If I can't make it, I'll ring."

She searched his lean face with quiet, curious eyes. Things had altered between them. She didn't understand how, but they had.

He sighed, catching her face in his hands to lift it. "I don't want to leave you," he whispered, bending to her mouth.

He kissed her softly at first, and then hungrily, deeply, slowly, so that she curled up against him and moaned under his demanding mouth.

He lifted his mouth slowly, reluctantly. His breath was as ragged as her own. "After church, we'll have a picnic. I'll pack something and we can pick it up after the service."

"I'll have to change."

"So will I." He kissed her eyelids, feeling the wonder of being with her. "I hope it doesn't rain."

"Me, too," she whispered.

He kissed her again, very gently. "See you in the

morning. Lock the door," he added firmly, glancing back as he left, his eyes dark and warm and possessive.

Kɪᴛᴛʏ ᴅɪᴅɴ'ᴛ sʟᴇᴇᴘ. Her heart raced every time she thought about the wonder of the dance. Drew had become entwined with her, so closely that she couldn't bear the thought of losing this magic.

Apparently he couldn't, either, because he was right on time to pick her up for church. They sat close together in the pew, barely aware of watching eyes, and shared a songbook. After the service, they held hands on the way to his Mercedes.

He dropped her off to change clothes and picked her up on his way back from changing his own clothes and retrieving the food he'd already packed for the occasion.

He drove them to a quiet riverbank with a small stone table and benches, and spread a disposable cloth over it to put the picnic basket on.

"This is fun." Kitty laughed, looking summery in her yellow-and-white sundress and sandals.

Drew glanced at her with pure appreciation. She looked young and pretty and very sexy with that low-cut bodice that left tantalizing skin bare.

He was wearing slacks and a green sports shirt. He looked younger, much more relaxed. As he unloaded the food, Kitty noticed his left hand and realized that they still had a very long way to go. He was wearing his wedding band. He never took it off. Of course, it was early days yet, and Kitty was more optimistic than she'd ever had reason to be before.

After they finished the cold lunch, Drew stretched out on the grass with a sigh.

He opened one eye as Kitty muffled a cough. "Brought your spacer, I hope?"

She nodded.

He closed the eye and smiled. "Good girl."

She lay down beside him, drinking in the peace and beauty of the secluded spot.

"A free Sunday," he murmured drowsily. "I haven't had a free Sunday in years."

"You haven't wanted one, I'll bet."

He smiled. "No. I haven't." He rolled over and stared at her. He searched her face quietly. "I want a lot of things lately that I thought I'd learned to live without. Come here, Kitty."

She went to him without protest, sliding into his arms as naturally as if she belonged there. He rolled her over beside him and kissed her.

Long, drowsy minutes went by while she savored his touch on her body, his kisses hard on her mouth. For a while, the world seemed very far away indeed.

Finally, she lay completely against him with her cheek on his rapidly moving chest, catching her breath.

"We should do this every Sunday," he murmured, his eyes closed. "I'm only really required to be on call one Sunday a month." He smiled, contented, and sighed. "All it needs is a child running around, doesn't it, Eve?"

Eve. Kitty froze in his arms. She felt as if every single hope died in her, right there.

He cursed under his breath. He heard himself say his late wife's name with complete shock, because it was Kitty he was holding, Kitty who was in his mind. Habit, he thought, died hard.

His regret was too little, too late. Kitty was already on her feet, gathering things together.

"I didn't mean to say it," he said when they were back at the car.

She shrugged. "I know." She managed a credible smile. "It's still too soon, isn't it?"

He looked at her hungrily, searching for words to repair the damage he'd done.

"It's all right," she said softly. Her eyes were sad, at variance with her light tone. "But can we go home? My favorite show is on tonight, and I really don't want to miss it. Okay?"

"Okay." He drove her home, and he still hadn't found the words to apologize when he left her at her door.

SHE CRIED HERSELF to sleep. She was so overwrought that she forgot to take her medicine; to compound it, she walked to work, right past a huge lawn that was being mowed. She'd no sooner made it inside the office than she collapsed on the floor, coughing so violently that she thought she was going to choke to death.

At some level she was aware of Drew bending over her and then slinging orders at Nurse Turner as he lifted her.

"Hold on, darling," he said at her ear. "Hold on! It's all right. Try not to panic!"

He sounded as if he needed those words spoken to him, Nurse Turner thought as she watched him rush out the door with Kitty in his arms. She phoned right through to the hospital emergency room and told them he was on the way, and gave them his instructions. The way he looked, he wasn't going to be in much condition to give orders when he got there.

Sure enough, Drew was half wild when he slammed on the brakes in front of the emergency room. A nurse and the resident physician rushed out with a gurney and scant minutes later, Kitty was in a cubicle being saturated with bronchodilators.

Drew was cursing steadily, while the staff stood by, wide-eyed, and listened. Probably learning new words, Kitty thought through her discomfort, because he was eloquent. His face was dark with color and his eyes were blazing like black fires. It was flattering that he was so concerned about her, but she wished he was quieter with it. The emergency room staff—the whole hospital staff—would have a gossip feast that would last weeks.

When she was able to draw breath again, she tried to explain. "They were…mowing grass, and I didn't have…a mask," she said before she was stuffed right back into the mask to inhale the rest of the bronchodilator he'd prescribed.

"Why the hell were you walking to work in the first place?" he demanded coldly. "When did you use your preventative?"

She grimaced. "I meant to have it refilled…"

"God deliver us from idiots!" he raged. He paced the room, mussing his hair. He glanced irritably at his watch. "I'll have patients screaming their heads off!"

"Go back to the office, then," she growled through the mask, and then coughed at the effort it took to speak.

"I'll go where I damned well please!"

She laid back, too worn to argue with him. He might have forgotten what he'd said the day before, but she hadn't. He'd called her Eve. They were never going to get past that, even if he did care enough to raise the roof of the emergency room because she'd had an asthma attack. Probably it made him mad *because* he cared.

He stood over her, glaring, until she'd finished the treatment. Then, leaving her long enough to fill out the paperwork, he went to check on a patient he'd admitted Saturday. He was back when she was ready to leave.

He didn't say a word. He helped her into the car and they drove straight to the pharmacy. She knew without being told why they were there. Fortunately the pharmacist wasn't busy and immediately refilled her inhalant.

She showed it to him when she got back into the car, subdued and a little surprised at his irritation.

"They're my lungs," she muttered.

"They work for me," he countered, reversing the car. "From now on, keep up with your preventatives."

"Yes, sir," she muttered.

He drove back to the office and marched her right to her desk, past an office full of surprised patients.

He pointed at her. "It's her fault. She forgot to use her medications and she had an asthma attack right here on the floor. We'll all be here until midnight because she won't take care of herself!"

He stormed off into his office, leaving behind a roomful of shocked and amused patients and a horribly embarrassed receptionist.

FOR A WEEK, Drew was cold and absolutely remote. Friday afternoon, he brought his father-in-law and mother-in-law in to meet Kitty.

"They're spending the weekend with me. We're going fishing," he told Kitty with a vindictive look in his eyes. "We're very close."

"Yes, I know," Kitty said gently, and smiled as she was introduced to them.

That seemed to make Drew even angrier. He bustled his in-laws out the door and gave Kitty a glare that would have stopped traffic.

"How very odd," Nurse Turner remarked as they were closing up the office for the weekend. "Goodness, he hasn't had them here for five years or more. I know he spends Christmas Day with them, but mostly he stays in a hotel and watches television to make everyone think he's enjoying himself. He doesn't have anything in common with them except Eve and fishing." She shook her head. "He's acting very oddly," she murmured, glancing at her co-worker. "I thought I was going to need an ambulance for him the morning he walked in and saw you on the floor. My goodness, normally nothing shakes him. Nothing at all."

"Maybe he has a terror of asthma attacks," she murmured self-consciously.

"Not him. I just don't understand him at all." She glanced again at Kitty. "Maybe he's in love."

"If he is, I feel sorry for her," Kitty said curtly. "She'll never be able to compete with his beautiful ghost."

"I wonder," Nurse Turner said, but she smiled and went home.

KITTY WAS INVITED to have Sunday dinner with Drew and his in-laws, whom he brought to church with him. But Kitty made sure she had other plans. She refused on the grounds that she'd accepted an invitation from Guy Fenton to go to a movie with him. She'd agreed to the date against her better judgment. He promised not to take up with another girl in the middle of the show, though, and it was a movie that she very much wanted to see. Drew's reaction to the news made her a little uneasy. He was furious and unable to hide it.

She settled into her seat at the theater, and Guy draped a gentle arm around her.

"I was surprised that you agreed," he commented quietly. "I wasn't very kind to you last time."

"I wanted to see this movie," she replied, smiling.

"I like science fiction, too," he agreed, smiling back.

It was a good movie, but her heart wasn't in it. She was remembering how hard Drew was trying to make her see her lack of importance in his life. If he was willing to have his in-laws practically live with him to keep her at bay, he must be serious about trying to keep her at arm's length. It made her sad to think how little she mattered. As long as she lived, she was going to hear him calling Eve's name on the banks of the river.

Guy took her home and kissed her gently, but he knew at once that she felt nothing for him.

He touched her nose gently. "Any time you're at a loose end, we can go to a movie. I'm not in the market for a wife or a steady girl, but I like you."

"Thanks," she said. "I like you, too."

"Don't grieve too much over the doctor," he advised quietly, and the familiar smile was temporarily in eclipse. "It wouldn't have worked. Everyone knows how he loved his wife. You just can't compete with a perfect memory."

"I know that."

"Of course you do. You're no dummy." He kissed her cheek. "Good night, pal."

"Thanks for the movie."

"You're welcome. Next time, we'll have pizza and then go to a movie."

She grinned. "I'd really like that."

"Me, too. I'll phone you."

He waved and made his way down the stairs. Watching his back, Kitty thought that he'd been a constant surprise. She wished she could have given her heart to somebody like Guy or Matt—someone who might want it.

She went into her apartment and sat down on the sofa. Alone, all the misery of the past week came back to haunt her. She was going to have to do something. She couldn't go on like this, seeing Drew every day and knowing that he didn't want her.

CHAPTER SIX

THE NEXT MORNING, Drew was eloquent about his visitors and how much he'd enjoyed his company. Nobody knew that he was lying through his teeth. Especially not Kitty.

Surprising everyone, mostly herself, she typed out her resignation and put it on Drew's desk. He glanced at her curiously before he read it.

"You want to leave?" he asked.

There was nothing in his face or voice to indicate that he gave a damn, so she said, "Yes, I do."

"All right," he replied. "I'll phone the agency right now and see when you can be replaced. If they have someone free, you can leave tomorrow. I'll write you a good reference and give you two weeks' severance pay."

She didn't argue. She was tired of the continual misery. "Thank you," she said, and walked out.

Drew stared at the closed door. He should have felt relief. His memories of Eve were safe now. He could live in the past, continue to be in love with his sweet ghost. Kitty, that pain in his heart, was about to depart forever. Why, oh, why, didn't he feel relief? He put his head in his hands and closed his eyes. If he felt anything, he had to admit in the privacy of his mind, it was grief. But this time, it wasn't for his ghost.

The agency came through. A new receptionist would be in the office the next morning. Kitty emptied her desk that afternoon and was ready to leave at the end of the day.

Nurse Turner was sorry to see her go, but too shrewd not to guess why she was going.

"I'm sorry it didn't work out for you," she said. "I'll miss you."

"I'll miss you, too." She picked up her sweater. "He won't eat breakfast. But maybe my replacement could bring him a roll or a bagel occasionally. He'll eat it if it's put in front of him with coffee."

"I noticed," Nurse Turner said dryly.

"It was just a thought."

She hugged Kitty. "Where will you go?"

"There are always jobs for a good typist," Kitty said simply. "I'll find something."

Nurse Turner hesitated. "Aren't you going to tell him goodbye?" she asked, nodding toward the back of the office.

Kitty hesitated, but only for a minute. "No," she said rawly. She left the office without another word.

TWO WEEKS LATER, she was enjoying a snatched cup of coffee when her new boss, Matt Caldwell, peered around the door.

"Got that disk copied yet?" he asked.

She grinned and held it up, in its jacket.

"Good thing for me you were tired of being a receptionist just when my secretary went into labor. You've saved my life. These are herd records for that group I've got at the Ballengers' feedlot. I want to show the birth weight ratios to a prospective buyer." He stuck the computer disk in its case into his pocket. "You're a jewel, girl. Don't know what I'd do without you."

She chuckled. "I doubt that. Probably half the women in Jacobsville would have come running if you'd advertised."

"That's why I didn't," he murmured. "I'm quite a catch, didn't you know? Handsome, rich, sophisticated and charming, and modest to a fault." He took a bow.

She burst out laughing. "I noticed the modesty right away."

He opened the door. "Go home early if you like. I'll be out for the rest of the day."

"I'll stick around to answer the phone."

"Where do you go from here?" he asked, scowling. "I could make a job for you quite easily…"

She shook her head. "I've got two interviews in Victoria."

He grimaced. "Listen, child, you don't have to leave the county just because Drew Morris can't live in the present."

"Yes, I do," she replied firmly. "I'm not going to sit around here eating my heart out every time I see him. I'll be happy in Victoria. I'll find another man and marry him and have five kids."

"You could marry me," Matt suggested. "I'm not interested in anyone seriously these days. And at least I'd be sure you weren't marrying me for my money."

She smiled warmly. "Thanks, Matt, but I don't think either of us could settle for a loveless marriage."

He shrugged and sighed. "I could."

She knew his past, and she doubted it, but she didn't say so. "I appreciate the offer," she told him sincerely. "I'll remember it and gloat every time a local belle swoons over you."

He threw her a wicked glance. "Likely story."

AFTER HE LEFT, she organized the filing and then just sat staring at the blank computer monitor. She was totally miserable. She hadn't really expected Drew to call, and he hadn't, but she'd hoped that he might miss her. That was wishful thinking, nothing else. He was probably happy that he didn't have her to divert him from his memories.

She was briefly ashamed of herself for being like that, when he'd loved his wife so much. She'd never be loved as Eve had, despite the feelings she harbored for Drew. Love that was unreturned was a bitter thing indeed.

As she filed the new jackets, she wondered how she'd ever come to this incredible low in her life. Not even the loss of her father had left her so depressed and miserable. If only she could work up just a spark of enthusiasm for a new job. Perhaps she'd find something in Victoria that would heal her wounds.

THE WORST THING about being in Jacobsville was that from time to time, she ran into Drew. It wasn't a tiny little town, but there were only two banks, and she and Drew both banked at the same one. She saw him there soon after she'd quit working for him. He was polite, but he acted as if he barely knew her. The next time they met, in the grocery store, he pretended not to see her. Her heart was breaking in two. The only thing for it was to get out of town as soon as possible, no matter what sort of work she got to do.

She couldn't find a single secretarial or receptionist job going spare in Victoria, but there was an opening at a nice-looking local café. In desperation, Kitty applied for it and was hired on the spot.

She didn't tell Matt what sort of job she had, just that she had one. She thanked him kindly for his temporary employment and packed her bags.

IT WAS INEVITABLE that Matt would run into Drew one day.

"You look like hell," Matt remarked bluntly when he saw the drawn, irritable-looking physician.

"I've been up all night with a patient," Drew muttered. He studied the other man. "I know Kitty's working for you. Are you making sure she uses her medicines? The pollen count's going to be out of sight this week, with no rain."

"Kitty's not here," Matt replied, faintly surprised. "She got a job in Victoria last week and moved there."

"What?"

The other man's shocked expression said a lot. "I only needed temporary help," Matt explained. "I have to have someone permanent, and Kitty didn't want to stay in Jacobsville."

"Why not?" Drew asked belligerently. "She was born here."

"Beats me. She couldn't wait to leave," Matt said with a shrewd idea of why Drew looked so bad. "She's a nice girl. I asked her to marry me."

Drew lost color again. His eyes widened, darkened.

"What did she say?" he asked, well aware of Matt's worth on the matrimonial market.

"She said no," Matt mused. "I guess I'm not as hot a marriage prospect as I thought."

Drew relaxed visibly. He stuck his hands into his pockets. "She doesn't know anyone in Victoria, does she? No family there, certainly."

"She didn't say," Matt said honestly. His eyes narrowed as he summed up the expression on Drew's face. "She's the kind of girl who's going to be snapped up soon, by some lucky man. She'll make a wonderful wife and a great mother. I'm sorry it won't be me."

Drew didn't look at him. He was so jealous he could hardly bear it. The last weeks had been endless, a nightmare of tortured thoughts and misery. Everywhere he looked there were memories of Kitty. He couldn't even bear to speak to her in the grocery store when he'd seen her there, for fear of choking up, of showing how much he missed her.

"For God's sake, are you going to let her go?" Matt demanded belligerently.

"Why shouldn't I?" came the terse reply.

"Because you love her," Matt replied with dead certainty.

Drew didn't seem to breathe for a minute. He searched Matt's eyes as if he sought answers he didn't have.

"Didn't you know?" Matt persisted gently.

Drew didn't speak. He turned on his heel and walked away in a daze. Loved her. He...*loved her*. His eyes closed as he reached his car. Good God, of course he loved her! Why else would he worry himself sick over her, making sure she used her medicines, wore warm things in winter, kept dry in the rain. He leaned against the hood of the car. He'd loved her for a long time, but he couldn't admit it, because it was disloyal to Eve. He'd loved Eve, too. But she was dead. And it occurred to him that she'd never have wanted him to end up like this, alone and bitter, living in the past, in a world that didn't exist anymore.

Eve had been tenderhearted, compassionate. She'd never have asked him to be faithful unto death. But he'd tried. He lifted his head and looked around him. Children were playing in the park across the street. He watched them hungrily. He remembered Kitty with his little patients on her lap, remembered her face as she looked at them. Kitty loved children.

He smoothed his hand over a spot on his hood. Kitty loved him, too. He'd seen it, felt it, knew it right inside his soul. But he didn't want to know, so he'd pretended not to see it. Now, it mattered more than anything else ever had. Kitty loved him. He loved her.

Then what in God's name was he doing standing here?

He got into the car and paused just long enough to phone his office and tell his new receptionist that he had an emergency out of town and wouldn't be back that day. She'd have to make new appointments for everyone, it couldn't be helped. He hung up and turned the car toward Victoria.

IT TOOK HIM several hours to track her down. Victoria was a good-sized little city and it had a surprising number of job agencies, none of whom had Kitty on their books. He found her accidentally, when his tired feet forced him into a café for a cup of coffee.

The first thing he saw was Kitty, standing at a table with a platter of chicken and mashed potatoes and gravy in her hands.

Without missing a step, Drew went right to her, and got down on one knee right there.

He took her hand in his and looked up into her stunned face. "Kitty Carson, will you marry me?" he asked loudly.

What happened next was, sadly, predictable. Kitty dropped the platter and his spotless silk jacket was anointed with the thickest, greasiest gravy in east Texas.

"Oh, Drew," she whispered, and got on her knees, too, in the gravy and mashed potatoes, put her arms around his neck, and kissed him until she had to stop for breath.

"You look tired. Are you using your medicines?" he asked worriedly. "Are you eating enough? You've gotten very thin."

"So have you," she whispered brokenly. "And you look so tired, Drew. Oh, darling, you look as if you haven't slept—"

He kissed her again, hungrily. "I haven't slept since you left. I need you. I love you. I want you for my wife. I want to have children with you…"

His mouth crushed against hers. They held each other hungrily, oblivious to the ruin in the middle of the floor, to the amused glances of the patron and the owner of the café. It was at least a break in the boring routine of the day.

At last, Drew managed to get up and draw a flushed,

radiant Kitty up with him. He glanced at the proprietor with a sheepish grin.

"Sorry about the mess. I almost let her get away."

"Shame on you," said Kitty's boss, and chuckled. "Get out of here, both of you, and best wishes! I hope you have ten kids."

"Oh, so do I," Kitty said fervently, and watched her prospective husband flush with fascinated interest.

EVERYBODY IN JACOBSVILLE turned out for the wedding. It was the major social event of the summer. The bride was radiant in a delicate white lace dress. Drew wore a morning coat and beamed with pride as they exchanged rings and vows.

Later, as Drew carried his new bride across the threshold, she noticed that the photo of Eve that had always stood on the mantel was gone.

Drew looked down into Kitty's soft eyes and kissed her. "I won't ever forget the past," he said gently. "But I promise you that I'm not going to live in it ever again. We start together, here, now. You're my wife, and I love you."

"I love you, too," Kitty whispered tearfully. She grinned even through the tears. "And now that we've made that clear, would you like to show me how much you love me?"

He chuckled as he picked her up, gorgeous gown and all, and carried her toward the bedroom. "I hope you ate a lot of cake," he said with a rakish grin. "Because this is going to take a very long time."

And it did.

* * * * *

JOBE

*"'Tis the last rose of summer,
Left blooming alone;
All her lovely companions
Are faded and gone."*

—Thomas Moore
Irish Melodies (1807–1834)
The Last Rose of Summer, st. 1

CHAPTER ONE

SANDY NOTICED THAT he looked absolutely disgusted. It was hard to get Jobe Dodd to stand still long enough to listen to anything she said. But when she was trying to get him to listen to her about computers, she might as well have saved her breath.

"It's my brother's ranch," Sandy Regan said hotly, glaring at the tall blond ranch foreman. "He says you're going to modernize the record-keeping, so you're damned well going to modernize it!"

Narrow gray eyes glittered down at her from an impossible height. Lean hands on lean hips made a visual statement about his opinion of her and her infernal machines without his saying a single word. He might not have a college degree, but he had arrogance down to a science.

"Did you hear what I said? Ted said we're doing it!" she persisted, pushing back a strand of unruly dark hair. She was recovering at the ranch from a rough bout of influenza, where Ted's wife and Sandy's best friend, Coreen, had been nursing her. She was better. Or she had been, until now.

"Ted still owns that ranch in Victoria," Jobe said pointedly in his deep, curt drawl, alluding to the ranch where he'd worked before Ted and Sandy had moved back to the old homeplace in Jacobsville. "No reason I couldn't go work up there."

"Great idea. You can work there until Ted has me convert those records to computer files, too!"

He gave her a level look guaranteed to provoke a saint. "I'll tell Ted you recommended it."

Her lips made a thin line. She was furious. It was her long-standing reaction to this man, who had been her nemesis since her fifteenth birthday. He'd started working for Ted just before she went away to college, and the more she studied, the more he provoked her. He had a good sound high school education, followed by some vocational training in animal husbandry, but he knew next to nothing about electronic equipment. She did, and he resented her expertise. Not that he'd have admitted it.

"You just can't stand it that I have a college degree, can you?" she raged. "It goes right through you that a mere woman understands something you don't!"

"I don't need to understand computers," he said smugly. "Not as long as you can't understand genetics. I guess your next step will be to stuff cows into that damned thing." He nodded toward the computer system she'd set up in the ranch office.

"As a matter of fact, I was coming to that," she said with a cold smile. "I want to use computer chip implants in the hides of the cattle—"

"Over my dead body," came the short reply.

"So that we can scan the cattle and get their records

simultaneously. It will save a lot of time and trouble with his breeding program, and hours of paperwork."

"I oversee the breeding program."

"You can do it better with a computer."

"And I'll tell you exactly what you can do with yours," he said in a deceptively pleasant tone, "and how far."

She sighed angrily. Her hand went to her forehead. She was still feeling rocky from the flu, and arguing with Jobe always gave her a headache. She tried to think of him as an occupational hazard, but it made the time she spent at home fraught with difficulties. In the past few months, she'd found excuses not to visit Ted and Coreen because it put her in such close contact with him. Then flu had struck, and she'd had no place else to go. Grown she might be, but Ted looked after his own.

Sadly he considered Jobe family, too, because he and Jobe's father had once been in the cattle business together. Sandy's antagonism for his ranch manager didn't bother Ted one bit. He knew that both of them were professional enough to overlook their small personality conflicts. From Sandy's point of view, that was going to take a lot of overlooking.

"You need to get some more meat on those little bones before you start arguing with me," he murmured, and his voice gentled. "You're frail."

"Hand me a stick and I'll show you how frail I am." Eyes almost as blue as her brother's blasted him.

"Did Ted tell you that you were going to have to learn how to use the computer and input records?"

He looked shell-shocked. "What?"

"I won't be here to program the computer," she continued. "You'll have to learn how to use it so that you can input herd records and breeding records and any other little thing you want access to."

He glared at her. "Like hell I'm going to learn to use a computer. If God had wanted men to use computers, we'd have been born with keyboards!"

She grinned at him. "Do tell?" She could imagine steam coming out of his ears. It made her feel superior, which was a rare sensation indeed when she was around him. "Well, Ted said you'd have to learn."

He cocked an eyebrow. "I'll learn to program computers when you learn to cook, cupcake," he offered.

Her pale blue eyes flashed fire. "I can cook!"

"Ha!" He was enjoying himself now. He had her on the run. "I still remember the last time you helped us with a company barbecue," he recalled, tongue-in-cheek. "First time in my life I ever saw cattlemen eat fish. I fried that, if you recall."

"The cowards," she remarked. "It was good barbecue. It had a crust. Good barbecue always has a crust!"

"Not black and halfway through the meat," he replied easily.

"I can cook when I feel like it!" She raised her voice.

There was a muffled laugh from behind them. She turned in time to see her brother, Ted, come in from the backyard. His prematurely silver hair gleamed in the light.

He glanced from Jobe's amused expression to his sister's outraged one and sighed.

"I fought in Vietnam," he recalled. "Amazing how much home reminds me of it lately."

Sandy flushed, but her glittering eyes didn't yield an inch. "He says he wants to work at the ranch in Victoria so he won't have to learn anything about computers!" she snarled.

Jobe didn't say a word, which somehow made it even worse.

Ted glanced at her and then back at his foreman. "We have to move into the twentieth century," he told the other man. "God knows, I resisted until the very last minute. But even the Ballengers yielded to the inevitable, and they did it some years ago."

"It's all those kids," Jobe mused. "They don't want their sons knowing how to do something they can't do."

"That's possible," Ted said knowingly, and grinned. "Our boy's barely a year old now and he's got a little computer of his very own."

"Indeed he does," Sandy chuckled, because she'd given little Pryce Regan that beginner storybook computer for his first birthday.

"If a little kid can do it, you can do it," Ted assured Jobe.

The other man lifted a blond eyebrow and a corner of his mouth in a full-scale grimace. "I don't like machinery."

"Just because the hay baler caught your jacket one time…!" Sandy began.

"It damned near caught my whole arm and jerked it off," he snapped back at her.

"Well, a computer can't jerk your arm off," she promised him.

His eyes narrowed. "So they say," he muttered. "But little kids can use one to build napalm."

"I'll be the first to agree that some chemical formulae shouldn't be posted on the Internet where any child can access it," Sandy agreed, "and that some sort of monitoring device should be available to parents."

"Nice of you," Jobe replied. "But my kids would be too busy to sit with their noses in a computer all afternoon. They'd be out working with livestock and learning how to track."

"All day and all night?" Sandy asked sweetly. "And pray tell where are you going to get these mythical well-occupied children in the first place? As I recall, you've never found a woman who lived up to your high standards!"

"Certainly not you," he agreed with a go-to-hell smile.

Sandy got up from her chair furiously, rocking a little on her feet.

"Whoa," Ted said, stepping between them. "The idea is to feed herd records into the computer, not start World War III over it." He looked from Jobe to Sandy. "I want you two to try and make peace. You have to work together on this thing. If you keep scoring points off each other, I'll never get my system up and running."

"I'd like to get him up and running!" Sandy flashed at Jobe.

Jobe looked haughty. "Don't be vulgar," he chided.

Sandy realized what she'd said and went as red as a radish.

Ted shook his head. "You two are going to be the death of me," he said sadly. "And all I want to do is move into the twenty-first century with my cattle operation."

"And your horses," Sandy added.

Jobe looked hunted. "Computers are a curse."

"Well, you're cursed, then," Ted answered, "because whether Sandy sets up the system or I have someone else set it up, you're going to have to learn to use it."

When Ted used that tone of voice, nobody argued. Jobe's broad shoulders rose and fell in silent acceptance, but he glared at Sandy.

"She's good at her job," Ted said pointedly. "She can do this better than anyone else I know."

"So let her do it. Foremen are thick on the ground." He nodded toward Ted and turned on his heel.

"You're not quitting!" Ted snapped.

Jobe glanced back over his shoulder. "Like hell I'm not." He kept walking.

"You can't find any place in Texas to work that doesn't use a computer!"

"Then I'll go to New Mexico or Arizona or Montana," he returned.

"What's the matter, Jobe, afraid you aren't smart enough to learn it?" Sandy asked in the softest, sweetest tone.

He stopped dead. When he turned, his eyes glittered like coals of fire. "What did you say?" he asked softly.

She'd seen grown men back down when he looked

like that. It was one of the reasons he was such a good foreman. He hardly ever had to use those big fists on anyone.

But she wasn't backing down. Although she respected Jobe, she wasn't afraid of him.

"I said, are you afraid you can't do it?" she persisted.

He stuck his hands on his hips. "I could. I just don't want to."

She shrugged and turned away. "If you say so."

"I could learn it!"

She shrugged again.

Jobe's high cheekbones were overlaid by dusky color. His nostrils looked pinched. Ted had to smother a laugh, because nobody got under Jobe's skin like Sandy. It often amazed him that two people with such violent feelings never noticed that there might be more to those emotions than just anger.

"All right, I'll give it a shot," Jobe said, but he was speaking to Ted. "And if I don't like it, I'm not staying."

"I'll accept that," Ted agreed. "But I think you're going to find that it saves you quite a lot of time."

Jobe stared at him. "And if it saves me all that time, what am I going to do with it?"

"Improve the breeding program," Ted replied at once. "Go to seminars. I'll send you to conferences to learn more about the newest theories in genetics. You can have more time to study, right down to finishing your degree in animal husbandry."

Jobe looked tempted. He thought about it. Finally, he nodded. "When do you want to start?"

"As soon as she's back on her feet again," Ted informed him, nodding toward Sandy. "She's had a bad time with the flu. I want her completely recovered before she takes on a project this size."

"I'm okay," she protested, and then ruined the whole thing by coughing.

"So I see," Jobe muttered. "You shouldn't have got out of bed so soon. Are you crazy!"

"Don't you call me names!" she snapped right back, and coughed again. "I can take care of myself."

"Sure," he nodded, "look what a great job you've done. If Ted hadn't come up to Victoria after you, you'd be dead of pneumonia, all alone in that apartment."

She really would have enjoyed disputing that theory, but she didn't have a leg to stand on. She blew her nose and tucked the handkerchief back into the pocket of her jacket.

"We'll shoot for next week," she promised. "That will give me a little time to work out hardware and programs. I'll probably have to do some engineering on the programs to make them work the way you want them to. But that's just a little thing, no problem."

"You go back to bed," Ted told her. "I've got some things to talk over with Jobe."

"Okay," she agreed. She felt weaker than ever, but she shot the foreman a smug look on her way out.

He glared at her. His hand clenched at his side. "For two cents," he began under his breath.

She went up the staircase, and Ted drew Jobe into his study and closed the sliding doors.

"Stop baiting her," he told the younger man.

"Tell her to stop baiting me," Jobe returned hotly.

"Good God, she lays in wait for me! Snide little remarks, sarcasm…do you think I'd take that from any man on the place?"

"You two have always rubbed each other the wrong way," Ted said pointedly. "Want something to drink?"

"I don't drink," Jobe reminded him.

"Lemonade or iced tea?" Ted continued.

Jobe chuckled. "Sorry. My mind wasn't working. Lemonade."

Ted took the pitcher out of his small icebox and filled two glasses. It was a hot day even for August, the air-conditioning notwithstanding.

The younger man sighed heavily and sipped lemonade, his pale eyes narrow as he stared out the window at the fenced pastures beyond.

"I don't mind so much that she knows computers inside out," Jobe murmured. "It's just that she can't resist rubbing it in. Hell, I know I'm not machinery-minded. But I know animal husbandry and genetics backward and forward!"

Ted knew hurt pride when he saw it. He wondered if Sandy even realized how thin Jobe's skin was. Probably not. She did her best not to notice the ranch foreman.

"Of course you do," Ted commiserated. "And she's not really rubbing it in. She loves her work. She's a little overenthusiastic about it, maybe."

Jobe turned, running an impatient hand through his thick hair. "She's a high-powered engineer with delusions of grandeur," he muttered. "Jacobsville was never big enough to suit her. She wanted bright lights and suave company."

"Don't most young people?" Ted asked.

Jobe's broad shoulders rose and fell. "I never did when I was young. I was happy with ranch life. There was all the time in the world, good people around me, the local bar if I needed cheering up, and plenty of friends when I needed them." He glanced at Ted curiously. "Didn't those things ever matter to Sandy?"

"They mattered," the older man replied. "But she had a good brain and she wanted to use it. She's made a career for herself in a field that wasn't overpopulated with women in the first place."

"Oh, yes," Jobe said harshly, "it was important to show people that a woman could do anything a man could."

"If it was, it was your fault," Ted said critically, and held up a hand when the other man started to speak. "You know it," he continued unabashed. "From the time she was a teenager, you were always lording it over her, making fun of her when she tried to help the mechanic work on machinery, taunting her when she couldn't lift bales of hay as easily as the men could. You gave her a hell of an inferiority complex. Sandy grew up with just one thought in mind, to prove to you that she could do something better than you could. And she has."

Jobe made an angry gesture. "She spent all those years complaining about how small Jacobsville was. She didn't want to spend her life in a hick town, she wanted sophistication. She said often enough that she didn't want to end up wearing cotton dresses married to a cowboy."

Ted's eyes narrowed thoughtfully as he stared at

the other man. He looked away. "Kids don't realize what's important until they become adults. I think you might find that Sandy's attitude toward Jacobsville has changed. She's crazy about our little boy, you know. She sits and plays with him all the time."

"He's not her kid," he said pointedly. "She can leave anytime the pressure gets too much. How would it be if he was her own kid, and she couldn't run away from him?"

"Ask her."

Jobe laughed coldly. "Who, me? If I ever marry, it's going to be some sweet small-town girl who doesn't give a damn about making a name for herself in a man's world. I want a mother for my children, not a computer expert."

Neither of them knew that Sandy had forgotten her glass of lemonade and had come back, silently, to get it. She'd paused just outside the door and that was when she'd heard Jobe's words.

Her face colored frantically. She turned and went silently, slowly, back up the staircase, feeling kicked in the stomach. Well, she'd always known that in Jobe's mind, the thought of her and marriage didn't follow each other. He wasn't in the market for a computer expert, and she wasn't going to settle for a male chauvinist who wanted a biddable little wife who'd stay pregnant half her life having his children.

She'd always known that. Curious, that it should come as such a shock now. But, then, Jobe had always had the power to hurt her more than anyone else ever could. He made her feel small, inferior, worthless. And she wasn't. She was as intelligent as any man on the place, and more intelligent than most; certainly more intelligent than *him*.

As for marriage, there were plenty of men in the world who'd be proud to have a wife who could engineer computer systems! Mentally she went back over her dates in the past year and grimaced. Well, there were plenty of men who'd have loved having an affair with her, she amended. She was a little short of marriage proposals.

That didn't matter. She was going to be a career woman. The world was her oyster. She could fit in anywhere now, and she didn't have to depend on any man to support her. She didn't want children, anyway, although she loved Ted and Coreen's little boy. Her eyes went dreamy as she thought about how cuddly he was.

Jobe wasn't cuddly. He was the most irksome man she'd ever known, and it was just unfortunate that she had to work with him on her brother's ranch.

If only Ted would fire him. There must be a dozen men who could do his job twice as well as he could do it. Men with college degrees, who knew genetics blindfolded, who could buy and sell livestock, improve breeding stock, and beat the hell out of any cowboy who got fresh with Ted's baby sister…

She didn't like remembering how protective Jobe had been about her when she was younger. Ted didn't get the chance to watch her; Jobe did it for him. He always seemed to turn up when she went out on dates, even if he only had a soft drink at a café where she was eating, or a bag of popcorn at any theater she went to. He'd been around during one of the worst nights of her life, when one of her boyfriends drank heavily and started trying to force her into the back seat of his car.

Jobe had dragged the boy out by his belt and pummeled him royally, before calling the police and having him arrested. His shocked parents had to come and bail him out. The boy had gone to live with a grandmother out of state the next day and he never came back. His parents, nice people, looked shellshocked for weeks afterward when they saw Jobe.

The men had razzed him about his special care of Ted's sister. They thought he was sweet on her. Sandy knew differently. He was just overbearing, obnoxious and determined to keep her from getting married to anybody locally. He'd even admitted it once. He wanted her out of town and out of his life. He wasn't taking any chances that she might marry a local boy and set up housekeeping nearby.

Meanwhile, Jobe went through women like water through a sieve. He was pleasant, attentive, courteous, but no woman was ever able to get a commitment out of him. He was the original bachelor, as slippery as an eel when wedding rings became the topic of conversation. He was thirty-six now and still seemed to have no aspirations toward being a husband and father.

Sandy didn't care. He could stay single forever as far as she was concerned. She hated him. Yes, she did! He was so cruel, so viciously cruel…

Tears were sliding down her cheeks when she got

back to her room and closed the door quietly behind her. Why, oh, why had she to love such a man, and for so long, with no hope at all of anything except rejection?

CHAPTER TWO

Coreen Tarleton Regan opened the door quietly, having heard the muffled sobs from the hallway. She sat down on the bed beside her best friend and slowly gathered her in her arms.

"I hate him," Sandy sniffed, savagely wiping away tears. "He's an idiot!"

"Yes, I know," Coreen said with a gentle smile. She pulled a tissue from the box beside the bed and handed it to Sandy. "Dry your eyes. Ted's sent him to Victoria for the rest of the day, to pick up some herd records at the office there."

"Good! I hope aliens kidnap him on the way back!"

"Now, now, think how we'd miss him around here."

"I wouldn't!"

Coreen's blue eyes smiled. "Didn't it ever occur to you that he might like you? All these little snips could be nothing more than a way to attract your attention."

Sandy's red-rimmed eyes glared at her. "No."

"He used to be your shadow," Coreen persisted. "Until you went away to college, at least."

"My keeper, you mean," she muttered. "Even then, he was making fun of me, putting me down."

"You're very intelligent. Maybe he felt threatened."

"He's intelligent enough," Sandy replied with a muffled cough. "He just doesn't like women who are smart. I heard what he just said to Ted downstairs. He said that all he wanted was a bunch of kids who didn't know one end of a computer from the other." Her eyes flashed. "As if I'd want kids with a man like that!"

Coreen just patted her shoulder, trying not to look as helpless as she felt. She wondered if Sandy knew how transparent her feelings for Jobe really were. Probably not, or she'd be horribly embarrassed. Sandy thought of herself as impervious to Jobe. Actually it was pretty much the reverse. Coreen, herself a veteran of turbulent relationships, knew exactly how her best friend felt.

"You feel lousy, don't you?" Coreen asked gently. "Why don't you try to sleep for a little while?"

"That might be a good idea." She forced a smile. "You're the best friend I ever had, you know."

"You're the best friend I ever had," Coreen replied warmly. "Don't you worry, if worse comes to worst, I'll help you push Jobe into a shark-infested ocean somewhere and I'll swear I don't have a clue where he is."

Sandy grinned through her tears. "Now that's real friendship."

Coreen nodded. "Exactly what I thought!"

But if Sandy had hoped that a day's absence would improve her situation, she was badly mistaken. Jobe came back from Victoria in a foul temper and avoided Sandy for the rest of the week. That suited her, because it gave her time to get a little better before she began the arduous job of teaching Jobe how to use a computer.

He presented himself in Ted's office the following Monday looking like a man facing imminent execution.

Sandy, in slacks and a tube top, had her hair in a bun and was cool and comfortable, at least on the surface. Jobe was wearing jeans and boots and a long-sleeved red-checked shirt. He looked the image of a rodeo cowboy. Sandy knew for a fact that he could ride anything on the place, from a bull to Ted's meanest stallion.

It amused her a little that he always buttoned his shirts to the top button. He was a modest man. She'd never seen him stripped to the waist or the least bit rumpled. Even his blond hair was neatly combed. He was one of the cleanest cowboys she'd ever known. Maybe that was an effort to make up for his nasty temper, she thought privately.

"All right," he said curtly. "Let's get to it."

"Sit down," Sandy invited, putting him in a chair in front of the computer.

He glared at it. "This is going to be a disaster," he muttered. "I'm not mechanical."

"Even you can't tear up this computer. It's almost foolproof."

"Where's the switch?" he asked, frowning at the console.

"This entire complex plugs into a surge spike. You push the red button, here, on the strip," she demonstrated, "and everything comes on, including the printer."

He watched the screen. "There's nothing there," he said pointedly.

"Give it a minute."

They waited and the menu came up.

"See?" she said, smiling. "Now take a look at the options. What you want is here." She moved the cursor with the mouse to a particular box and clicked on it. A screen opened up with all Ted's herd records on it.

"Where did that come from?" he asked.

"I typed it in while you were away last week. This is only a partial listing. You'll have to do the rest when you have time. Now this is how you select options and make changes."

It was slow going. He'd never even played computer games before. It was like teaching a child, and every bit as aggravating. He hated every minute of it, and made his dislike apparent.

"It's a waste of time," he said shortly when they'd gone through the preliminaries six times. "I keep all these records in my head. I can tell you everything there is to tell about any particular breeding cow on the place, and every bull to boot."

"I know that," she replied calmly. Jobe's memory was legendary. "But what if you get sick or have to go away? Who knows it then?"

He shrugged. "Nobody." He glanced at her. "Is Ted planning on firing me?" he asked cannily. "Is that why he wants all this on a computer?"

She grinned. "He's waited a long time, hasn't he? You were working here before I went away to college."

"So I was." He didn't like being reminded. It showed. He looked back at the computer screen. "Now that we've made changes, how do we keep them there?"

She showed him how to save the file and then how to pull it back out again.

He sighed. "Well, I guess I'll get used to it eventually."

"Sure you will," she assured him. "It's not hard. Even little kids do it. They grow up with computers now."

"One day," he murmured, "the power will all go off, and nobody will know how to do math or write. Civilization will vanish in a heartbeat, and all because people trusted machines to do the work."

She hesitated. "Well, maybe not right away," she said.

He looked up at her with narrow gray eyes. "How am I supposed to supervise the daily operation of this place, and the ranch in Victoria, and input all these damned records at the same time?"

Sandy pursed her lips and whistled. "I wonder if Ted thought about that?" she mused. She studied his lean face. "Do you really need to sleep and eat?"

"Yes."

"In that case, I guess Ted is going to have to hire somebody with computer experience to put the records in files."

"I guess he is."

"We'll advertise…"

"No need," Jobe said, getting to his feet. "Missy Harvey just graduated from the technical school with a diploma in computer programming. She needs a job and she's fun to have around."

"Ted will have to decide about that," Sandy said stiffly, because she knew that Jobe had been dating Missy on and off for a few weeks.

"I'll speak to him," Jobe said, and walked out.

Sandy stared after him with confusing emotions. She didn't want Missy here, in this house. But what sort of protest would she be able to make without sounding like a jealous shrew? As if she'd be jealous of Jobe! Ha!

All the same, when Jobe mentioned it to Ted at supper that night, Coreen shot a quick look at Sandy.

"We wouldn't need her permanently," Jobe emphasized. "But I can't handle what I have to do every day and spend several weeks typing in herd records one letter at a time, too."

Ted was frowning thoughtfully. "I didn't consider that," he said after a minute. He glanced in Sandy's direction. "I don't suppose you'd like to do it?"

She grimaced. "I've already taken all my sick days for the year, Ted," she confessed. "I have to go back to work or I could lose my job."

"God forbid," Jobe murmured nastily.

She shot a vicious look his way. "I love my job as much as you love yours," she replied. "Stop baiting me."

He slammed his fork down on the table, gray eyes blazing. "You're the one who does the baiting, honey."

"Don't call me honey! It's demeaning!"

Jobe stood up, bristling with anger. "To you, just being a woman is demeaning," he said icily, ignoring Ted's glare. "You don't have a clue, do you? You dress like a man, work like a man, think like a man. Hell, you even act like a man. You always have to know more, do more, than any man on the place!"

She stood up, too, shaking with fury. "Not any man," she said, correcting him. "You! I have to be better than you!"

"Sandy," Ted said warningly.

"Oh, why try to protect him?" she demanded, throw-

ing down her napkin. "He started it, making hurtful remarks and downgrading me when I was barely sixteen.
To hear him tell it, I couldn't do anything!" She lowered
her voice. "Well, I'm twenty-six now, and I can do a
hell of a lot of things that he can't. And if you want to
know, it feels really good to get to talk down to Jobe
Almighty Dodd for a change!"

Jobe's high cheekbones had gone a ruddy color as
he glared at Sandy. "That'll be the day, when you can
talk down to me, lady," he returned.

"It isn't hard to do, when you can't tell the difference between the enter key and the delete key on a computer!" she said with a haughty smile.

He didn't have a comeback. He gave her a look that
could fry bread, turned on his heel and left the room
without another word.

Sandy, still shaking, stared after him with a sick,
empty feeling.

"That," Ted remarked, "was the worst mistake you've
ever made. You don't ridicule a man like Jobe."

"Why not?" she raged, near tears. "He ridicules me
all the time!"

"Sit down."

She sat, defeated, deflated, tired to the bone.

Ted leaned forward on his elbows and glanced at his
wife, who seemed to understand what he was feeling—
as usual.

"Sandy, Jobe's mother was a scientist," he said quietly.

"Ted, no," Coreen tried to head him off.

He held up a hand. "She needs to know." He looked
back to his sister's fixed expression. "Jobe's mother

worked in nuclear research. His father was a cowboy, like he is, who knew the weather and animals and not much more. His mother had several degrees and spent his young life making his father feel stupid and inadequate. She did it so well that he shot himself when Jobe was ten."

Sandy thought she might faint. She picked up her glass of iced tea and pressed it to her cheek. "Oh, my God," she whispered.

"It didn't even seem to bother her," Ted recalled coldly. "Not even when Jobe packed his bag and went to live at the juvenile hall."

"I thought you had to be arrested and sent there," Sandy ventured.

"Bingo," Ted said, smiling humorlessly. "He stole a horse and even though the owner wouldn't press charges, he was arrested and arraigned. His mother didn't want him—not intelligent enough to stay with her, she said—so the state provided for him until he was old enough to get a job and go to work. He's been here ever since." His face was colder than his sister had ever seen it. "Pity you didn't ask me why I wanted you to teach him to use a computer. The herd records could have waited, but Jobe was losing ground with the men because most of them are more computer literate than he is."

Sandy put her face in her hands. "I'm sorry," she whispered.

"Tell him, not me," Ted said relentlessly.

"She didn't know, Ted," Coreen interjected. She got up and put her arms around Sandy. "I don't suppose either of us thought you needed to know," she told the other woman.

Sandy brushed away tears. "He isn't stupid," she said angrily. "His mother must have realized that!"

"She didn't want him in the first place," Ted said sadly. "She was one of those straitlaced people who put appearances before everything, and she'd had a major fling with a cowboy and got herself pregnant. She married him only to please her parents and friends, and made him pay for it every day he lived."

"Where is she now?" Sandy asked.

"Nobody knows. Jobe never speaks of her." He shook his head. "It's a good thing you don't like him, I suppose, in the circumstances. Because he'll never forgive what you said today."

Sandy felt sicker. She averted her eyes. Coreen handed her a handkerchief and patted her back awkwardly, giving Ted a helpless look over Sandy's bent head.

"You'll hire Missy, I guess?" Sandy asked without looking up.

"Yes," Ted said flatly. "She's the kind of woman who builds a man up. She'll repair the damage you did, and then some. She's a gentle soul."

"I wouldn't have said that Jobe needed a gentle woman," Sandy said through her teeth.

Ted cocked his head and stared at her. "How would you know what he needs?" he asked. "You've never cared a hoot what he did."

"I suppose not." She shifted in the chair and uncrossed her legs. "Missy doesn't like me."

"I'm not surprised," Ted replied. "She thinks Jobe's sweet on you."

Sandy's heart leaped. "Do you?"

Ted laughed. "You're better off not knowing what he says when you aren't around. You've damaged his pride, but no woman can touch his heart. They say his mother buried it alive."

Sandy put down the handkerchief Coreen had given her, slumping a little. "I didn't mean to put it like that. He's always attacking me. I just had enough, that's all."

"Oh, I'm not protecting him," Ted remarked. "Jobe can take care of himself. But hitting below the belt is pretty low."

"I won't do it again."

"You won't get the chance," her brother predicted. "I don't imagine he'll let you within clawing distance a second time." He gave her a curious look. "As for Missy, I think you can handle anything she can dish out, can't you?"

She smiled back at him. "I guess so. I'm your sister, after all."

TED'S REMARK ABOUT Jobe's attitude toward his sister turned out to be a pretty accurate prediction. Jobe never mentioned what Sandy had said to him, but his manner changed overnight. He treated her the same way he treated Ted, with courtesy and respect, but nothing more. Even the old antagonism was gone. Apparently, he'd decided to be indifferent.

Missy wasn't. Her devotion to Jobe was evident the minute she stepped into a room with him. Her long straight black hair fell in a curtain around her oval face and big brown eyes. She had a pretty mouth and a nice smile, and although she was very thin, she wasn't unpleasant to look at.

But she didn't like Sandy, and it showed. She listened silently while Sandy told her what she would be expected to do. She didn't have to speak; her eyes said plenty.

Sandy was dressed for work, in an expensive gray silk suit with neat little plain low-heeled shoes and her hair in a French pleat. She handed the last of Ted's files to Missy and looked around to see if she'd forgotten anything.

"If you have any questions and you can't find Ted, Coreen will know where to look for him," she assured the young woman.

"If I have any questions, I'll ask Jobe," Missy said coolly without looking at her. "After all, he's the boss around here, not you— Oh!"

She gasped as Sandy caught the back of her chair and swung it around sharply. "You work for the Regans," Sandy said curtly, "which makes me your boss as well." She leaned closer to the girl with threats in her whole posture. "You're only here because my brother wanted to do Jobe a favor. I don't owe Jobe any favors, so, given the least excuse, I'll shoot you out the door like a bomb," she added with a cold smile. "I hope that's clear."

Missy, suddenly white-faced and shaking, nodded.

"Good," Sandy said, standing erect. Her eyes blazed at the younger woman.

"I'm sorry," Missy stammered.

Sandy didn't even answer her. She whirled and went through the door, almost colliding with Jobe.

He glanced past her at the tears running down Missy's cheeks. "Had your razor blades for breakfast, I see," he said coldly. "If you've got a problem in this office, take it up with me."

"This is my home," Sandy reminded him with fury. "And nobody here talks to me as if I were the family pet! You might relay that to your girlfriend. She seems to think she works for you."

She pushed past him and walked out, her face so red that she looked positively feverish.

Missy ran into Jobe's arms and cried. "She was hateful to me!" she whimpered.

He smoothed her dark hair involuntarily, fuming over Sandy's remarks. "It's okay. I'll protect you."

Missy snuggled closer with a sigh. "Oh, Jobe, you're so strong…!"

Sandy heard that last remark as she went up the staircase and she could have chewed nails. It was all an act, surely Jobe could see through it? Or, perhaps he couldn't. If his mother had been a strong, independent woman, a woman like Missy might appeal to him as an opposite type from his despised parent.

Well, Sandy had too much pride to act like a simpering simpleton for the benefit of any man. Since girlhood, Ted had taught her that she wasn't a second-class citizen. She was a Regan.

She packed her suitcase and went down to her car without sparing a glance for the office. Let Ted see how much work got done with Missy making eyes at the foreman every waking hour. When he'd had enough, Missy was going to find herself on the receiving end of much worse than Sandy had given her.

SHE DIDN'T GO back for a week, having traveled most of east Texas on business. She was worn to a frazzle when she pulled her small white sports car into the driveway at Ted's house and parked it. With her travel bag over one arm and her shoulder bag over the other, she marched up the front steps with weariness in every step.

She had her key in her hand, but the front door was unlocked. She pushed it open and went inside, closing it gently behind her in case the baby was asleep. Ted and Coreen got precious little time together these days while their son was cutting teeth.

A sound coming from Ted's office caught her attention. The door was open, and as she neared it, the sounds grew louder. They were unmistakable, even without the deliberate soft moan.

She stopped at the doorway, her eyes as cold as a winter sky. Missy was lying across Jobe's legs, her head in the crook of his arm. He looked up and saw Sandy standing there, and an odd expression crossed his handsome face.

"Oh, don't mind me," she drawled, all too aware of Missy's sudden, frantic haste to get to her feet and rearrange her clothing. "I gather that Ted is now paying the two of you to test the springs in his sofa."

She turned on her heel and went up the staircase, ignoring the stern voice calling her name.

She should have known that she couldn't walk away

from Jobe. He followed her right up the staircase and into her bedroom without hesitation.

"For God's sake," she said angrily, turning on him, "I'm tired! Have this out with Ted. He's your boss, as you like to remind me. I have no voice in the business except in an advisory capacity."

She averted her eyes from his shirt, unbuttoned to the collarbone, and showing a disturbing amount of thick dark hair. She hated the very sight of him.

"I don't want Missy blamed for something that was my fault," he persisted.

She sat down on the edge of her bed with a hard sigh, pushing back strands of loosened hair. She still wouldn't look at him. "I won't say anything," she said stiffly. "But Ted would have."

"I'm aware of that."

She rubbed her fingers against her forehead. "I've got a splitting headache. Close the door on your way out, would you?"

He didn't leave. "Shall I send Mrs. Bird up with some aspirin?"

"I have aspirin of my own, if I want them." She looked at him then, with accusing eyes that gave away her contempt.

His jaw tautened. "Tell me that you've never kissed your boss in his office, Sandy."

The mocking remark didn't hit a nerve. "My boss is a gentleman," she said quietly. "He has a business degree from Harvard and he's quite reserved. It would never occur to him to wrestle any woman down on a couch, much less an employee."

His eyes narrowed. They skimmed over her loose jacket to the firm thrust of her breasts under it, and his face changed imperceptibly. "Would he know what to do with you if he did wrestle you down on a couch?" he asked in a tone he'd never used with her.

She stared at him blindly, aware of the sudden silence in the room, of his gray eyes holding hers, of the ragged sound of her own breathing, the uneven throb of her heart at her rib cage.

"You have…no right…to say such things to me," she choked.

"Maybe I have more right than you realize," he said grimly.

"Missy's the one with the rights," Sandy said curtly.

"At least," he said softly, "she knows that she's a woman."

Sandy stared at him without blinking. It was ridiculous that she should feel betrayed. But she did. "Lucky you," she replied in a baiting tone.

"That's the one thing you've never tried—throwing yourself at me," he continued in a conversational tone. "Pity. You might have learned a few things."

She flushed uncomfortably. "I don't throw myself at men," she said unsteadily.

"Of course not," he replied. "You're much too superior to think about it seriously. Your mother should have taught you how to manage men."

She stood up. "Don't you make remarks about my mother!"

His eyebrows rose. "Was I?"

"Everyone knows what she was," she said angrily.

"She left our father and ran away with another man, and shortly afterward, she left him for yet another one. No man could ever satisfy her," she said bitterly. "Well, I'm not like her and I never will be. I don't need a man!"

Jobe was oddly silent. He searched her white face for a long moment before his gaze fell to the hands clenched at her sides.

"So that's it," he said, almost to himself. "I knew Ted didn't like women until Coreen came along. I never really knew why." His jaw tautened. "I guess she did a job on both of you, didn't she?"

She drew herself up to her full height. "My mother is none of your business."

"That's a matter of opinion, but we'll let it drop for now."

"If you're through goading me, I'd like to rest. It's a long drive from Houston."

He stuck his hands into his jean pockets and watched her with keen eyes. "We're having a barbecue tomorrow, to coincide with Ted's horse auction."

"I'm sure you and Missy will enjoy it," she said pointedly. "I have no intention of attending, if that reassures you."

He scowled. "Why should you think that?"

She laughed mirthlessly. "For God's sake, I know how you feel about me," she said in a hollow tone, turning away. "I've always known."

"How do I feel about you?" he asked in a strange tone.

"You despise me," she replied without turning. "Didn't you think I knew?"

CHAPTER THREE

JOBE STARED AT her straight back with conflicting emotions. "Who told you that?" he asked finally.

"Nobody had to," she said in a defeated tone. "When I was younger, nothing I did ever measured up to your expectations. I spent years trying to be what you wanted, and I always fell short." She wrapped her arms around herself, as if she were cold, and stared out the window. "Finally I gave up."

He was scowling. "I don't understand," he said. "You don't care what I think. You've always been at my throat."

She laughed bitterly. "Haven't I, though?"

"Why?"

She wouldn't have told him ordinarily. But she was worn out and half sick from what she'd seen downstairs. There was no hope left where he was concerned, she knew that now. Her shoulders lifted and fell. "So you wouldn't realize that I was in love with you," she said, without looking at him. Even so, she could feel the sudden tension in the room. She let out a breath. "Oh, don't worry, I got over it," she said, her eyes on a distant horse out in the pasture.

"That's a relief." His voice sounded choked.

She nodded. "I imagine so. I didn't know anything about you. If I had…" She closed her eyes. "I suppose you had your fill of career women a long time ago."

"Who told you about my mother?" he asked curtly.

"Ted." She smoothed her hands over her forearms. "I'm sorry about what I said to you that day," she added quietly. "I meant it to hurt, but I'm sorry."

There was a long pause. "No harm done."

That wasn't quite true, she thought, but she didn't pursue it. She leaned her head against the cool windowpane. "You'll have things to do," she said, closing her eyes. "And I really have to lie down now. My head's splitting."

After a minute, she heard footsteps and the closing of the door. Until they died away, she didn't even realize that she was crying.

LATER, SHE WAS horrified at what she'd admitted to Jobe. He must have had a good laugh about it, probably with Missy. God knew, the girl looked smug enough every time Sandy saw her. And as the barbecue got underway, it seemed that Missy had suddenly become the hostess.

Coreen put a stop to that immediately, her blue eyes flashing fire at the girl even as she gently sent her to the kitchen to make coffee. Sandy noticed that Jobe held her hand and drew her along to the kitchen to soften the blow.

"Honestly," Coreen exclaimed shortly thereafter, "did you see that? She's getting a little big for her britches!"

"Jobe indulges her," Sandy said without emotion.

"He can indulge her someplace else if she tries that

again," Coreen said. "I'm not putting up with that sort of nonsense."

Sandy didn't say a word.

Coreen scowled at her. "Sandy, what's wrong?" she asked gently. "You haven't been yourself at all lately. Isn't your boss supposed to come down today to bring those papers you left in Houston?"

"You saw the fax he sent, I guess?" Sandy mused. "He said he might, but I doubt it. Mr. Cranson isn't much on parties. He's strictly a businessman."

"Does he drive a black Mercedes?" Coreen asked conversationally.

"Well, yes, he does."

Coreen grinned. "Then he's here." She let out a soft whistle as the big, dark man climbed out of the car. "Good grief, you didn't say he was a dish!"

"He is, isn't he?" Sandy murmured, smiling. "I'm very fond of him. But he's in love with someone else."

"Pity."

"Yes, it is," Sandy agreed. She went to meet her dark-eyed boss. "Glad you could come, Mr. Cranson."

"You might as well call me Phillip, under the circumstances," he said, handing her a thick file. "This is the dossier you mislaid, I believe."

"Yes, it is. Mr.—Phillip," she amended, "this is my sister-in-law, Coreen. Coreen, Mr. Cranson."

"Nice to meet you," Coreen said, smiling. "Ted and I have heard a lot about you."

"Hopefully some of it was good," he murmured with a dry glance at Sandy. He looked down at his expensive suit. "I seem to be overdressed."

"We're having a barbecue and later there'll be square dancing," Coreen said. "I hope you'll stay."

He pursed his lips and glanced at Sandy.

"I'd love it if you would," she said honestly.

He chuckled. "In that case, I'd be delighted."

He walked around the gathering with Sandy beside him, looking very comfortable now that he'd taken off his jacket and rolled up his white shirtsleeves. He was rakishly handsome, and Sandy had often wondered what had happened to sour him against women so much. He never spoke of the past, but sometimes he sat in his office and glowered, intimidating young employees.

"Have you always lived here?" he asked Sandy when they paused to get coffee.

"Most of my life," she agreed. "I love Jacobsville. It may be a small town, but it has a big history."

"Does it? Tell me about it."

She did, and he listened attentively. Neither of them noticed a pair of gray eyes glaring in their direction.

Jobe paused beside Ted and Coreen. "Who is he?" he asked curtly.

"Her boss," Ted murmured, avoiding the other man's eyes. "Nice-looking man, isn't he? I wondered what he was like. She's been very secretive about him."

Jobe's eyes narrowed. "He's older than she is. A good bit older. And for all her age, Sandy is a babe in the woods where men are concerned."

If Ted was shocked at Jobe's words, and he was, it never showed in that poker face. "Well, she's twenty-six, Jobe," he reminded the other man. "It's past time she thought of settling down and having children."

Jobe's eyes flashed. "She won't marry. She's a career woman."

"Nonsense," Coreen said shortly. "She loves kids, and there's nothing she enjoys more than riding around the ranch."

"She can't cook," Jobe muttered.

"She's never had to," Ted interjected. "We've always had housekeepers. She does pretty needlework, though, and she knits." He studied Sandy and her boss. "They look good together," he remarked. "Of course, he's a city boy. You can tell."

"He probably knows computers inside out," Jobe said irritably.

"Actually he doesn't," Coreen replied. "He's good at business, but he's pretty much limited to marketing. He doesn't ride, either."

"That's a shame," Ted added. "Because I can't see Sandy living anywhere that she can't ride. She loves horses."

"If he cared enough, he'd do what pleased her," Coreen remarked.

Jobe's face paled. He murmured something and went off alone, to be waylaid by Missy shortly afterward.

"I see Lady Boss has somebody to hang on to," Missy remarked pertly. "He isn't bad, but he's old."

Jobe didn't reply. He was glaring at them.

Missy pressed close. "Want to go somewhere we can be alone?" she purred.

He scowled down at her. He didn't know why he'd let himself be tempted. She was cute and sweet, but she had no maturity at all. A few kisses, and she'd become horribly possessive. He wondered if anyone else had noticed.

"Listen," he said quietly, "we work together and I like you. But that's as far as it goes. We aren't a couple."

Missy's eyebrows lifted. "You kissed me."

"I kiss lots of girls," he said honestly. "You're sweet, honey, but I'm not in the market for an affair."

She colored. "Well, neither am I!"

"Or marriage," he added firmly. "I don't want it. Not ever."

Missy looked as if he'd hit her with a brick bat. She moved a little away from him. "I…see."

"No, you don't," he said sharply. "It's not that I don't like you. I don't want a relationship, that's all."

She looked so young. Tears swam in her eyes. He felt guilty and ashamed as he looked at her. He should never have given her ideas.

"I'm sorry," he said quietly.

She pressed against him, crying softly. He gathered her close.

"Damn it, Missy!" he muttered.

"Don't fuss," she pleaded, sniffing. "I won't stand in your way, or anything. I'll just be around when you're lonely."

He only half heard her. His eyes were on Sandy. Her boss had put his arm around her as they walked toward the barbecue pit, and his heart leaped with fury. He felt jealousy as if it were acid in his stomach, and wondered at the intensity of it.

Missy felt him stiffen and pulled away, dabbing at

her eyes with a tissue she'd produced from her pocket. "What's wrong?"

He didn't answer and she followed his angry gaze to Sandy and the big, dark man beside her.

"You don't like her at all, do you?" Missy said with evident satisfaction. "I'm glad. Maybe she'll marry her boss and go away. I hate to see her upset you like she does."

"She doesn't upset me," he said stiffly. "Her opinion doesn't matter."

"Good. Then you can come and dance with me, can't you?" She coaxed him onto the dance floor. He went, but his heart wasn't in it. If only he could keep his eyes off Sandy, damn her!

Sandy, unaware of the reaction she was causing, ate barbecue with her handsome boss and then sat and talked computers until the music changed to slow, sultry songs.

"Care to dance?" Jobe asked suddenly.

She jumped. She hadn't realized he was so close. She hesitated.

"Oh, go ahead," Mr. Cranson chided. "You've been talking business with me all evening. Go enjoy yourself."

Jobe glared at the man, but he nodded politely as he took Sandy's hand and pulled her along with him.

She was stiff in his arms, so tense that she felt brittle.

"Relax," he muttered angrily. "What can I do to you on a dance floor?"

He'd be amazed, she thought wildly. Her heart was acting up, so was her breathing. Her legs felt like jelly under her. Only by holding her body rigid could she retain some semblance of dignity. She wanted nothing more than to press close, as Missy had earlier, and feel his strength. But that was the one thing she didn't dare do.

His big hand spread between her shoulder blades. His fingers linked into hers. His cheek rested against her temple as he moved slowly to the music. His sigh was warm in her hair.

"You always smell like violets," he murmured.

She didn't know how to answer that. He had his own unique fragrance, a spicy smell that clung to his face, one that she always associated with him. Odd how keen her senses were when he was close. Not that he ever was. She'd only danced with him once before in her life, and that had been a square dance. This was different. It was far too close, too intimate. She was vulnerable, and she didn't want to be.

"I'm...tired," she protested, weakly pulling against his arm.

"No, you aren't," he replied, holding her in place. His head lifted and he caught her eyes relentlessly. "Now, relax," he commanded softly.

He seemed able to make her body obey. Little by little, she relaxed into him and shivered slightly at the reaction their closeness provoked in her. All her senses seemed to come alive at once, in a riot of sensation.

His big hand smoothed up and down her spine, riveting her to the lean, powerful length of him. She shivered again. Involuntarily, her cheek went to his warm, muscular shoulder and she gave in to all the forbidden longings of the past.

He sighed unsteadily. He was having his own problems with her closeness. It was good. It was better than he'd ever imagined it would be. His eyes closed. She felt soft and sweet against him, womanly soft. The lights were low and they were a little apart from the other dancers, in the shadows. Impulsively he lowered his head until he could feel her soft mouth under his searching lips. He made a sound, deep in his throat, and stopped dancing. His mouth opened, became demanding, fierce and hard on her trembling lips. They parted for him. She stiffened a little and then pressed close, a sobbing moan rising from her chest.

His hand was at her neck, coaxing, guiding. He lifted his mouth only to lower it again, in soft biting kisses that made her tremble.

"Sandy," he groaned, looking around him in agonized hunger. There was a big tree close by and nobody was paying attention to them just yet.

He maneuvered Sandy behind the tree and levered his body down against hers in a fever of need, crushing her gently between the tree and himself.

His mouth covered hers again, with slow, sweet ardor that brought her arms around him. He kissed her until she would have fallen, but for the support of the tree and his arms. So many dreams came true in that space of minutes, so many painful longings. She hadn't dreamed that the two of them would generate such sweet desire between them. She wanted him with all her heart, loved him, needed him. The world spun away and there was only the two of them and the desire that grew like a seedling.

Eventually he had to stop. His body ached, but he ignored it, pulling Sandy free of the tree trunk and into arms that were suddenly gentle and protective.

She couldn't stop trembling. She shivered helplessly in his arms while he rocked her in the warm evening silence, broken by sweet, muted strains of music.

He buried his face in her warm, scented throat, hanging there as he fought to control the raging desire she'd kindled in him.

Her eyes opened. She saw the shadowy leaves above them, and beyond them, the stars. It was like a moment out of time. She was afraid to break the silence, to speak. She didn't dare ask why. She didn't want to know. It was enough that he'd wanted her, even for such a brief time. She could live on it forever. Her eyes closed again and she stood against him without a protest, without a sound.

He let her go inch by inch, his face as hard as stone. He didn't say anything. She could feel his eyes, but it was too dark to see them. Her head lowered and she felt cold as he moved back.

The sound of her own breathing was unusually loud. She didn't look up. Her arms wrapped around herself to warm her in the chill of his withdrawal. Her legs still felt unsteady.

They didn't speak. A full minute later, Missy's shrill voice calling to Jobe brought his head up. He cursed silently, but he turned and went to her. He didn't want her to see Sandy like this, vulnerable and defenseless.

He didn't think any of his own turmoil would show in the dim light.

"There you are," Missy said, linking her arm through his. "They're about to play the last song. I'm ready to go when you are. Wasn't it fun?"

He didn't answer her. His mind was spinning.

Sandy got her breath back and went in search of Phillip Cranson, smiling blandly at people she passed. No one looking at her would ever guess that she'd been so abandoned in a man's arms only minutes earlier. For the rest of the evening, she was the perfect co-hostess. She even managed a nice smile for Missy and Jobe as they left after the last dance. But she didn't meet his eyes. She wondered if she would ever be able to look at him again after the way she'd behaved.

BY THE NEXT MORNING, she'd convinced herself that it hadn't happened, anyway. She slept late and had to be dragged out of bed by a disapproving Coreen.

"Come on, sleepyhead, you can't spend your life in bed! I want to go riding."

Sandy blinked. "Riding? Before daylight?"

"It's almost noon, you idiot," Coreen chuckled. "Ted's going to babysit while we're out."

That got her attention. "This I've got to see," she said, and got up.

Sure enough, Ted was in the living room with his son, his face radiant as he held the little boy in his arms. It was amazing, the change in Ted since he and Coreen had married. Her taciturn brother was the picture of a contented parent, and a loving husband. It hadn't always been that way. He'd given Coreen a lot of pain before he'd finally given in to his feelings for her and stopped dwelling on the age difference between them.

He looked up as the women entered. "Take as long as you like," he said generously. "I'll stay home."

Coreen snuggled up to him and kissed him tenderly before she pressed her lips to her son's tiny forehead. "Isn't he a miracle?" she sighed.

Ted was looking at her instead of the baby. "My life is one long miracle since I put that ring on your finger," he replied.

Sandy felt like an interloper. "I'll go out and saddle the horses," she offered with an approving grin.

"I told Jobe to do that," Ted said. "But he may need help."

Sandy's eyes flashed. "Is Missy with him?"

"Missy doesn't work Saturdays," Ted reminded her.

"Amazing," Sandy said under her breath. "I've got to get my hat," she said aloud, because she didn't want to go to the stables and be alone with Jobe, not after last night.

"Don't take long," Coreen called after her. "It's going to rain later, they said."

"Okay!"

She was back within five minutes, and Coreen went out the door with her.

Jobe was lounging against a bale of hay when they walked in. He didn't say anything, but the look he gave Sandy in her trim, well-fitting jeans, would have made any woman's knees weak. He didn't smile or joke or say a word. He just looked.

"Thanks, Jobe," Coreen called to him as they mounted.

He shrugged. "No problem. I'm going out to check on the baler. They were having trouble with it earlier, and it's due to rain. Mind if I tag along as far as the bottoms?"

"Of course not," Coreen said, ignoring Sandy's hunted expression.

Jobe drew his own horse, already saddled, out of a nearby stall and swung gracefully into the saddle. They rode along in a pleasant silence for a few minutes.

"Don't hold those reins so tight," Jobe chided Sandy. "You'll hurt his mouth."

She loosened them at once. She didn't argue or snap back, which was so uncharacteristic that Coreen shot her a startled look. But when she saw her friend's face, she hid a smile.

"I'm going to ride over and talk to Hank for a minute about the new foal we've got in the barn," she said. "Be right back!"

Sandy wanted to call after her, but she couldn't admit that she was afraid to be alone with Jobe. Alone, she mused humorously, in the middle of a ranch with cowboys everywhere. What a laugh!

Jobe's gloved hand rested on the pommel. He didn't look at her, but off into the distance, his broad-brimmed hat pulled low over his gray eyes. "That rain would be welcome two days from now. I hope it holds off until we've got this hay up."

"Will it be hard…to fix the machine?"

He turned his head and looked into her eyes under the brim of her wide-brimmed straw hat, seeing the nervousness there, the unfamiliar vulnerability. He maneuvered his horse closer to hers.

"Don't be afraid," he said unexpectedly, holding her gaze.

She laughed unsteadily. "Afraid? Of you?"

"I wasn't going to follow up on what happened last night, Sandy," he said solemnly. "It was a moment out of time. Nothing to worry about."

Her heart fell. She didn't look at him. "I see."

"Unless…"

She glanced up. "Unless?"

His narrow eyes fell to her mouth. "Unless you're willing to take a chance with me."

Her breath caught in her throat. "What…sort of… chance?"

He searched her drawn face carefully. "The sort we tried together last night," he replied. "It was good. Better than I'd ever thought it could be. We've both had our share of false starts with the opposite sex. Why don't we see how we do as a couple for a while?"

She felt her heart stop in her chest. It was the last thing she expected him to say to her. "What about Missy?" she choked.

"What about her?" His face hardened. "I haven't made her a single promise."

"Yes, I remember. You don't make promises to women."

"Don't make a joke of it," he said flatly. "I'm not kidding. This is serious business."

She caught her lower lip between her teeth and stared at him, half-afraid. "You're a single man. You like it that way. I'm not…not in the market for an affair. I'm sorry."

She started to move away, but his hand caught hers where it held the reins.

"I'm not talking about an affair, Sandy," he said. He managed a smile. "Ted would kill me. He lives in the past, too."

She glared at him. "So I'm old-fashioned. So what?"

"I don't mind," he mused, chuckling. "In some ways, I'm old-fashioned myself."

She moved in the saddle and heard the leathers creak. "What did you have in mind?"

"Suppose we go out to eat and take in a movie?" he suggested. "Or is that too middle-class for you?"

She flushed. "I'm middle-class, too."

"Like hell you are," he countered. "You and Ted were born to money. You've never been without it."

"I earn my own way now," she reminded him, refusing to admit why she'd decided to go out to work when she stood to inherit a fortune from a trust when she turned twenty-eight.

"Yes, I know you do," he replied. "And I know why."

She met his eyes, shocked. "You...do?"

He started to speak, and just as he opened his mouth, Coreen came galloping up beside Sandy.

"We'd better get moving," she said with an apologetic smile, indicating the black clouds building. "That hay will be a dead loss if the rain gets it."

"So it will," Jobe agreed. He shot a wistful glance at Sandy, tipped his hat and rode away.

"Sorry I interrupted," Coreen began.

"In the nick of time," Sandy said, forcing a laugh. "Don't worry. Everything's fine."

CHAPTER FOUR

IF SANDY HAD hoped to avoid Jobe's offer of a date, the rain didn't stop him. He came looking for her late that afternoon, after the hay was in.

It was dark and rainy outside and Sandy had been sitting in the garden room out back, watching the rain come down on the pecan trees.

Jobe found her there, curled up on a sofa in white slacks and a brief blue top.

"Avoiding me?" he asked quietly.

She sat up abruptly, flustered. "Why, no, of course not."

He moved right into the room, took off his hat and sat down beside her on the sofa. "I like thrillers," he said without preamble. "There's one at the theater downtown. If you'd rather see something else, I believe there's a comedy at the Grand."

"I like thrillers."

He nodded. "We can have a pizza or a burger and fries before we go to see it. Or there's a cafeteria, if you'd like that better."

He was testing her, she concluded, to see if she minded an inexpensive meal.

She searched his eyes for a long moment. "I don't

have to go to the best restaurants or to the opera or a play, in case that's what you were thinking," she said gently. "I like a burger and fries, and movies suit me very well."

"It isn't what you're used to, though," he added. He sighed. "To tell you the truth, I had second thoughts about asking you out at all." He twirled his hat in his hands. "Maybe it's a bad idea."

She didn't know what to say. She shifted a little. "Whatever you want to do is fine," she said.

"Is that so?" His eyes glittered. He threw his hat on the floor, caught her around the waist and bore her down on the sofa, finding her mouth with his at the same instant.

She couldn't get enough air to breathe, much less to protest. He was rough with her, as if her reply had angered him. There was no hesitation, no tenderness, in his demanding mouth or the weight of his body over hers.

She made a soft sound of protest and he relented, lifting his head to glare at her.

"This is what I want to do," he said harshly, looking at her as if he hated her. "It's what I've wanted to do since you were seventeen, damn it!"

She paled, seeing the self-loathing written all over his face. He wanted her and hated himself for it. If she had dreams of happily ever after, they turned to ashes from the look in his eyes.

Suppressing quick tears of anger and disappointment, she put both hands against his shirtfront and pushed.

"Let me up, please," she said through her teeth.

To her surprise, he did. He got to his feet and whipped his hat off the floor with an angry hand.

"I don't want to go out with you, thanks all the same," she said in a choked tone. She sidestepped him and the instant she was an arm's length away, she ran all the way upstairs, into her room, locking the door behind her.

Tears ran down her cheeks, and she wiped them away angrily. He was the cruelest man she'd ever known. How could he treat her like that, after all the years they'd known each other? It broke her heart that he had no more respect for her than that. It made her furious that she'd let her guard down at all.

She went into her bathroom and washed her face, cold with suppressed rage.

She didn't even think as she dragged her suitcase out of the closet and started packing. No way was she going to stay here after that.

A quick change of clothing, from jeans into a neat beige suit, her hair in a bun and her purse over her arm, and she was on her way down the staircase.

She paused at the kitchen doorway, where Mrs. Bird was cooking supper.

"I have to go back to Victoria," she told the woman. "An emergency."

"Oh, did the phone ring, then?" Mrs. Bird asked. "I was out in the yard getting in the throw rug, I must have not heard it."

"You must not have," Sandy agreed with a straight face. "Tell Ted and Coreen that I'll phone them later, would you?"

"Of course, Miss Sandy."

She smiled at the housekeeper and marched out the front door and down to the garage.

Jobe was leaning against the trunk of her car. She stopped short when she saw him, but only for an instant.

"If you'd move, I could put my suitcase in the trunk," she said with ice dripping from every word.

He searched her wan face, noting the redness of her eyes. "You're always running away," he remarked.

"And you don't think I have good reason to?" she demanded.

"This time, yes, you do," he replied. His narrow gaze slid over her face. "I'm just as hesitant about getting involved as you are. I didn't mean to hurt you," he added heavily, noting with a grimace the swollen place on her lower lip where his teeth had caught it.

"No harm done," she replied tightly. "Would you move?"

He stepped aside, watching irritably as she put her case in the trunk and closed it.

"Wouldn't it be better to get it out of our systems?" he asked.

She straightened. "Didn't you do that, on the sofa?" she asked with cold irony.

His jaw tautened. "I don't make a practice of hurting women. I'm sorry."

"You wanted me to leave."

He let out an angry breath. "All right, maybe I did," he said shortly. "There are so many obstacles..."

"Yes, there are," she agreed at once. "Missy's just

your style, uncomplicated and sweet. I'm sure you'll be very happy together."

"As happy as you'll be with your boss?" he asked harshly.

She turned at the door. "Mr. Cranson is in love with someone else," she said. "I like him very much, but I'm not romantically involved with him."

He was surprised at her lack of guile. "You seemed affectionate with him."

"I like him," she repeated. "I don't like you," she added with a venomous look. "Not one bit."

"I could work on that, if you'd let me," he replied.

She avoided his eyes. "You don't want me here," she said perceptively, bringing a fleeting surprised look to his features. "Maybe you were flattered by what I told you, about the way I used to feel toward you, but you don't want me here and it shows. You needn't feel guilty on my account, because of an old crush that I'm over. You don't owe me anything."

He scowled faintly.

"For God's sake, you don't even like me," she said heavily. "You never have. You said you knew why I went away to work. That explains it all, doesn't it?"

"You were seventeen," he recalled, "when you went to college. I knew it was to get away from me. I just didn't know exactly why."

"You were dating Liz Mason," she replied sadly. "We all thought you'd probably marry her." She moved one shoulder. "I wasn't pretty like Liz, and I couldn't talk cattle. It was no surprise to me that I rubbed you the wrong way. You picked at me all the time. I left because it hurt too much to be around you."

"It wasn't because I didn't like you," he returned.

She managed a smile. "I understand that now," she said with what dignity she could muster. "You wanted me, didn't you?"

He nodded, a curt, angry nod of his head.

"And you still do," she said with gathering misery. "Maybe I should be flattered, but I'm not. Bodies are cheap, a dime a dozen."

"The sort of chemistry we have together isn't all that usual," he remarked. "In fact, it's quite rare."

"I want more than a few nights in bed with a man who has nothing but desire to offer," she said honestly. "That's why I've never been a rounder. I'm much too serious for lighthearted affairs."

His chin lifted and he didn't even blink. The intensity of his gaze made her heart race. "I could take you to bed anytime I liked," he said quietly. "That was true when you were seventeen and it's true now. I've always known it."

She flushed. "You arrogant...!"

"Oh, hell, don't fidget," he muttered. He stuck his hands into his pockets. "I haven't done anything about it. And if I've antagonized you, it was for your own protection. Just how much willpower do you think I've got? If you'd ever thrown yourself at me, neither of us would have had a prayer."

She stiffened. "I don't throw myself at men."

"Good thing," he replied. "Otherwise, you'd have found yourself standing in front of the nearest minister

I could produce. I don't play around with women who don't know the score."

"I'm not some ignorant schoolgirl!"

He drew in a long breath. "I know exactly what you are, Sandy," he said quietly. "It hasn't made things easier." He searched her face. "If you're determined to leave, I won't try to stop you. Maybe you're right. We'd both have a lot of adjusting to do. I don't know if you could really settle for a middle-class life, and I'm not the sort to give up my job and live on my wife's income."

"I don't want to get married," she said through her teeth.

He saw through the pretense, but he didn't say anything. "Have a safe trip," he remarked, and turned away.

Sandy watched him walk off, her heart down around her ankles. She didn't know what he really wanted, and he wasn't going to tell her. As usual, he was going to force her to read his mind.

"I hate men," she muttered to herself.

She climbed into the car, started it and drove away. All the way to Victoria, she kept the radio playing as loud as she could stand it, just to stop the thoughts that plagued her. She shouldn't have left, she should have stayed and let things take their course. But she was afraid of being hurt. Jobe couldn't guarantee her that they'd find anything more than desire in each other's arms, and desire wasn't enough.

But she'd never know what he was offering. She'd been too afraid to risk her heart with him. Now she was going to pay the price.

PAY IT SHE DID, for two solid miserable weeks, trying desperately to put Jobe to the back of her mind. But he wouldn't stay there. He kept popping up all the time, especially in conversations with Coreen.

"He won't even talk to Missy lately," Coreen mused over the phone. "He's so morose that one of the men asked if he'd had a relative die or something. It's strange, you know, for Jobe to be anything but pleasant and easygoing."

"Maybe he had bad news," Sandy said stiffly.

"Oh, no, it's not that. He's been this way since you left."

Sandy's heart jumped. "Pull the other leg."

"I'm not kidding," Sandy told her. "He misses you."

She didn't say a word. After a minute, she changed the subject and Coreen didn't say anything else about the ranch foreman.

But two days later, Ted called.

"We've run into a snag with the computer," he told Sandy. "The files won't come up, and I have to have them for a production sale. Can you come down and have a look?"

"Okay. I'll be home first thing tomorrow."

"Good girl!"

He hung up and she considered the workings of providence. Fate was taking a hand. She wondered what would be waiting for her in Jacobsville.

She packed her case and left early the next morning, refusing to admit to herself how much she'd missed Jobe, how much she cared for him.

He wasn't in the office when she went to have a look at the computer, but Ted was.

He glowered. "I never did trust the damned things," he muttered while Sandy checked files on the hard drive. "Now see what it's done, it's eaten my damned herd records!"

"It hasn't," Sandy replied. "They've been erased, but I can recover them. Just stop cursing and give me a little time to do it."

He made a rough sound. "Are you sure you can?"

"Yes." She ran through the files. "How did it happen?"

"Missy was upset and hit the wrong keys, or so Jobe said."

She looked at her brother curiously. "What upset her?"

"I don't know," he replied dryly, "but I think it was because Jobe didn't want to go with her to some party in town. She bought a new dress just for the occasion."

"Why didn't he want to go?"

"Ask him." He perched himself against the desk. "He's been hell to talk to lately. He snaps, no matter what you say to him. Irritable as all hell, since you left that day. Odd, isn't it?" he added with a cool smile and narrow, intent eyes.

Sandy colored in spite of herself. "We both agreed that we're better off with the status quo."

"In other words, you're too scared to take a chance on him, is that right?"

She stopped working with the computer and whirled around in her chair. "We're both scared," she replied.

"He doesn't think I can settle for a middle-class life, and I don't think he's capable of any feelings that aren't physical. Does that put things into perspective for you?"

Ted chuckled. "I thought it was something of the sort." He folded his arms across his chest. "But sometimes you have to take a chance," he added gently.

"You'd know," she replied, remembering how hard he'd fought Coreen's influence. Her eyes softened. "I guess you and Coreen had to make adjustments when you decided to get married."

"You don't know the half of it," he replied, tongue-in-cheek. "We were explosive together. Well, we still are, but not quite in the same way."

"I get your meaning." She studied her hands folded neatly in her lap. "I ran."

"I know."

She shifted in the chair and crossed her long legs. "Actually, I think he ran, too. We've spent a long time at each other's throats. It's hard to make peace."

"Especially the sort of peace he wants to make?" Ted probed gently.

She flushed. "Yes."

He took a long breath. "Honey, I can't tell you what to do with your life. I can't promise you that things would work out if you and Jobe put your differences aside. But I've been alone and I've been married. Believe me, married is better."

"I don't think he wants marriage."

His face hardened. "He'd better."

"Now, Ted, don't start playing big brother."

"Don't you start with lectures on modern morality, either," he snapped back. "This is a small town in Texas."

"And you're going to tell me that women don't live with men if they aren't married and that all kids are born in wedlock here."

He made a face. "Of course not. But you're family."

"Yes, I am. I think you're terrific, in case I haven't said so," she murmured. "But I'll live my own life, whether you like it or not."

He glared at her.

She shrugged. "Actually I'm not much on loose relationships, either, which is why I ran. Jobe isn't a marrying man."

"All men are, with the right woman," Ted replied.

"I thought Missy was the right woman."

His eyebrow jerked. "You wouldn't think so if you'd seen her light out of here yesterday, madder than a wet hornet."

"Everybody argues. Usually they make up."

"Why don't you?" Ted returned.

She studied her hands again. "He isn't around."

"Yes, he is."

A soft sound in the hall caught her attention. She turned just as Jobe came in the door. But not the man of her memories. This one was cold-faced and looked as hard as steel. He barely nodded at her before he turned to Ted.

"We've got six horses in the road. The fence broke out on Jasper Road."

"How?" Ted asked, all business as he stood up.

"A truck had a flat going the speed limit and ran through it. I've got men out looking for them."

"I'll go and help. Sandy says she can get the files back for you," he added, nodding toward Sandy. "You can help her while I see about my horses."

He left, and Jobe cursed under his breath.

"I don't like it any better than you do," Sandy said with a speaking glance in his direction. "But we seem to be stuck here together."

He paused by her chair, watching her fingers race across the keys. "What are you doing?" he asked, diverted.

"I'm using a program to recover files. If you wipe something out accidentally, most of the time you can get it back if you know how." She went on to explain about temporary files and the manner of their storage, and the use of the recovery program.

"That's incredible," he said.

"Yes, isn't it?" She smiled. "I grew up watching *Star Trek* reruns. I wanted to be a computer expert, just like Mr. Spock."

"A lot of kids did," he agreed, smiling back. "You make this look easy. It isn't."

"I've been doing it for a lot of years. Practice improves most things. Look how good you are with horses and cattle," she added, punching more keys. "Because you grew up with it."

He stood behind her, watching the screen. His lean hand touched her hair lightly. "I missed you," he said suddenly.

She caught her breath. "Did you?"

"Ted said he was on the verge of firing me," he continued. "He knew what was wrong, I think, but he wouldn't put it into words." He paused. "How's your temper been, while we're on the subject?"

"Not much better than yours, according to my co-workers."

He drew her up from the chair and pulled her into his arms. "Then I think it's time we made some decisions," he said.

"What sort?"

He smiled and bent his head. "This sort," he whispered against her warm mouth.

It was like coming home. She pressed close, savoring the muscular warmth of his body in the silence that followed. She hadn't a protest left. She followed where he led, eagerly, without reservation.

When he lifted his head, she looked up at him with her heart in her eyes.

He looked oddly hesitant, his gaze intent and a little worried.

"What's wrong?" she asked.

He touched her cheek. "Cold feet," he murmured, chuckling.

"I know how you feel." She sighed. "But I'm miserable, just the same."

"We know each other pretty well by now," he remarked thoughtfully. "God knows, we aren't kids. Let's just take it one day at a time and see how it goes."

She nodded. "Okay."

He bent and kissed her again, lightly this time. "No

heavy stuff, either," he murmured against her lips. "We could be in over our heads much too quick."

She sighed and laid her cheek against his chest. It felt familiar, safe. Her eyes opened and she studied the office across his patterned shirt.

"Remember when my puppy died, and you found me crying in the barn so Ted wouldn't see?" she recalled.

He chuckled. "You didn't want me to see, either."

"Nothing ever seemed to bother you and Ted. I felt like a sissy. But you picked me up and held me until the tears stopped. Remember what you said?"

"That tears healed a broken heart," he murmured. "Do they?"

"You wouldn't know. You never cry."

His hands linked behind her waist. "I did when my father killed himself," he replied. "He was a good, decent man, but he wasn't smart enough to suit my mother. She said she needed a man with a proper education, with the mind of a genius."

"Do you know what happened to her?" she asked gently.

He stiffened. "No."

"Sorry."

"It's all right. I didn't mind the question. I lost track of her after he died. I suppose she's still doing research in some top-secret lab somewhere. Maybe she's even found a man smart enough to suit her, but I don't imagine she stayed with him. You see, if he was too smart, she wouldn't like the competition."

"My mother wasn't all that smart, she was just a rounder," she volunteered. "It warped Ted, really badly.

If Coreen hadn't come along, I doubt he'd ever have married."

"She's a peach," he agreed. He looked down at her with a tender smile. "So are you. Under that hard exterior and that computer brain, you're a sweet woman."

"Is that a compliment?"

His mouth brushed hers. "Oh, I think so," he murmured. His breath whispered across her nose. "I've spent years trying to pretend that you were just another career woman like my mother. But when I see you with that little boy of Ted and Coreen's in your arms, you don't look much like a hard-boiled career woman, Sandy."

She searched his pale eyes curiously. "You've never talked about children, except once," she recalled, and looked uncomfortable. "You told Ted that you didn't want a bunch of little computer experts…"

He put a long forefinger over her lips. "We all say things we don't mean," he told her. "I didn't mean that. I've been fighting a losing battle with you for years. It's hard to stop."

"I know. I thought my life was exactly as I wanted it. Then I'd come home and see you…"

He nodded. "I understand perfectly." He drew her closer and bent to kiss her again, softly. "This feels nice."

"Mmm, doesn't it, though?" She chuckled. She closed her eyes. "Eventually I should do something about Ted's files."

"They can wait."

"I suppose so. But…"

The front doorbell rang. They looked toward it. Mrs. Bird went to let a visitor in, and they both frowned when they saw who it was.

Jobe let go of Sandy as Missy approached. She looked very cool and pretty in a yellow sundress. She had her purse and a file folder in both hands.

"I thought you might need these herd records," she said with a sweet smile at Jobe. "I accidentally took them with me when I left." She glanced mutinously toward Sandy. "I guess you came to look for those lost files?"

"I found them," Sandy said smugly.

Missy looked uncomfortable. "I didn't think you could recover lost files."

"Where *did* you train?" Sandy asked pointedly.

"It's a good school," Missy said defensively, flushing. "They taught us how to recover stuff. I just forgot."

"Bad business," Sandy returned coolly. "Especially when so much depends on stored information. Fortunately for Ted, I knew how to get his herd records back. There's a production sale this month, as I'm sure Jobe must have mentioned."

Missy smiled. "Well, I guess he did, but then we didn't talk about business *all* the time, did we, honey?" she asked Jobe.

He looked very uncomfortable. He'd made it seem as if he and Missy were involved to protect himself from Sandy, and now it was going to get him in serious trouble. He could tell from the expression on Sandy's face that she still had doubts about him and Missy, and he didn't exactly know how to dispel them.

CHAPTER FIVE

Missy saw Jobe's uneasiness and decided to let her remarks sink in for a while. "Well, I'll be off now. See you Monday," she told Jobe with a flash of dark eyes and a secretive smile.

"Sure," he returned.

Missy had left the herd records on the desk. Sandy glanced through them. These were the missing ones that Missy apparently thought she'd successfully deleted. She must have had ideas of spending today inputting them again in Jobe's company.

"Too bad," she murmured. "She missed out on a whole day here reinstating them. Shame."

Jobe looked worried. "I didn't encourage her to do that. I know it looks bad..."

She moved toward him, her clear eyes steady and bright. "I've seen Missy in action," she said. "I'm not jealous. Well, not much," she murmured.

He chuckled. "A little?"

She shrugged. "Microscopic."

He bent his head and kissed her slowly. "Do you like Chinese food?"

"I love it," she whispered.

"Good. Get your purse and let's go."

"But Ted's files…!"

"They can wait until you've eaten. Aren't you hungry?"

"Ravenous."

"All right, then. Come on!"

He caught her hand and held it all the way to the black pickup he drove. He put her inside and buckled her in, watching her possessively the whole time.

"Pickup trucks make good bait for catching women," he murmured dryly. "Look what I caught." He bent his head and kissed her.

She traced his upper lip. "Works both ways," she whispered, and kissed him back.

"What the hell…!" Ted exclaimed as he drew up beside them and got out of his car. "What are you doing? What about my herd records?"

"We're hungry," Jobe explained. "Want to get Coreen and the baby and eat Chinese?"

Ted let out a rough sigh and glanced from his flushed sister to his smug ranch foreman. "But I guess you have to eat sooner or later. Oh, get out of here," he muttered. "The records can wait a while."

"Thanks, Ted." Sandy grinned at him.

He grinned back. "Problem solved?" he asked.

"Just beginning," Jobe replied before she could. "But we're no sissies, are we?"

"Not us," Sandy agreed.

They waved at Ted and drove away.

FOR THE NEXT few days, life took on a dreamlike quality for Sandy. She didn't go back to Victoria, opting to take a week off—the vacation time she'd never used.

She and Jobe were inseparable, to Missy's irritation. They went riding and one day, he took her to Turner's Lake nearby. It was a popular fishing hole, where customers paid a fee to throw their lines into a lake stocked with game fish.

"Isn't this fun?" he asked, slapping at a mosquito as he adjusted the tension in his line.

She was sitting beside him with her bare feet dangling off the pier. "Heavenly," she agreed, and meant it. She hadn't been fishing since childhood. It was peaceful here, even with other fishermen scattered around, and being with Jobe was sheer joy.

"I've never taken a woman fishing before," he mused, glancing at her from under his bibbed cap. He drew up one long, blue-jeaned leg. "You're pretty good at it."

She glanced at the two fish on her string and the three on his. "Well, I'm a fish behind," she remarked.

"Oh, you're doing fine. It looks better if you let the man catch more fish."

She tossed her pole aside and, laughing, threw herself across him to the ground.

"You chauvinist pig," she murmured.

He linked his arms at her back and grinned up at her, his blond hair disheveled, his hat in the grass. "You might as well get used to it," he reminded her. "I'm consistent as all hell."

"I noticed." She sighed and bent to put her mouth softly over his hard lips.

He held her there, savoring the taste of her in the early-afternoon heat. A mosquito stabbed into his wrist and he never noticed.

She felt a surge of joy like an explosion deep in her body and sighed as he turned her in the long grass and his powerful leg eased between both of hers. His mouth became suddenly demanding. She felt her lips part as her heart rocketed under her rib cage. His searching hand found her breast and seconds later, so did his hungry mouth.

She cried out softly.

It wasn't a protest, but it brought him to his senses. He lifted his head, grimacing as he realized where they were.

"Sorry," he murmured, helping her up with a rueful smile. "We came here to fish. I forgot."

"So did I."

He chuckled. "Maybe you'd better wear this, just so people don't get the wrong idea when we do things like that."

He tossed a small, gray velvet-covered box into her hands. "Go on," he coaxed. "Open it."

She hesitated, because she had a pretty good idea what it was. A question came with it, and he was going to expect an answer pretty quickly. She looked up into his eyes and knew what the answer would be. There was, after all, only one possible.

Her hands fumbled and she opened the box. Her gasp was audible. "You pig!"

She closed the box over the cartoon character lapel pin and threw it at him. "How could you?"

"Wait a minute, wait a minute, it's the wrong box! Here!"

He had to stop laughing before he could dig the right

one out of his pocket. "That was for my little cousin… tomorrow's her birthday. Here. This is yours."

He put it into her fingers and pulled it open. His eyes never left her face.

"It isn't the Hope diamond," he said quietly, watching her look at the small diamond engagement ring. "But the sentiment that goes with it is every bit as large. I love you. I want to share my life with you."

She felt the tears rushing down her cheeks, leaving hot, wet tracks behind them. The ring blurred. The way he put the proposal was shattering. Until that moment, it had never occurred to her that he might love her.

She looked up, seeing him through a mist.

"Don't you want it?" he asked solemnly. "Am I totally mistaken about what you feel for me?"

She shook her head. "Oh, no," she whispered. "I love you. I just didn't know that you loved me."

"Blind as a bat," he mused, although relief was in his voice. He took out the ring and slid it on her finger. "If I'd loved you less, I never would have picked on you. We only hurt the ones we love. Don't you listen to old sayings?"

"You must love me terribly…"

"Do shut up…"

He kissed her again, much more possessively this time, and eased her down into the grass, regardless of chiggers and mosquitoes and yellow flies and possible snakes. She didn't notice the wildlife population being potentially crushed beneath her. Every sense was caught up in the feel of Jobe's hard mouth on her lips, his caressing hands on her body.

"I like kids," he whispered.

"So do I."

"Good thing," he murmured hungrily, "because I have in mind buying us a big ranch one day, and we'll need lots of kids to help us manage it."

She chuckled. "What about my job?"

"What about it?" he murmured. "Although you might try to spend less time on the road, later on."

She looked at him possessively. "You don't mind if I work?"

He shook his head. "That's up to you, sweetheart. I can support you. Not the way you've been supported," he said firmly, "but adequately."

She put a finger against his mouth. "I'll settle for whatever we can earn together. Our kids can inherit my trust."

His expression lightened. "You'd do that?"

"I know how proud you are, Jobe," she confessed. "I wouldn't want to make you uncomfortable. I'm used to working for my living. In fact, I like it. If we can build something worthwhile together, with our own hands, I'd much rather have it than all the money in the world."

"I didn't give you enough credit," he murmured.

"I didn't give you enough, either," she said. "I thought you only wanted me."

"I do," he said quietly. "Very much."

"Yes, but I didn't know you loved me." She searched his lean face lovingly. "It means the world."

"To me, too," he whispered, and bent again. "God, Sandy, don't make me wait too long." His arms became demanding. "I want you with me all the time. We'll have the foreman's house, and you can plant all the flowers you like, and cook for...me..."

He lifted his head and grimaced. "Oh, my God, we'll starve," he said, so plaintively that she burst out laughing.

She nuzzled her smiling face into his throat. "Don't you worry, my darling, I've already enrolled in a cooking course at one of the schools in Victoria. I'm not *cordon-bleu*, but I can produce an unburned steak and scalloped potatoes anytime you like."

"Can you, really?" He rested his weight on his elbows and looked down into her eyes lazily. "I can make a cake."

"You can?"

"A pound cake, nothing fancy." He traced her eyebrows. "I guess we won't starve, after all. Although," he added wickedly, "I don't think we'll spend much time worrying about food the first week we're married."

She touched his mouth. "Are we going to wait until then?" she asked without meeting his eyes.

He stiffened. "Of course we are!" he said shortly. "Good Lord, woman, you aren't trying to seduce me, are you?"

Her eyebrows arched. "Who, me?"

"Good thing," he murmured, "because I'm not that sort of man. I plan to wear a white suit at our wedding..."

She hit him. "I can just see that!"

"I am," he repeated.

"Because you're a virgin," she said, tongue-in-cheek. He didn't smile.

Her eyes widened. "You're thirty-six!"

He still didn't smile.

Her heart jumped into her throat. "You have got to be kidding!"

"You came along at a traumatic time in my life," he recalled lazily, fitting her small hand to his big one. He grinned at her. "I fell head over heels in love with you the day we met, and I never wanted anyone else." He shrugged. "I guess we start even, don't we, honey?"

She drew him down to her and kissed him with all her heart. Tears burned her eyes. "I can't believe it."

"You will," he said with a wistful sigh. "I expect we'll fumble a bit at first. But it comes naturally for birds and things, so I guess it will for us, too."

She laughed through her tears. "Of course it will! Oh, Jobe...!"

The sound of footsteps finally broke them apart. Jobe looked up at a big, bearlike man in a bibbed cap carrying a fishing rod.

"I never even caught a fish," the big man said gruffly, "and your spinning rods are on a tour of the lake. Some people have all the damned luck."

He stomped off. Jobe sat up with a dazed Sandy, and they watched the progress of their rods across the lake.

"I guess we might as well go home, unless you want to swim out after them," Jobe offered.

She shook her head. "Not in that water," she said dryly.

"I see what you mean." He retrieved their strings of fish and they wandered back to the truck, pausing just long enough to kiss each other on the way.

THE WEDDING WAS arranged by a gleeful Coreen. As much as she hated to, Sandy had to leave Jobe long enough to get some work done in Victoria.

Her boss, Mr. Cranson, gave them a crystal bowl for a wedding gift, and her co-workers went in together to buy a set of dishes and some flatware. Coreen and Ted gave them towels and sheets and small appliances. They'd have enough to start housekeeping, at least, and the bathroom in the foreman's house was being remodeled by Ted as another small gift.

Missy hadn't said a word about the wedding. But Sandy was uneasy, just the same, because she knew how possessive and vengeful the woman was. It wasn't like Missy to waltz off without a word when she'd lost a man she had her heart set on.

Sure enough, the last day Sandy was to spend in the apartment in Victoria, there was a knock on the door.

Expecting Jobe, she was surprised to find a tearful Missy on her doorstep. The tears were real, too.

"Come in," Sandy invited.

"Thanks." Missy sniffed, holding a handkerchief to her eyes. "I'm so sorry to come here and bother you at a time like this," she confessed, blowing her nose noisily, "but there are things you simply have to know before you marry him."

"Sit down."

Missy perched herself on the sofa. "I'm really sorry."

"You said that," Sandy reminded her.

Missy cleared her throat. She contrived to look tragic. "Well, it's like this," she began. She took a deep breath. "I'm pregnant."

Sandy's eyebrows rose. She smiled. "Congratulations."

Missy looked taken aback. "You don't understand. It's Jobe's."

Sandy searched the other woman's face. For one instant—of which she was very ashamed—she let herself imagine that it could be true. Then she measured Missy's word against Jobe's and all her doubts went away at once.

"Do tell me all about it. Do you want some iced tea?" Sandy offered, and went to get it.

"You're taking this very well," Missy said, shocked.

"I suppose I am. Come on. Tell me all about it."

"He seduced me," Missy said, sobbing.

"You poor thing," Sandy commiserated. "The louse!"

Missy's eyes widened. "You believe me?"

"Of course I do," Sandy lied. "I'm so sorry for you. The pig. How could he do such a thing to such a sweet girl?"

Missy sipped her iced tea and peered at Sandy, trying not to grin. This was going better than she'd ever dreamed it would.

"He said he loved me," Missy continued. "He took me out to eat and then we parked on this lonely, deserted road. He started kissing me and one thing led to another, and…it just happened."

"And naturally, you aren't on the Pill?"

Missy glanced at her. "How…how did you know?"

"Well, if you're pregnant…"

"Oh. Right. Yes. Well, I'm about six weeks along," she added. "At least, I think I am. I haven't been to the doctor. But I'm sure it couldn't be anything else. And you know, Jobe will surely marry me if there's a baby on the way, what with Jacobsville being such a small town, and my reputation, and his reputation."

"Of course," Sandy agreed readily.

Missy put down her tea. "You do understand that he can't marry both of us?"

Sandy smiled. "Certainly, I do."

"Well...then what are you going to do?"

"I'm going right down to Jacobsville with you to tell him what I think of him," Sandy said flatly. She got to her feet. "Let's go."

Missy's indrawn breath was audible.

"Come on!"

She got up. "Right now?" she exclaimed.

"Right now. You've got your car, haven't you?"

"Y...yes."

"You can follow me. I'll just get my purse..."

They went out the door together. Sandy was enjoying herself. She couldn't wait to see the look on Jobe's face. It would be something to tell their grandchildren. It would also show Missy exactly where she stood.

"Two birds with one stone," Sandy said to herself as she led the way down the highway to Jacobsville.

MISSY PARKED NEAR the front door, but she was slow to get out of her car. Jobe's black pickup was parked nearby. He was probably in the office, cursing the computer, Sandy mused.

She led the way into the house, with Missy dragging behind, and went right into the office.

Jobe was sitting on the edge of the desk, talking on the phone. He looked up and saw the two women, and ended his conversation.

"This is a surprise," he said.

Sandy smiled. "I'll bet it is. Uh, Missy has something to say. Go ahead, dear," she coaxed the other woman, waving a hand in her direction. She sat down in the nearest chair and prepared to be amused.

Missy cleared her throat. She was flushed as she looked from Sandy to Jobe.

"I'm pregnant," she blurted out.

Jobe looked hunted. His eyes went immediately to Sandy, and he scowled, as if he was daring her to believe what any normal person would at the moment.

She didn't crack a smile. She did arch an eyebrow, and the twinkle in her eyes grew more noticeable.

"I said, I'm pregnant!" Missy returned. She folded her arms over her chest and smiled smugly at Jobe. "What are you going to do about it? I've already told her," she added, nodding toward Sandy.

"What did she say?" Jobe asked curiously.

"She understood that you're going to have to marry me."

Jobe's lip curled up. "We'll call the newspapers and the television people, too," he mused. "You're going to make history if I'm the father of your child."

She looked uneasy. "I don't understand."

He picked up the telephone. "Of course, I'm certain that the real father of this child will be eager to learn about it. I'll set you up with an appointment this very afternoon at Coltrain's clinic. They can take a blood sample to check if you are pregnant and then when the baby is born they can do a DNA test. That will rule me out immediately as the father."

Missy's face went red. "They…they can't do that sort of thing!"

"Sure they can," he said. "Coltrain has a lab in Houston do his important work. You'd be amazed at what a test will reveal these days. And if you're pregnant, you should be seen at once." He held on to the receiver. "Betty? This is Jobe Dodd. I want you to set up an appointment today for…"

"No!" Missy cried.

She rushed forward and hung up the receiver at once, panting for breath. "No, I…uh, I don't want to do that!"

"Why not?" Sandy asked. "I'd think a pregnancy test would be the first thing on your mind right now."

Missy looked hunted. She stared at Jobe, who had his arms folded across his chest. He wasn't smiling.

He glanced at Sandy. "While we're on the subject," he began, "I'd like to know right now if you believe her," he added, nodding toward a frozen Missy.

Sandy smiled softly, her eyes full of love and trust. "Don't be silly," she said gently.

"You said you believed me!" Missy accused.

Sandy got up. "I wanted to see how far you'd go," she replied simply. "Now stop this play-acting and tell the truth, Missy. You don't want to do something like this to Jobe. You're not a bad enough person to try to ruin his life deliberately."

Missy's lower lip stuck out. "I love him!"

"No, you don't," Sandy said. "If you did, you wouldn't

be trying to trap him into marriage. You want people to be happy if you love them. We all know that Jobe wouldn't be happy with you unless he really loved you. And he doesn't."

Missy's eyes clouded. She looked mutinous. "I could love him enough for both of us!"

Jobe shook his head. "That isn't possible. I love Sandy. I always have. You're a sweet kid, honey, but it wasn't love."

Missy's shoulders slumped. "I guess I knew that all along. I didn't want to admit it." She flushed even more. "I guess I made a real fool of myself."

"Not to me," Sandy said. "Not to Jobe, either. I imagine he's flattered, in a way. But it's time to stop pretending."

"Okay," Missy admitted, "I'm not pregnant. He only kissed me once, like you'd kiss a kid who was hurt. I built a lot of dreams on it." She drew in a long sigh. "I guess there's somebody out there for me. Maybe I'll find him one day."

"Of course you will," Sandy said gently. "But in the meantime, I think it might be better if you found a different job. One where there's an eligible man or two."

"Not here," Missy mused.

"Not here," Sandy agreed. She looked at Jobe quietly. "This one belongs to me," she said, and watched his high cheekbones go ruddy.

Missy saw it, too. She managed a smile on her way out. "Well, I hope I get invited to the wedding, at least," she said. "I'm not a bad loser."

"No, you're not," Jobe agreed. He smiled at her. "Stay out of trouble, sprout."

"I'll do my best. I'm really sorry," she added sheepishly. "It seemed like a good idea at the time. Maybe I wasn't really grown up until now." She went out the door quickly, closing it behind her.

Jobe got up from the desk with a sigh and walked to Sandy, pulling her into his arms. "You didn't believe a word of it, hmm?"

She shook her head. "I know you too well. You've never lied to me. Not even when it would have been kinder. It was pretty simple to tell where the truth was. Besides," she added, pulling his head down, "I love you."

"I love you, too," he whispered, and kissed her back hungrily.

CHAPTER SIX

Two weeks later, they were married. They didn't plan on a honeymoon, but Ted sent them off to Nassau on an airplane and neither of them had the heart to argue with him.

Nassau was the most unexpected, glorious sight of Sandy's life. Despite the wealth that she and Ted enjoyed, it was the one place she'd never been. The day they arrived, she and Jobe didn't even wait to change clothes. They tipped the bellboy who carried their luggage to their sixth-floor room at the huge, gaudy hotel on Cable Beach and then took a cab into downtown Nassau, where they walked down the narrow streets past the gaily colored straw market and friendly people, idly gazing at passenger ships at Prince George Wharf and pausing to look in store windows.

The air smelled of the ocean and adventure. They saw the statue of the island's first royal governor, Woodes Rogers, in front of one of the older hotels in town, and then strolled along Bay Street, holding hands and dreaming.

When they got back to the hotel, they started to change for dinner when Jobe turned and just stared at

Sandy as she stood there in only her lace teddy, with her dark hair down around her shoulders.

He had his shirt off. His broad chest, hair-covered and muscular and deeply tanned, drew her like a magnet. With her breath in her throat, she went to him, her heart racing.

She looked up at him, noting his own tension, the ragged sound of his breathing. "Now," she whispered huskily.

He reached for her, gently, and brought her to him. "Now," he whispered back, and bent to her mouth.

Several feverish minutes later, they were on the bed, trembling against each other with the sound of the ocean loud even outside the closed window as they fought layers of clothing to get to the skin underneath.

"Oh, Lord… I've torn it," he groaned as he finally got the teddy out of the way and his mouth burned against her small, taut breasts.

"Who cares?" she panted, clutching his head to her. "Oh, Jobe, oh, dear God!"

She arched as the suckling motion of his mouth sent thrills of pleasure into the most secret places of her body.

Her soft cries made him wild to have her. He managed to get out of the last of his clothing and his mouth bit into hers as he eased quickly between her long, trembling legs.

"I'm sorry," he whispered urgently. "I'm sorry, it's going to be…rough."

"I don't care!"

She adjusted her body to his in a violent fever of

need, so hungry for him that nothing else mattered. She barely felt the flash of pain as he went into her, the pleasure that followed drowning her in such exquisite sensations that she stretched like a wanton under his powerful body and sighed loudly.

"Yes," he groaned, searching for her mouth as his hips moved down and he shivered. "Did you even dream…that it would feel like this?" he asked huskily.

"Never!" She met his mouth and lifted to him, matching his rhythm, trembling with each new contact. "This is wicked!" she whispered when he paused and looked down the length of their joined bodies, coaxing her to look as well.

"We're married," he whispered unsteadily. "Two of the oldest virgins in the continental United States… Good God!"

Her sudden urgent movement caught him off guard and he cried out as she moved again, twisting up to him.

He ground his mouth into hers with a sharp groan and suddenly there was no time to savor it, to lengthen it. There was tension and urgent need. He drove into her, drowning in her sweetness, her husky little cries of ecstasy. When he felt her arch and cry out, he was already in the throes of his own fulfillment. He seemed to black out as the most harshly sweet pleasure he'd ever experienced pulled his powerful body so tight that he thought he might actually faint…

Minutes later, drenched in perspiration and shaking in the aftermath of their frenzied lovemaking, Sandy lifted her head to look at her new husband and she couldn't resist a huge, wicked grin.

"I guess it was worth waiting for, huh?" she teased.

He rolled over, his face aglow with love and happiness. He laughed like a boy. "Oh, yes, my darling. Well worth it," he replied. He bent to her mouth and rolled over in the same instant. "I love you insanely. And just in case you didn't get the message the first time…!"

He wasn't the only one insanely in love and aching to prove it. Sandy's last conscious thought was that marriage to Jobe was going to be one long, sweet adventure. And this was only the beginning!

* * * * *

TOM

"If love were what the rose is,
And I were like the leaf,
Our lives would grow together
In sad or singing weather."

—Algernon Charles Swinburne
A Match (1866), st. 1

PROLOGUE

THE CHRISTENING WAS a delightful affair. It seemed that everyone in Jacobsville, Texas, was there to give their best wishes to Dr. Jebediah Coltrain and his wife, Dr. Louise Coltrain, on the birth of their son, John Daniel.

Afterward, at the reception, the champagne flowed like water. The beautiful day in mid-June was clear and warm.

Dr. Drew Morris was standing close to the punch bowl enjoying the company of his friends. Beside him stood Ted Regan and Ted's foreman, Jobe Dodd, along with Ted's sister, Sandy. Sandy was giving Jobe a black glare, which he was returning with interest. On the other side of him stood newcomer to town Tom Walker, who'd just opened an investment firm.

"I need to talk to you about some investments next week," Drew told Tom with a grin. "I had a good year and I want to do something with my cash overflow."

"I'll be glad to do whatever I can for you, Dr. Morris," Tom said with a grin on his dark, handsome face.

"By the way," Drew added, "if you're in the market for any computer equipment, Ted's sister there is the lady to see." He nodded toward Sandy. "She works for one of the big computer franchises, and she's a whiz with electronics."

"Sure is," big blond Jobe Dodd said mockingly. "Pity she can't stay on a horse."

"The devil I can't!" Sandy shot back, her blue eyes flaming.

"Now, now." Ted separated them. "Go fight some-where else. We're here to celebrate a christening, not to start a war."

They glared at him and went their separate ways.

"Whew!" Ted sighed. "It's like that all the time lately! Coreen and I are about to the point of taking our baby and running for cover. I wish they'd kill each other and get it over with."

"They do seem volatile," Drew agreed, sipping punch.

"How's your new employee working out?" Ted asked him.

"She can't dress herself, she can't walk through the office without tripping over something and she's forever trying to work without her glasses because she thinks she looks better that way." He threw up his hands.

"So you like her, then?" Ted murmured.

Drew glared at him and stalked off.

Ted chuckled. His prematurely silver hair sparkled in the light as he glanced at Tom, the only companion left. "That just about clears away the group around the punch bowl," he mused, and helped himself to another cup of champagne punch. "Don't you want to glare at me and storm off, too?"

Tom grinned, his green eyes twinkling. "I don't have any reason to, just yet. Besides, this punch is really good."

"How's business?"

"Going great," Tom told him, sipping the drink. "Coming down here was one of the best moves I ever made. Matt Caldwell was right. I do have an open field here. I can't keep up with all the work, and I've barely set up my office."

"Glad to hear it." Ted studied the younger man over his cup of punch. "Old man Gallagher said you had a dog."

"He's sort of a toothache with fur," Tom murmured and then grinned at the other man. "I found him in a storm, under a city mailbox in Houston. He was just a little ball of fur and scared to death, so I took him home." He took a swallow of champagne punch. "Now he weighs ninety pounds and he's uncivilized. He is housebroken, in a sense, but I'd actually call him a housebreaker. I only have one ceramic thing left." He glanced at Ted. "I don't suppose you need a cattle dog?"

Ted chuckled. "No. Thanks. I gave Coreen a pup before we got married. He's grown now and he's smart enough to do what little herding I need around the place."

"I wouldn't really give Moose up, anyway," Tom confessed. "I'm all alone, and he's company." His eyes had a sad, faraway look for an instant, before he wiped it away. "The Coltrain baby's cute."

"So he is," Ted agreed, glancing at the two doctors with the baby. "I wonder if he'll be a redhead like his dad or a blonde like his mom?"

"No telling," Tom said. "How old is your boy?"

"Just a few months," Ted said, sighing. "Never

dreamed I'd become a father at my age. Hell, I never dreamed I'd get married." His eyes searched the room and found Coreen's blue ones. She had their little boy in her arms. They never left him for a minute, even with so many willing babysitters around. He was a treasure, like their love for each other.

Drew Morris saw that look, and poignant memories flooded through him as he rejoined the men. He'd loved his wife. After she died he'd never thought of finding someone else. He still mourned her. He glanced at Tom, who looked as alone and sad as he felt. Farther away, Jobe Dodd was glaring at Sandy Regan, who was standing near Coreen. He wondered if all that hostility had something beneath it?

He sighed and lifted his cup. Ted and Tom lifted theirs, too. The others in the room caught on, and Jobe Dodd lifted his with theirs toward the two doctors and their son. It was going to be quite a summer in Jacobsville.

"Cheers!" they all said in unison.

Three men in the privacy of their own minds stared at the child and wondered how it would be if they had families. Each of them was sure that he never would.

CHAPTER ONE

THERE WAS A muffled crash from the living room and Tom Walker let out a weary sigh as he turned from unpacking the few small kitchen appliances that had come with him from Houston.

"Moose!" he grumbled. He got up from the floor and left the box sitting to see what latest disaster his pet had caused.

It had all started with a rainstorm and a tiny, frightened little ball of fur hiding under a metal mailbox in downtown Houston. Somebody had abandoned the puppy and Tom had been unable to leave it there on the side of a busy street. But the act of compassion had repercussions. Big ones. The tiny puppy had grown into a gorgeous but enormous German shepherd mix whom he had named Shep, but who was later rechristened Moose.

As he stood watching the huge animal settle himself among the remains of a once-elegant antique bowl on the big coffee table, he reflected that the new name was appropriate. It was like having a moose in the house.

"Kate will never forgive you," he said pointedly, remembering how happy his sister had been when, newly married, she had given him the bowl as a Christmas gift. "That was a Christmas present. It was handmade by a famous Native American potter!"

"Woof," Moose replied in his deep dog voice, and grinned at him.

The vet had said that Moose was still going through his puppy stage.

"Will he outgrow it?" Tom had asked plaintively, having taken the big dog to the vet after Moose had gone swimming in a neighbor's outdoor goldfish pond.

"Sure!" the vet had assured him, and just as Tom began to sigh with relief, he added with a wicked grin, "Four, five years from now, he'll calm right down!"

Resigned, he took the big dog back home and hoped he could adapt to living among pottery shards and disemboweled furniture for the next few years of his life.

One of his neighbors had offered to buy Moose who, while a walking disaster, was absolutely beautiful, with a black coat of fur that shone like coal in sunlight, and stark white markings with medium brown eyebrows and facial markings.

Tom had replied that he liked the man too much to sell Moose to him.

He gave the coffee table one last look, shook his head and went into the kitchen to make coffee. Just as he started the coffeemaker, he heard a crunching noise and turned to find that while he'd been occupied with coffee, Moose had overturned the kitchen trash can and spread the contents all over the linoleum floor. He was munching contentedly on an apple core amidst coffee grounds, banana peels and empty TV dinner cartons.

"Oh, Lord," Tom prayed silently. He took the apple

core away, set the trash can upright and went to find a broom. What a good thing that he wasn't entertaining thoughts of marriage. No woman in her right mind would put up with his canine companion.

He was thirty-four. He should have been long-since married, but he and his sister, Kate, had been victims of a shocking, terrible upbringing that had stunted them sexually. Their father had beaten both of them as children and raised the devil every time one of them so much as smiled at the opposite sex. In fact, sex, he lectured, was the greatest sin of all. He was a lay minister, so they believed him.

What they hadn't known at the time was that he had a brain tumor that modified his once-loving personality and eventually killed him. Their long-missing mother had been found by Jacob Cade, his sister Kate's husband, and presented to them both at Jacob and Kate's wedding, over six years ago. It had been a painful reunion until they learned that far from deserting them as children, their mother had never dreamed that their father would kidnap them and spirit them away from her. But he had done just that. She'd spent half a lifetime using money from her meager salary trying to find them again. She lived in Missouri, but they both saw her frequently. Now that Kate was married and had a son, their mother often visited her.

Tom wondered if he could ever marry. Kate had, but then Jacob Cade had been the love of her life since her early teens. Presumably Kate's fear of the physical side of marriage had been overcome. She and Cade had a son, who was five years old. And although they'd tried to have a second child, they hadn't been able to just yet.

He'd have liked children. But his one sexual experience had left him sick with guilt. Kate's wedding had pointed out, as nothing else ever had, how very alone he was. He'd gone back to his job with an advertising firm in New York City and that weekend, to a local bar to drown his sorrows.

She'd been there at a going-away party for one of the girls in the office. Elysia Craig had been his secretary for two years. She was a pretty blonde with gray eyes and a neat little figure who was teased by her co-workers for being so prim and prudish. Tom thought it was a joke. He never realized that she was as inexperienced as he was. Not until it was far too late. His most vivid memory of Elysia was of her crouching in the full-size bed in his apartment with a white sheet clutched to her breasts, weeping like a widow. He'd hurt her without meaning to, and the tears had been the last straw. He couldn't remember saying a single word to her as she dressed and got into the cab he called for her. He'd been far too inebriated and sick to drive by then.

He hadn't known how to apologize, or explain. His behavior had shamed him. He couldn't even meet her eyes the next morning, or speak to her. Most of the women in the office where he worked were sophisticated and savvy, but Elysia wasn't. His inability to communicate with her provoked her into quitting her job that very day and going back home to Texas. To his shame, he hadn't even looked for her. He'd still been fighting feelings of shame and guilt, holdovers from his brutal childhood, despite the aching hunger he'd felt for Elysia.

Her gentle, kind nature was what had attracted him to her in the first place, but except for his excessive drinking he would never have approached her. His feelings for her he'd kept secret, never dreaming that he might one day end up in bed with her. It had been the most exquisite experience of his life, but the guilt had made him sick, so he pushed it to the back of his mind and tried to forget it.

Not long afterward, he'd given up his advertising job and studied the investment business. His first job had been as an assistant advisor with a well-known national company. Then he'd moved to Houston, Texas, to open his own office in the building with a friend, Logan Deverell. But he'd gotten wanderlust again when Logan had married his long-suffering secretary.

He'd arrived in Jacobsville three weeks ago, thanks to another mutual friend, Matt Caldwell, who owned a stud farm out of town. Matt was friends with the Ballenger brothers, Calhoun and Justin, who owned a huge feedlot and liked to invest their earnings. They were all mutual friends of the Tremayne brothers, who owned properties all over Texas. Before he'd even had time to unpack, Tom had all the business he could handle.

A real-estate agent in town had dabbled in the properties market, but since she'd remarried her ex-husband, a pilot, they'd moved house to Atlanta. The nearest investment counselor now was in Victoria. Tom had no competition at all, for the moment, in Jacobsville. It seemed like a dream come true.

Then, yesterday, out of the blue, a new client had walked in the door—Luke Craig—and the bottom had fallen out of Tom's life. Luke had a sister, recently widowed with a small daughter. Her first name was Elysia.

Tom poured himself a cup of coffee and sat down on the sofa. Moose jumped up beside him to rest his chin on his master's leg.

He petted the big dog absently. "Don't think I'm forgetting the broken pot or the garbage," he murmured.

Moose sighed and gave him a baleful look.

Tom sipped coffee and wondered what he was going to do. Of all the quirks of fate, to land himself in the one town in America where he couldn't bear to live. No wonder it had all seemed too good to be true. Fate was playing a monstrous joke on him. The woman he'd seduced lived right here. Apparently she'd married and had a child after she'd come home. He wondered if she remembered him, and then chided himself for his own stupidity. Of course she did. He'd been her first experience, just as she'd been his. She didn't know that. She'd still think that he'd seduced and abandoned her, like some big city playboy without a conscience. What a joke.

He put the coffee cup down. Moose was snoring softly. He stroked the huge head and thought how nice it was to have a companion, even such a one as this.

He didn't know how he was going to cope, but he knew he would. Jacobsville was a small town, but not all that small. He might never run into Elysia. Worry at this stage was premature. He had all this unpacking to do that he'd put off for almost a month. He'd do better to go to work and stop tormenting himself with things that might never happen. He probably wouldn't recognize the woman, anyway. It had been years ago, after all.

FATE MUST HAVE been howling the next morning when he drove to work, parked his car and started into the office. Next door to his office was an insurance agency. And heading toward it was a blonde woman in jeans, boots, a T-shirt under a flannel shirt and a neat French braid.

Elysia.

She stopped dead when she was close enough to recognize him. Gone were the big-rimmed spectacles she'd worn when she worked for him. Gone was the racehorse thinness. She'd filled out. She still wasn't pretty, but she was very attractive. He couldn't help staring at her.

She moved closer, not shy or reticent as she had been. She looked right at him. "I heard you'd moved here to open an investment office. My brother said you looked strange when he mentioned my name. I told him I used to work for you, nothing else." She laughed bitterly. "So you don't have to worry about being lynched. Feel better, Mr. Walker?"

The unexpected assault had tied his tongue. She wasn't the same girl he'd known at all.

His dark green eyes lanced down into hers. "You've changed, Miss Craig."

"Mrs. Nash," she corrected him.

His eyebrow jerked. "Mrs. Nash," he said.

She seemed less assertive all at once. "My husband died last year. He had cancer."

"I'm sorry."

"He was sick for a long time," she murmured. "It's trite to say it, but he really is better off."

"I see."

"You're not married yet?"

He searched her soft oval face without expression. "That'll be the day," he replied.

"Yes, I remember. You're the original love-'em-and-leave-'em bachelor." The bitterness was back in her voice. "I guess you're still shaking the women out of your bed…"

He stepped closer, his eyes kindling. "My love life is none of your damned business!" He never raised his voice, but the whip in it cut almost physically. It disconcerted her.

"No…of…of course not!" she stammered.

She actually took a step backward, and he cursed himself inwardly.

"I'm sorry," he said curtly. "You probably think you were one in a line. That's the joke of the century."

"Ex…excuse me?"

He checked his watch, feeling self-conscious. "I have to get to work."

His behavior puzzled her. She'd spent years blaming him, hating him. But he didn't look like a philanderer. *Sure,* she reminded herself, *and most ax-murderers probably don't look like killers, either.*

She stood aside to let him pass. He hesitated, though, the wind blowing his thick black hair around over a face that was deep olive. He had an untamed look about him. He was still very handsome, although she was sure that he was in his middle thirties by now. His build was that of a much younger man, lean and muscular.

"You have Native American ancestry, don't you?" she asked involuntarily.

"Sioux," he agreed. "Our great-grandfather."

"How is your sister?" she asked without wanting to.

"Fine. She and Jacob have a son. He's five now."

"I'm happy for her."

"So am I. It wouldn't have surprised me if she'd never married, either."

There was a deeper meaning to what he was saying. She wished she could read between the lines. Her eyes searched his curiously. If only she could hate him.

He looked down his long, straight nose at her with dark green eyes that didn't blink. "We're both older. I'm glad you found someone you could love. I hope he was good to you."

She flushed. "He was very good to me," she said.

"And I wasn't." His lean hand reached out, almost touched her hair, withdrawing before it made contact. He laughed at his own inability to show affection. "I regret you most of all, Elysia," he said numbly. "I was afraid. Maybe I still am."

He turned and went into his office, leaving her staring blankly after him.

She'd hated him so much when she'd come back to Jacobsville after his cold rejection. It hadn't even been much of a memory, that short night she'd spent in his arms. He'd been ravenously hungry for her, but rough and at times, oddly hesitant. When he'd hurt her, he'd even tried to draw away, but it hadn't been possible. His harsh groan as he gave in to his hunger had stayed with her all these long years. He'd sounded as if he hated himself for wanting her, blamed her for it. He hadn't said a single word. Not before, during, or after.

It was painful to remember how desperately she'd loved him. She'd gambled everything on giving in to him, that once. But instead of bringing them closer, it had destroyed their tenuous friendship. She'd come home and he'd never tried to contact her at all. Perhaps that was best. She didn't really want him to know about Crissy. Eventually he might notice that the child bore a striking resemblance to him, but he wouldn't know what her late husband looked like, so there was little danger of her secret coming out.

She wondered what he would say if he knew that their one intimacy had produced such a beautiful little miracle. She couldn't tell him. Everyone in town thought that her late husband had fathered the child, but poor Fred had been far too ill for intimacy, even when they married soon after her flight to Jacobsville six years before. His illness had been a long-drawn-out one, with brief periods of remission that became even briefer as time passed. He'd been kind to her, though, and she'd had affection for him. He'd loved the child. Poor man, whose wife had divorced him to marry someone richer, just when he was diagnosed with cancer. They'd both been deserted by the people they loved most. Marriage had been a sensible solution. He wouldn't have to die alone, and her child would have a name.

The thought of telling Tom Walker about his daughter had never occurred to her. His cold avoidance of Elysia after they were intimate had told her all she needed to know. He no longer wanted her. Certainly he wouldn't want a child.

She went into the insurance office to pay her bill without a backward glance. Their time was over, before it even began. He would never have to know about Crissy, anyway. And if he could bear to live here with the constant sight of her to remind him of the past, she could endure it as well. She was a successful businesswoman with rich clients at her exclusive fashion boutique that shipped couture and locally designed garments all over the world. She had a wonderful child and a bright future. She didn't need Tom Walker to complete her life, even if the sight of him had knocked the breath out of her all over again. She'd just have to exercise some strong self-control, that was all. Because judging by his behavior, he hadn't missed her. She wished that she could have said the same.

Tom sat down behind his desk, shaken. Elysia looked as lovely to his eyes as she ever had. She was more mature, much more desirable. He felt ashamed all over again. She'd married and had a child. He couldn't have had much of a place in her heart after what he'd done. He wished things had gone differently for them. If he'd been able to communicate, a little less proud about his past, a little more open with her, who knew what might have happened. But he'd let his chance for happiness slip right by him. He'd given her the idea that he found her easy and undesirable after one night. How could he blame her for being bitter?

The phone rang. He picked it up. It was a potential client. He put on his best business manner and forced the thought of Elysia to the back of his mind for the moment.

IT WAS INEVITABLE that he was going to run into the Craigs sooner or later. As it happened, it was Luke he saw first, and he had Elysia's daughter with him.

Tom stopped dead at the sight of the child. There was something about her that reminded him vividly of his sister, Kate. The child had olive skin and light green eyes. Her hair was long and straight and jet black. She was almost the image of Kate. He smiled in spite of himself. What a beautiful child!

"Hi, Tom," Luke said with his easy friendliness. He had the little girl by the hand. He drew her forward. "I'm taking my niece to a movie. Crissy, honey, this is Mr. Walker. He's Uncle Luke's investment counselor."

"Hello," the child said politely, eyeing the tall man curiously. "You look like an Indian."

His eyebrow quirked. He smiled faintly. "I had a Sioux great-grandfather."

"I like to wear my hair in braids. Mama took me to an Indian powwow. That's a festival where you can learn all about their culture and history, and all sorts of crafts. I had fun."

That interesting fact piqued Tom's curiosity, but before he could say anything, Luke cut the child off.

"Christine, you're babbling," Luke chided gently, chuckling as he glanced at Tom. "She'll talk your leg off. She's only in kindergarten, too."

"Uncle Luke thinks I talk too much," the little girl muttered, glowering up at her uncle.

"No, I don't, pet," her relative assured her. "She wants to see the pig movie." He sighed. "I'm not keen, but I don't have much to do around the ranch today, so I was free. Elysia's at home with every pot we own on the stove putting up sauce. We're going to die of tomato poisoning. Honest to God, she's put up enough sauce to float a small ship!" He eyed Tom. "I don't guess you like spaghetti? I could give you twenty or thirty jars of spaghetti sauce for Christmas."

"I love it, as it happens," Tom admitted, amused. "Why does she put up so much of it?"

"Just between us, I think something's upset her," he confessed. "She's been like this for several days. She's cleaned the house twice and washed both cars, now she's determined to corner the tomato sauce market."

"Mama always works when she's upset," Crissy volunteered. "Last time was when Miss Henry told her I pushed Markie down the steps."

Tom's eyebrows both rose. "Did you?"

Her lower lip thrust out. "He called me a sissy," she said belligerently. "Just because I made him stop throwing rocks at a little frog." She brightened. "I told his mama what he did, and he got whipped. His mama has an aquarium with lots of little fire toads in it. She let me see them."

"Poor Markie," Luke said under his breath.

"Good for you," Tom told the child.

"Do you like cows?" she asked Tom. "We've got lots. I'll bet Uncle Luke would even let you pet one, if you want."

"He can pet all I've got," Luke replied, his blue eyes dancing as he glanced at the other man.

"I'm a city boy," Tom mused, his hands in his pockets. "Lately, anyway."

"Yes, you're from Houston, aren't you?" Luke asked.

"Originally, I'm from South Dakota," he replied. "I grew up around Jacob Cade's ranch near Blairsville. He taught Kate and me how to ride when we were young. He's a whiz at it."

"I know that name," Luke replied. "He and I were at a cattle auction in Montana a couple of years back. He's your brother-in-law? Well, well. I have to say I was impressed. He knows cattle."

"So does Kate. I'm the odd one out."

"You know how to invest money," Luke said pointedly. "That's no small talent."

Tom smiled. "Thanks."

Luke was frowning. "Jacob said something about you… Oh, I remember," he added with a grin. "You threw a client out the door in Houston for making remarks to your secretary, as I recall."

"He was a—" he glanced at the little girl "—chauvinist." He amended the word he'd been about to use. "It was no great business loss. I don't like people hassling my employees."

"Didn't Elysia used to work for you, when you were working at that ad agency in New York?" Luke asked suddenly.

Tom's face showed no expression at all, but he felt a sinking feeling inside. "Yes, she did. I was sorry to lose her. She was a terrific secretary."

"She said she got tired of New York," Luke replied easily. "I don't blame her, what with all that noise and concrete. Anyway, it was a good thing she came home, or she'd never had married Fred and had Crissy. It's been nice having her back here. I expect you missed her."

"More than she'll ever know," Tom replied absently, his eyes with a faraway look. He shook himself mentally. "I have to go. Nice to have met you, Miss Nash," he told Crissy, extending a lean hand.

She shook it warmly. "Nice to meet you, too, Mr. Walker."

"Great manners," he remarked to Luke.

"Oh, Elysia's a stickler for them. Crissy's much loved, but she doesn't lack for discipline, either."

"What does Elysia do now?"

"She owns an exclusive fashion boutique, actually," he told Tom. "She enrolled in college after Crissy was born and got her degree in business and marketing. She has a backlog of designers and dressmakers and despite the small size of our town, she's getting an international reputation for her fashion sense. She gets orders from all over. She even does a little designing as well. I knew she could draw, and she's always been good at numbers, but I don't think she really applied herself until she married Fred. He had contacts in the fashion world and in business and he pushed her—gently, of course. All that hidden talent came out. She's only been in business a few years, and she already makes more on her boutique than I do on my cattle. Kills my ego."

"I can imagine."

"She and Crissy live with me. I don't have any marriage plans and it's our old family home—one of those big Victorian horrors. Of course, Matt Caldwell's sweet on her. She may give in and marry him one day and move out."

For some reason, that casual remark played on Tom's mind all day long, and into the night. Matt hadn't mentioned Elysia at all when they'd talked, before he moved to Jacobsville. He wondered if the omission had been deliberate. Maybe Matt had known that Tom and Elysia were acquainted and was protecting what he thought of as his property. It was odd that he hadn't mentioned her.

MOOSE WAS WAITING for him when he got home. The dog really was huge, he thought, as he fended off huge paws on his chest and an affectionate tongue the size of a washcloth.

"Down, you moose," he muttered, laughing as he patted the dog's head. "Hungry, are you, or desperate for a fire hydrant? Come on."

He led the way to the back door and opened it. The backyard was fenced and reinforced on the bottom, fortunately, because Moose liked to dig. Local gardeners wouldn't appreciate a visit from his pet.

He waited until Moose was ready to come back in and opened the door for him. He filled the food and water dishes and left the big animal to have his supper.

Tom went through his cabinets looking for something to tempt his appetite. He finally settled on a bowl of cold cereal. He had no appetite at all. Too many questions were plaguing him.

CHAPTER TWO

TOM'S OPINION OF the new Elysia underwent a series of changes in the following few weeks. There was still plenty of gossip about her in Jacobsville, and he heard it all in bits and pieces of conversation when Elysia's comings and goings were noticed by local citizens. One acquaintance thought she'd only married Fred Nash for his money, and that it was this inherited wealth that had made her exclusive fashion boutique possible. It was known that their union was one of friendship, not passion, and that there was a great age difference. And that Fred had been very, very rich.

He didn't believe the unpleasant remarks at first, but it was impossible not to notice how prosperous she was. She'd bought into her brother's cattle farm and held half ownership of it. She also had investments of several kinds, including some very expensive oil stock. She had her daughter enrolled in a very well-known girls' school in Houston for the fall term, and she drove a Mercedes convertible. Poor, she wasn't.

With her investments and the nearest counseling office in Victoria, it was inevitable that Luke was going to suggest that she bring her portfolio to Tom.

"I don't think that's a good idea," she told her brother after supper that night.

"Why not?" Luke asked. "He's a whiz. Ask the Ballenger brothers."

"I know he's good at picking stocks that increase in value," Elysia replied calmly. "But he's an intelligent man and he isn't blind. I don't want him around Crissy."

Luke sat back with a soft sigh, his blue eyes sympathetic. "She's almost six years old," he said pointedly. "She's already in kindergarten. Don't you think it's time he knew he was a father?"

She grimaced, leaning forward with her forearms crossed over her knees. "I don't know how he'd react," she said. "He was…less than encouraging when I left the office for good. I think he was relieved that I went away." She shrugged. "I don't think he's lacked female company."

"Then isn't it interesting that he doesn't date?" he asked shrewdly. "That was the case in Houston, too. And since I haven't heard any gossip about Mr. Walker liking men, I gather that he's amazingly selective about his dates. One woman in over six years, I believe…?"

She flushed red. "He was drinking. I told you."

He leaned forward, too, his face serious. "Jacob Cade and I became fairly good friends over the years. He never came right out and said anything, but he intimated that his wife and Tom had a very brutal childhood. Their father had a brain tumor and went stark-raving mad before he died. He attacked Kate physically because she just smiled at a young man."

"Wh…what?"

He nodded. "That's right. In his distorted mind, he equated sex with evil and made his kids believe it. Neither of them had anything to do with the opposite sex, even after he died. He warped them, Ellie. Now imagine how it would be, to have a parent who browbeat you into repressing your sexuality for years and years. And then imagine how it would be if you grew older with no experience whatsoever with the opposite sex? Do you think a man, especially, would find it easy to become involved with a woman?"

She was barely breathing. "You aren't going to tell me that you think Tom is a…a…"

He nodded. "That's exactly what I think. He and Kate were very close. When she married Jacob, Tom had nobody. He was totally alone. Probably getting a snootful of liquor was the only way he could let go of those repressed desires."

She sat back with a rough sigh. It actually made sense. She felt her heart beating wildly in her chest as she recalled how it had been with Tom. At the office, he'd avoided the female staff. He and Elysia had become close because she didn't make eyes at him. She wasn't aggressive, as some of the women were. She was shy and reserved, and she must have been the least threatening female he knew. He'd opened up with her, just a little. And then right after Kate had married, he'd had too much to drink and Elysia had been nearby. Perhaps he'd given in to feelings he couldn't express, and then been ashamed of what he'd done, because of his childhood teachings.

The thought made her heart race. Could it be possible that she was Tom Walker's first, only, woman in that way? Her lips parted.

"Do you think it's possible?" she asked hesitantly.

"That it was his first time?" He nodded. "He's no rounder. Nobody would accuse him of being a playboy. He's courteous to women, but there's an icy tone to his dealings with them. He's polite, but nothing more." He smiled. "He was very impressed with Crissy. You've never seen his sister Kate, have you?"

"No."

He chuckled softly. "Well, I have. Crissy could be her daughter. I'm sure the resemblance didn't escape Tom, even if he hasn't quite recognized it yet."

"What should I do, Luke?" she asked.

"Why don't you go and talk to him honestly?"

"It would be hard."

"Of course. Doing the right thing usually is."

"I can't go today. I'm meeting with a European buyer to open a new market."

"There's always tomorrow."

She sighed. "I guess I always knew that I'd have to tell him one day. He won't like it."

"He will."

She smiled. "You're a nice brother. Why don't you get married?"

"Bite your tongue, woman," he said. "I'm not putting my neck in that particular noose. There are too many pretty girls around who like to party," he chuckled, rising.

"One day, you'll run head-on into someone who doesn't."

"I'll pity the poor girl, whoever she is," he said with a grin.

"You're hopeless."

"At least I'm honest," he said pointedly. "A confirmed bachelor has to protect himself any way he can against you devious females!"

She threw a small sofa pillow at him.

SHE'D PLANNED TO stop by Tom's office the next day, but an unexpected meeting early that morning had unfortunate consequences.

She'd just seen her European buyer off, very early that morning, from her shop in the middle of town. He was a determined would-be suitor who had to be convinced that a young widow didn't need a man. She'd pushed him away with a cold smile right there on the sidewalk and wished him a pleasant trip.

"Pleasant, ha!" the handsome Frenchman had called. "Without you in my bed, I shall be very lonely, *cherie*. I hope that the business I send you will compensate you for my loss. After all, Elysia, to you, money is much more important than a mere lover, *n'est pas?*"

Sadly for Elysia, this bitter remark, loudly made by her angry rejected suitor, reached Tom Walker's ears. He was less than ten feet away and heard every word.

Before Elysia could reply angrily to the Frenchman, he climbed into his sports car and roared away. She could have the business she wanted overseas, but the cost was too high. She wasn't going to accept the merger. Better to rest on her American sales record than have to deal with a man like that!

"Is that how you get clients?" Tom asked, pausing beside her, his dark green eyes furious in that lean, dark face. "By sleeping with them?"

She looked at him blankly. "I get clients by providing quality service."

"Oh? Really?" His gaze went up and down her body in the simple silk suit, to her long hair twisted into a neat chignon. She looked cool and desirable and very flushed. He hated her in that moment for the way she'd twisted his heart.

His contempt was visible. It hurt her, and it also made her furiously angry, that he should misjudge her so.

She pulled herself up to her full height. "Think what you like," she said coldly. "Your opinion and fifty cents will buy you a cup of coffee at any café in town!"

He made a rough sound and put his hands into his pockets. "How was he in bed?"

Her face went scarlet. She slapped him. It wasn't premeditated, but it felt good afterward. She turned on her heel and stalked away to her Mercedes convertible. Several people had seen what she did, but she didn't care. She knew that she was gossiped about—most wealthy people were. She didn't care anymore. She'd send her daughter away to a private school where she wouldn't have to suffer the speculation and contempt of the neighbors. As for herself, people could think whatever they liked. And that included Tom Walker!

TOM, NURSING A stinging cheek, stalked back into his own office, foregoing the sweet roll he'd gone out to get for his breakfast. He'd never been slapped by a woman in his life. It was an experience he didn't relish.

He walked past his curious middle-aged secretary and closed his office door. Elysia had never seemed spirited in the old days. Perhaps her marriage had made her bitter.

As he recalled what he'd said to her, he had to admit that he'd provoked her into the action. He hadn't meant to say the things he had, but the thought of her with that Frenchman—a man who had probably been to bed with hundreds of women from the look of him—made him sick with jealousy. He hadn't known that he still felt so strongly for Elysia in the first place. Apparently his feelings for her were buried so far inside him that they couldn't be removed.

Was this how Kate had felt about Jacob Cade? His sister had been enamored with the man most of her adult life. She'd kept photos of him in the damnedest places. It wasn't until her job as a reporter had sent her into a terrorist standoff and she'd been shot that Jacob had revealed his own violent feelings for her. Theirs had been a rocky, volatile romance that eventually ended in a happy and lasting marriage. Kate had adjusted to it with joy.

But except for Elysia, Tom had never felt a rush of joy at just the sight of a woman. He'd often wondered as he grew older what it would be like to share his life and his heart as well as his bed with a woman. He'd always been sure that no woman would accept him with his hangups and his chaste status. Elysia had, but then, she hadn't known that she was the first. He'd been too proud to admit that he was innocent. Now, he was glad he hadn't shared that knowledge with her. She obviously wanted no part of him in her life.

He leaned forward and began to deal with the stack of mail on his desk, his sore cheek forgotten. Elysia was in the past. He might as well keep her there.

IF ONLY IT had been that easy. Jacobsville was small enough that the monied class congregated everywhere. There was an endless social round that included chamber of commerce meetings and various charity and business gatherings of all sorts. Tom, as the town's only investment counselor, was included in all of these. So, unfortunately, was Elysia.

Their stiff courtesy with each other didn't go unnoticed. People remembered that Elysia had worked for Tom in New York before she'd come home to marry Fred Nash. They began to wonder about these two people because of their obvious hostility toward each other.

The gossip was unavoidable.

Tom found himself seated next to Elysia at the monthly meeting of businessmen. It was a lunch affair, served in the private dining room of the largest local restaurant. Tom, in a dark suit, and Elysia, in a neat gray pantsuit, her hair in a chignon, was secretary of the group. She couldn't avoid him at this function, or the gossip would have been even worse.

But it was obvious to the most unobservant of guests that they barely tolerated each other. When Elysia passed around the neat copies she'd made of the financial report, she made sure that her hand didn't touch

Tom's. When she passed the cream and sugar holders to him, again, she kept her fingers from making contact.

Tom was keenly aware of her bitter avoidance of him. He understood it, but that didn't make it any easier. He was astonished that such a mercenary woman still had feelings to hurt.

After the meeting, she went straight to her car.

Tom followed right behind her, keenly aware of eyes following his progress to his own somber Lincoln, which was parked beside her Mercedes convertible.

Elysia fumbled with her keys and dropped them in her haste to get away before he came to his car. She muttered curses, hating the door because it wouldn't cooperate.

"Don't worry," he murmured coolly from across the top of her car, "whatever I seem to have probably isn't contagious a car length away."

She glared at him, flushed. "That works both ways, Mr. Walker!"

"Listen, if you want to sleep your way up in the fashion world, it's none of my business," he said with icy venom.

She bit back a curse as the president of the chamber of commerce passed them with a curious glance.

"Nice meeting, Mr. James," she said through her teeth with a smile.

"Yes, it was. Nice to have you aboard, too, Mr. Walker," he said, pausing to shake Tom's hand. "You be good to him, Mrs. Nash, we need new blood in the community!" he added with a wave of his hand as he went along to his own car.

"Oh, how I'd love to show him some of yours," Elysia said fervently, glaring at Tom.

"You need to work on that attitude problem," he replied somberly. "You seem to have lost your knack for diplomacy."

"Only with you," she shot right back. "I get along fine with everyone else."

"Especially French buyers, hmmm?"

"Damn you!"

His eyebrows arched as she pulled off a high heel shoe and threw it at him.

"Wouldn't you know I'd miss?" she demanded of the parking lot. "Give me back my shoe."

"Come over here and get it," he challenged.

"You're not my type," she purred. "You can't speak French!"

His eyes went cold. He threw the shoe onto the top of her car, got into his own, backed out and drove away without even looking in her direction.

"I love you, too, you sweet man!" she called after him.

"Can I print that?" the local newspaper editor whispered in her ear.

She shrieked. "John, don't sneak up on me like that!"

He grinned wickedly. "Can't you see the headlines? Boutique Owner Shouts Love For Financial Advisor At Top Of Lungs…"

"Do you need a shoe?" she asked, holding it over her head in a threatening manner.

He cleared his throat. "Not my size. Thanks, anyway."

He beat a hasty retreat. She glared after him. This was getting totally out of hand.

TOM WAS KEPT busy for the rest of the week, and Elysia took a back seat in his mind as he dealt with one financial crisis after another. By Saturday, he was ready for some rest and recreation. He decided that fishing might be a nice way to relax, and a local man had a stocked private pond where he rented poles and bait for a small all-day fee.

He put on jeans and went on his way. Fortunately the fish were biting, since he did love a nice fried bass. It brought back memories of his youth in South Dakota, when he and Kate had gone fishing with Jacob Cade on the older man's sprawling ranch.

His boots were worn, but serviceable, like the old beige Stetson he'd had for years. Dressed like that, he looked every inch a cowboy. Kate had always wondered why her only brother had chosen city life. She'd never realized that the very anonymity of a big city was kind to his ego. In a small town, his aloneness would have been so much more noticeable.

In fact, it worried him here. He hadn't considered how curious small-town people were about strangers, or how gossip, though kind, ran rampant. It was rather like being part of a huge family, having everyone know all about you. The comforting thing about it was that, also like family, people tended to accept each other regardless of human frailty.

For instance, everyone knew that old Harry was an alcoholic, and that Jeff had been in prison for killing his wife's lover. They also knew that a local spinster bought copies of a notorious magazine that contained vivid photos of nude men, and that a certain social worker lived with a man to whom she wasn't married. These were open secrets, however, and not one person ridiculed these people or treated them as untouchables. They were family.

Tom began to understand that even the talk about Elysia wasn't vicious or brutal.

In fact, as Tom spent more time around local people, and heard more gossip about her, he learned that Elysia's marriage had been looked upon more as a charitable act on her part, despite her husband's wealth.

"Took care of him like a nurse, she did," old man Gallagher had said, nodding with approval as he filled Tom's order at the office supply store the week before, when talk had turned to Elysia's similar taste in stationery for her boutique. "Never shirked, not even at the end when he was bedridden and needed around-the-clock nursing. She had a nurse, but she stayed, too." He smiled. "She may have inherited a lot of money, that's true, but most people feel like she earned it with the care she took of old Fred. Never doubted that she was fond of him. And that kid doted on him." He sighed. "She mourned him, too, and so did the kid. Nice young woman. Most folks remember her dad." His eyes had darkened and narrowed.

Tom frowned. "In a kind way?" he asked, because the old man's voice had shaded a bit.

"Hardly. Old man Craig drank like a fish. Beat Elysia's mother and Luke. Day came when Luke was old enough to realize he had to do something. He called the police, even though his mama wouldn't. Swore out a warrant for his dad and signed it, too." He chuckled.

"They put the man away. He died in prison of a heart attack, but I think it was a relief to all of them. Would never have stopped beating her, if they'd ever let him out. I reckon they all knew it."

That had sounded painfully familiar to Tom, who'd had his share of beatings. His and Kate's father had never touched alcohol, but the brain tumor had made a monster of him. The two of them had been "disciplined" frequently by their unpredictable parent, especially if they ever showed a flicker of interest in the opposite sex.

Tom threw his line into the water and leaned back against the trunk of an oak tree with a sigh. He wasn't really interested in fishing, but it was something to do. His days had been empty for a long time. In the city, there was always something to do in the anonymity of crowds. Here, he either sat at home with rented movies or fished. Fishing was much preferable.

"Hi!"

The bright greeting caught his attention. He turned his head to find Luke and Crissy with tackle boxes and fishing poles.

"I never expected to find a big city dude in a place like this," Luke murmured dryly. "Bored to death or do you just enjoy eating cheap fish?"

"This isn't cheap," Tom murmured on a chuckle. "Ten dollars a day and the price of renting the tackle. Plus fifty cents a pound for whatever you catch. It adds up."

"Bobby Turner's no fool," Luke said with a grin. "He

figures people will pay to catch clean fish in a good location. He does a roaring business."

Tom, glancing out over the dozens of people around the big lake, had to admit that the warm weather drew scores of fishermen.

"Mind if we join you?" Luke asked. "The best spots are already taken."

"Is this one of them?" Tom queried.

"It sure is," Crissy piped up. "I caught a big fish last time, didn't I, Uncle Luke?"

"She caught a four-pound bass," Luke agreed, settling in. "But I had to land him. She's a bit small yet for pulling in fighting fish on a line."

"It pulled me down," Crissy explained solemnly. Then she grinned. "But we ate it for supper. It tasted very good."

Tom laughed in spite of himself. The child had an incredible variety of facial expressions.

Crissy looked at him for a long time, her little face studious and quiet. "You have green eyes and dark hair," she noted. "Just like me."

He nodded. "So I do." He paused, glancing at Luke, who'd gone to the small shed where bait was sold. "I guess your dad had green eyes, too, huh?"

She frowned. "No," she said, shaking her head. "My daddy had red hair."

Tom's heart jumped up into his throat. The most incredible thoughts were gathering speed in his head. He stared down at the child. She had his own olive skin, his eyes, his hair. She was in kindergarten, that would make her at least five years old. He couldn't stop looking at her as a shocking idea took shape in his mind.

Luke came back with bait. "Go put this on your hook," he told Crissy, "and watch that you don't get it stuck in your finger like poor old Mr. Hull did last time he went with us."

"Yes, sir," she said at once. "I don't want my finger cut open!"

She rushed off, a miniature whirlwind in jeans and a short-sleeved cotton shirt.

"She loves to fish," Luke said. "I had a date, but I broke it." He made a face. "My latest girl doesn't like fishing or any other 'blood sport.'"

"Fishing is a blood sport?" Tom asked.

"Sure is," came the reply. "So is eating meat." He grinned sheepishly. "I'm not giving up my cattle, so I guess this girl will go the way of the others pretty soon. She's a looker. Pity."

Tom knelt down beside Luke, glancing warily toward the child. "She said her dad was redheaded."

Luke's indrawn breath was audible, although he recovered quickly enough. "Did she? She was barely older than a toddler when he died..."

"Red is red, whatever age you are," Tom said doggedly. His green eyes met the blue ones of the other man. "She's mine."

Luke cursed silently. Elysia was going to kill him.

"She's mine," Tom repeated harshly, his eyes demanding verification.

Luke bent his head. "She's yours," he said heavily.

Tom looked at the little girl again, his face white,

his eyes blazing. He'd never thought much about getting married, much less about having children, and all
at once, he was a father. It was a shattering thought.

"Dear God," he breathed.

Luke put a hand on his shoulder, noting how the other
man tensed at once. He didn't like being touched. Luke
withdrew the comradely gesture. "She thought you were
a big city playboy," he explained. "She never considered
trying to get in touch with you, especially after the way
you acted before she left town."

Tom grimaced.

"If it's any consolation, Fred had leukemia when
they married, and he was already infirm. They lived
together as friends, nothing more, and she was fond of
him. She needed a name for Crissy. For a small town
like this, we're pretty tolerant, but Elysia couldn't bear
having people gossip about us more than they already
do." He searched Tom's eyes. "You'll have heard about
our father, I imagine?"

Tom nodded. He drew in a long breath. "My father
was a madman," he confided quietly. "I've had my share
of beatings, too," he added, and a look passed between
the two men. "The difference was that my father died
of a brain tumor—while he was beating my sister for
smiling at a boy she liked. He called her a slut, if you
can imagine being labeled that for a smile."

Luke grimaced. "Good God, and I thought I had it
bad."

Tom laughed coldly. His eyes were on the child. "One
time," he said half to himself, "in my entire life, and
there was a child."

Luke looked down at the ground. "Elysia was your first?"

Tom hesitated, but he was too stunned by what he'd learned to conceal it anymore. "Yes," he said bluntly. "And the last. There hasn't been anyone else, ever."

Luke looked up, quietly compassionate. "Not for her, either," he said. "Not even her husband."

"You're not serious."

"Yes, I am," Luke countered. "He was too ill most of the time, and she never felt like that about him. She was honest. Then when Crissy was born, they seemed to find common ground. That child was wanted and very much loved."

Tom's hand clenched by his side. "And now that I know about her—" he nodded toward the child "—what the hell do I do?"

CHAPTER THREE

"ON THAT SUBJECT," Luke mused, "I would say that you've got a real problem on your hands. Elysia never meant for you to find out about Crissy. And here I've given the game away."

He shook his head. "Crissy gave it away," he replied, "when she said her dad was redheaded. I believe in recessive genes, of course, but not to that extent. She's a dead ringer for my sister, Kate."

"I noticed that, too," Luke replied.

"What am I going to do?" Tom groaned, pushing his hands through his hair in frustration. "I can't walk up to Elysia after all this time and demand my rights to my daughter. I let her leave New York pregnant, although I swear I didn't suspect that she could have been after one night, and I never even tried to see her again. She won't understand why."

"Care to tell me?"

Tom laughed coldly. "Because I was too ashamed," he said. "I got drunk and had sex," he said with self-contempt. His eyes closed. "My God, I thought I was sure to go to hell after that. I didn't realize that the hell was going to be living with myself afterward. I missed her," he confided. "She'd been with me for two years, and it was like losing part of my own body. But every time I thought about what I'd done, I was too ashamed to try to contact her. I never thought of a child," he added huskily. He shook his head. "I wasn't very clued-up for a twenty-eight-year-old man. And Elysia thought I was a playboy. How's that for irony?"

"You should have told her the truth," Luke told him. "She's not the sort of woman who would think less of you. I'd guess that it would impress her very much."

"How could I have told her something like that? I'm thirty-four now, but when I knew Elysia I was twenty-eight already. How many male virgins of that age have you ever known?" Tom asked him with an irritable glance.

Luke grinned. "One."

Tom burst out laughing. It didn't seem so terrible now, that he'd had a woman and a child had come of the experience. In fact, the more he thought about it, the more pleasure he felt. Those pangs of conscience were receding at least a little. But he was knee-deep in problems, with no solutions in sight. Elysia was the biggest one of all. He remembered the things he'd said to her recently and he wanted to throw back his head and scream. Even if she'd have let him come around Crissy before, she'd never allow him close to the child now. He'd burned his bridges by accusing her of sleeping her way up the corporate ladder. He groaned aloud. How could he have been so blind?

"You might come to supper tonight," Luke said.

Tom's eyebrows lifted. "She'd have me stuffed and

baked if I walked in the door. Either that, or she'd smother me in all that tomato sauce you said she made."

"No guts, no glory," Luke reminded him. He looked at the child, who was just joining them. "Crissy, what would you think if Mr. Walker came to dinner tonight?"

"I'd like that," the child said seriously, grinning up at him. "I'd like to know all about Indians."

Tom sighed. "I only know family lore, and not much of that," he confided. "Kate and I went to live with our grandmother, and she didn't like that side of our family at all. She refused to let us talk about it."

"How mean," Crissy muttered.

"It was, wasn't it?" Tom agreed, having just realized that it was a form of discrimination on the old woman's part. "But my sister's husband knew someone on the Sioux reservation who was related to our great-grandfather—and therefore to us. He asked for the history, and Kate went to see the woman and wrote it all down." He searched the little face so much like his own. "One of our ancestors was at the Little Bighorn, and we have distant relatives in Canada and South Dakota among the Sioux."

"Do you visit them?" Crissy asked, wide-eyed.

"I haven't yet. I think I might like to," he added. He smiled. "Maybe you and your mom could come along."

"You could ask her," Crissy said doubtfully. "She doesn't like to go places."

"You said she took you to a powwow," Tom reminded her, cherishing the memory.

"She liked it," Crissy agreed. "She told me all about

the Plains Indians and about that place where General
Custer got shot, too."

"Colonel Custer," Tom told her. "He had a Civil War
battlefield promotion to Brigadier General, but that was
a brevet commission. He was only a colonel in the 7th
Cavalry."

"Touchy subject, hmmm?" Luke teased.

"Very," Tom replied. "And isn't it a hell of a thing
that it should be? I haven't paid a lot of attention to my
ancestry before now." He looked at Crissy. "But it's in
the genes."

"It sure is," Luke replied amusedly.

"I want to catch a big fish for you to eat at our house,"
Crissy said. She tried to throw the hook into the water,
but she wasn't tall enough to cast the line out.

Tom squatted just behind her, holding her with one
arm while he guided the small hand holding the line.
"Like this, sweetheart," he said gently.

She grinned at him over one shoulder. "Thanks. You
smell nice," she added.

He chuckled, hugging her close. "So do you, tidbit."

He got up, leaving her to hold the pole tight in both
hands. He'd never used endearments, but the child
seemed to invoke them effortlessly. He stared down
at her with pure pride, unaware that Luke could see
that pride.

"She's very like you," Luke remarked quietly.

"Yes," came the reply. Tom went back to his own
pole, baited the hook and tossed the line out into the
lake. His thoughts were dark ones. He knew Elysia
wasn't going to want him in her house, but he had to

try to make his peace with her. He glanced at his daughter and knew that it was worth the effort.

THEY CAUGHT FIVE big bass between them, which Luke volunteered to clean. "Come over about six," he told Tom.

Tom glanced from the child's eager face to Luke's. He grimaced. "I don't know…"

"You have to," Crissy pleaded. "Me and Uncle Luke and Mama can't eat all these big fish alone. Please?"

"Okay," he relented. "I'll see if I can rent some body armor," he murmured to himself. "Boy, am I going to need it!"

He went home to clean up, wondering how Luke was going to fare when he broke the news to Elysia. It would probably be bloody.

"YOU WHAT?" ELYSIA EXPLODED.

Luke held up a hand. "Go upstairs and clean up, pumpkin," he told Crissy.

She hesitated. "Mommy, you have to say it's okay," she told her mother somberly. "I invited Mr. Tom to come help us eat the fish. He helped us catch them. I like him," she added belligerently. "He's going to tell me all about Indians."

"Go on," Luke prompted, smiling. "It will be all right."

Crissy went, glowering at her white-faced parent on the way.

"You can't," Elysia cried when her daughter was out of sight. "You can't have him here! If he's around her enough, he'll see…!"

"He already has," Luke said.

He jumped forward and helped her into a chair, because she looked as if she might faint.

"You told him," she accused hoarsely.

"I did not. Crissy did."

"Crissy? But she doesn't know!"

"She told him that her dad was redheaded," he explained. "It wasn't a great leap of logic from that to the way she resembles his sister—not to mention himself."

"Oh, dear God," Elysia whispered, closing her eyes. "Dear God, what'll he do?"

"Nothing, judging by this afternoon," Luke said. He knelt by her chair, one hand on hers in her lap. "Listen, he's not vindictive. He doesn't blame you. He's got secrets of his own," he added, hoping to get her attention.

That did. She looked at him through misty eyes. "He does?"

"You remember what we were speculating about?" he asked. "Well, we were right on the money. Sex was a taboo at home. Their father beat them for showing the slightest interest in the other sex. He said his conscience was eating him alive about you. He thought he'd go to hell for sleeping with you."

She gasped. "Good heavens!"

"He said that it's taken all these years for him to come to grips with it," he continued quietly. "The main thing that came out is that he was angry at himself, not at you. It was guilt and shame that caused him to let you go without a word, and kept him from coming after you. He didn't even consider that you might become pregnant. His father taught him that desire was nothing more than sick lust."

She closed her eyes and shivered. "How he must have felt," she whispered.

"He's a case," he agreed. "I don't suppose there was a woman brave enough to chase him at all until you came along. That cold reserve of his is rather formidable, even to other men."

"I'll say," she agreed, remembering the Tom of six years ago. She looked up. "Why is he coming to dinner?"

"Because I invited him." He held up a hand. "This can't go on," he informed her. "Half the town's talking already about the way the two of you avoid each other. We all have to live here. It's time to make peace. Or at least, a public peace. This is the first step."

"He'll be lucky if he gets in the door unwounded," she said coldly. "Do you have any idea what he's been saying to me lately?"

"No," he said warily.

"He's accused me of sleeping with that damned Frenchman to market my boutique's designs," she said furiously. "He thinks I'm a slut!"

"No, he doesn't…"

"You can't imagine the things he said to me at the business meeting just the other day," she added. "Not to mention that we were about to have lunch in Rose's Café downtown and when he saw me come in the door, he gave up his place in line and left."

He pursed his lips. "He didn't mention that."

"He was probably too busy thinking of ways to get

to my child," she raged. "Well, he won't get her. He can come here tonight, but you are never to invite him into this house again while I'm living in it, Luke! I won't be persecuted by him, not even for my little girl's sake!"

"He's not out for revenge," he reminded her. "He's had as rough a time as we had. Maybe rougher. You can at least try to be sociable, can't you? Crissy likes him." He searched her wan face. "You loved him once."

"A long time ago," she replied, "and he never felt the same way, even then. He talked to me, but it was never more than that, until he got drunk. He doesn't love me. He wanted me that once, and now he doesn't anymore. He thinks I'm a gold digger, out for money and nothing else. He told me so. That was a week or so before the business meeting."

"Tom actually accused you of that?" Luke was surprised, because Tom hadn't said anything about that to him, either.

"We had words on the street, and I slapped him." She flushed at her brother's level look. "Well, he deserved it! He made me out to be cheap, and all because that French buyer had humiliated me loud enough for the whole town to hear." Her eyes flashed. "Hell will freeze over before I give him a contract for our designs," she added coldly. "He did that deliberately because I wouldn't have an affair with him."

"Did you tell Tom that?"

"He didn't let me tell him anything," she replied. "He made a lot of nasty accusations and I hit him. I'm glad I hit him," she added. "I only threw a shoe at him and missed at the business meeting, but I'll practice," she assured herself. "Next time, I'll knock his brains out!"

Luke had to bite back a grin. "He has got quite a few hang-ups," he reminded her. "It will take a brave woman to live with a man like that, if she can even get him in front of a minister to get married. He's frozen halfway through because of his father."

"I wish I'd known that in New York. It's too late to matter much now. A man that age isn't going to change." She stared out the window and grimaced. "But I'm sorry he had a bad time of it." She glanced back at her brother with a rueful smile. "I guess his upbringing was like ours."

He smiled sadly. "I guess it was," he agreed. "The world is full of wounded children who grow up to be wounded adults. Sometimes they get lucky and find solace in each other."

"Sometimes they withdraw and strike at anyone who comes close," she replied.

He chuckled. "An apt description of our Mr. Walker. But he has a weakness. Crissy. She winds him around her finger."

"He really likes her?" she asked.

"He's crazy about her," he said. "She likes him, too. If you're wise, you won't try to separate them. There's already a bond growing."

"I wouldn't deny him access," she said defensively. "But it's going to complicate things. He doesn't like me at all, and it's mutual."

"He doesn't know you, Ellie. Give him a chance."

"Even if I would, he'll never give me one," she said finally.

He saw that arguing with her wasn't going to solve anything. He winked at her instead. "I'll clean those fish for you."

SHE WAS A bundle of nerves by five-thirty. Crissy, in a neat little pink skirt and tank top, was setting the table. She glanced at her mother with wry amusement for such a young child. Elysia, in a sedate denim dress and loafers, was pacing the floor. Her hair, in a neat chignon, gleamed in the sunlight filtering through the window.

Luke came down the hall with a grin on his handsome face. "You'll wear holes in the floor," he told her. "Quit that."

"I'll go mad long before six o'clock," she moaned. "Oh, Luke, why did you…" Her voice trailed off into a faint gasp as she heard the crunch of car tires on the gravel driveway. She looked out the window, and there was the gray Lincoln.

"He's here," she choked.

"Is it him?" Crissy called, running into the living room. She looked out the screen door. "It is!" She opened the door and ran to him. "Hi, Mr. Tom!"

The sight of the child running toward him aroused odd sensations in Tom Walker. He opened his arms and caught her, lifting her high, his eyes twinkling with the joy that raged inside him. This was his own, his child, his blood. Amazing how attached he'd become to her in such a short time. He hugged her close, laughing.

She returned the enthusiastic hug, and chattered

brightly about the meal they were going to have as he carried her effortlessly into the house.

"Gosh, you're strong, Mr. Tom," she said with a grin. "I'll bet you could lift my pony."

"Not quite," he mused, setting her back on her feet. He shook hands with Luke and then turned to Elysia.

Her face was drawn. She looked frustrated and even a little frightened.

He reacted to her expression rather than to her cold greeting. "It's all right," he said gently, searching her eyes quietly. "We'll call a truce for tonight."

She drew in a steadying breath, ignoring the comment. "Dinner's ready, if you'd like to sit down."

"Come on and help me bring in the food, Crissy," Luke said to the child, herding her out of the room.

Tom heard the kitchen door close and he searched Elysia's worried face for a long moment. "I'm not very good at this," he began slowly.

"At what?" she asked tersely.

He shrugged. "Apologies. I don't think I've made two in my entire life. But I'm sorry about what I said to you the other day."

"You needn't butter me up because you like Crissy," she said coldly. "Regardless of your opinion of me, I'm not vindictive."

He searched her eyes. "She's a unique young lady. You've done a good job with her."

She moved restlessly. "Thank you."

He stuck his hands into his slacks pockets with a long sigh. "Are you and Luke close?" he asked suddenly.

The question should have surprised her, but it didn't.

"Yes," she said. "We were physically abused children, so I guess we were closer than kids who had a normal upbringing."

His face grew very hard. "It's a damnable world for some children, isn't it? Even with the new protective laws, the secrecy hangs on. It's so hard for a child to accuse a parent, even one who deserves a prison term."

"I know." She searched his lean face with quick, curious eyes. "You want to know if Luke told me what you said to him, don't you?"

"He did, of course," he said knowingly.

She nodded. "He thought…it might help if I knew it all."

"And did it?"

She lowered her eyes to his chest, flushing. She'd been more intimate with this man than with anyone in her whole life. It hadn't bothered her before, but now it did. Vivid memories flooded her mind of that night with him. They were embarrassing and they made her self-conscious around him.

"I won't stop you from seeing Crissy, if that's what you mean," she said, evading a direct answer, her tone cold with her inner turmoil.

"Thanks," he replied.

Neither of them spoke, having too much trouble finding the right words.

When Luke and Crissy came back, two pairs of eyes looked toward them with open relief.

"Shall we eat?" Luke murmured.

Crissy reached up and took Tom's hand. "You have

to sit beside me, Mr. Tom, so you can tell me about Indians."

"Native Americans." Elysia corrected her without thinking and then flushed at Tom's keen glance.

"Is that right?" Crissy asked her companion.

"Actually it is," he told her. "Or, if you prefer, indigenous aborigines." He grinned. "Those two words get a workout lately."

Crissy tried to pronounce it and finally succeeded.

After they were well into their meal, Tom explained the divisions of Sioux to his young daughter. "There are Lakota, Nakota and Dakota," he said, "which refers to the use of the *l* and *n* and *d* in each of those languages. Then, there are Brule, or burned thigh, Sioux, Nez Perce, Blackfoot and Sans Arc." He explained to her that Sans Arc meant "without bows" and came from a sad incident in that tribe's history during which the group were advised by a shaman to put their bows and arrows into a pile. They were subsequently attacked, with tragic results.

"Tell me about your great-grandfather," Crissy persisted.

"He was one of the warrior subchiefs," he explained. "He fought and was wounded in the Little Bighorn fight."

"Massacre," Crissy said knowingly.

He gave her a long look. "A massacre is when one group is totally unarmed and defenseless. Custer and his men had plenty of weapons."

"Oh," Crissy said respectfully.

"Back in the old days, trackers could tell by the shape

of a moccasin which tribe he was tracking. The arrows were unique to each tribe, and even to each warrior."

"Goodness," Crissy exclaimed. "Can you track?"

He chuckled. "I can track my way to the nearest burger stand," he mused. "But out in the woods, I don't think I'd be much good at it. Now my sister's husband is a real tracker. And he's got Native American blood, too. Their little boy is just your age. He looks a lot like you," he mused, studying Crissy. "He has green eyes, too, despite his dark skin and hair."

"Have you seen the Cades lately?" Luke asked.

Tom shook his head. "I've been too busy, what with this move to Jacobsville. But I thought I might go up there for a few days next month. I don't know what I'll do with Moose while I'm away, though," he added thoughtfully.

"You got a moose?" Crissy asked, wide-eyed.

"That's his name," Tom said, correcting her. He chuckled. "Moose is sort of like a walking disaster. I've been around dogs most of my life, but he's unique. Kate saw him once and called him an albatross."

"What's that?" the little girl wondered aloud.

"There was a poem by Coleridge. The ancient mariner was forced to wear one around his neck—"

"I read that in school," Luke interrupted. "It was one of the only poems I liked."

"We could keep your dog for you," Crissy volunteered.

"No, you couldn't," Tom said before Elysia or Luke could speak. "Moose would shatter every fragile thing your mother and uncle have, and you'd have to recarpet the floor. He's a digger. If he can't get his paws into dirt, he'll try to unearth the carpet. Everything I own is saturated in lemon juice to keep Moose out of it. He really hates the taste of lemon."

"Why do you keep him?" Luke asked.

Tom made a face. "I don't know. I like him, I guess. He was a stray. I felt sorry for him. Now I feel sorry for myself. But he'll grow up. One day."

"We have two cats that somebody abandoned," Luke murmured, with a speaking glance at his sister. "I was going to take them to the pound, but she—" he gestured toward Elysia "—wouldn't hear of it. They went to the vet instead, for shots. Good thing she makes a good living at her boutique, or their appetites would bankrupt her."

"They eat an awful lot," Crissy agreed. "Especially Winter."

"Winter?" Tom ventured.

"It was when we found her," she replied. "And the other one is named 'Damn—'"

"Crissy!" Elysia burst out.

"Well, that's what Uncle Luke calls her," Crissy muttered.

"Her name is Petunia," Elysia said, smothering laughter. "But she likes shaving lotion, so every morning when Luke uses his, Petunia leaps into his lap and tries to lick him."

"Moose has several other names, too," Tom murmured, "But I won't repeat them in mixed company."

Luke chuckled.

"Would you like to see our cats?" Crissy asked when they finished dessert. "They live in the barn."

"Go ahead," Elysia told the other three occupants of the table. "I have to clear away."

Tom hesitated, but Crissy caught his hand and coaxed him out the back door.

Luke hesitated before he followed. "You okay?" he asked his sister.

She managed a smile. "I suppose so. Not that we've settled anything, but we're not attacking each other, either. I don't mind if he sees Crissy."

"They seem to be forming a bond."

"I noticed." She sighed. "Luke, you don't think he'll try to take her away from me?" she asked worriedly.

"No, I don't. He isn't that kind of man."

"I do hope you're right. I've only been around him for a few…"

The sound of tires on the gravel outside caught their attention. A tall, dark-haired man was just getting out of a racy red foreign sports car.

"Why, it's Matt!" Elysia exclaimed. "Whatever is he doing here?"

CHAPTER FOUR

MATT CALDWELL WAS a handsome devil, dark-eyed and lean-faced and dark-browed. He moved with a lithe, sure gait and he was the favorite target of most of the single women in Jacobsville. Not that Matt ever seemed to notice any of them, except Elysia, and only on a friendly basis. His full name was Mather Gilbert Caldwell. But everyone called him Matt.

He grinned as he approached the people on the front porch, showing perfect white teeth.

"Are you a delegation?" he queried.

"You'd better hope we're not a lynch mob," Luke chuckled. "What brings you out here?"

"I'm looking for your dinner guest. Where is he? I've got a message for him from his sister."

"It must be a pretty important one to bring you out here," Elysia said. "And how did you know he was here?"

"Mr. Gallagher," he murmured dryly.

She groaned. "He's out in the barn with Crissy."

"Mind if I deliver the message?"

"Of course not," Elysia said.

He caught her by the hand and pulled her along. "You come, too."

She let him lead her away with an amused glance toward her brother.

"Is it bad news?" she asked as they approached the barn.

"Not at all." He glanced down at her. "Why is your dinner guest in the barn with Crissy?"

"She's introducing him to our cats."

"I heard she and Luke spent today out at Turner's Lake fishing with Tom."

"They did."

"Is he Luke's friend, or yours?" Matt asked, pausing to stare down at her.

She fidgeted. "That's personal. You and I are just friends, Matt."

"Of course we are," he agreed. "But friends take care of each other. Our Mr. Walker has a cold, nasty temper and he seems to be going out of his way to antagonize you. I felt a little guilty about it, so I came out to see why Luke brought him home."

His wording went right by her. "Crissy likes him," she said.

"Crissy likes me, too," he said pointedly.

She couldn't say any more without giving away secrets. She grimaced. "Matt, be a dear and stop grilling me, could you?"

"Is he why you left New York so suddenly?"

She glared at him. "Hey. That's too personal!"

"Sure it is. We've already agreed that we're friends, haven't we?" His dark eyes narrowed. "Crissy looks a lot like him, don't you think?"

"Matt!"

He let out a long sigh. "Well, she does. I'm not blind or stupid, and I knew more about Fred Nash than most people. He wasn't in any shape to become a father…"

"Oh, God, not you, too?" she groaned.

"Yes. Me, too. For heaven's sake, hasn't it dawned on you that I was responsible for Tom being in Jacobsville? That I planted the seed in his mind, encouraged him to do a market study of the area and move down here?"

She actually gasped. "You didn't!"

"I did," he said firmly. "He had a right to know. Not that I said anything about Crissy to him. I thought fate would take care of that. And it has. He knows, too, doesn't he?"

She glowered up at him.

"Of course he knows," he answered his own question. "He isn't blind, either. And he's been giving you fits ever since he moved here. Damn, I'm sorry."

She slumped. "Matt, you were only trying to help. But it's all such a mess."

"Most messes can be cleaned up with the right broom." He tilted her face up, smiled and bent to kiss her on the cheek. "Cheer up. The world isn't going to end. In fact, things are going to work out beautifully. All you have to do is give them a chance."

The squeak of the barn door opening brought both heads up. Tom was standing there with Crissy beside him, glaring blackly at the newcomers.

"There you are," Matt said genially, still clinging tightly to Elysia's hand. "Kate phoned. When she couldn't find you, she found me. She has news."

Tom stilled. "Bad news?"

"Hell, no," Matt said, chuckling. "She's pregnant. You're going to be an uncle again."

Tom whistled through his teeth. "Imagine that. They've tried for years to have a second child." He laughed with pure delight. "I'll bet they're both over the moon."

"Kate sounded that way when I spoke to her," Matt agreed. "She said Jacob's already planning a new nursery. He wants a girl this time. I think Kate does, too."

"They'll be happy with whatever they get. They're both crazy about kids."

"Their son will like having a playmate."

"And Kate is a wonderful mother," Tom added. "I'll call her as soon as I get home. Why are you holding Elysia's hand?" he added so abruptly that it caught Matt by surprise.

"Was I?" He loosened her fingers with a smug look that neither of them saw.

"He can hold my hand if he wants to," Elysia told Tom.

"I noticed," he said coldly. "You must like him. You haven't thrown anything at him. What's the matter, can't get your shoe off?"

"Just you give me a minute and we'll see…!" She struggled with a loafer, using Matt's arm for a prop, but she was immediately tugged upward.

"Stop that," Matt muttered.

"Did she throw a shoe at you, Mr. Tom?" Crissy asked, wide-eyed.

"Yes, she did," he replied curtly. "A high-heeled one, at that. She could have knocked my head off."

"That was the idea, all right," Elysia said sharply.

"Now, now." Matt stepped between them. "This isn't setting a good example for the shortest member of our little friendly group."

Tom and Elysia stopped glaring at each other and glanced at Crissy, who was watching them with growing worry.

Tom wiped the anger from his face and smiled nonchalantly. "It's just a slight disagreement, cupcake," he said. "Nothing to worry about. Isn't that right, Elysia?"

She cleared her throat. "Of course."

"Then why did my mommy throw a shoe at you?" Crissy asked the tall man.

"Because he called me a—!"

"Ellie!" Matt interrupted.

Elysia clenched her teeth and forced a smile in Tom's general direction. "Never mind."

"Don't you like each other?" the child asked plaintively. "Mommy, you have to like Mr. Tom because he's my friend."

Those green, green eyes would have melted stone, which Elysia wasn't. She went down on one knee. "I like Mr. Tom," she told the child. "I really do."

"And do you like my mommy?" the child asked the man.

He drew in a short breath. "Sure. I think she's just spiffy."

"Huh?"

He glanced at Elysia with cold green eyes. "Terrific. Super. A truly wonderful person."

"Thank goodness," Crissy said, smiling her relief. "Now you have to stop yelling at each other, okay?"

Tom and Elysia stared at each other. "Okay," they chorused gruffly.

"Let's have a cup of coffee," Matt said quickly. "Elysia, do you mind?"

"Not at all." It was something to do, to get her out of range of that…that man!

The men followed slowly back toward the house with Crissy in tow. By the time they arrived in the dining room, Elysia was calm and coolly friendly, even to her daughter's hated friend. But she was relieved when Tom left, just the same.

HE BECAME A regular visitor to the ranch after that. Sometimes he came when Luke was there alone with the child, but occasionally he showed up for Sunday dinner. Elysia tolerated him, but she couldn't forget the horrible things he'd said to her, his cold treatment of her. Even understanding his past didn't make him any more welcome in her home. She knew that he was just pretending to tolerate her company so that he could spend time with his daughter.

She still wasn't sure if he might try to claim custody of Crissy, and it made her nervous. She saw the way he looked at the child, with pride and tenderness. Crissy was equally fond of him. It was going to complicate Elysia's life, but she didn't know what to do. Tom had every right to see his child. But it cut right into Elysia's heart every time she saw him. The past might be over, but her feelings for him had never wavered. They grew harder to contain as she saw that rare tenderness he displayed with Crissy. With no one else was he as open, as vulnerable. To make matters worse, when Elysia came into a room, he seemed to freeze over.

She didn't know that it was jealousy motivating him, that seeing her with Matt that evening had provoked all sorts of doubts about her feelings.

She was getting Sunday dinner when Tom came into the kitchen to ask for cups to go with the carafe of coffee.

"They're in that cupboard." With her hands busy making rolls, she had to nod with her head toward the cabinets.

"I'll get them."

She kneaded risen dough, trying not to notice how nice he looked in slacks and a dark jacket with a delicately red striped shirt and paisley tie. He wore his hair short and neat but she had fantasies about how he might look with his hair tousled or down around his shoulders like his Native American ancestors...

"Crissy wants to know if you'll let her come home with me to meet Moose," he said.

She froze. She knew she shouldn't be thinking of making up excuses, but she was.

"I know you don't approve," he said quietly. "But she's my child, too."

She glanced at him worriedly and then away again. "It isn't that I don't approve," she faltered.

He put the cups down and went to stand close behind her. "But you want her to like Matt, is that it?" he demanded.

She whirled. "Whatever made you ask that?"

He searched her wide eyes. "You're involved with him, aren't you?" he demanded.

She grimaced. "No, I'm not," she said through her teeth. "But I wish I were. He's handsome and sexy and…"

"Experienced," he said for her, bitterly.

The tone of his voice slowed her down. She looked at him quietly, seeing emotional scars that probably were invisible to most people. They were vivid to her, perhaps because they shared the same sort of past.

"Experience doesn't make a man," she replied. "There are many things much more important."

"Such as?"

"Tenderness," she said promptly. "The ability to carry on a conversation. Intelligence. A sense of humor."

He glared down at her. "I suppose Matt has all those qualities," he said.

"He's my friend," she told him. "Only my friend."

His green eyes narrowed. "And what am I?"

Her heart jumped. She didn't want to be pinned down with such a question. She turned her attention back to her dough.

"We were friends once," he continued, as if she'd spoken. "I valued your opinion. We got along well together."

"All that changed," she reminded him.

"Yes. I got drunk and made the mistake of my life," he said bitterly. "I've lived with it, but it hasn't been easy. Probably not for you, either," he added perceptively. "You were no more a rounder than I was."

She looked at him wide-eyed. "Excuse me, that's not

what you said when that French Don Juan made some loud remarks about me on the street."

He grimaced. "I was jealous," he said flatly.

Her hands stilled in the dough as she stared at him. "You were what?"

He shrugged. "I hated his guts," he said shortly. "I couldn't imagine you with a man like that, but I wasn't thinking clearly. You're very attractive," he added reluctantly. "I can't blame other men for wanting you, too."

His almost unnoticed slip fascinated her. She glanced at him hesitantly. "Do you…want me?" she asked daringly.

His heart jumped in his chest. His face hardened.

She backtracked. "Sorry. Unfortunate question—"

His mouth cut off the words. He'd moved so quickly that she didn't even see him coming. He kissed her a little clumsily, because it had been a long time. But after a minute, as she began to respond shyly, he started to get the hang of it again.

"Of course I want you," he growled against her mouth.

He pulled her close, ignoring her floury hands, and wrapped her up against him from head to toe. His lips were hungry, ardent. It had been years, and she was as soft and sweet as he remembered her. He groaned under his breath and deepened the kiss.

She felt as if she'd died and gone to heaven. He wanted her. She wanted him, too. She pressed closer and whimpered.

Tom forgot that there were people in the other room. He lifted her clear off the floor and kissed her until his mouth hurt. He hadn't realized how much he'd missed.

Now, his lack of love came home with a violence that made him oblivious to everything else. In all the world, there was only one woman for him, and he had her in his arms right now.

She felt him stiffen finally and her feet touched the floor. He was breathing roughly, but he didn't look as if he felt the least bit guilty. He touched her face gently and brushed the hair back from her face.

"You don't look a day older than you did in New York," he said unsteadily. "You're as lovely as you were then."

She searched his face with eyes that were just as inquisitive as his. She wanted to believe him, she wanted to trust him. But they weren't married and he wanted his daughter. She hesitated.

He drew in a slow breath. "It's too soon, isn't it?" he asked. "All right. Suppose you go out with me, just the two of us, tomorrow night? I'll take you out to eat and we'll find somewhere to dance."

"In Jacobsville?"

"In Houston," he informed. "We'll need to leave about five. Can you close up early?"

"I will," she said immediately.

He smiled, and his whole face changed. "Maybe they're right about second chances," he said. "I've missed you."

She knew those words came hard to him. She smiled back. It was like the sun coming out after a long storm.

BUT THE SHADOWS LINGERED, TOO. That night, after he went home, Tom had nightmares. His father's mocking, hateful words echoed over and over again in his ears. He wanted Elysia, but the barrier between his brain and his body still existed. Love was a weakness. Sex was a bigger one. His one taste of her had left him aching for months afterward. What would it be like, now, if he gave in to her? Could he really trust her not to want revenge for the emotional pain she'd suffered after his cold rejection, for leaving her alone to bear their child?

He was tormented by doubts and irrational fears. By morning, he was already regretting his impulsive invitation to Elysia for supper. If he could have found a single logical excuse for backing out, he would have. But as things went, he was forced to go.

WHEN HE WENT to pick her up, he found Elysia wearing a very pretty black lacy dress with short sleeves and a black velvet jacket. She looked elegant and expensive. Considering her inherited wealth, and the amount of money she seemed to earn with her exclusive boutique, it was no wonder that she had the right sort of clothes for any occasion. He remembered painfully well the simple black crepe sheath she'd worn the night he'd seduced her in New York City. It had been a cheap dress, and looked it. The one she was wearing tonight was probably a designer model. With her blond hair in a neat chignon and her pretty feet in simple black high heels, she was a knockout.

"You're staring," she said.

He chuckled. "I suppose I am. You look very nice."

"Thanks. So do you." He was wearing a dark suit, which emphasized his own dark complexion. He looked remote and elegant and very sexy. She lowered her eyes and spoke to his chin. "Are you sure you want to do this?"

Hearing her repeat aloud his own doubts startled him.

She glanced up into his eyes and saw the indecision there. "I thought you might be regretting it," she said with a forced smile. "All of this was rather forced on you, wasn't it? You just wanted someone for a night, and now you have a past and a child to show for it." She sighed heavily. "I'm sorry. If I'd been more streetwise than I was—"

"Crissy is a treasure," he said, interrupting her. "I'll never regret her."

She brightened a little. "Honestly?"

He smiled. "Honestly." He glanced around. "Speaking of Crissy, where is she?"

"There's a carnival in town. Luke took her to eat cotton candy and go on the rides," she replied. "After he'd made sure they were safe, of course." She grinned. "He's very protective of her."

"I noticed. I like Luke," he added.

"So do I. He was my guardian angel when our father was still alive." She searched his bitter eyes. "Oh, Tom, we didn't have much of a childhood, either of us, did we?"

His jaw tautened. "No. It wasn't my father's fault, but that doesn't make the memories any easier." He reached out slowly and touched her soft hair. He grimaced as he moved a little closer, his smile almost apologetic. "I'm not used to touching, or being touched. It's hard for me to talk about how I feel, much less show it."

"I understand."

His dark green eyes narrowed thoughtfully. "Yes, I think you do." He searched her face. "Could you live with it, though, from day to day? You'd have no guarantee that I could ever be like a normal man."

"If by normal you mean ready, willing and able to sleep with every woman you date, then I'd just as soon have you the way you are," she said flatly. "I'm not risking my life with a man who sees women as a party favor."

He chuckled softly. "Funny, that's just how I feel about women who are rounders."

"See? We have plenty of things in common."

"We always did. You were the only thing that made New York City bearable, and I never even told you. Just seeing you at your desk every morning, smiling and cheerful, made my day." He sighed. "Not that I realized it until you were gone, of course," he added ruefully.

"They say we never know what we're missing until we don't have it anymore."

"So they do."

She frowned suddenly. "You asked if I could live with the way you are," she recalled.

He shrugged, sliding his hands into his pockets. "Maybe it was too soon to say anything. But eventually, I'd like it if we got married. I hope you would, too."

She whistled silently. "There'd be a lot of adjustments to make," she said.

"Oh, yes, there would," he agreed. "Crissy's never

known any father except your late husband. This house has been home for you both for a while. She's used to Uncle Luke being around constantly. I'm not an easy companion, and I like my own way—I expect you do, too. We'd have to do a lot of compromising."

"I like paying my own way," she added.

"So do I." He smiled. "So what?"

"I don't plan to give up my boutique."

His eyebrows arched. "Did I ask you to?"

"It takes up a lot of my time," she began.

"My work takes up a lot of mine," he told her. "But we'd have weekends with each other and Crissy. She'd have a balanced family."

"She doesn't know that you're her father," she said worriedly.

"One day, she will. We don't have to decide anything in the next five hours, do we?"

She laughed out loud. "Tom, you make it all seem so simple."

"Generally life is simple. People complicate it when emotions get in the way." He looked at her openly, with tender appreciation. "You're amazingly pretty."

She flushed. "I am not. I'm five pounds overweight for my height and I have wrinkles."

"I'd be getting there, myself, if I didn't spend so much time chasing Moose out of things."

"Your dog?"

"My small horse. Once you meet him, it will take a while to get used to him. It would be all right as long as you don't have anything fragile."

She cocked her head at him. "This sounds serious."

"It is. He's still a puppy and he has no respect for personal property, unless it's his."

"I like dogs," she said.

"That's because you haven't met Moose."

"When am I going to?"

He eyed her warily. "I was hoping to put that off until the very last minute, just in case. But if you have to, you have to. How about tomorrow? You can bring Crissy with you."

"She'd like that."

He checked his watch. "We'd better get going. I made reservations for supper."

"This sounds like serious eating," she said as he led her to the Lincoln.

"It is. I hope you still like seafood."

Her breath caught. "I do. How did you remember that, after all this time?"

He got in beside her and cranked the engine. "You'd be surprised at some of the things I remember about you," he replied. "You were memorable."

She averted her eyes. "So were you."

He drove quietly for several minutes. "I hurt you."

"Inevitably," she agreed. "But, before…" She cleared her throat.

"Before?" he prompted.

She turned her purse over in her lap. "Before…it was…wonderful."

"For me, too," he said stiffly. "A feast of first times. I'd never touched a woman that intimately in my life."

She smiled shyly. "I know. I'm glad."

He glanced at her ruefully. "Thank God you weren't experienced," he murmured.

"Why?"

"You'd have laughed your head off at all that fumbling."

"Don't be silly," she replied. "No matter what you'd done, it would have been wonderful. I loved you, you know," she added huskily, and she didn't look at him.

"Well, that's nice to know," he told her. "Because I was head over heels in love with you, too."

CHAPTER FIVE

SHE GAPED AT HIM. *"You were?"*

He didn't look at her. "Didn't you know?" he asked softly. "Everyone else did. It was why I couldn't face you the next morning. It had been the most exquisite experience of my life. But I had no way of knowing for sure if you were innocent, even though I suspected it. I was afraid you'd laugh at me."

"As if I could, ever!" she exclaimed. "I worked for you for two years. Didn't that give you some clue to my character?"

"I never knew you intimately," he explained. "And most women these days are very experienced and they expect a lot in bed. I wasn't sure I could measure up to those expectations. That's one reason I shied away from being intimate. At least, until you came along." He glanced at her. "I didn't plan it, either. I drank too much and things just seemed to happen."

"I know. It was like that for me, too, nothing planned." She smiled, the first time she'd been able to smile about her naiveté. "You might have noticed the lack of precautions…"

He chuckled with delight. "All four feet of her," he said with a nod.

She dropped her gaze to his chest and shook her head. "I guess we were both pretty naive."

"I'm sorry," he said gravely, and his eyes were somber when hers lifted to them. "About the way I behaved, and most especially about the way things worked out for you and Crissy. I've missed so much of her life," he added. "I have years to catch up on. If you're going to let me."

She felt startled. "Why wouldn't I?"

His broad shoulders lifted and fell. "You have every right to hold a grudge against me for the past. I couldn't really blame you for wanting me out of your life all over again."

The statement shocked and relieved her. She'd been afraid that he might sue for full custody of his daughter, but he didn't sound vindictive at all. He sounded as if the past left him guilty and empty.

"I won't deny you access to your daughter, Tom," she said honestly. "I wouldn't do that."

He let out the breath he'd been holding. "Thank you for that. I'd worried, you know."

"So had I," she had to confess. "I thought you might feel vengeful toward me for not contacting you when I knew I was pregnant."

"It was bad, wasn't it, having to have her without a husband?"

"Fred Nash gave me respectability," she reminded him. "He was a good man, Tom. You'd have liked him. He was in a terrible condition, with no family to care for him, and he was dying. I needed a husband, he needed a companion and nurse. We helped each other. He loved Crissy as if she were his own."

He grimaced at the thought of Elysia having to marry someone she didn't love in order to live in this small community. Respectability was important in small towns. He remembered when he and Kate had gone to live with their grandmother, and how careful she was about relating any of their past. Elysia had her brother to think of, and his business. It must have been very difficult for her. And she'd gone back to school, managing that as well as a child and a husband with cancer. His mind boggled at the stress she'd lived under.

"What a life you must have had," he murmured out loud.

She met his searching gaze. "It was difficult at times, but I have a lot to show for my sacrifices. I've grown up."

"So have I," he mused. "I didn't realize it until I landed here, but I suppose you had a lot to do with the maturing process. I was a late bloomer."

"So was I," she told him. "I've learned a lot. I'm independent now. I can take care of myself and Crissy."

His eyes narrowed. Was she telling him that she had no need of him in her life?

"What I meant," she said when she saw the uncertainty in his dark face, "is that I wouldn't ever be a financial burden to any man. And that I wouldn't be left dangling if he left me or died."

"I see."

"Not that I expect you to die anytime soon," she added quickly.

His green gaze slid over her flushed face and he smiled. "I'll do my best not to."

She glanced at him shyly as he stopped at a traffic light. It seemed unreal to be sitting beside him in a car after so many lonely years of nothing but memories. When she'd worked for him in New York, they'd often spent their lunch hours talking about the places they'd seen, the people they met. He always had time for those conversations. It had never occurred to her that, as busy as he usually was, he was making the time he gave her. Now, it mattered.

His head turned toward her and he caught her searching gaze. He smiled. "I still can't quite get over it," he mused. "You don't look like a woman who's had a child."

"Thank you," she replied.

"Did you have her naturally?" he asked.

She shook her head. "That wasn't possible. I have a quirky little heart defect—nothing serious, except when I have a lot of physical stress. I had an arrythmia that wouldn't stop and they had to take Crissy. I have a scar. It's faint, but noticeable."

"I should have been there," he said quietly, reproaching himself mentally. "Your husband couldn't be, could he?" he added suddenly.

She grimaced. "He'd just had chemotherapy and he was so sick… Luke drove me to the hospital and stayed with me all the time. I don't know what I'd have done without him."

He was somber, and he didn't speak again until they were almost to Houston.

"You could have died," he said.

She studied his hard face. "I didn't."

He drew in a heavy breath. "All that suffering, all that loneliness, because I was too ashamed to tell you the truth."

"I understand." And it was true, she did. She smiled gently at him. "A man's pride is a hard thing to give up. But I wouldn't have made fun of you if you'd told me. I think…"

"You think…" he prompted, when she didn't finish her sentence.

"I think it would have made it easier," she confessed. "I was very nervous and upset because I thought you'd had dozens of women, and I was so inexperienced. I didn't even know what to do exactly." She flushed, averting her eyes to the darkness outside the window, broken intermittently by the lights of Houston in the distance. "I thought you wouldn't talk to me because I'd disappointed you."

"I was thinking the same thing, about myself," he added. He shook his head. "What a couple of prize idiots we were. At least you had your age as an excuse. All I had was an overdose of pride. I'm sorry."

"You said yourself that we have a second chance, Tom," she replied.

His breathing was audible. "We do. And we're going to make the most of it." His eyes darted toward her face. "You won't get away from me this time, Mrs. Nash," he mused. "No matter how far or fast you run."

"I don't think I want to run anymore," she told him.

"Good. Because I'm getting too old to run."

She chuckled. "You'll get over that if you're around Crissy much more. She loves all sports. Just wait until school starts!"

"I'm rather looking forward to a real Christmas for once," he said. "I haven't had one since Kate and I left our grandmother's house. I miss decorating a tree and having presents to open."

"We'll see that you have both," she promised, her gray eyes twinkling.

THE RESTAURANT HE took her to was in the best section of Houston, an elegant one with no prices on the menu at all and a table near the window overlooking the canal that brought sea traffic into the city. Huge ships were visible in the distance, and she imagined that in the daylight, sea gulls dipped and soared everywhere here.

"This is very nice," she remarked.

"Yes, it is," he agreed. "I used to come here with business clients when I worked in Houston. Never with a woman, though, except once," he added with a cold look.

"Bad experience?" she queried softly.

"She was one of those very aggressive business-women who liked sex as a sideline. I wouldn't play ball and I lost a very big contract." He glanced at her warmly. "If you could have seen the look on her face. She was very attractive and she tried every trick in the book."

"And you wouldn't?" she asked, fascinated.

"I couldn't," he replied. He smiled softly, searching

her lovely face. "I haven't ever wanted another woman. Only you."

She flushed. "Isn't that…unusual?"

"I don't know," he said honestly. "I'm not experienced." Amazing how easy it was to admit that to her. He toyed with his fork. "I just didn't feel anything at all, not even when we danced and she plastered herself against me. She was experienced enough to know that she wasn't having an effect. She walked out of the restaurant in a huff, without finishing her food."

"I guess her pride was hurt."

He smiled. "She called me the next week to apologize," he added.

"I'll bet that surprised you."

"Shocked me," he agreed. "But she was sure she'd guessed why it was like that. She said that I'd been an idiot to let the right woman get away, and that I was worth ten of the men she'd done business with. I got the contract after all."

"I hope you don't still have it," she said icily.

His eyebrows shot up with patent delight. "Yes, I do," he told her. Then he added, "Hers, and her brand-new husband's."

She flushed again. "Oh."

"Jealous?" he teased.

She glared at him. "Of course I'm jealous," she said irritably. "You're the only man I've ever known…that way."

He stared down at the fork instead of at her. "I've wondered ever since that night how it would be if we were totally honest with each other, if we had no secrets at all." His thumb pressed the fork down absently and his jaw tautened. "I've read a lot of books since that night. I think I could make it more pleasurable...now."

She lifted her eyes to his. Her breath seemed to catch in her throat as she met that smoldering glance. "Tonight?"

His cheeks went ruddy. "I hadn't thought about it that soon."

She didn't drop her gaze. "But you want to."

His jaw clenched. "My God, of course I want to," he said in a harsh undertone. "It's all I think about lately."

"I'm glad," she replied. "Because it's all I've thought about since we kissed last night in my kitchen."

His hand slipped across the small table and caught hers, fingers interlacing. His skin felt as hot as her own did. His eyes were steady, unblinking.

"I love you," he said roughly.

Her eyes seemed to melt into his. "I love you, too, Tom," she whispered.

The heat that look generated made her body swell uncomfortably. Her gaze dropped to his mouth and she ached to feel it on her mouth, on her body.

"Dear God, we've ordered food," he whispered with wry humor. "I'll choke!"

"So will I," she confessed, taking a slow breath. "But now that we're here..."

"We might as well eat."

She laughed self-consciously, and so did he. The waiter came seconds later with seafood platters. And they did eat, but lightly. Dessert was bypassed, along with second cups of coffee.

THERE WAS A good hotel downtown. Elysia felt uneasy about going there with Tom, but she was as hungry for him as he seemed to be for her.

He paid for the room very nonchalantly for an inexperienced man, and escorted her into the crowded elevator, holding her hand tightly until they reached the right floor.

He opened the door, guided her inside and didn't even turn on the light. His arms enveloped her, like his mouth. He didn't say a single word.

The bed was king-size, huge. There was only a little light filtering in through the window from the city streetlights and scattered neon signs. She couldn't see him very well. It was like their first time. Except that now they knew each other and it would be an act of love.

When she felt his nudity against her own, she moaned softly with unexpected pleasure. She hadn't remembered that exquisite sensation until she felt it again. Her arms reached up around his neck, her hands buried themselves in his thick black hair as his mouth gently teased her neck and then her breasts.

He must have been reading more than a few books, she thought as she began to gasp and move helplessly under the expert caresses of his hard mouth.

"Here?" he whispered roughly. "And here?"

"Y…yes!" she cried out, arching.

"Dear God, this is sweet," he murmured as his mouth moved against hers again. "So sweet!"

Her legs parted for him. She buried her face in his hot throat and held on, shivering a little as he touched her and then moved down.

But it wasn't like the first time.

He paused to kiss her, until her tense body relaxed, opened itself to the most intimate caresses. She sighed under the teasing of his mouth and lifted her body to meet the slow descent of his hips.

It was a little painful, because it had been so long. But after a few seconds, her body accommodated him easily. He slid into her and lay there, unmoving, his kiss soft on her closed eyelids, her cheeks. His hands lifted her and he pushed, tenderly. She shivered. He did it again, listening to her breathing as it changed. He moved with slow sensuality from side to side, and then again in the tender rhythm. She cried out and clutched him.

"We're like children learning to dance," he breathed into her mouth, and she could feel the smile on it. "I want it to last forever. I don't want to climax. I don't want you to. I want to move against you and inside you this way until we grow old."

"I can't…live…" she said, choking.

He moved again, hearing her soft cry of pleasure. "Yes, you can, sweetheart," he breathed. He rolled over onto his back and moved her on his body, laughing with wicked pleasure at the sounds she was making. His hands bit into her hips, demanding now, pulling and pushing and maneuvering until she lost her head and bit his shoulder in anguish.

"Do it," she sobbed against his collarbone. "Oh, please, please, do it…now!"

"I forgot that part," he whispered at her ear as he moved her onto her side and eased one slender leg over his hip to ease his passage. "Your body is capable of more than one fulfillment. Here…let me…"

He moved sharply and she cried out and convulsed. He felt her body contract and then expand as she shook and sobbed her ecstasy against his damp chest. When she relaxed, he kissed her eyes and soothed her. But he was still capable and showed no signs of tiring.

"Didn't…you?" she whispered shyly.

His lean hand smoothed over her disheveled hair. "Not yet," he whispered back, smiling. "I'm enjoying you far too much to let it end for me just yet." He hesitated. "I'm not hurting you?"

"No!"

"Not even when I do this?" he breathed, and pushed down hungrily.

She groaned, her legs wrapping around him hungrily. "No!" she gasped.

He laughed wickedly as he turned her a little roughly under him and began to kiss her all over again. "If only I could stop time," he whispered into her open mouth. And then he felt the heat rising in him, too, and it was impossible to say anything else.

"Elysia."

She heard the deep voice and opened her eyes. The light beside the bed was on. But it wasn't her bed. And there was a masculine face that needed a shave looming just above her own.

Her eyes opened wider. "Tom?"

He nodded. He touched her swollen lips tenderly. "It's two in the morning. Wake up."

She searched his eyes. There was no reticence there now, no shame or guilt. But there was love, and deep pride.

She smiled.

He smiled back. He bent and touched his mouth lightly to hers. "Come on," he whispered. "Get up now."

He pulled the covers off slowly and looked at her while she looked at him. Her face colored a little, but she didn't avert her eyes until they were full of him. She looked up into his eyes.

"I've never seen a man without his clothes. Not even you, before."

"I've never seen a woman," he whispered. "You look as sweet as you feel."

She smiled. "So do you."

He cocked a wicked eyebrow. "I feel sweet?"

She colored again. "You tortured me," she whispered.

"I know." He bent and touched his lips tenderly to the tip of her firm breast. "I tortured myself, too. I never dreamed it would feel like that. The first time was good, but this was…indescribable," he said finally.

"You cried out," she whispered, searching his eyes. "Your whole body convulsed for so long that it frightened me."

"You aren't the only one it frightened," he managed to say huskily. "No book I ever read prepared me for what I felt."

"Yes, I understand what you mean." She touched his chest, letting her fingers curl into the thick, black hair on it. "You aren't ashamed?" she asked, because she had to know.

He shook his head. His eyes narrowed. "Unless you were taking something, we made a baby," he whispered.

She let out her breath very slowly. "I never thought of taking anything," she confessed. "I…would like another child, with you."

His face fascinated her. It was like the sun coming out. He gathered her against him in a rough, affectionate hug and growled into her throat. "Oh, God, how I love you!" he said roughly. "Love you, with all that I am, all I know, all I feel. I'll never stop, not as long as I live."

"Neither will I," she moaned, holding him close. "Oh, Tom, we're not married and I'm going to be pregnant again…!"

"I've got a license in my pocket," he murmured huskily. "That's why you have to wake up and get dressed."

She was confused. "What? But how, when…?"

"I applied for it two weeks ago, and told them to get your blood test from your doctor."

"He said I had to have a blood test because someone who'd been in my shop had meningitis, the wicked devil!" she gasped.

"Dr. Morris is a good man," he murmured. "So when I mentioned this license to him, he was glad to help me out."

"I'll have him shot," she muttered.

He chuckled. "No, you won't, because we can be married in a couple of hours." He glanced at the clock. "We'll have to put on some clothes, though, or people will stare. Especially at you," he added when he drew back. "God, what a body!"

She chuckled, all her shyness gone. She got to her feet and stared down at him. "I could say the same," she mused.

He got up, too, and hugged her close with a sigh. "I suppose we should call Luke and tell him where we are."

"You can tell him where we are," she agreed. "But not exactly."

"Coward."

She grinned at him. "Where do we find a minister?"

"I'm glad you asked that," he said. "Because I just happen to have an appointment with one at five a.m.!"

"That's three hours away," she reminded him, glancing at the clock. "Not two!"

He glanced down at her body and then at his own, and he smiled wickedly. "Well, I can think of a few ways to pass the time," he murmured, and he reached for her. "After all, practice makes perfect…"

SHE NEVER ASKED how he'd managed to talk a minister into getting up at five in the morning to marry them. It was enough that he had. She spoke her vows in the same black cocktail dress she'd worn to dinner, flushed from the bath they'd shared as well as the excitement of becoming a much-loved and wanted wife.

He kissed her at the altar, and the look in his eyes made her heart run wild. It was like no other look he'd ever given her. He whispered her married name and kissed her with a tenderness that made her knees weak. She'd never dreamed of such happiness.

They called Luke to tell him where they were, and then they spoke to an excited Crissy to tell her their news.

"We'll be home in two days," Elysia promised Luke, blushing even over the phone at his low laughter. "And you can stop that," she muttered.

He cleared his throat. "Sorry. Anyway, I'll take great care of my little buddy Crissy here, and we'll see you two when you get back."

Tom spoke to both of the people at the other end, too, and his heart swelled when Crissy called him "Daddy." He thought he'd never felt so happy in his life. And when he looked at his new wife, he was certain of it.

THEY SPENT TWO days and nights in a romantic haze, barely taking time to eat. They talked and talked and made love and talked some more. By the time they left Houston, they were closer than ever.

When they got back to Jacobsville, two days later, it was to find themselves guests of honor at a surprise evening wedding reception hosted by Dr. Drew Morris and Luke. Half the people in town were there to wish them well, along with Crissy in a delightful little party dress with lace trim. And the crowning surprise was Tom's sister, Kate, along with her husband, Jacob Cade, and their young son, Hunter.

Tom embraced his sister warmly and shook hands with Jacob before he bent to lift Hunter in his arms.

"You look just like your dad, young man," he told the boy, "except for those green eyes."

"I have eyes like my mom," Hunter assured him with a somber gaze. "Yours are green, too, Uncle Tom."

"So they are." He put Hunter down, and watched the child scowl in a perfect imitation of his father when Crissy ran up to join them.

"Gee, you look like me, too," Crissy told Hunter. "Of course, you're a boy."

"Of course I'm a boy," Hunter said belligerently. He made a subtle face at the newcomer. "I can hunt and fish just like my dad."

"So can I," Crissy said with equal belligerence. "I caught a four-pound bass, didn't I, Daddy?" she asked Tom.

His heart leaped as he looked down at her. "Yes, you did, sweetheart," he agreed.

Kate was looking at her brother with open curiosity.

"Why don't you show your fishing rod to Hunter, sweetheart?" Elysia suggested.

Crissy agreed eagerly, and motioned to Hunter to follow her. When they were out of earshot, Kate glanced from Elysia's flushed face to Tom's bland one.

"She's the image of you," Kate said bluntly.

"She was a reporter for years in Chicago," Jacob told Elysia with an amused smile. "I can never keep secrets from her. You might as well just tell her what she wants to know. It's easier."

Elysia grinned. "Well, she's Tom's daughter," she confessed shyly. "He never knew," she added, so that nobody would blame her handsome husband. She clung to his hand.

"He never even suspected," Tom added dryly with a sheepish look at his sister.

Kate smiled at him with pure love. "It looks as though everything has worked out very well, despite the obstacles."

"Indeed it has," Tom said, pulling his new wife close. "Better than I ever dreamed it would."

Elysia pressed against him with a sigh. "Oh, yes," she said.

Jacob put an arm around his own wife and grinned down at her. "Now are you going to stop worrying?" he asked. "If you can't tell a happy couple when you see one, I'm going to get Hank to give you one of his herbal potions to improve your little brain."

"Hank's his dad," Kate explained to Elysia. "He's always poking around in my greenhouse with this herbal medicine book he bought, making up potions for everything from poison ivy to sore feet." She cleared her throat. "And other things."

Jacob chuckled wickedly. "Go ahead, make fun of him, but this last one worked, didn't it?" he asked, and glanced down at her stomach with a mixture of pride and delight.

Kate flushed and hit him. "Jacob!"

"If you like, we'll get him to fix one up for you," Jacob added, tongue-in-cheek. "This one was for a girl, but since you already have one of those…"

"I think we can manage, Jacob, but thanks just the same," Tom chuckled.

A small commotion caught their attention. Crissy

came plowing through the crowd of people with Hunter right behind her.

"She's got a spinning reel," Hunter told his parents in a wounded tone. "All you gave me was an old cane pole with corks and sinkers and hooks!"

"It was my old pole," Jacob told him. "It's an heirloom!"

"I want my own spinning reel," Hunter muttered. "She's a girl and she's got one!"

"She's your cousin," Kate replied. "And you be polite, young man. Manners!"

"Yes, ma'am," he muttered, glaring at his smug little cousin. "I could catch a four-pound bass if I had a nifty spinning reel," he hinted, looking at his father for support.

Jacob sighed. "Okay, son, as soon as we get home we'll go right to the sporting goods store and buy one."

Hunter grinned. "Thanks, Dad!"

"You could have asked me to take you," Kate prompted. "I like to fish, too, you know."

"Thanks, Mom," Hunter said, moving close to his dad's side. "But this is a man sort of thing, you know?"

Kate had to smother laughter. She exchanged a glance with Elysia. "He doesn't think women are the weaker sex, in case you're wondering," she explained. "But every once in a while, he plays with our neighbor's son Buck and Buck's dad is a…well, how shall I put it?"

"A throwback to our more primitive ancestors?" Jacob said helpfully.

She leaned against him. "Thank you, darling. Yes,

that's about the size of it." She looked down at Hunter. "Is Mommy the weaker sex, dear?"

"Heck, no!" Hunter said immediately. "My mom can shoot a shotgun," he said proudly. "And you should see her on a horse!"

Kate made a victorious gesture, and all the adults laughed.

It was after everyone had gone, Kate and Jacob and Hunter on their way to the airport with Luke as chauffeur, that Crissy came up to Tom and gave him a loving smile. "We're a family now, aren't we, Mr. Tom?" Crissy said heartily. "Now you get to be my daddy, and I get to be your own little girl, and you can just tell me everything about Indians."

"Everything I know, pumpkin," he agreed with a loving smile. He hugged her close with a sigh. "And I'm very happy that you'll be my very own little girl. I promise to love you just as much as I love your beautiful mommy, too."

"Oh, I do love you…Daddy," she whispered, and hugged him just as hard as she could.

His eyes closed on a mist that he had to blink away before anyone saw it. But they opened again and Elysia was there. He looked at her with fierce delight over his daughter's shoulder. And if she'd had one lingering doubt about his motives for marrying her, they were all gone in a rush of love. No man could look at a woman like that unless he loved her obsessively.

CHAPTER SIX

TOM HAD MANAGED to get a willing Luke to take Moose to be boarded at the vet's while he and Elysia were still in Houston. But when Elysia and Crissy had moved into the house with Tom, he had grave misgivings about how it was going to work out. He hadn't had time to introduce Moose to his new family, and he was going to hate having to give away the animal. He just knew that Moose was going to be too much of a headache for the other two members of his household.

But he brought Moose home and turned him out into the backyard anyway.

"Can I go play with him?" Crissy asked excitedly.

Tom hesitated. Moose was a happy, playful pup, but he was an elephant compared to the little girl.

"Go ahead," Elysia said, solving the problem, "but be careful."

"Okay, Mommy!"

Tom watched her go out the back door. "We should watch her," he suggested. "I don't think there's a chance that he'd hurt her…"

A sudden scream and the sound of growling made their hearts stop. Tom raced for the back door, cursing himself for not having gone right outside with the child.

But the scene he expected to see wasn't what met his eyes. Crissy was standing beside the steps with her hands over her mouth, shivering. A few yards away, Moose stood grinning at them with a huge dead rattlesnake in his mouth.

Crissy ran to Tom and Elysia. "Oh, Daddy, I didn't even see it! I didn't see it and it rattled, and Moose went right over and grabbed it! He saved me!"

Elysia hugged her little girl close, crying tears of relief. She looked toward Moose, who was playing with the snake now.

"If you ever try to get rid of that dog," she told Tom, "it's grounds for divorce."

He chuckled delightedly. "I'll remind you that you said that," he said, so proud of his dog and so relieved over Crissy's well-being that he was almost euphoric.

SEVERAL WEEKS LATER, as he watched Moose drop something at Elysia's feet and then lay a guilty head on her lap in the living room and saw her wide-eyed shock, he was glad about the snake.

"You said he was worth his weight in dog bones," Tom reminded her quickly. "You said getting rid of him was grounds for divorce."

She looked up at her husband with her mouth open and then closed it, grimacing. With a sigh, she started stroking Moose's huge head.

Beside her lay the remnants of a beautiful lacy black bra, in elegant wet tatters.

"He likes you," Tom assured her. "He only eats clothes if he *really* likes the person."

"That's right, Mommy," Crissy said enthusiastically. "He ate my old orange socks, both of them! He likes me a lot!"

Elysia and Tom exchanged resigned glances.

"He does kill poisonous snakes," Tom reminded her.

She kept staring at him.

He raised both eyebrows. "Love me, love my dog?"

She burst out laughing. "I guess that says it all, doesn't it? Okay." She hugged Moose and then got up and hugged her husband, pausing to kiss him warmly before she retrieved the remnants of her lacy underwear. "But if he eats my new maternity dress, he's had it."

"Your new...what?" Tom stammered.

She gave him a wicked grin. "Remember those herbs Hank Cade sent us from South Dakota?" She wiggled her eyebrows. "Guess what?"

Moose's enthusiastic barks were drowned out by Tom's cry of delight. He whirled her in his arms high in the air and kissed her until his mouth was sore.

Crissy petted Moose's big head and sighed as she stared at the grown-ups. "They do that all the time," she told Moose. "I think it's silly, don't you?"

"Woof!" Moose replied.

"Come on, Moose, I'll give you a doggie biscuit. Honestly, adults are just the silliest people..."

Neither of the silly adults saw or heard them leave. They were in a world of their own, just for the moment, and it was too sweet for words.

* * * * *

GRANT

CHAPTER ONE

THE SUMMER SUN was rising. Judging by its place in the sky, Dana Mobry figured that it was about eleven o'clock in the morning. That meant she'd been in her present predicament for over two hours, and the day was growing hotter.

She sighed with resigned misery as she glanced at her elevated right leg where her jeans were hopelessly tangled in two loose strands of barbed wire. Her booted foot was enmeshed in the strands of barbed wire that made up the fence, and her left leg was wrapped in it because she'd twisted when she fell. She'd been trying to mend the barbed-wire fence to keep cattle from getting out. She was using her father's tools to do it, but sadly, she didn't have his strength. At times like this, she missed him unbearably, and it was only a week since his funeral.

She tugged at the neck of her short-sleeved cotton shirt and brushed strands of her damp blond hair back into its neat French braid. Not so neat now, she thought, disheveled and unkempt from the fall that had landed her in this mess. Nearby, oblivious to her mistress's dilemma, her chestnut mare, Bess, grazed. Overhead, a hawk made graceful patterns against the cloudless sky.

Far away could be heard the sound of traffic on the distant highway that led around Jacobsville to the small Texas ranch where Dana was tangled in the fence wire.

Nobody knew where she was. She lived alone in the little ramshackle house that she'd shared with her father. They'd lost everything after her mother deserted them seven years ago. After that terrible blow, her father, who was raised on a ranch, decided to come back and settle on the old family homeplace. There were no other relatives unless you counted a cousin in Montana.

Dana's father had stocked this place with a small herd of beef cattle and raised a truck garden. It was a meager living, compared to the mansion near Dallas that her mother's wealth had maintained. When Carla Mobry had unexpectedly divorced her husband, he'd had to find a way of making a living for himself, quickly. Dana had chosen to go with him to his boyhood home in Jacobsville, rather than endure her mother's indifferent presence. Now her father was dead and she had no one.

She'd loved her father, and he'd loved her. They'd been happy together, even without a huge income. But the strain of hard physical labor on a heart that she had not even known was bad had been too much. He'd had a heart attack and died in his sleep. Dana had found him the next morning when she went in to his room to call him to breakfast.

Hank had come immediately at Dana's frantic phone call. It didn't occur to her that she should have called the ambulance first instead of their nearest, and very antisocial, neighbor. It was just that Hank was so capable. He always knew what to do. That day he had, too. After a quick look at her father, he'd phoned an ambulance and herded Dana out of the room. Later he'd said that he knew immediately that it was hours too late to save her father. He'd done a stint overseas in the military, where he'd seen death too often to mistake it.

Most people avoided Hayden Grant as much as possible. He owned the feed and mill store locally, and he ran cattle on his huge tracts of land around Jacobsville. He'd found oil on the same land, so lack of money wasn't one of his problems. But a short temper, a legendary dislike of women and a reputation for outspokenness made him unpopular in most places.

He liked Dana, though. That had been fascinating from the very beginning, because he was a misogynist and made no secret of the fact. Perhaps he considered her safe because of the age difference. Hank was thirty-six and Dana was barely twenty-two. She was slender and of medium height, with dark blond hair and a plain little face made interesting by the huge dark blue eyes that dominated it. She had a firm, rounded chin and a straight nose and a perfect bow of a mouth that was a natural light pink, without makeup. She wasn't pretty, but her figure was exquisite, even in blue jeans and a faded checked cotton shirt with the two buttons missing, torn off when she'd fallen. She grimaced. She hadn't taken time to search for a bra in the clean wash this morning because she'd been in a hurry to fix the fence before her only bull got out into the road. She looked like a juvenile stripper, with the firm, creamy curves of her breasts very noticeable where the buttons were missing.

She shaded her eyes with her hand and glanced around. There was nothing for miles but Texas and more Texas. She should have been paying better attention to what she was doing, but her father's death had devastated her. She'd cried for three days, especially after the family attorney had told her about that humiliating clause in the will he'd left. She couldn't bear the shame of divulging it to Hank. But how could she avoid it, when it concerned him as much as it concerned her? Papa, she thought miserably, how could you do this to me? Couldn't you have spared me a little pride!

She wiped stray tears away. Crying wouldn't help. Her father was dead and the will would have to be dealt with.

A sound caught her attention. In the stillness of the field, it was very loud. There was a rhythm to it. After a minute, she knew why it sounded familiar. It was the gait of a thoroughbred stallion. And she knew exactly to whom that horse belonged.

Sure enough, a minute later a tall rider came into view. With his broad-brimmed hat pulled low over his lean, dark face and the elegant way he rode, Hank Grant was pretty easy to spot from a distance. If he hadn't been so noticeable, the horse, Cappy, was. Cappy was a palomino with impeccable bloodlines, and he brought handsome fees at stud. He was remarkably gentle for an ungelded horse, although he could become nervous at times. Still, he wouldn't allow anyone except Hank on his back.

As Hank reined in beside her prone body, she could

see the amused indulgence in his face before she heard it in his deep voice.

"Again?" he asked with resignation, obviously recalling the other times he'd had to rescue her.

"The fence was down," she said belligerently, blowing a strand of blond hair out of her mouth. "And that stupid fence tool needs hands like a wrestler's to work it!"

"Sure it does, honey," he drawled, crossing his forearms over the pommel. "Fences don't know beans about the women's liberation movement."

"Don't you start that again," she muttered.

His mouth tugged up. "Aren't you in a peachy position to be throwing out challenges?" he murmured dryly, and his dark eyes saw far too much as they swept over her body. For just an instant, something flashed in them when they came to rest briefly on the revealed curves of her breasts.

She moved uncomfortably. "Come on, Hank, get me loose," she pleaded, wriggling. "I've been stuck here since nine o'clock and I'm dying for something to drink. It's so hot."

"Okay, kid." He swung out of the saddle and threw Cappy's reins over his head, leaving him to graze nearby. He squatted by her trapped legs. His worn jeans pulled tight against the long, powerful muscles of his legs and she had to grit her teeth against the pleasure it gave her just to look at him. Hank was handsome. He had that sort of masculine beauty about him that made even older women sigh when they saw him. He had a rider's lean and graceful look, and a face that an advertising agency would have loved. But he was utterly unaware of his own attractions. His wife had run out on him ten years before, and he'd never wanted to marry anyone else since the divorce. It was well-known in the community that Hank had no use for a woman except in one way. He was discreet and tight-lipped about his liaisons, and only Dana seemed to know that he had them. He was remarkably outspoken with her. In fact, he talked to her about private things that he shared with nobody else.

He was surveying the damage, his lips pursed thoughtfully, before he began to try to untangle her from the barbed wire with gloved hands. Hank was methodical in everything he did, single-minded and deliberate. He never acted rashly. It was another trait that didn't go unnoticed.

"Nope, that won't do," he murmured and reached into his pocket. "I'm going to have to cut this denim to get you loose, honey. I'm sorry. I'll replace the jeans."

She blushed. "I'm not destitute yet!"

He looked down into her dark blue eyes and saw the color in her cheeks. "You're so proud, Dana. You'd never ask for help, not if it meant you starved to death." He flipped open his pocketknife. "I guess that's why we get along so well. We're alike in a lot of ways."

"You're taller than I am, and you have black hair. Mine's blond," she said pointedly.

He grinned, as she knew he would. He didn't smile much, especially around other people. She loved the way his eyes twinkled when he smiled.

"I wasn't talking about physical differences," he explained unnecessarily. He cut the denim loose from the wire. It was a good thing he was wearing gloves, because the barbed-wire was sharp and treacherous. "Why don't you use electrified fence like modern ranchers?"

"Because I can't afford it, Hank," she said simply.

He grimaced. He freed the last strand and pulled her into a sitting position, which was unexpectedly intimate. Her blouse fell open when she leaned forward and, like any male, he filled his eyes with the sight of her firm, creamy breasts, their tips hard and mauve against the soft pink mounds. He caught his breath audibly.

Embarrassed, she grasped the edges of her shirt and pulled them together, flushing. She couldn't meet his eyes. But she was aware of his intent stare, of the smell of leather and faint cologne that clung to his skin, of the clean smell of his long-sleeve chambray shirt. Her eyes fell to the opening at his throat, where thick black hair was visible. She'd never seen Hank without his shirt. She'd always wanted to.

His lean hand smoothed against her cheek and his thumb pressed her rounded chin up. His eyes searched her shy ones. "And that's what I like best about you," he said huskily. "You don't play. Every move you make is honest." He held her gaze. "I wouldn't be much of a man if I'd turned my eyes away. Your breasts are beautiful, like pink marble with hard little tips that make me feel very masculine. You shouldn't be ashamed of a natural reaction like that."

She wasn't quite sure what he meant. "Natural… reaction?" she faltered, wide-eyed.

He frowned. "Don't you understand?"

She didn't. Her life had been a remarkably sheltered one. She'd first discovered her feelings for Hank when she was just seventeen, and she'd never looked at anyone else. She'd only dated two boys. Both of them had been shy and a little nervous with her, and when one of them had kissed her, she'd found it distasteful.

She did watch movies, some of which were very explicit. But they didn't explain what happened to people physically, they just showed it.

"No," she said finally, grimacing. "Well, I'm hopeless, I guess. I don't date, I haven't got time to read racy novels…!"

He was watching her very closely. "Some lessons carry a high price. But it's safe enough with me. Here."

He took her own hand and, shockingly, eased the fabric away from her breast and put her fingers on the hard tip. He watched her body as he did it, which made the experience even more sensual.

"Desire causes it," he explained quietly. "A man's body swells where he's most a man. A woman's breasts swell and the tips go hard. It's a reaction that comes from excitement, and nothing at all to be ashamed of."

She was barely breathing. She knew her face was flushed, and her heart was beating her to death. She was sitting in the middle of an open field, letting Hank look at her breasts and explain desire to her. The whole thing had a fantasy quality that made her wide-eyed.

He knew it. He smiled. "You're pretty," he said gently, removing her hand and tugging the edges of the blouse back together. "Don't make heavy weather of it. It's natural, isn't it, with us? It always has been. That's why I can talk to you so easily about the most intimate things." He frowned slightly. "I wanted my wife all the time, did I ever tell you? She taunted me and made me crazy to have her, so that I'd do anything for it. But I wasn't rich enough to suit her. My best friend hit it big in real estate and she was all over him like a duck on a bug. I don't think she ever looked back when she left me, but I didn't sleep for weeks, wanting her. I still want her, from time to time." He sighed roughly. "And now she's coming back, she and Bob. They're going to be in town for a few weeks while he gets rid of all his investments. He's retiring, and he wants to sell me his racehorse. Hell of a gall, isn't it?" he muttered coldly.

She felt his pain and didn't dare let him see how much it disturbed her. "Thanks for untangling me," she said breathlessly, to divert him, and started to get up.

His hand stayed her. He looked studious and calculating. "Don't. I want to try something."

His fingers went to the snaps of his chambray shirt and he unfastened it all down his chest, pulling the shirttail out of his jeans as he went. His chest was broad and tanned, thick with hair, powerfully muscled.

"What are you doing?" she whispered, startled.

"I told you. I want to try something." He drew her up on her knees, and unfastened the remaining buttons on her shirt. He looked searchingly at her expression. She was too shocked to protest, and then he pulled her close, letting her feel for the first time in her life the impact of a man's seminudity against her own.

Her sharp breath was audible. There was wonder in her eyes as she lifted them to his in fascinated curiosity.

His hands went to her rib cage and he drew her lazily, sensuously, against that rough cushion of his chest. It tickled her breasts and made the tips go harder. She grasped his shoulders, biting in with her nails involuntarily as all her dreams seemed to come true at once. His eyes were blazing with dark fires. They fell to her mouth and he bent toward her.

She felt the hard warmth of his lips slowly burrow into hers, parting them, teasing them. She held her breath, tasting him like some rare wine. Dimly she felt his hand go between them and tenderly caress one swollen breast. She gasped again, and his head lifted so that he could see her eyes.

His thumb rippled over the hard tip and she shivered all over, helpless in his embrace.

"Yes," he whispered absently, "that's exactly what I thought. I could lay you down right here, right now."

She barely heard him. Her heart was shaking her. His fingers touched her, teased her body. It arched toward him, desperate not to lose the contact.

His eyes were all over her face; her bare breasts pressed so close against him. He felt the touch all the way to his soul. "I want you," he said quietly.

She sobbed, because it shouldn't have been like this. Her own body betrayed her, giving away all its hard-kept secrets.

But there was a hesitation in him. His hand stilled on her breast, his mouth hovered over hers as his dark eyes probed, watched.

"You're still a virgin, aren't you?" he asked roughly.

She swallowed, her lips swollen from the touch of his.

He shook her gently. "Tell me!"

She bit her lower lip and looked at his throat. She could see the pulse hammering there. "You knew that already." She ground out the words.

He didn't seem to breathe for a minute, then there was a slow, ragged exhaling of breath. He wrapped her up in his arms and sat holding her close, rocking her, his face buried in her hot throat, against her quick pulse.

"Yes. I just wanted to be sure," he said after a minute. He released her inch by inch and smiled ruefully as he fastened her blouse again.

She let him, dazed. Her eyes clung to his as if they were looking for sanity.

Her mouth was swollen. Her eyes were as round as dark blue saucers in a face livid with color. In that moment she was more beautiful than he'd ever known her to be.

"No harm done," he said gently. "We've learned a little more about each other than we knew before. It won't change anything. We're still friends."

He made it sound like a question. "Of...of course," she stammered.

He stood up, refastening his own shirt and tucking it back in as he looked at her with a new expression. *Possession.* Yes, that was it. He looked as if she belonged to him now. She didn't understand the look or her own reaction to it.

She scrambled to her feet, moving them to see if anything hurt.

"The wire didn't break the skin, fortunately for you," he said. "Those jeans are heavy, tough fabric. But you need a tetanus shot, just the same. If you haven't had one, I'll drive you into town to get one."

"I had one last year," she said, avoiding his eyes as she started toward Bess, who was eyeing the stallion a little too curiously. "You'd better get Cappy before he gets any ideas."

He caught Cappy's bridle and had to soothe him. "You'd better get her out of here while you can," he advised. "I didn't think you'd be riding her today or I wouldn't have brought Cappy. You usually ride Toast."

She didn't want to tell him that Toast had been sold to help settle one of her father's outstanding debts.

He watched her swing into the saddle and he did likewise, keeping the stallion a good distance away. The urge to mate wasn't only a human thing.

"I'll be over to see you later," he called to her. "We've got some things to talk over."

"Like what?" she asked.

But Hank didn't answer. Cappy was fidgeting wildly as he tried to control the stallion. "Not now. Get her home!"

She turned the mare and galloped toward the ranch, forgetting the fence in her headlong rush. She'd have to come back later. At least she could get out of the sun and get something cold to drink now.

ONCE SHE WAS back in the small house, she looked at herself in the bathroom mirror after a shower and couldn't believe she was the same woman who'd gone out into the pasture only this morning. She looked so different. There was something new in her eyes, something more feminine, mysterious and secretive. She felt all over again the slow, searching touch of Hayden Grant's hard fingers and blushed.

There had been a rare and beautiful magic between them out there in the field. She loved him so much. There had been no other man's touch on her body, never another man in her heart. But how was he going to react when he knew the contents of her father's will? He didn't want to marry again. He'd said so often enough. And although he and Dana had been friends for a long time, he'd drawn back at once when he made her admit her innocence. He'd wanted an affair, obviously, but discovered that it would be impossible to justify that with his conscience. He couldn't seduce an innocent woman.

She went into her bedroom and put on a blue sundress, leaving her freshly washed and dried hair loose around her shoulders. He'd said they would talk later. Did that mean he'd heard gossip about the will? Was he going to ask her to challenge it?

She had no idea what to expect. Perhaps it was just as well. She'd have less time to worry.

She walked around the living room, her eyes on the sad, shabby furniture that she and her father had bought so many years ago. There hadn't been any money in the past year for reupholstery or new frills. They'd put everything into those few head of beef cattle and the herd sire. But the cattle market was way down and if a bad winter came, there would be no way to afford to buy feed. She had to plant plenty of hay and corn to get through the winter. But their best hand had quit on her father's death, and now all she had were two part-time helpers, whom she could barely afford to pay. A blind woman could see that she wouldn't be able to keep going now.

She could have wept for her lost chances. She had no education past high school, no real way to make a living. All she knew was how to pull calves and mix feed and sell off stock. She went to the auctions and knew how to bid, how to buy, how to pick cattle for conformation. She knew much less about horses, but that hardly mattered. She only had one left and the part-time man kept Bess—and Toast, until he was sold—groomed and fed and watered. She did at least know how to saddle the beast. But to Dana, a horse was a tool to use with cattle. Hayden cringed when she said that. He had purebred palominos and loved every one of them. He couldn't understand anyone not loving horses as much as he did.

Oddly, though, it was their only real point of contention. In most other ways, they agreed, even on politics and religion. And they liked the same television programs. She smiled, remembering how many times they'd shared similar enthusiasms for weekly series, especially science fiction ones.

Hank had been kind to her father, too, and so patient when a man who'd given his life to being a country gentleman was suddenly faced with learning to be a rancher at the age of fifty-five. It made Dana sad to think how much longer her father's life might have been if he'd taken up a less exhaustive profession. He'd had a good brain, and so much still to give.

She fixed a light lunch and a pot of coffee and thought about going back out to see about that downed fence.

But another disaster would just be too much. She was disaster-prone when Hank was anywhere near her, and she seemed to be rapidly getting that way even when he wasn't. He'd rescued her from mad bulls, trapped feet in corral fences, once from a rattlesnake and twice from falling bales of hay. He must be wondering if there wasn't some way he could be rid of her once and for all.

It was nice of him not to mention those incidents when he'd rescued her from the fence, though. Surely he'd been tempted to.

Tempted. She colored all over again remembering the intimacy they'd shared. In the seven years they'd known each other, he'd never touched her until today. She wondered why he had.

The sound of a car outside on the country road brought her out of the kitchen and to the front door, just in time to see Hank's black luxury car pull into the driveway. He wasn't a flashy sort of man, and he didn't go overboard to surround himself with luxurious things. That make of car was his one exception. He had a fascination for the big cars that never seemed to waver, because he traded his in every other year—for another black one.

"Don't you get tired of the color?" she'd asked him once.

"Why?" he'd replied laconically. "Black goes with everything."

He came up onto the porch, and the expression on his face was one she hadn't seen before. He looked as he always did, neatly dressed and clean-shaven, devastatingly handsome, but there was still a difference. After their brief interlude out in the pasture, the atmosphere between them was just a little strained.

He had his hands in his pockets as he glanced down at her body in the pretty ruffled blue sundress.

"Is that for my benefit?" he asked.

She blushed. She usually kicked around in jeans or cutoffs and tank tops. She almost never wore dresses around the ranch. And her hair was long and loose around her shoulders instead of in its usual braid.

She shrugged in defeat. "Yes, I guess it is," she said, meeting his eyes with a rueful smile. "Sorry."

He shook his head. "There's no need to apologize. None at all. In fact, what happened this afternoon gave me some ideas that I want to talk to you about."

Her heart jumped in her chest. Was he going to propose? Oh, glory, if only he would, and then he'd never even have to know about that silly clause in her father's will!

CHAPTER TWO

SHE LED THE way into the kitchen and set out a platter of salad and cold cuts and dressing in the center of the table, on which she'd already put two place settings. She poured coffee into two mugs, gave him one and sat down. She didn't have to ask what he took in his coffee, because she already knew that he had it black, just as she did. It was one of many things they had in common.

"What did you want to ask me, Hank?" she ventured after he'd worked his way through a huge salad and two cups of coffee. Her nerves were screaming with suspense and anticipation.

"Oh. That." He leaned back with his half-drained coffee cup in his hand. "I wondered if you might be willing to help me out with a little playacting for my ex-wife's benefit."

All her hopes fell at her feet. "What sort of acting?" she asked, trying to sound nonchalant.

"I want you to pretend to be involved with me," he said frankly, staring at her. "On this morning's showing, it shouldn't be too difficult to look as if we can't keep our hands off each other. Should it?" he asked with a mocking smile.

Everything fell into place; his odd remarks, his "experiment" out there in the pasture, his curious behavior. His beloved ex-wife was coming to town and he didn't want everyone to know how badly she'd hurt him or how he'd grieved at her loss. So Dana had been cast as his new love. He didn't want a new wife, he wanted an actress.

She stared into her coffee. "I don't guess you ever want to get married again, do you?" she asked with studied carelessness.

He saw right through that devious little question. "No, I don't," he said bluntly. "Once was enough."

She grimaced. Her father had placed her in an intolerable position. Somehow, he must have suspected that his time was limited. Otherwise why should he have gone to such lengths in his will to make sure that his daughter was provided for after his death?

"You've been acting funny since your father died," he said suddenly, and his eyes narrowed. "Is there something you haven't told me?"

She made an awkward motion with one shoulder.

"Did he go into debt and leave you with nothing, is that it?"

"Well…"

"Because if that's the case, I can take care of the problem," he continued, unabashed. "You help me out while Betty's here, and I'll pay off any outstanding debts. You can think of it as a job."

She wanted to throw herself down on the floor and scream. Nothing was working out. She looked at him in anguish. "Oh, Hank," she groaned.

He scowled. "Come on. It can't be that bad. Spit it out."

She took a steadying breath and got to her feet. "There's a simpler way. I think…you'd better read Dad's will. I'll get it."

She went into the living room and pulled out the desk drawer that contained her father's will. She took it into the kitchen and handed it to a puzzled Hank, watching his lean, elegant hands unfasten the closure on the document.

"And before you start screaming, I didn't know anything about that clause," she added through her teeth. "It was as much a shock to me as it's going to be to you."

"Clause?" he murmured as he scanned over the will. "What clause… Oh, my God!"

"Now, Hank," she began in an effort to thwart the threatened explosion she saw growing in his lean face.

"God in heaven!" He got to his feet, slamming the will back on the table. His face had gone from ruddy to white in the space of seconds. "What a hell of a choice I've got! I marry you or I end up with a stock car racetrack on the edge of my barn where my mares foal! Moving the damned thing would cost half a million dollars!"

"If you'll just give me a chance to speak," she said heavily. "Hank, there may be a way to break the will—"

"Oh, sure, we can say he was crazy!" His black eyes were glittering like diamonds.

She flushed. He was flagrantly insulting her. She might love him, but she wasn't taking that kind of treatment, even from him. She got to her own feet and glared up at him. "He must have been, to want me to marry you!" she shouted. "What makes you think you're such a prize, Hank? You're years too old for me in the first place, and in the second, what sane woman would want to marry a man who's still in love with his ex-wife?"

He was barely breathing. His anger was so apparent that Dana felt her knees go wobbly, despite her spunky words.

His black eyes slewed over her with contempt. "I might like looking at your body, but a couple of kisses and a little fondling don't warrant a marriage proposal in my book."

"Nor in mine," she said with scalded pride. "Why don't you go home?"

His fists clenched at his sides. He still couldn't believe what he'd read in that will. It was beyond belief that her father, his friend, would have stabbed him in the back this way.

"He must have been out of his mind," he grated. "I could have settled a trust on you or something, he didn't have to specify marriage as a condition for you to inherit what's rightfully yours!"

She lifted her chin. "I can hardly ask what his reasoning was," she reminded him. "He's dead." The words were stark and hollow. She was still in the midst of grief for the passing of her parent. Hank hadn't considered that she was hurting, she thought, or maybe he just didn't care. He was too angry to be rational.

He breathed deliberately. "You little cheat," he accused. "You've had a crush on me for years, and I've tolerated it. It amused me. But this isn't funny. This is low and deceitful. I'd think more of you if you admitted that you put your father up to it."

"I don't give a damn what you think of me," she choked. Her pride was in tatters. She was fighting tears of pure rage. "When you've had time to get over the shock, I'd like you to see my attorney. Between the two of you, I'm sure you can find some way to straighten this out. Because I wouldn't marry you if you came with a subscription to my favorite magazine and a new Ferrari! So I had a crush on you once. That's ancient history!"

He made a sound through his nose. "Then what was that this morning out in the pasture?" he chided.

"Lust!" she threw at him.

He picked up his hat and studied her with cold contempt. "I'll see what I can do about the will. You could contact your mother," he added pointedly. "She's wealthy. I'm sure she won't let you starve."

She folded her arms across her breasts. "I wouldn't ask my mother for a tissue if I was bleeding to death, and you know it."

"These are desperate circumstances," he said pointedly, a little calmer now.

"My circumstances are no longer any of your business," she said in a voice that was disturbingly calm. "Goodbye, Hank."

He slammed his hat over his eyes and went to the front door, but he hesitated with the doorknob in his hand and looked over his shoulder. She was pale and her eyes were shimmering. He knew she was grieving for her father. It must be scary, too, to have her inheritance wrapped around an impossible demand. If he didn't marry her, she was going to lose everything, even her home. He winced.

"Goodbye," she repeated firmly. Her eyes startled him with their cold blue darkness. She looked as if she hated him.

He drew in a short breath. "Look, we'll work something out."

"I'm twenty-two years old," she said proudly. "It's past time I started taking care of myself. If I lose the ranch, I'll get a grant and go back to college. I've already completed the basic courses, anyway."

He hadn't thought that she might go away. Suddenly his life was even more topsy-turvy than before. Betty was on her way back to town, Dana's father had tried to force him into a marriage he didn't want and now Dana was going away. He felt deserted.

He let out a word that she'd never heard him use. "Then go, if you want to, and be damned," he said furiously. "It will be a pleasure not to have to rescue you from half a dozen disasters a day."

He slammed the door on his way out and she sank into a chair, feeling the sudden warm wetness of the tears she'd been too proud to let him see. At least now she knew how he felt about her. She guessed that she'd be well-advised to learn to live with it.

The rest of the day was a nightmare. By the end of it, she was sick of the memories in the house. Grief and humiliation drove her to the telephone. She called Joe, the oldest of her two part-time workers on the ranch.

"I'm going away for a couple of days," she told him. "I want you and Ernie to watch the cattle for me. Okay?"

"Sure, boss lady. Where you going?"

"Away."

She hung up.

It only took her a few minutes to make a reservation at a moderately priced Houston hotel downtown, and to pack the ancient gray Bronco she drove with enough clothes for the weekend. She was on her way in no time, having locked up the house. Joe had a key if he needed to get in.

She spent the weekend watching movies on cable and experimenting with new hairstyles. She drifted around the shops downtown, although she didn't buy anything. She had to conserve her money now, until she could apply for a grant and get into college. On an impulse she phoned a couple of colleges around the area and requested catalogs be sent to her home address in Jacobsville.

The runaway weekend had been something of an extravagance, but she'd needed to get away. She felt like a tourist as she wandered around all the interesting spots, including the famed San Jacinto monument and the canal where ships came and went into the port city. Heavy rain came on the second day, with flash flooding, and she was forced to stay an extra day or use her Bronco as a barge, because the streets near the hotel were too flooded to allow safe travel.

It was late Monday before she turned into the long driveway of her ranch. And the first thing she noticed as she approached the farmhouse was the proliferation of law-enforcement vehicles.

Shocked, she pulled up and turned off the ignition. "What's happened? Has someone broken into my home?" she asked the first uniformed man she met, a deputy sheriff.

His eyebrows went up. "You live here?" he asked.

"Yes. I'm Dana Mobry."

He chuckled and called to the other three men, one of whom was a Jacobsville city policeman. "Here she is! She hasn't met with foul play."

They came at a lope, bringing a harassed-looking Joe along with them.

"Oh, Miss Mobry, thank the Lord," Joe said, wringing her hand. His hair was grayer than ever, and he looked hollow-eyed.

"Whatever's wrong?" she asked.

"They thought I'd killed you and hid the body!" Joe wailed, looking nervously at the law officers.

Dana's eyes widened. "Why?"

"Mr. Grant came over and couldn't find you," Joe said frantically. "I told him you'd gone away, but I didn't know where, and he blew up and started accusing me of all sorts of things on account of I wouldn't tell him where you were. When you didn't come back by today, he called the law. I'm so glad to see you, Miss Mobry. I was afraid they were going to put me in jail!"

"I'm sorry you were put through this, Joe," she said comfortingly. "I should have told you I was going to Houston, but it never occurred to me that Mr. Grant would care where I went," she added bitterly.

The deputy sheriff grinned sheepishly. "Yeah, he said you'd had an argument and he was afraid you might have done something drastic…"

She glared at him so furiously that he broke off. "If that isn't conceit, I don't know what is! I wouldn't kill myself over a stuck-up, overbearing, insufferable egotist like Mr. Grant unless I was goofy! Do I look goofy?"

He cleared his throat. "Oh, no, ma'am, you don't look at all goofy to me!"

While he was defending himself, Hank came around the side of the house to see where the search party had disappeared to, and stopped when he saw Dana. "So there you are!" he began furiously, bare-headed and wild-eyed as he joined her. "Where in hell have you been? Do you have any idea how much trouble you've caused?"

She lifted her chin. "I've been to Houston. Since when is going to Houston a crime? And since when do I have to inform you of my whereabouts?"

He snorted. "I'm a concerned neighbor."

"You're a royal pain in the neck, and I left town to get away from you," she snapped. "I don't want to see you or talk to you!"

He straightened his shoulders and his mouth compressed. "As long as you're all right."

"You might apologize to poor Joe while you're about it," she added pointedly. "He was beside himself, thinking he was going to jail for doing away with me."

"I never said any such thing," he muttered. He glanced at Joe. "He knows I didn't think he'd done you in."

That was as close as he was likely to come to an apology, and Joe accepted it with less rancor than Dana would have.

"Thanks for coming out," Hank told the deputy and the others. "She was missing for two days and I didn't know where she was. Anything could have happened."

"Oh, he knows that," the city policeman, Matt Lovett, said with a grin, jerking his thumb at the deputy sheriff. "He and his wife had an argument and she drove off to her mother's. On the way her car died. She left it on the river bridge and caught a ride into town to get a mechanic."

"Matt...!" the deputy grumbled.

Matt held up a hand. "I'm just getting to the best part. He went after her and saw the car and thought she'd jumped off the bridge. By the time she got back with the mechanic, the civil defense boys were out there dragging the river."

"Well, she might have been in there," the deputy defended himself, red-faced. He grinned at Hank. "And Miss Mobry might have been eaten by one of her young steers."

"Or carried off by aliens," Matt mused, tongue in cheek. "That's why our police force is always on the job, Miss Mobry, to offer protection to any citizen who needs it. I'd dearly love to protect you at a movie one night next week," he added with twinkling green eyes. "Any night you like. A good movie and a nice big burger with fries."

Dana's eyes were twinkling now, too.

Hank stepped in between her and the policeman. "I think she'll need some rest after today's excitement, but I'm sure she appreciates the offer, Matt."

The words didn't match the dark threat in his eyes.

Matt had only been teasing, although if he'd really wanted to take Dana out, all the threats in the world wouldn't have stopped him.

"You're probably right," Matt agreed. He winked at Dana. "But the offer stands, just the same."

She smiled at him. He really was nice. "Thanks, Matt."

The law enforcement people said their farewells and went off to bigger tasks, leaving Dana and Joe and Hank standing aimlessly in the front yard.

"I'll get home now, Miss Mobry. So glad you're all right," Joe said again.

"Thanks, Joe," she replied. "I'm sorry for all the trouble you had."

"Not to worry."

He ambled off. Dana folded her arms over her breasts and glared furiously at Hank.

He had his hands deep in his pockets. He looked more uncomfortable than she'd ever seen him.

"Well, how was I to know you hadn't done something desperate?" he wanted to know. "I said some harsh things to you." He averted his eyes, because it disturbed him to remember what he'd said. In the few days Dana had been missing, he'd done a lot of remembering, mostly about how big a part of his life Dana was, and the long friendship he'd shared with her. He'd had no right to belittle the feelings she had for him. In fact, it had rocked his world when he realized how long he'd been deliberately ignoring them. He was torn between his lingering love for Betty and his confused feelings for Dana. It was an emotional crisis that he'd never had to face before. He knew he wasn't handling it very well.

Dana didn't budge an inch. "I've already decided what I'm going to do, in case you had any lingering worries," she told him coolly. "If you can find a loophole, a way for us to break the will, I'm going to sell the place and go back to school. I have catalogs coming from three colleges."

His face went rigid. "I thought you liked ranching."

She made an amused, bitter sound. "Hank, I can't even use a fence tool. I can't pull a calf without help from Joe or Ernie. I can feed livestock and treat wounds and check for diseases, but I can't do heavy lifting and fix machinery. I don't have the physical strength, and I'm running out of the financial means to hire it done." She threw up her hands. "If I even tried to get a job at someone else's ranch, with my lack of skills, they'd laugh at me. How in the world can I run a ranch?"

"You can sell it to me and I'll run it for you," he said curtly. "You can rent the house and stay here."

"As what?" she persisted. "Caretaker? I want more than that from life."

"Such as?" he asked.

"Never you mind," she said evasively, because a ready answer didn't present itself. "Did you talk to my lawyer?"

"No."

"Then would you, please?"

He stuck his hands into his pockets. "Listen, Dana, no court in Jacobsville is going to throw out that will on the grounds that your father was incompetent. His mind was as sound as mine, and he knew business inside out."

Her heart fell. "He might have been temporarily upset when he inserted that clause."

"Maybe he was," he agreed. "Maybe he'd had some chest pain or a premonition. I'm sure he meant it as a way to make sure you weren't left alone, with no support, after he was gone. But his reasons don't matter. Either you marry me or we both stand to lose a hell of a lot of money."

"You don't want to marry me," she reminded him with painful pleasure. "You said so."

He drew in a long, weary breath and searched her wan little face. "God, I'm tired," he said unexpectedly. "My life is upside down. I don't know where I'm going, or why. No, Dana, I don't want to marry you. That's honest. But there's a lot riding on that will." He moved his shoulders, as if to ease their stiffness. "I'd rather wait a few weeks, at least until Betty's visit is over. But there's a time limit as well. A month after your father's death, I believe, all the conditions of the will have to be fulfilled."

She nodded miserably.

"In a way, it would suit me to be married right now," he reflected solemnly. "I don't want Betty to see how badly she hurt me, or how much I still want her. I might be tempted to try and break up her marriage, and that's not the sort of man I want to be."

"What about her husband?"

"Bob doesn't care what she does," he replied. "He's totally indifferent to her these days, and he's no longer a financial giant. I don't think it would take too much effort to get her away from him. But she left me because he had more money, don't you see?" he added pointedly. "My God, I can't let myself be caught in that old trap again, regardless of what I feel for her!"

She felt sorry for him. Imagine that. She linked her hands together over her stomach. "Then what do you want to do, Hank?" she asked quietly.

"Get married. But only on paper," he added deliberately, his dark eyes steady and full of meaning. "Despite the physical attraction I felt for you out in the pasture that day, I don't want a physical relationship with you. Let's get that clear at the outset. I want a document that gives you the right to sell me that land. In return, I'll make sure the figure you receive is above market price, and I'll put you through college to boot."

It sounded fair enough to Dana, who was wrung out from the emotional stress. "And I get to stay here, in my own house," she added.

"No."

Her eyebrows shot up.

"I'll want you to stay up at the homeplace with me," he replied, "as long as Betty and Bob are in town. Even though this is a legal marriage, I don't want Betty to know that I'm only a paper husband."

"Oh, I see," she replied. "You want us to pretend that it's a normal arrangement."

"Exactly."

She didn't want to agree. He'd hurt her feelings, made horrible remarks, insulted her and embarrassed her with today's womanhunt. But she needed to be able to sell the ranch. It would be her escape from the emotional poverty of loving where there was no hope of reciprocation.

"Okay," she said after a minute. "Will we have to get a blood test and a license at the courthouse?"

"We'll fly to Las Vegas and get married out there," he told her. "As soon as we've completed the legal maneuvers and Betty is safely out of my hair, we'll get a divorce there, which will be just as easy."

Easy marriage. Easy divorce. Dana, with her dreams of returned love and babies to raise, felt the pain of those words all the way through her heart.

"An annulment will spare you any hint of scandal afterward," he continued. "You can get your degree and find someone to spend your life with. Or part of it," he added with a mocking smile. "I don't think anybody has illusions about marriage lasting until death these days."

Her parents had divorced. Hank had divorced. But Dana had seen couples who'd stayed together and been in love for years. The Ballenger brothers with their happy marriages came instantly to mind.

"I'm not that cynical," she said after a minute. "And I think that children should have both parents while they're growing up if it's at all possible. Well," she added, "as long as it isn't a daily battleground."

"Was your family like that?" he asked gently.

She nodded. "My mother hated my father. She said he had no ambition, no intelligence, and that he was as dull as dishwater. She wanted parties and holidays all the time. He just wanted to settle down with a good book and nibble cheese."

She smiled sadly, remembering him, and had to fight the easy tears that sprang so readily to her eyes.

"Don't cry," he said shortly.

She lifted her chin. "I wasn't going to," she said roughly. She remembered him holding her at her father's funeral, murmuring comforting words softly at her ear. But he had little patience with emotion, as a rule.

He took a deep breath. "I'll set everything up and let you know when we'll go," he said.

She wanted to argue, but the time had long passed for that. She nodded. He waited, but when she didn't say anything else, he went back to his car, got in and drove away.

CHAPTER THREE

LAS VEGAS SAT right in the middle of a desert. Dana had never been there, and the sight of it fascinated her. Not only was it like a neon city, but the glitter extended even to the people who worked at the night spots. Dana found the way women dressed on the streets fascinating and almost fell out the window of Hank's hired luxury car trying to look at them. It wasn't until he explained what they did for a living that she gave up her surveillance. It was interesting to find that what they did was legal and that they could even advertise their services.

"Here we are," he said gruffly, stopping at one of the all-night wedding chapels.

It looked flashy, but then, so did the rest of them. Hank offered her an arm but she refused it, walking beside him with her purse tight in her hand. She was wearing a simple off-white suit. She didn't have a veil or even a bouquet, and she felt their omission all the way to her toes. It was so very different from the way she'd envisioned her wedding day.

Hank didn't seem to notice or care. He dealt with the preliminaries, they signed a document, he produced a ring that she didn't even know he'd bought. Five minutes later, they were officially married, ring, cool kiss and all. Dana looked up at her husband and felt nothing, not even sorrow. She seemed to be numb from head to toe.

"Are we flying right back?" she asked as they got into the car once more.

He glanced at her. She seemed devoid of emotion. It was her wedding day. He hadn't given her a choice about her wedding ring. He hadn't offered to buy her a bouquet. He hadn't even asked if she wanted a church wedding, which could have been arranged. He'd been looking at the whole messy business from his own point of view. Dana had deserved something better than this icy, clinical joining.

"We can stay at one of the theme hotels overnight, if you like, and take in a show."

She didn't want to appear eager. The only show she'd ever seen was at a movie theater in Victoria.

"Well," she said hesitantly.

"I'll introduce you to the one-armed bandit," he added, chuckling at her expression.

"If you think we could," she murmured, and that was as far as she was willing to commit herself. "But I didn't pack anything for an overnight stay."

"No problem. The hotel has shops."

And it did. He outfitted her with a gown, a bag and everything in the way of toiletries that she needed. She noticed that he didn't buy any pajamas, but she thought nothing of it. Surely they'd have separate rooms, anyway.

But they didn't. There were too many conventions in town, and they got the last suite the hotel had—one with a king-size bed and a short sofa.

Hank stared at the bed ruefully. "Sorry," he said. "But it's this or sleep on the floor."

She cleared her throat. "We're both adults. And it's only a paper marriage," she stammered.

"So it is," he mused, but his dark eyes had narrowed as they assessed her slender, perfect figure and he remembered the sight of her in the pasture with her blouse open and the feel of her breasts pressed hard into his bare chest.

She glanced up, meeting that hot, intent stare. She flushed. "I'm not having sex with you, Hank," she said shortly.

His eyebrows went up. "Did I ask?" he drawled sarcastically. "Listen, honey, the streets are full of prime women, if I'm so inclined."

Her eyes blazed at him. "Don't you dare!" she raged. "Don't you dare, Hank!"

He began to smile. "Well, well, aren't we possessive already?"

"That's not the point. You made a vow. Until we have it undone, we're married." She stared at her shoes. "I wouldn't go running to some gigolo on my wedding night."

"Of course you wouldn't." He moved closer, his hands finding her small waist, and brought her gently to him. His breath feathered her forehead. "I can hear you breathing," he whispered. "Nervous?"

She swallowed. "Well...yes...a little."

His lips brushed her hair. "There's no need. It's a big bed. If you don't want anything to happen, it won't."

She felt disappointed somehow. They were legally married. She loved him. Did he really not want her at all?

He tilted her face up to his dark, curious eyes. "On the other hand," he said softly, "if you want to know what it's all about, I'll teach you. There won't be any consequences. And you'll enjoy it."

She felt the words to the very tips of her toes. But she wasn't going to be won over that easily, even if she did want him more than her next breath.

"No dice, huh?" he mused after a minute. "Okay. Suppose we go downstairs and try our luck?"

"Suits me," she said, anxious to go anywhere away from that bed.

So THEY WENT the rounds in the casino and played everything from the one-armed bandits to blackjack. The glittery costumes of the dancers on stage fascinated Dana, like everything else about this fantasy city. She ate perfectly cooked steak, watched the shows, and generally had a wonderful time while Hank treated her like a cherished date. In fact, that's what it was. They'd never been out together in all the years they'd known each other. During that one evening they made up for lost time.

They returned upstairs just after midnight. Dana had gone overboard with piña coladas, the one drink she could tolerate. But she'd underestimated the amount of rum the bartender put in them. She was weaving at the door, to Hank's patent amusement.

He slid the coded card into the slot and when the

blinking green light indicated that it was unlocked, he opened the door.

"Home again," he murmured, standing aside to let her enter.

She tugged up the strap of her black dress that had slipped off her shoulder. Like the rest of her abbreviated wardrobe, it was the result of the afternoon's quick shopping trip. In addition to the knee-length cocktail dress and hose, she had a far too revealing black nightgown and no robe. She hoped Hank was agreeable to letting her undress in the dark.

"You can have the bathroom first," he invited. "I'll listen to the news."

"Thanks." She gathered her gown and underwear and went into the bathroom to shower.

When she came out, Hank was sitting on the edge of the bed. He'd removed everything except his slacks. He got up, and she had to suppress a shiver of pleasure at the sight of him bare from the waist up. He had muscular arms and a sexy dark chest with a wedge of curling black hair running down it. His hair was mussed and down on his forehead. He looked rakish because he needed a shave.

"Good thing I packed my razor," he mused, holding up a small pouch that had been in the attaché case he always carried when he traveled. "I have to shave twice a day." His dark eyes slid over her body in the abbreviated gown, lingering where her arms were crossed defensively over the thin fabric that didn't quite cover her breasts from view. "We're married," he reminded her. "And I've seen most of you."

She cleared her throat. "Which side of the bed do you like?" she asked shyly.

"The right, but I don't mind either one. You can have first pick."

"Thanks."

She put her discarded clothing on a chair and climbed in quickly, pulling the covers up to her chin.

He lifted an eyebrow. "Stay just like that," he coaxed, "and when I come out, I'll tell you a nice fairy tale."

She glared at him through a rosy haze. "I'll probably be asleep. I haven't ever had so much to drink."

He nodded slowly. "That may be a good thing," he said enigmatically, and went into the bathroom.

SHE WASN'T ASLEEP when he came out. She'd tried to be, but her mind wouldn't cooperate. She peered through her lashes and watched him move around the room turning out lights. He had a towel hooked around his hips and as he turned out the last lamp on his side of the bed, she saw him unhook the towel and throw it over the back of the vinyl-covered chair.

She stiffened as he climbed in beside her and stretched lazily.

"I can feel you bristling," he murmured dryly. "It's a big bed, honey, and I don't sleepwalk. You're safe."

She cleared her throat. "Yes, I know."

"Then why are you shivering?"

He rolled over and moved closer. She could feel the heat of his body through her thin gown. She trembled even more when his long leg brushed against hers.

"Shivering," he continued, moving closer, "and

breathing like an Olympic runner." He slid a long arm under her and brought her sliding right over against him. "I haven't forgotten the signs when a woman wants me," he whispered as his hands smoothed the gown right down her body. "And you want me, Dana."

She started to protest, but his mouth was already covering hers. He turned and pulled her to him, so that she felt his nude body all the way down hers. He was warm and hard, and even in her innocence she was aware that he wanted her badly.

His lean hands smoothed over her flat belly, tracing down to the juncture of her long legs. His thumb eased between them and he touched her softly in a place that she hadn't dreamed he would.

She jerked.

"No," he said gently. "Don't pull back. This isn't going to hurt. It's only going to make it easy when I take you." His fingers were slow and sensual and insistent. She shivered, and the pressure grew. His mouth teased over her parted lips while he taught her body to yield to building pleasure.

"Does it feel good?" he whispered.

"Yes," she sobbed.

"Don't fight it," he breathed. His mouth slid down to her breasts and explored them in a silence that grew tense as the movement of his hand produced staggering sensations that arched her body like a bow.

He was doing something. It wasn't his finger now, it was part of his body, and he was easing down and pushing, penetrating…!

"It hurts," she whispered frantically.

"Here," he whispered, shifting quickly. He moved again, and she shivered, but not with pain. "Yes, that's it," he said quickly. "That's it, sweetheart!"

She was unconsciously following his lead, letting him position her, buffet her. She felt his skin sliding against her own, heard the soft whisper of it even as the sensations made her mind spin. She was making sounds that she didn't recognize, deep in her throat, and clinging to him with all her strength.

"I…wish…!" she choked.

"Wish what?" he bit off, fighting for breath. "What do you want? I'll do anything!"

"Wish…the light…was on," she managed to say.

"Oh, God…" he groaned.

He tried to reach the light switch, but just at that moment, a shock of pleasure caught him off guard and bit into his body like a sweet, hot knife. He gave up any thought of the light and drove against her with all his might, holding her thrashing hips as she went with him on the spiral of pleasure. He heard her cry out and thanked God that she was able to feel anything, because his only sane thought was that if he didn't find release soon, he was going to die…

"Dana!" he cried out as he found what he craved, shuddering and shuddering as he gave himself to the sweetness of ecstasy.

Her hands soothed him as she came back down again, shivering in the aftermath. She stroked his hair and his nape, pressing tender kisses on his cheeks, his eyes, his nose.

"It was good," she whispered. "It was so good, so sweet. Oh, Hank, do it again!"

He couldn't get enough breath to laugh. "Sweetheart, I can't," he whispered huskily. "Not just yet."

"Why? Did I do something wrong?" she asked plaintively.

He turned his head and kissed her soft mouth. "A man's body isn't like a woman's," he said gently. "I have to rest for a few minutes."

"Oh."

He kissed her lazily, stretching his strained muscles and drawing a deep breath before he laced her close against him again and sighed.

"Did it hurt very much?" he murmured drowsily.

"A little, at first." She stretched against him. "Heavens, it's just like dying," she remarked with wonder. "And you don't care if you die, because it's so good." She laughed wickedly. "Hank, turn on the light," she whispered.

"I thought you were a prude," he taunted.

"No, I think I'm a voyeur," she corrected him. "I want to look at you."

"Dana!"

"And don't pretend to be shocked, because I know you aren't. I'll bet you want to look at all of me, too."

"Indeed I do."

"Well, then?"

He turned on the light and peeled the covers away. She looked at him openly, coloring just a little at the sight of his blatant nudity. He didn't blush. He stared and stared, filling his eyes with her.

"God, what a sight," he murmured huskily. He held out his arms. "Come here."

She eased into them, felt him position her and lift her, and then bring her down over him to fit them together in a slow, sensual intimacy.

"Now," he whispered huskily, moving his hands to her hips. "Let's watch each other explode."

"Are we…going to?" she whispered back, moving slowly with him.

He nodded, because he couldn't manage words. His black eyes splintered as the sensations began to build all over again. His last sane thought was that he might never be able to get enough of her…

HE WAS DISTANT the next morning. Dana had expected a new and wonderful closeness because of their intimacy in the night, but Hank was quiet and reserved in a way he'd never been before.

"Is something wrong?" she asked worriedly.

He shrugged. "What could be wrong?" He checked his watch. "We'd better get a move on. I have an appointment in the office late this afternoon, and I can't afford to miss it. Got your stuff together?"

She nodded, still a little bewildered. "Hank…you aren't sorry about last night, are you?" she asked uneasily.

"Of course not!" he said, and forced a smile. "I'm just in a hurry to get home. Let's go."

And so they left and went home.

CHAPTER FOUR

DANA PEERED AGAIN at the thick gold wedding ring on her hand. They'd been back in Jacobsville for two weeks, and she was living in his big sprawling brick mansion now. The housekeeper, Miss Tilly, had been with Hayden for a long time. She was thin and friendly and secretly amused at the high-handed manner Hayden had managed his wedding, but she didn't say a word. She cooked and cleaned and kept out of the way.

Dana was uneasy at first. Her brand-new husband didn't wear a wedding band, and she didn't like to suggest it to him for fear of sounding possessive. But it made her uncomfortable to think that he didn't want to openly indicate his wedded state. Surely he wasn't thinking of having affairs already?

That was a natural thought, because despite his ardor in Las Vegas on their wedding night, he hadn't touched her since. He'd been polite, attentive, even affectionate. But he hadn't touched her as a lover. He was like a friend now. He'd insisted on separate bedrooms without any explanations at all, and he'd withdrawn from her physically to the point that he wouldn't even touch her hand. It wore on Dana's nerves.

HIS BEHAVIOR BEGAN to make sense the next morning, however, when Tilly went to answer the doorbell and a strange couple entered the house as if they belonged there.

"Where's Hank? He saw Bob at the bank and invited him to lunch," the woman, a striking brunette, announced flatly. "Didn't he say he'd be back by this time, Bob?" she asked the much older, slightly balding man beside her. He looked pale and unhealthy, and he shrugged, as if he didn't much care. He glanced at Dana with an apologetic smile, but he seemed sapped of energy, even of speech.

"I don't know where he is. I just got home," Dana said. She was very conscious of her appearance. She was wearing jeans and boots and a dusty shirt, because she'd been down to her own place to check on her small herd of cattle. She smelled of horses and her hair wasn't as neat in its braid as it had started out.

"And who are you, the stable girl?" the woman asked with a mocking smile.

Dana didn't like the woman's attitude, her over-polished look, or the reek of her expensive perfume that she must have bathed in.

"I'm Mrs. Hayden Grant," she replied with curt formality. "And just who do you think you are, to come into my home and insult me?" she added for good measure, with sparks in her blue eyes.

The woman was shocked, not only by the name she'd been given, but by that quick hostility.

She fumbled her words. "I'm Betty Grant. I mean, Betty Collins," she amended, rattled and flushed. "I didn't know Hank…had remarried! He didn't say anything about it."

"We've known each other for years, but we've only been married a few weeks," Dana replied, furious at Hank for putting her in this position so unexpectedly. He hadn't said anything about his ex-wife paying a visit. "Tilly, show them into the living room," she told the thin housekeeper. "I'm sure Hank will be along," she added curtly. "If you'll excuse me, I have things to do." She spared the man a smile, because he hadn't been impolite, but she said nothing to Betty. Her feelings had been lacerated by the woman's harsh question.

She walked to the staircase and mounted it without a backward glance.

"She isn't very welcoming," Betty told her husband with a cold glance toward the staircase.

"She wasn't expecting you," Tilly said with irritation. She'd never liked the ex–Mrs. Grant and she liked her even less now. "If you'd like to wait in here, I'll bring coffee when Mr. Grant comes."

Betty gave the housekeeper a narrow-eyed look. "You never liked me, did you, Tilly?"

"I work for Mr. Grant, madam," she replied with dignity. "My likes and dislikes are of concern only to him. And to Mrs. Grant, of course," she added pointedly.

As the blood was seeping into Betty's cheeks, the housekeeper swept out of the room and closed the door. She went down the hall to the kitchen and almost collided with Hayden, who'd come in the back door.

"Whoa, there," he said, righting her. "What's got you so fired up?"

"Your ex-wife just slithered in, with her husband," she said grimly, noticing the pained look the statement brought to his face. "She's already had a bite of Mrs. Grant, which she got back, with interest," she added with a smile.

He sucked in his breath. "Good Lord, I forgot to phone and tell Dana I'd invited them. Is she very upset?"

"Well, sir," Tilly chuckled, "she's got a temper. Never raised her voice or said a bad word, but she set Betty right on her heels. Betty asked if she was the stable girl."

His face grew cold and hard. "How does she look?"

"Dana?"

He shook his head. "Betty."

"She looks very rich, very haughty and very pretty, just as she used to." She frowned. "Sir, you aren't going to let her knock you off-balance again, are you?"

He couldn't answer that. The memory of Betty in his bed had tormented him ever since the divorce, despite the ecstasy Dana had given him that one night they'd had together.

"No," he said belatedly. "Certainly I'm not going to give her any rope to hang me with."

"Might think about telling Dana that," Tilly mused. "She won't take kindly to the kind of shock she just got. Especially considering the sleeping arrangements around here."

He opened his mouth to reply hotly, but she was already through the door and into the kitchen. He glared after her. Tilly's outspokenness was irritating at times. She was right, which didn't help the situation.

"Bring a tray of coffee to the living room," he bellowed after her.

There was no reply, but he assumed that she heard him. So, probably, had half the county.

He strolled into the living room, trying not to think about how it was going to affect him to see Betty. He wasn't as prepared as he'd thought. It was an utter shock. She'd been twenty when she left him, a flighty girl who liked to flirt and have men buy her pretty things. Ten years had gone by. That would make her thirty now, and she was as pretty as ever, more mature, much more sensuous. The years rolled away and he was hungry for this woman who'd teased him and then taken him over completely.

She saw his reaction and smiled at him with her whole body. "Well, Hank, how are you?" she asked, going close.

With her husband watching, she reached up and kissed him full on the mouth, taking her time about it. She laughed softly when he didn't draw back. She could feel the tension in him, and it wasn't rejection.

He hated having her know how he felt, but he couldn't resist the urge to kiss her back. He did, thoroughly. His skill must have surprised her, because he felt her gasp just before he lifted his head.

"My, you've changed, lover!" she exclaimed with a husky laugh.

He searched her eyes, looking for emotion, love. But it wasn't there. It never had been. Whatever he felt for her, Betty had never been able to return. Her victorious smile brought him partially back to his senses. Ten years was a long time. He'd changed, so had she. He mustn't lose sight of the fact that despite her exquisite body and seductive kisses, she'd left him for a richer man. And now Hank was married. Dana was his wife, in every sense of the word.

He blinked. For the space of seconds he'd kissed his ex-wife, Dana had gone right out of his mind. He felt guilty.

"You look well," he told Betty. His eyes shifted from her to his friend Bob in the distance. He held out his hand. "How are you, Bob?" he asked, but without the warmth he could have given the man before the divorce.

Bob knew it and his smile was strained as he shook the proffered hand. "I'm doing all right, I guess," he said. "Slowing down a little, but it's time I did. How've you been?"

"Prosperous," Hayden replied with a faint, mocking smile.

"So I've seen," the older man said congenially. "You've made quite a stir among breeders, and I hear one of your two-year-olds will debut this year at the track."

"That's the long and short of it. How's the poultry business?"

"I've divested myself of most of my holdings," Bob said. He grimaced. "I was so busy traveling that I didn't realize I'd lost control until there was a proxy fight and I lost it," he added, without looking at Betty. "Then I had a minor stroke, and even my shares weren't worth the trouble. We're living comfortably on dividends from various sources."

"Comfortably is hardly the word," Betty scoffed.

"But we've got one prize possession left that may put us in the black again. That's one reason we're here today." She smiled flirtatiously at Hank, who looked very uncomfortable, and deliberately leaned back against his desk in a seductive pose. "When did you get married, Hank? When you heard we were moving back here?"

His face hardened. "That's hardly a motive to get married."

"I wonder. Your new bride is frightfully young, and she seems to prefer the great outdoors to being a hostess. She wasn't very friendly. Is she the little farm girl whose father just died? She's not even in your league, socially, is she?"

"Oh, I wouldn't say that," came a voice from the doorway.

Hank turned his attention to his wife and didn't recognize her. Her blond hair was down around her shoulders, clean and bright, and she was wearing a silk sundress that even made Bob stare.

She was wearing just enough makeup, just enough perfume. Hank's eyes went down to her long, elegant legs and he felt his whole body go rigid as he remembered how it felt to kiss her. His face reflected the memory, to Betty's dismay.

Dana walked in, her body swaying gracefully, and took Hank possessively by the arm. She was delighted that she'd bought this designer dress to wear for Hank. The occasion hadn't arisen before, so she'd saved it. "I thought you'd forgotten the invitation," she said idly, glancing at Betty. "We're so newly married, you see," she added with indulgent affection.

Betty's face had flushed again with temper. She crossed her legs as she leaned back further into the desk. Her eyes narrowed. "Very newly married, we hear. I was just asking Hank why the rush."

Dana smiled demurely and her hand flattened on her stomach. "Well, I'm sure you know how impetuous he is," she murmured huskily, and didn't look up.

The gesture was enough. Betty looked as if she might choke.

Hank was surprised at his wife's immediate grasp of the situation, and her protective instincts. He'd been horrible to her, and here she was saving his pride. He'd been set to go right over the edge with Betty again, and here was Dana to draw him back to safety. Considering his coolness to her since their marriage, and springing this surprise on her today, it was damned decent of her.

His arm contracted around her waist and he smiled down at her with genuine appreciation. "A child was our first priority, but we sort of jumped the gun," he added, lying through his teeth as he helped things along. "We're hoping for a son."

Bob looked wistful while Betty fumed. "I'd have liked a child," he told them. "It wasn't on the cards for us, though."

"Children are a nuisance," Betty murmured. "Little irritations that grow."

"Aren't you lucky that your mother didn't have that opinion?" Dana returned smoothly.

Betty stood up. She'd been expecting a pushover, and she was getting one until the venomous child bride walked in and upset her cart. Things weren't going at all according to her plan. "Has Bob asked you about the racehorse? He hoped you might be willing to come down to Corpus Christi with us and take a look at him, Hank," she said, getting straight to the point. "He's a proven winner, with good bloodlines, and we won't rob you. We'll make you a good price."

Why hadn't he realized that Betty might have had an ulterior motive when Bob had all but invited himself and Betty for lunch? He'd thought she'd put Bob up to it because she wanted to see him again, perhaps because she'd regretted the divorce. But it was just like old times. She was after money and saw him as a way to feather her nest—and Bob's. Her body had blinded him again. Angrily he drew Dana closer. "I don't think Dana would feel up to traveling right now," Hank replied, continuing with the fiction of pregnancy.

"We don't have to take her with us," Betty said curtly.

Bob laughed. "Betty, they're newlyweds," he said with noticeable embarrassment. "What are you trying to do?"

"That would have been *my* next question, Mr. Collins," Dana replied quietly. "Although I'll tell you right now that my husband doesn't travel without me." She caught his hand in hers, and he was surprised at how cold it was, and how possessive.

"Oh, you don't surely think *I'm* after your husband," Betty scoffed. "I…we…only want to see our racehorse placed in good hands. Nobody knows thoroughbred horses like Hank." She shifted her posture, for effect. She had a perfect figure and she didn't mind letting it show whenever possible, if it was to her benefit. "You must be very insecure in your marriage, dear, if you don't trust your husband out of your sight with a married woman and her husband. And that's rather a sad statement about your relationship."

Dana flushed. She could tell that Hank was suddenly suspicious. He looked down at her with narrowed eyes, as if he'd taken Betty's taunt to heart. And his hand was dead in hers, as if he felt nothing when he touched her.

Dana felt his withdrawal. She drew her fingers away. So much for the pretense, she decided. "Hank and I have only been married for two weeks," she said.

"Yes, dear, but if you're pregnant, it hardly means you've only been sleeping together since you married, or can't I count?" she asked pointedly.

Which put Dana between a rock and a hard place. She couldn't admit that she and Hank had only slept together since their wedding, unless she wanted to make herself a liar about the pregnancy. She glanced at Hank, who'd started the fabrication, but he wasn't helping her now. In fact, he looked as if he hated being tied to her when Betty was within his grasp. Her husband didn't seem to be jealous at all. It was a frightening thought to a woman in love with a husband whose motives for the marriage had been suspect from the start, and who had admitted that he still felt something powerful for his ex-wife. He'd said, too, that he had no love to offer Dana; only affection.

"Besides, it isn't as if I'm trying to break up your marriage," Betty continued. "Bob and I are in terrible financial shape. That's one reason we're having to give up our holdings all over Texas and our racehorse. Even if Hank doesn't want to buy the horse, he might be able to help us find someone who'll want him. Surely you don't begrudge us a little advice, for old times' sake? It's only Corpus Christi, after all, not some foreign country. It would only mean a night away from home."

Hank was wavering, so Betty advanced on Bob and draped herself against him with a seductive smile, as if she was making him an offer. "Tell him, honey," she drawled seductively.

Bob's face burned with color as he looked at her and he shifted restlessly. "Come on, Hank," he said. "The stable where this horse is kept is right down the road, about ten miles from where we live. We've got plenty of room. You can spend the night and come back tomorrow." He smiled weakly. "We really can't afford to wait any longer. I've had some health problems, so I have to get this settled now. We were good friends once, Hank."

You're being suckered, Dana wanted to scream. *She's using him to get to you, she's bribing him with her body to coax you down to Corpus Christi so she can seduce you into buying that horse.*

Hank felt Dana's tension. His eyes narrowed as he looked down at her and recognized the jealousy, the distrust. He was feeling much too threatened already by Betty, and he was puzzled by the stormy indecision his own feelings brewed inside him. He felt trapped between two women, one whom he wanted to the point of madness and the other who'd discarded his heart and now seemed to want him again—despite her husband.

He glanced from Dana's set, angry face to Betty's coaxing one and felt himself wavering.

"Your wife doesn't have you on a leash or something, does she?" Betty asked pointedly.

That did it.

CHAPTER FIVE

MALE PRIDE ASSERTED ITSELF. "I can spare a day or two," Hayden told Bob with a meaningful glare down into Dana's flushed face. "After all, we're civilized people. And the divorce was years ago. It's stupid to hold a grudge."

Betty beamed. She'd won and she knew it. "What a nice thing to say, Hank. But you always were sweet."

Dana felt left out. The other two took over the conversation, and in no time, they were recalling old times and talking about people Dana had never met. She poured the coffee that a disgruntled Tilly had brought on a tray, with cake, and served it to the guests. But she might have been invisible, for all the attention Hank paid her. After a few minutes she excused herself and left the room, without being really sure that he'd even noticed her absence.

Tilly was headed toward the kitchen with her tray right ahead of Dana's retreat, muttering to herself about men who couldn't see their own noses. Normally Tilly amused Dana by talking to herself, but she was far too preoccupied today to notice.

She went up the stairs to the room she occupied alone and began to pack. If Hank was going away, so was she. She'd had enough of being an extra person in his life, in his house. If she'd had any hopes that he might one day learn to love her, they'd been killed stone dead with the arrival of his ex-wife. Anyone could see how he still felt about her. He was so besotted that he hadn't even noticed Dana once Betty flashed that false smile at him. Well, let him leave with his ex-wife, on whatever pretext he liked, and good luck to him!

It took her ten minutes to pack. She threw off the sundress and put on jeans and a knit top and her boots. She braided her hair and looked in the mirror. Yes, that was more like it. She might have been a society girl once, but now she was just a poor rancher. She could look the part if she liked, and Hank surely wouldn't miss her if she left, not when Betty was ready, willing and able.

Apparently it didn't matter at all to Hank that Betty was still married, avaricious, and only using Hank to make a profit on that horse. God knew he could afford to buy it, and the woman looked as if she wouldn't mind coming across with a little payment in kind to reimburse him.

She was going through drawers to make sure she hadn't left anything when the door opened and Hank walked in.

He'd expected to find her crying. She had a sensitive nature and he'd been unkind to her, especially downstairs in front of their guests. Betty's remarks had made him feel like a possession of Dana's, and he'd reacted instinctively by shutting Dana out. Now he was sorry. His conscience had nipped him when she walked out with such quiet dignity, without even looking at him, and he'd come to find her, to comfort her, to apologize for making her feel unwelcome. But apparently it was going to take a little more than an apology, if those suitcases were any indication of her intentions.

"Going somewhere?" he asked politely, and without a smile.

"I'm going home," she said with quiet pride. "You and I both know that this was a mistake. You can get a divorce whenever you like. The will only required a paper marriage. The property is now mine and I promise you that I won't sell it to any enterprise that might threaten your horses."

He hadn't been prepared for this. He stared at her with mixed feelings.

"It's a big house," he said, because he couldn't think of anything else to say.

"You and Tilly won't miss me. She's busy with domestic things and you're never here, anyway." She didn't meet his eyes as she said that, because she didn't want him to see how much his frequent absences had made her feel unwanted. "I thought I might get a dog."

He laughed coldly. "To replace a husband?"

"It won't be hard to replace a husband who won't even sleep with me…!" She stopped dead, cold, as she realized that the door was standing open and Betty was right there, listening.

Her abrupt cessation of conversation and her horrified gaze caused him to turn, too.

Betty wasn't even embarrassed. She smiled victoriously. "I was looking for a bathroom. Sorry if I interrupted anything."

"The bathroom's down the hall, as you know, third door on the right," Hank said shortly.

"Thank you, darling." Her eyes swept over the suitcases and Dana's pale face, and she smiled again as she left them.

Hank's face had no expression in it at all. Dana picked up her suitcase. "I'll take this with me. If you wouldn't mind, could you have one of the men drop off the rest of my things? I've still got my Bronco in the garage, I hope?"

"I haven't done anything with it."

"Thanks."

She walked past him. He caught her arm, feeling the stiffness, the tension in her.

His breath was warm at her temple. "Don't," he said through his teeth.

She couldn't afford to weaken, to be caught up in some sordid triangle. Betty wanted him, and he'd always loved her and made no secret of it. Dana was an extra person in his life. She didn't fit.

Her dark blue eyes lifted to his brown ones. "Pity isn't a good reason to marry. Neither is breaking a will. You don't love me, any more than I love you," she added, lying through her teeth, because she'd always loved him. Her eyes lowered. "I don't want to stay here anymore."

His hand dropped her arm as if it was diseased. "Get out, then, if that's what you want. I never would have married you in the first place except that I felt sorry for you."

Her face was even paler now. "And there's the way you feel about your ex-wife," she returned.

He stared at her blithely. "Yes. There's Betty."

It hurt to hear him admit it. She went past him without looking up. Her body was shaking, her heart was bursting inside her. She didn't want to leave but she had no choice, it had been made for her. Even as she went down the staircase, she could hear Betty's softly questioning voice as she spoke to Hank.

Dana headed for the front door, and a voice called to her from the living room.

"Good Lord, you aren't leaving, are you?" Bob asked, aghast. "Not because of us?"

She stared at him without expression. "Yes, I'm leaving. You're as much a victim as I am, I guess," she said.

His mouth opened to refute it, and the sadness in his eyes killed the words. He shrugged and laughed shortly. "I guess I am. But I've lived with it for ten years, with taking Betty away from Hank with my checkbook. Funny how life pays you back for hurting other people. You may get what you want, but then you have to live with it. Some choices carry their own punishment."

"Don't they just?" she replied. "So long."

"She doesn't really want him," he said softly, so that his voice didn't carry. "She wants a way to live as high as we used to, on an unlimited budget. I've lost my bankroll so I've become expendable. It's his money she wants, not the man. Don't give up if you love him."

She lifted her chin. "If he loved me, I'd stay, I'd fight her to my last breath," Dana replied. "But he doesn't. I'm not brave enough to have my heart torn out by the roots every day of my life, knowing that he looks at me and wants her."

Bob winced.

"That's what you've done for ten years, isn't it?" she continued perceptively. "You're much braver than I am, Mr. Collins. I guess you love her so much that it doesn't matter."

"It isn't love," he said coldly, with the most utter self-contempt she'd ever heard in a man's voice.

She sighed. The needs of men were alien and inexplicable to her. "I guess we're both out of luck." She glanced toward the staircase with eyes that grew dark with pain. "What a fool I was to come here. He told me he had nothing to give me. Nothing except wealth. What an empty, empty life it would have been."

Bob Collins scowled. "Money means nothing to you, does it?" he asked, as if he couldn't comprehend a woman wanting a poor man.

She looked at him. "All I wanted was for him to love me," she said. "There's no worse poverty than to be bereft of that, from the only person you care about in the world." She made a little face and turned away. "Take care of yourself, Mr. Collins."

He watched her go, watched the door close, like the lid on a coffin. *Oh, you fool,* he thought, *you fool, Hank, to give up a woman who loves you like that!*

DANA SETTLED BACK into her house without any great difficulty, except that now she missed more than just her father. She missed Hank. He hadn't been home much, probably because he was avoiding her, but at least he'd given her the illusion of belonging somewhere.

She looked at her bare hands as she washed dishes. She'd left the rings behind, both of them, on her dresser. She wondered if he'd found them yet. She had no reason to wear wedding rings when she wasn't a wife anymore. Hank had married her because he didn't want Betty to know how he felt about her. But his ex-wife was so eager to have him back that a blind man could see it. He'd never made any secret of his feelings for Betty. What an irony, that his wife should come back now, of all times, when Dana might have had some little chance to win his heart. Betty had walked in and taken him over, without a struggle. She wondered if she could ever forget the look in Hank's dark eyes when he'd stared at his ex-wife with such pain and longing. He still loved her. It was impossible not to know it. He might have enjoyed sleeping with Dana, but even so, he'd never shown any great desire to repeat the experience.

She put away the dishes and went to watch the evening news. Her father had liked this time of the day, when he was through with work, when they'd had a nice meal and he could sit with his coffee and listen to the news. He and Dana would discuss the day's events and then turn off the television and read. She'd missed that at Hank's elegant house. It was empty and cold. The television was in his study, not in the living room, and she'd never felt comfortable trespassing in there to watch it. She had none of her own favorite books, and his were all about horses and livestock and genetics. He read biographies, too, and there were some hardcover bestsellers that looked as if they'd never been opened at all.

Hank didn't make time to read for pleasure, she supposed. Most of his material seemed to be business-related.

She curled up in her father's armchair with tears stinging her eyes. She hadn't given way to tears in all the time she'd been married, and she wasn't going to cave in now, either, but she felt entitled to express a little misery while there was no one to see her.

She dabbed at tears, wondering why Hank had tried to stop her from leaving since he'd said he didn't want her anymore. Maybe it was the thought of ending their brief marriage so soon. It would be hard on the pride of a man like that to have failed more than once as a husband.

After a while, she got up and turned on a movie. It was one she'd seen half a dozen times but she only wanted the noise for company. She had to consider what she was going to do for the rest of her life. At this point, she was certain that she couldn't go on trying to keep the wolf from the door while she fought to maintain the small cattle ranch. She didn't have the working capital, the proper facilities or the money to trade for more livestock. The best way to go would be to just sign the whole thing over to Hank before it bankrupted her, and use the trust fund her mother had given her to pay for a college education. With that, she could find a job and support herself. She wouldn't need help from anyone; least of all from a reluctant husband. There was no alimony in Texas, but Hank had a conscience and he'd want to provide for her after the divorce. She wanted to be able to tell him she didn't want it.

Her plans temporarily fixed in her mind, she turned her attention to the movie. It was nice to have things settled.

HAYDEN GRANT DIDN'T have anything settled, least of all his mind. He was on the way to Corpus Christi with Bob and Betty, only half listening to the radio as he followed behind the couple, they in their Mercedes, he in his Lincoln.

He could have gone in the car with them; something he thought Betty was secretly hoping for. But he wanted to be alone. His ex-wife had fouled everything up with her untimely reappearance. Her taunts had caused him to be cruel to Dana, who'd had nothing from him except pain. He'd forced her into marriage whether she wanted it or not, seduced her in a fever of desire, and then brought her home and literally ignored her for two weeks. Looking back, he couldn't explain his own irrational behavior.

Since the night he'd been with Dana, his only thought had been of how sweet it was to make love to her. He hadn't dreamed that he could want anyone so much. But his feelings had frightened him because they were so intense, and he'd withdrawn from her. Betty's intervention had been the coup de grace, putting a wall between himself and Dana.

But desire wasn't the only thing he felt for his young wife, and for the first time he had to admit it. He remembered Dana at the age of sixteen, cuddling a wounded puppy that some cruel boy had shot with a rifle and crying with anger as she insisted that Hank drive her to the vet's. The puppy had died, and Hank had comforted the young girl whose heart sounded as if it might break. Dana had always been like that about little, helpless things. Her heart embraced the whole world. How could he have hurt her so, a woman like that?

He groaned out loud. He wondered if he'd lost his reason with Betty's return. He'd dreaded it because he thought he was still in love with Betty. He wasn't. He knew it quite suddenly when he saw Dana with tears in her eyes and her suitcase in her hand. Dana had lived with him for two weeks, and he hadn't even touched her since their wedding night. He thought of it with incredulity. Now he realized what his behavior had masked. He'd been afraid of falling so deeply in love with her that it would be as it had been with Betty. Except that Dana wasn't mercenary. She wanted him, and seemed to be ashamed of feeling that way. But she had a tender heart, and she'd cared about him. If he'd tried, he might have made her love him. The thought, once dreaded, was now the essence of heaven.

It was too late, though. He'd let her leave and he wouldn't be able to get her back. He'd lost her. What the hell was he doing driving to Corpus Christi with two people he didn't even like?

As he thought it, he realized that they were already driving into its city limits. It was too late to turn back now. He'd do what he'd promised, he thought, but after that, he was going home to Dana. Whatever it took, he was going to get her back.

IF ONLY IT had been that easy. They'd no sooner gotten out of the car at the Collins's white brick mansion when Bob groaned and then fell. He died right there on the green lawn before the ambulance could get to him, despite Hank's best efforts to revive him. He'd had another stroke.

Betty went to pieces and Hank found himself in the ironic position of arranging a funeral for his ex-wife's second husband; and his former friend.

Back home, Dana heard about Bob Collins's death; it was all over the radio. He'd been a prominent man in the state's poultry industry and was well-known and liked. His funeral was very big and many important people attended it. Dana saw newspaper clippings of Hank supporting the grieving widow. She couldn't imagine that cold-eyed woman grieving for her husband. If Betty was crying, it was because Bob's life insurance policy had probably lapsed.

Dana chided herself for her uncharitable thoughts and threw the newspaper into the trash. Well, one thing was certain, Hayden Grant would be asking for a divorce so that he could remarry the woman he really loved. If Betty was what he wanted, he should have her. Dana remembered what she'd said to Bob Collins about not wanting to eat her heart out for the rest of her life with a man who wanted someone else. Poor Bob, who'd done exactly that, steadfastly, for ten long years. Dana offered a silent prayer for him. At least now perhaps he would have peace.

TWO LONG WEEKS PASSED, with no word from Hank. The next morning, Dana went to see the family lawyer and asked him to initiate divorce proceedings. It would mean dipping into her small trust fund to pay for it, but that didn't matter. She wanted Hank to be happy.

"This isn't wise," the attorney tried to advise her. "You've been upset and so has he. You should wait, think it over."

She shook her head. "I've done all the thinking I care to. I want the deeds made up for my signature and delivered to Hank, along with the divorce papers. I'm throwing in the towel. Betty's free now and Hank deserves a little happiness. God knows he's waited long enough to get her back."

The attorney winced as he looked at the vulnerable, pale woman sitting in front of him. She'd suffered, judging by the thinness of her face and those terrible shadowed blue eyes. He couldn't imagine a man crazy enough to turn down a love that violent and selfless. But if she was right, that's exactly what Hayden Grant had already done. He sighed inwardly. Talk about throwing gold away in favor of gloss! Some men just didn't know their luck.

"I'll have everything ready by tomorrow morning. You're absolutely sure?"

She nodded.

"Then consider it done."

She thanked him and went home. The house was very empty and she felt the same. There would be a new life ahead of her. She was closing a very firm door on the old one, starting tomorrow. That thought was fixed firmly in her mind until the morning came and she began to throw up as if she were dying. She made it to the attorney's office to sign the papers, but she was too sick to travel.

Fearful that she had some virus that would prevent her plans to move, she made an appointment to see Dr. Lou Coltrain, a newly married member of the local medical community.

Lou examined her, asked pertinent questions and began to whistle softly while Dana looked at her with horror.

"It must have been some wedding night," Lou said, tongue in cheek, "because you've only been married a month and I know Hayden Grant. He wouldn't have touched you until the ring was in place."

"Lou, you're awful!" Dana groaned, flushing.

"Well, I'm right, too." She patted the younger woman on the shoulder. "It's two weeks too early for tests to tell us anything positive. Come back then. But meanwhile, you watch what medications you take and get plenty of rest, because I've seen too many pregnancies to mistake one. Congratulations."

"Thanks. But you, uh, won't tell anyone, right?" Dana asked gently.

"Your secret is safe with me." The doctor chuckled. "Want to surprise him, I guess?"

"That's right," Dana said immediately, thinking what a surprise it would have been.

"Come back and see me in two weeks," Lou repeated, "and I'll send you to Jack Howard up in Victoria. He's the best obstetrician I know, and it's a lot closer than Houston."

"Thanks, Lou."

"Anytime."

Dana went home in a cloud of fear and apprehension and joy. She was almost certainly pregnant, and her marriage was in tatters. But she knew what she was going to do. First she had to find her way to Houston, get an apartment and find a job. She'd handed the deeds to her father's property and the divorce petition over to the attorney for disposition. Presumably, he'd have already forwarded them to Hank in Corpus Christi in care of the bereaved Mrs. Collins. She'd burned her bridges and there was no going back.

Unaware of what was going on in Corpus Christi, Dana set out for Houston the next morning, painfully working out a future without Hank while a tall man with shocked dark eyes was served a divorce petition and cursed her until he went hoarse.

HANK JERKED UP the phone, oblivious to Betty's shocked stare, and dialed the phone number of the attorney, who was also a friend of his.

"Luke, what the hell's going on?" he demanded, shaking the divorce papers at the receiver. "I didn't ask her for the deeds to the ranch, and I sure as hell don't remember asking for a divorce!"

"There, there, old fellow, calm down," Luke said firmly. "She said it was the best thing for both of you. Besides, you're going back to Betty anyway."

"I am?" he asked, shocked.

"That's what Dana told me. See here, Hank, you're throwing over a good woman. She never thought of herself once. It was what you wanted, what you needed to make you happy that she considered when she arranged all this. She said it would give you a head start on all the happiness you'd missed out on ten years ago, and she was glad for you."

"Glad for me." He looked at the papers and glanced irritably at Betty, who'd been practicing bereavement for two weeks while trying to entangle Hank in her web again. She hadn't succeeded. He was untangling Bob's finances for her, and they were in one major mess. It had taken time he didn't want to spend here, but for Bob's sake he'd managed it. Now he only wanted to go home and reclaim his wife, but he was holding proof that she didn't want to be reclaimed.

"She knew you'd be happy to have the matter dealt with before you came back," he continued. "Listen, if you don't contest the divorce—and why should you, right?—I can get it through in no time."

Hank hesitated, breathing deliberately so that he wouldn't start swearing at the top of his lungs. The words on the pages blurred in his sight as he remembered the last time he'd seen Dana. He mentally replayed the cruel, hateful things he'd said to her. No wonder she was divorcing him. She didn't know how he felt; he'd never told her. She thought he hated her. What a laugh!

"Can you hold it back for a few weeks?" he asked the attorney. "I've got some things to untangle down here for Bob's widow, and I can't get back home for a week, possibly longer."

"I can, but she won't like it," Luke said.

"Don't tell her."

"Hank…"

"Don't tell her," he repeated. "Leave it alone until I get back."

There was a heavy sigh. "If she asks me, point-blank, I won't lie to her."

"Then make sure she doesn't have the opportunity to ask you."

"I'll try."

"Thanks."

He hung up. He felt sick. God, what a mess he'd made of his life!

Betty sidled close and leaned against his arm, wearing a wispy negligee. "Poor old dear, is she leaving you?" she asked softly. "I'm sorry. Why don't you come upstairs with me and I'll kiss you better?"

He looked at her as if he hadn't heard correctly. "Betty, your husband was buried week before last," he said.

She shrugged. "He'd run out of money and he was barely able to get around by himself." She smiled in a shallow, childlike way, and he realized that she was just that—childlike. She had no depth of emotion at all, just a set of wants and needs that she satisfied the best she knew how, with her body. He'd lived with her for two years, ached for her for ten more, and he'd never known the sort of person she really was until he became involved with Dana. Now he could see the real difference between the two women.

He removed her hand from his arm. "I have some things to finish," he told her. "We'll talk later. Okay?"

She smiled. "Okay, lover."

CHAPTER SIX

IT TOOK ALL of another ten days for Hayden to wrap up the odds and ends of Bob's life and get his affairs safely into the hands of a good local attorney. Bob had an attorney, but the man had been evasive and almost impossible to locate. Finally it had taken the threat of litigation to get him to turn over needed documents. And afterward, the man—who had a degree in law from an interesting but unaccredited law school overseas—had vanished. It was no wonder that Bob had lost most of his money. The charlatan had embezzled it. Fortunately there would be enough left, added to the life insurance, to keep Betty fairly secure if she was careful.

It was only as he explained things to her and she realized that he wasn't going to propose marriage that she came apart for real.

"But you love me," she exclaimed. "You always have. Look at how quickly you married that child just so I wouldn't think you were carrying a torch for me!"

"It might have started that way," he replied quietly. "It didn't end that way. I can't afford to lose her now."

"Oh, she's got money, I guess."

He frowned. "No. She hasn't a dime in the world.

Do you always ascribe mercenary reasons to every decision?"

"Of course I do," she said, and smiled faintly. "Security is the most important thing in the world. I didn't have anything when I was a child. I went hungry sometimes. I promised myself it would never happen to me." She made an awkward gesture with her shoulder. "That's why I left you, you know. You were heading into debt and I was scared. I did love you, in my way, but there was Bob and he had a lot of money and he wanted me." She smiled. "I had no choice, really."

"I don't suppose you did." He was remembering that Dana had nothing, and she was giving him the only thing of worth in her possession, those deeds to the land, so that he wouldn't face the threat of some dangerously noisy neighbor. He could have kicked himself for letting her walk out of the house in the first place.

"I felt sort of sorry for her," she added thoughtfully. "She isn't sophisticated, is she? She was afraid of me." Her eyebrows met. "Why won't you sleep with her?"

He averted her eyes. "That's none of your business."

"It is, in a way. You won't sleep with me, either. Why?"

He grimaced. "I don't want you," he admitted reluctantly. "I'm sorry."

"You used to," she recalled. "You wanted me all the time. I thought it was going to kill you when I walked out."

"It damned near did. But things have changed." His eyes were sad and quiet. "I am sorry, Betty. For your loss, for everything."

"Bob wasn't a bad man," she said. "I was fond of him. I guess I'll miss him, in a way." She looked up. "You're sure about not wanting me?"

He nodded.

She sighed and smiled again. "Well, that's that. At least I'll have enough money to make ends meet, thanks to you. And I'm still young enough to make a good third marriage!"

On that note, he said his goodbyes and went back to the motel where he'd been staying. It felt nice to have the weight of Betty's disastrous finances off his shoulders, although he'd enjoyed untangling the mess. Now he was going to go home and work on his own problems.

He looked at the divorce petition and the deeds and his eyes narrowed. Dana had wasted no time at all turning over the ranch to him. He began to frown. Where was she going to live without her house?

He picked up the phone and dialed the attorney's number, but he was told that Luke was in court on a case and couldn't be reached. Really worried now, he dialed the Mobry ranch number. It rang twice and the line was connected. He started to speak. Just as he did, a mechanical voice informed him that the number had been disconnected.

Frustrated and worried, his next call was to his own house, where he found Tilly.

"All right, what the hell's going on? Where did Dana go?" he demanded without preamble.

"She wouldn't let me call you," Tilly said stiffly. "I begged, but she wouldn't budge. I gave my word. Couldn't break it."

"Where is she?"

"She's left," came the terse reply. "Said you had the deeds and that Joe and Ernie would keep watch over the place until you made other arrangements, but you'd have to pay them."

"Oh, to hell with the ranch!" he snapped. "Where is she?"

"Took a cab to the bus station. Got the bus to Houston. I don't know where she went from there."

Hope raised its head. "Houston! Tilly, you're a wonder!"

"There's, uh, something else. The nurse who works for Dr. Lou Coltrain is a cousin of mine. Seems Dana went to see Lou before she left town. If you don't find her pretty soon, you're going to be looking for two people instead of one," she said, and hung up.

He stared at the telephone blankly and felt all the blood draining out of his face. Dana was pregnant? He counted back to their wedding night and realized that neither of them had even thought about precautions. His Dana was going to have a baby, and she'd left him! What an idiot he'd been!

He called the airport. Houston was a good place to start, thanks to Tilly, who'd saved him hours of tracking. But it was a big city, and he didn't even know where to start. He cursed himself for every painful thing he'd ever said to her. It couldn't be too late to convince her how much he cared, it just couldn't!

HE SOON REALIZED how impossible it was going to be to locate Dana in Houston. She had a little money, but it would soon run out if she didn't get a job. He had to find her quickly, so he went straight to one of the better-known Houston detectives, and told him everything he knew about Dana including a description.

"Do you have a photo of your wife, Mr. Grant?" Dane Lassiter asked the man across the desk from him. A former Texas Ranger, Dane had built his agency from scratch, and now it had a fine national reputation for doing the impossible.

The question startled Hank, who hadn't expected it. He looked uncomfortable. "No," he said.

The other man didn't comment, but his eyes were steady and curious. No wonder, because the table behind Lassiter's desk carried a family photo of the detective, his attractive wife and two young sons who looked just like him.

"We're newlyweds," Hayden felt constrained to explain. "It was a quick marriage."

Dane didn't say a word. He was busy writing things down. "Did she run away, Mr. Grant?" he asked suddenly, and his black eyes pinned the other man.

Hayden took a sharp, angry breath. "Yes," he said through his teeth. "I did something stupid and I deserve to lose her. But I don't think I can stand to, just the same." He leaned forward and rested his forearms on his splayed legs in a defeated position. "And she's pregnant," he added through his teeth.

Hank's predicament sounded very familiar to Dane Lassiter. He knew all about pregnant women who ran away.

"We'll find her," Dane told the man, not so distant

now. "You've given us some good leads, we'll check them out. Where can I reach you?"

Hayden gave the name of a local hotel. "I'll be here until I hear from you," he added, and he had the look of a man who planned to stay there until the turn of the century if that's how long it took.

"Okay. I'll get right on it." He stood up and shook hands. "Women need a lot of tenderness. They get hurt easily, and they keep secrets," he said surprisingly. "But if it helps, you learn how to cope with it after a while."

Hayden smiled. "Thanks."

Dane shrugged. He smiled back. "I've been married a long time. Nobody starts out in paradise. You sort of have to work up to it."

"I'll remember that. I hope I get the chance to find out firsthand."

It took two days for Dane to track Dana to a small boarding house outside Houston. During that time, Hayden lost sleep and thought torturously of all the things that could have happened to his errant, pregnant wife. It didn't improve his temper, or his heartache.

When Dane called, he was over the moon. He wasted no time at all getting to Mrs. Harper's Boarding House, but when he pulled up at the front steps in the Lincoln he'd rented at the airport on his arrival in Houston, he didn't know quite what to say. He stared at the big white house with longing and apprehension. His wife was in there, but she didn't want him. She'd tried to divorce him, had moved here and she'd made a good effort to erase her presence from his life. She hadn't even said a word to him about her pregnancy. How did he talk to her, what did he say to cancel out all the hurts he'd dealt her?

He got out of the car and approached the house slowly. His steps dragged, because he dreaded what was coming. He went up and rang the doorbell. A plump, smiling elderly woman opened the door.

"May I help you?" she asked politely.

"I'm Hayden Grant," he said in a subdued tone. "My wife lives here, I believe. Her name is Dana."

"Miss Mobry is your wife?" she asked, puzzled. "But I'm sure she said she wasn't married."

"She's very much married," he replied. He removed his cream-colored Stetson, belatedly, and let the hand holding it drop to his side. "I'd like to see her."

She gnawed on her lip, frowning. "Well, she's not here at the moment," she said. "She went to see that new adventure movie playing at the shopping center. With Mr. Coleman, that is."

He looked vaguely homicidal. "Who's Mr. Coleman?" he asked shortly.

"He lives here, too," she stammered, made nervous by the black glitter of his eyes. "He's a very nice young man..."

"Which shopping center and which movie?" he demanded.

She told him. She didn't dare not to.

He stomped back to his car, slammed into it and skidded on his way out the driveway.

"Oh, dear, oh, dear," Mrs. Harper mumbled. "I wonder if I shouldn't have mentioned that David is eleven years old..."

SADLY UNAWARE OF the age of Dana's "date," Hank drove to the shopping center, parked the car and went straight to the theater. As luck would have it, the feature was just ending, so people were pouring out of three exits. He stood, glaring, until he spotted Dana.

She was talking to a small boy in a baseball cap, her face animated, smiling. His heart jumped as he watched her come out of the big building. He loved her. He hadn't known. He honestly hadn't known. His heart accelerated wildly, but his eyes began to glow from within, quiet and watchful and adoring.

Dana was too far away to see his expression. But she spotted him at once and stopped dead in her tracks. The boy was saying something, but she wasn't listening. Her face was stark white.

Hank approached her, alert to any sudden movement. If she tried to run, he'd have her before she got three steps.

But she didn't run. She lifted her chin as if in preparation for battle and her hands clenched the small purse she was holding against the waist of her denim skirt.

"Hello, Dana," he said when he was within earshot.

She looked at him warily. "How did you find me?" she asked.

"I didn't. A detective agency did."

She looked paler. "I signed all the necessary papers," she told him curtly. "You're free."

He stuck his hands deep into his pockets. "Am I?"

Dana turned to David and handed him a five-dollar bill. "Why don't you go back in there and play the arcade machine for a minute or two while I speak to this man, David?" she asked.

He grinned. "Sure, Miss Mobry, thanks!"

He was off at a lope.

"So you came with the boy, not with some other man," Hank murmured absently.

She flushed. "As if I'd trust my own judgment about men ever again! David's mother is at work, so I offered to treat him to a movie."

"You do like kids, don't you?" he asked, and his eyes were very soft as they fell to her waistline. "That's fortunate."

"That isn't what I'd call it," she said stubbornly.

He sighed. He didn't know what to say, but this certainly wasn't the ideal place to talk. "Look, suppose you go fetch the boy and we'll go back to your boarding house? Did you drive here?"

She shook her head. "We got a city bus." She wanted to argue, but he looked as if he was going to dig his heels in. She couldn't understand why he was here, when Betty was free. Perhaps that's what he wanted to explain. She seemed to have no choice but to do as he said, for the time being, at least.

"A city bus!" he muttered, and in her condition! But he didn't dare mention that he knew about her pregnancy. Not yet. "Get the boy," he said shortly. "I'll take you home."

She went to find David, and Hank drove them back to the boarding house. David thanked her and deserted her. Mrs. Harper hovered, but a hard glare from Hank dispatched her soon enough. He closed the door behind her and sat down in the one chair in Dana's room, while she perched on the bed a little nervously.

"Where's Betty?" she wanted to know.

"In Corpus Christi, I guess," he said. "I'm alone."

"You won't be alone for long," she reminded him. "You're getting married again."

"I'm already married," he said quietly. "I have a young and very pretty wife."

She flushed. "I divorced you."

He shook his head. "I stopped it."

"Why?" she asked miserably, her eyes eloquent in a face like rice paper. "You don't have to stay married to me now that she's free!"

He winced. He reached over and touched her cheek, but she jerked away from him.

He averted his face and stared down at the floor. "I don't want to remarry Betty."

She stared at his averted features, unconvinced. "You've never gotten over her, Hank," she said sadly. "You said yourself that part of the reason you married me was so she wouldn't know how you'd grieved since she divorced you."

"Maybe it was the old story of wanting what I couldn't have, or the grass being greener on the other side of the fence," he ventured.

She drew in a long breath. "Or maybe it was just that you never stopped loving her," she added, and the eyes that searched his were wistful and sad. "Oh, Hank, we can't love to order. We have to settle for what we can have in this life." Her eyes went to the floor. "I'll go back to school and work toward my degree and I'll be happy."

His eyes slid up to hers. "Without me?" he asked bluntly.

She wasn't sure how much he knew. She blinked and gathered her scattered wits. "Doesn't Betty want to marry you?" she asked suspiciously.

"More than ever," he affirmed.

"Then what's the problem?"

"I told you. The problem is that I don't want to marry her."

"I don't understand," she said uneasily.

He smiled wistfully. "I used to envy other men taking their sons on camping and fishing trips with them. I never thought I might have one of my own. But a girl would be nice, too. I guess girls can fish and hunt as well as boys can, if they're so inclined." His eyes lifted to hers. "You like to shoot, as I recall."

"I don't like to hunt," she replied, uneasy at the way he was talking about kids. He couldn't possibly *know*...

He shrugged. "I'll teach you to shoot skeet."

"Okay, but I won't cook them."

He chuckled. "Concrete won't tenderize."

"I know what a skeet target is made of." She drew in another breath. The way he was touching her made her toes tingle. "Betty might change her mind about having a child."

He shook his head. "And even if she did, she wouldn't want it, or love it. You will. You'll want our kids and spoil them rotten if I don't watch out." His eyes lifted. "Tilly's already looking forward to it. She's bought a food processor so she can make fresh baby food for him."

She flushed. "She's jumping the gun."

"No, she isn't," he said with a grin. "Tilly's kin to Dr. Lou Coltrain's office nurse."

"Oh, my God!" she said in a burst.

He shrugged. "So I know. The world won't end because you didn't tell me." His eyes darkened. "I'm sorry that I made it so rough on you that you didn't feel you could tell me."

She glared at him. "I'm not going back."

His shoulders seemed to fall. "I know I've made a lot of mistakes," he said. "You have to make allowances. Until a couple of weeks ago, I thought I was still in love with my ex-wife. I had to get to know her again to realize that she was an illusion. The reality of Betty was pretty harsh, after you."

"I don't understand."

"Don't you?" He sighed. "Well, Dana, I suppose I made an idol of her after she left. The one that got away is always better than anything that's left."

"You didn't act like someone who wasn't in love with his ex-wife," she reminded him as all the painful things he'd said to her returned in a flash of anger.

"All it took was two weeks in Corpus Christi to cure me," he returned. He leaned forward with his forearms resting on his knees and stared at the floor. "She's shallow," he said, glancing at Dana. "Shallow and selfish and spoiled. And I'd been away from her so long that I forgot. It cut the heart out of me when I realized that you went away because you thought I wanted Betty instead of you. I'm sorry for that."

"You can't help wanting someone else…"

"I want you, Dana," he said with a quizzical smile.

She clasped her hands hard at her waist. "You're just making the best of it, aren't you? You know about the baby and how I feel about you and you're sorry for me."

His heart jumped. "How you feel?" he prompted.

"You know that I'm in love with you," she said, avoiding his penetrating gaze. "That I have been since I was seventeen."

His heart wasn't jumping anymore, it had stopped. He barely could breathe. He certainly was robbed of speech.

She jerked one shoulder as she assumed his silence was one of regret for her sake, because he had nothing to give her. "Shameful, isn't it? I was still a kid. I couldn't even let boys kiss me, because I kept thinking about you. I've lived like a nun all these years, waiting and hoping, and it has to happen like this…you have to be forced into marriage just when your ex-wife is free again."

He hadn't known that she loved him. He'd known she wanted him, which was a very different thing altogether. He was stunned for a moment, and then overwhelmed, overjoyed.

"I'm sorry," she said on a long breath. "I guess we're both trapped."

"You'll need some maternity clothes," he remarked, clearing his throat. "Things to wear when we give parties. After all, I'm a rich man. We wouldn't want people to think I couldn't afford to dress you properly, would we?"

She frowned. "I'm not coming back…"

"We can turn that third guest room into a nursery," he continued, as if she hadn't spoken. "It's next door to the master bedroom, and we can leave the door open at night. I'll get a monitor, too," he added thoughtfully. "So if the baby has any problems at night, it will set off an alarm next to our bed. Or we could get a nurse for the first month or two. Would you like that?"

He'd made her speechless with plans. "I haven't thought about any of that," she stammered.

"Don't you want a settled life for our baby, with a mother and father who love him?" he persisted.

He cut the ground right out from under her with that last question. What could she say? Of course, she wanted a settled life for their child. But if Hank still loved Betty, what kind of life would it be?

Her eyes mirrored all her worries. He touched her cheek, and then smoothed back her disheveled hair. "I was trying to live in the past because I didn't have much of a present, or a future, unless you count making money. That's no longer true. I have something to look forward to now, something to challenge me, keep me going." He smiled. "I guess Tilly will make me miserable for a week, paying me back for the way I treated you. I won't be allowed to forget one rotten thing I said to you, and she'll burn the banana pudding every time I ask her to make it." He sighed. "But it will be worth it, if you'll just come home, Dana. Tilly's all aglow at the thought of having a baby in the house."

"We've already discussed this," she began.

He bent and drew his lips tenderly across hers. "Not really," he murmured. "Open your lips a little, I can't taste you like this."

"I don't wa…"

"Ummm, that's it," he whispered gently, and deepened the kiss.

She forgot what she was trying to think to say to him. Her arms curled up around his neck and she let him lift her over his legs, so that he could hold her gently across his body. He was gentle and slow, and very thorough. When he finally lifted his head, she couldn't think at all.

"I'm going to like being a father," he assured her. "I won't mind sitting up with you when he's teething or giving bottles or changing diapers."

"That's nice."

He smiled. "Do you have a lot to pack?"

"Just a few skirts and blouses and shoes. But I haven't said I'm going with you."

"What's holding you back?" he asked gently.

"You haven't explained why you don't want Betty back."

"Oh. That." He shrugged. "I don't love her. I'm not sure I ever did. I wanted her, but there's a big difference in lust and love."

"Are you sure?"

"Considering the sort of man I am—and I think you know me pretty well by now—do you think I'm capable of making love to one woman when I'm in love with someone else?"

She searched his eyes. "Well, no, I don't think so. You're pretty old-fashioned like that."

He nodded. "So how could I have made love to you so completely that one time if I'd really been in love with Betty?"

"I'm sure most men wouldn't have refused something that was offered."

"We're talking about me. Would I?"

She grimaced. "No."

"That being the case, making love to you was something of a declaration of my feelings, wasn't it?"

It was. She caught her breath. "Oh, my goodness. I never considered that."

"Neither did I until I was well on my way to Corpus Christi," he admitted. "I called it guilt and remorse and misplaced emotion, I denied it to you and myself. But in the end, I came back because I loved you. And you weren't there." He smiled sadly. "I thought you'd fight Betty. I never expected you to run."

"I didn't think you wanted me. Women only fight when they know they're loved. I didn't." She searched his eyes, fascinated. "I don't guess you'd like to…say it?"

He grimaced. "Not really."

"Oh."

"But I could. If it matters that much." He looked down at her stomach. "I guess kids like to hear it, too, don't they?"

She nodded. "All the time."

He cleared his throat. "Okay. Give me a minute to get used to the idea."

She smiled with excitement and growing delight. "You can have as much as you need."

"Okay. I...love you."

Her eyebrows rose.

"I love you," he repeated, and this time it sounded as if he meant it. He stared down at her with wonder. "By God, I do," he whispered huskily. "With all my heart, Dana, even if I didn't realize it."

She moved closer and slid her face into his hot throat, curling into him like a kitten. "I love you, too, Hank."

He smiled crookedly, staring past her head to the door. He hadn't expected it to be so easy to confess his deepest emotions. He'd never done it before, not even with Betty. His arms contracted. "I guess we're not the first people who ever fell in love."

"It feels like it, though, doesn't it?" she asked drowsily. "Oh, Hank, I wish my dad was still alive, so he'd know."

His hand smoothed over her hair. "He knows, Dana," he said at her temple, his voice deep and quiet and loving. "Somehow, I'm sure he knows."

She curled closer. "Perhaps he does."

CHAPTER SEVEN

THE BABY WAS born at two o'clock in the morning. Tilly sat in the emergency room cubicle in her robe and slippers, her hair in curlers, glaring at the disheveled man across from her who was sitting up, pale-faced, on the examination table thanking the doctor for his new son.

"It's a boy!" he exclaimed when the doctor moved out of sight. "And Dana's fine! I can see her as soon as they bring her out of the recovery room!"

"You saw her already," she muttered at him and cocked an eyebrow at his red face. "Just before you fainted…"

"I never!" he said. "I tripped over that gown they made me wear in the delivery room!"

"The one that only came to your knees?" she asked knowingly. "Dana was laughing so hard, she didn't even have to push. The baby just popped right out."

"I've had a hectic night," he began defensively.

"Sure, denying that it was labor pains, right up until her water broke. 'It's just false labor, sweetheart, you're only eight months and three weeks along,' you said. And there we were, rushing her to the hospital because you were afraid to wait for an ambulance, me in my nightgown, too! And then we no sooner get her into the delivery room when you see the baby coming out and faint dead away!"

He glared at her. "I didn't faint, I tripped…!"

She opened her mouth to argue just as a nurse peeked around the corner. "Mr. Grant, your wife is asking for you."

"I'll be right there."

"Are you feeling all right now?" she asked.

"I tripped," he said firmly.

The nurse and Tilly exchanged amused glances, but he didn't see them. "Yes, sir, I know you did, but we can't overlook any fall in a hospital."

"Sure. I knew that."

He followed the nurse down the hall until she stopped at a private room and stood aside to let him enter.

Dana was sitting up in bed with their son in her arms, tears of pure joy in her eyes as she watched the nurse stuff Hank into a gown and mask.

"Hospital rules," he muttered.

"Yes, sir, but all for baby's protection, and we know you don't mind," she replied with a grin.

He chuckled. "Of course not."

She tied the last tie and left him with his small family.

"Are you okay?" she asked.

He nodded. "Just a little shaky, and I did not faint," he added.

"Of course you didn't, darling," she agreed. "Come see what I've got."

She pulled back the flannel and exposed a perfect

little boy. His eyes weren't even open just yet, and he looked tiny.

"He's going to grow, isn't he?" Hank asked worriedly.

"Of course he is!"

He touched the tiny head, fascinated. The baby was smaller than he'd expected, so fragile, so new. Tears stung his eyes as he looked at his very own son.

Seconds later, the tiny mouth opened and began to cry. Dana chuckled as she fumbled with the gown and got it off one shoulder, exposing a firm, swollen breast. While Hank watched, spellbound, she guided the tiny mouth to a hard nipple and caught her breath as he began to suckle.

Flushed, she looked up to find an expression of pure wonder on her husband's face.

"I know we talked about bottle feeding," she began.

"Forget we said a word," he replied. He stood over her, his eyes so full of love that they sparkled with it. "I hope you can do that for a year or so, because I love watching it."

She laughed a little self-consciously. "I love feeling it," she confessed, stroking the tiny head. "Oh, Hank, we've got a baby," she breathed ecstatically. "A real, live, healthy little boy!"

He nodded. He was too choked for speech.

"I love you."

He took a steadying breath. "I love you, honey," he replied. His eyes searched hers hungrily. "With all my heart."

"My paper husband," she murmured.

"Remembering?" he teased. "Me, too. But I feel pretty flesh and blood right now."

"You look it, too." She drew him down and kissed him through the mask. "Have you forgotten what day it is?"

He frowned. "Well, in all the excitement…"

"It's your birthday!"

His eyebrows arched. "It is?"

"Yes, it is." She grinned at him. "Like your present?" she added, nodding toward the baby feeding at her breast.

"I love it," he returned. "Do I get one of these every year?" he teased.

"I won't make any promises, but we'll see."

"That's a deal."

Tilly joined them minutes later, still in her gown and robe with her hair in curlers.

"Good Lord, haven't you gone home yet?" Hank asked, aghast.

She gave him an amused grin. "How?"

"You could…" He pursed his lips. "No money for a cab, and you can't drive."

"Got it."

He looked sheepish. "I'll drive you home right now." He bent and kissed Dana and his child. "I'll be back as soon as I drop off Tilly. Anything you want me to bring you?"

She nodded. "Strawberry ice cream."

"I'll be back in a flash!"

And he was. For years afterward, the small hospital staff talked about the day young Donald Mandel Grant was born, when his proud dad satisfied Dana's craving for strawberry ice cream by having a truckload of the most expensive made delivered to the hospital. Dana said that it was a shame their baby was too young to enjoy it, but Hank promised that he wouldn't miss out. Hank had just purchased an ice cream company, and he was waiting for their son's first birthday party with pure glee!

* * * * *

"The Joshua trees and saguaros sure are pretty," Jack
said reflectively. "This sort of looks like the land west
of the Three Rivers Ranch house. Where you showed
me the North Star, remember?"

Remember? Those moments had been burned into
Vanessa's memory. Even if she never saw him again
for the rest of her life, she'd always have those special
moments to relive in her mind.

The thought unexpectedly caused her throat to
tighten, and she wished the waitress would get back
with their drinks. She didn't want Jack to think she was
getting emotional. Especially because she could feel
their time together winding to a close.

"I do. And I just happen to know a place not too far
west of here where there's another special view of the
evening star."

His eyelids lowered ever so slightly as he looked across the table at her. "After we eat, you should show me."

Did he expect her to look at him in the moonlight and not feel the urge to kiss him? Or maybe she'd get lucky, Vanessa thought, and the moon would be in a new phase and the light would be too weak to illuminate his face.

Damn it, Vanessa. Who are you fooling? You could find Jack's lips in the darkest of nights.

Thankfully, a waitress suddenly approached their table, and the distraction pushed the mocking voice from her head…but not the idea of being in Jack's arms again. She was beginning to fear she'd never rid herself of that longing.

Don't miss
The Other Hollister Man *by Stella Bagwell,*
available August 2022 wherever
Harlequin books and ebooks are sold.

Harlequin.com

HARLEQUIN
SPECIAL EDITION

**Believe in love. Overcome obstacles.
Find happiness.**

Save **$1.00**

off the purchase of ANY
Harlequin Special Edition book.

Available wherever books are sold,
including most bookstores, supermarkets,
drugstores and discount stores.

Save $1.00

off the purchase of ANY Harlequin Special Edition book.

Coupon valid until October 31, 2022.
Redeemable at participating outlets in the U.S. and Canada only.
Limit one coupon per customer.

52617371

5 65373 00076 2   (8100)0 12526

Get 4 FREE REWARDS!

We'll send you 2 FREE Books plus 2 FREE Mystery Gifts.

FREE
Value Over
$20

Both the **Romance** and **Suspense** collections feature compelling novels
written by many of today's bestselling authors.

Love Harlequin romance?

DISCOVER.

Be the first to find out about promotions,
news and exclusive content!

 Facebook.com/HarlequinBooks

 Twitter.com/HarlequinBooks

 Instagram.com/HarlequinBooks

 Pinterest.com/HarlequinBooks

You Tube YouTube.com/HarlequinBooks

ReaderService.com

EXPLORE.

Sign up for the Harlequin e-newsletter and
download a free book from any series at
TryHarlequin.com

CONNECT.

Join our Harlequin community to
share your thoughts and connect
with other romance readers!
Facebook.com/groups/HarlequinConnection

HSOCIAL2021